UNPREDICTABLE
WEBS

UNPREDICTABLE
WEBS

A NOVEL

DARLENE QUINN

RIVER GROVE
BOOKS

This book is a work of fiction. Names, characters, businesses, organizations, places, events, and incidents are either a product of the author's imagination or are used fictitiously. Any resemblance to actual persons, living or dead, events, or locales is entirely coincidental.

Published by River Grove Books
Austin, TX
www.rivergrovebooks.com

Distributed by River Grove Books

Design and composition by Greenleaf Book Group
Cover design by Greenleaf Book Group
Cover Image: ©iStockphoto.com/Steve Greer

Publisher's Cataloging-in-Publication data is available.

Print ISBN: 978-1-63299-504-9

eBook ISBN: 978-1-60832-425-5

First Edition

DEDICATION

To Jack, my husband—the absolute best partner and support system on planet Earth.

And in loving memory of my ninety-three-year-old aunt Marguerite Page (Auntie Marnie) who passed away on December 28. Although her wit and sense of fun will be missed, she will always be in our memories and in our hearts.

ACKNOWLEDGMENTS

While writing the type of novels I like to read, I endeavor to create realistic backgrounds and remain true to the world of retail. Maintaining accuracy and authenticity is important to me (although I never allow it to get in the way of page-turning suspense), and so I owe a great deal to the following individuals.

As always, I owe my firsthand retail education and the ring of truth that reverberates throughout this work of fiction to the former executives and the sales and sales-support associates of Bullock's/Bullocks Wilshire. Also, I must express my gratitude to the following people:

Allen Questrom—master of merchandising, retail, and company turnarounds, who led Federated Department Stores out of bankruptcy and on to the acquisition of The Broadway/Emporium Stores and R. H. Macy & Company, Inc.

Terry Lundgren—chairman, president, and CEO of Macy's, Inc. (formerly known as Federated Department Stores). Under Terry's leadership Macy's Inc. has become a national brand, blanketing our nation: More than eight hundred Macy's department stores plus forty Bloomingdale's stores are flourishing under the Macy's umbrella.

Special thanks to Rosemary Troy of Troy's upscale boutique on El Paseo in Palm Desert; and to Glenn Ellison, currently with Tommy Bahama in Palm Desert.

Loretta Cahill, sales associate beyond compare at Bloomingdale's Newport Beach, who recently retired and is greatly missed.

Michael Dervos, senior vice president Macy's North, and regional director of stores; Andrea J. Schwarts, vice president media relations and cause marketing, Macy's North & Midwest Regions; and Vicki Musial, manager, Macy's By Appointment, Macy's East.

James McKay; Ward Miller; Gayle Soucek; Deputy Coroner John P. Kenney, DDS, MS; Gloria Evensen; Pete Soucek; and Eric Bronsky—all dedicated fans of Marshall Field's.

Ken Price, director of public relations, Palmer House, Chicago.

Cynthia Clampitt, author of *Waltzing Australia*, for her assistance with the hot spots in Chicago.

In matters outside the world of retail, I would like to thank Gary Olson, former first vice president of wealth management with Morgan Stanley/Smith Barney, and Bob Hughes, MDRT with American General, who assisted in regard to financial ramifications; Chief of Detectives Thomas M. Burn, Chicago PD; private investigator Raymond P. Lombardo, previously an LAPD lieutenant and officer in charge of the Hollywood precinct; Steve Fritch, retired LBPD forensic unit; and my son, John Fields, who added insight into the unknown.

I owe a special thanks to my granddaughter, Jamie Dominguez, for introducing me to the world of dance. Also aiding in my education and bringing me up to speed were granddaughters Jennifer, Jessica, and Juliana Dominguez; Victoria Fields; and my "adopted" granddaughter, Odessa Porter (my assistant's daughter and Jamie's friend since they met in musical theater at age six). The girls entered the dance world at the age of four; Jamie, Victoria, and Odessa celebrated their twenty-second birthdays in 2012.

I would also like to thank my wonderful review committee members: Nanci Gee, Shirley Williams, Barbee Heiny, Sally Williams Szabo, Peggy Kuntzelman, Barbara McClousky, Mike McNeff, Glenda A. Bixler, Dolores Ayotte, Jon Batson, Brenda Minor, Cynthia Clampitt, Stefanie Jackson, Kevin Keeny, Toni Rakestraw, Sue Senden, Kami Weeks, Shirley Nyquist, Samantha Noelle Golt, Sally Fritch, Sue Short, and Ginnie Wilcox.

I couldn't do without the folks at EMSI: Marsha Friedman, Steve Friedman, Senior Campaign Manager Alex Hinojosa, Rich Ghazarian, Russ Handle, Jeni Hinojosa, Ginny Grimsley, and Rachel Friedman. It's a joy to work with this savvy group of publicists, all of whom are dedicated professionals with a great sense of humor.

I must also thank Greenleaf Book Group, particularly Justin Branch, director of consulting; Bryan Carroll, project manager; Neil Gonzalez, cover designer extraordinaire; Corrin Foster, marketing manager; Steve Elizalde, distribution account executive; my incredible editor, Linda O'Doughda, who shapes my stories and makes them so much better; and freelance copy editor Amy D. McIlwaine, for assuring accuracy and order with her fabulous sense of time and place. Your collective enthusiasm and dedication have not only enhanced this work of fiction but also made the journey to publication an exciting and enjoyable adventure.

Thanks also to Brennan Harvey, an award-winning author who attempted to keep my former website as current as possible; to Joe Thomas, director at Left Brain Digital, for developing my new website at darlenequinn.net; and to Eddie Velez, content coordinator with Left Brain Digital.

And finally, a special thanks to my fantastic administrative assistant Kathy Porter, who is an invaluable part of my team and the international award–winning author of *Earth's Ultimate Conflict* (Gray Guardian Series).

Halting midstride, Marnie whirled around, defiance flashing in her deep brown eyes as well as the biting set of her jaw.

Caught in her daughter's cold glare, Ashleigh Taylor found herself temporarily speechless. *When did this precious child become so hostile?* she thought. *It's all my fault.* She had hundreds of questions that needed to be answered, but every one of them stuck in her throat.

"I don't belong here. I never have." Marnie's words split the silence of the room. But in the next instant, her gaze dropped to the kitchen floor, and her voice fell to a level barely above a whisper. "I want to live with my mother."

I am your mother! Ashleigh wanted to scream, but she never would. The last thing she wanted to do was to put her angry young daughter on the defensive. Unbidden, the name she dared not speak aloud thundered through her head and hammered in her heart: *Cassie. Oh, my Cassie.*

Taking a restorative breath, Ashleigh willed herself not to slip back in time. If she allowed *what-ifs* or *should haves* to cloud her mind, she'd be immobilized. She had no power to rewrite the past. What had been done could not be undone.

Nearly sixteen years earlier, on the day Ashleigh had given birth to perfect twin daughters, Cassie had been abducted from the cradle beside Ashleigh's bed. That heinous crime had trapped two utterly different families in a heartbreaking tangle of secrets and lies for eight long years.

For those critical years, Erica Christonelli, the wife of Cassie's abductor, was the only mother her Cassie had known. How much easier it might have been if Ashleigh could have despised the woman. But Erica was no less a victim than she and her husband had been. Unaware that the baby she was raising as her own was Callie's kidnapped twin sister, Erica had named *her* child Marnie.

Ashleigh had never deluded herself with thoughts that the road to making her family whole again would be an easy one. There was bound to be a multitude of treacherous bumps along the path she'd chosen. Yet she never dreamed how difficult it would be to stay that course. Unwilling to deny her daughter time with the "mother" she had known since birth, Ashleigh had turned a blind eye to the obstacles and instead looked into her heart, drawing upon the old African proverb, *It takes a village to raise a child*. In time she had worn down Conrad's resistance. He'd come to terms with what was best for their daughter. They had agreed to make Erica a member of their extended family. But their "family village" was filled with so many pitfalls, so many side roads, so many voices. Far too many voices.

Ashleigh looked past the hard set of her daughter's jaw to her pain-filled eyes and quickly closed the distance between them. "Marnie. I love you with all my heart," she said softly. "If you don't belong here, then neither do I." She reached out to brush the loose hairs from Marnie's cheek.

Marnie stepped back. "That's a lie. I hate it when you say things you don't mean. I know you wish I'd never been born." Dissolving into tears, she averted her eyes, jammed her arms into the sleeves of her parka, and bolted for the kitchen door.

CHAPTER

2

From the pantry, Elizabeth heard every word of the exchange between Ashleigh and her rebellious daughter. Momentarily frozen in place, her mind quickly raced through the options. *Ashleigh doesn't deserve this. She's a wonderful mother. She tries so hard to be fair and do what's right, not only for the twins and Juliana but for everyone.*

Over the years, Elizabeth had become more like a member of the family than part of their household staff. She had grown to love and care for the entire Taylor family as she had for Ashleigh's beloved grandfather. Right or wrong, she could no longer remain silent. "Marnie," she called out, moving swiftly toward the door.

Ashleigh, just a few steps behind Elizabeth, reached it first and placed her hand over Marnie's on the doorknob. "Don't open that door," she warned. Her words came out sharper than she'd intended. *Well, maybe not.* After all, she could not keep tiptoeing around. Marnie was in need of a firm hand.

"What is this?" Marnie spun around, her gaze shifting from Elizabeth to Ashleigh. "Am I under house arrest?"

In the thundering silence, Elizabeth glanced from Ashleigh's troubled expression to Marnie's stormy defiance. If only she could shake some sense into the young rebel. If only she could find a way to help Marnie drink in all the love that surrounded her.

"Marnie," Ashleigh began, "it's sixteen degrees outdoors. Even if we didn't have a lot to discuss, you aren't entirely dressed for this weather." She looked down at Marnie's bootless feet.

"Whatever," Marnie sighed. "I'm sorry." Not meeting Ashleigh's eyes, she added, "I should just totally keep my mouth shut."

Before Ashleigh could respond, the kitchen door burst open. Juliana called out, "We finished our choreography and we're ready—"

As she slid to a stop in her soft-soled jazz shoes, her eyes flashed from her mother to Elizabeth before resting on Marnie. "Oops," said Juliana. "Guess this isn't such a good time."

Torn between her unusually perceptive eleven-year-old's excitement and Marnie's pain, Ashleigh glanced up at the wall clock. *Quarter to ten.* "How about we come upstairs to see your duet at ten thirty? That will give—"

"Can't we go up to the studio *now*?" Marnie pleaded, her face suddenly brightening. "I want to see how much of my part had to be changed."

Ashleigh glanced across the room to Elizabeth for a fraction of a second, but she did not hesitate in making up her mind. Looking straight into Marnie's damp eyes, which now seemed to sparkle in anticipation, she said, "Sure, we'll check out the new rendition of your duet. Then we need to talk."

Marnie nodded and took off toward the broad staircase in the foyer.

As they headed toward the dance studio, Ashleigh's mind reeled. Marnie's sudden mood swings were nothing new, and yet they never failed to astound her. Since Marnie's recent return from spending the last few days of Christmas vacation with Erica and her brother-in-law, Mike Christonelli, Ashleigh felt as if she were tiptoeing though a field of hand-blown glass baubles. As if the emotional turmoil that visit had stirred in the teenager weren't enough, Ashleigh realized that Marnie's being eliminated from the upcoming dance competition and forced to give up practice for the past few weeks—to give her twisted ankle time to repair—had taken their toll. And now that Marnie was walking without a limp, she resisted following through with the strengthening exercises she needed to avoid further injury to her ankle. Ashleigh knew the additional blow of handing over her role in the duet with Callie to her younger sister had to be far more devastating than Marnie was letting on.

"Okay, Midget," Marnie teased as she followed Juliana to the dance studio on the top floor of the family's suburban home. "Let's see how many of my pirouettes you had to take out."

"Only two," Callie called out from the top of the stairs. "She's taken on the challenge like a champ."

Once Juliana had assumed her place on the dance floor, Callie pressed PLAY on the CD player and the two girls fell into their opening pose. For the duet competition, the twins had adapted choreography from Twyla Tharp's *Sinatra: Dance with Me.*

While Ashleigh joined Marnie as a spectator in the home studio, she wondered how much effort it took for her daughter to plant that smile on her face, when just moments before . . . *How much of who Marnie is today was preordained by DNA, and how much by her environment during those critical early years?* Ashleigh was not alone in her inability to solve the age-old controversy of Nature versus Nurture. She only knew—based on the books she had devoured about the care and development of identical twins—that both genes and upbringing played a vital part.

Good, bad, or indifferent, Marnie had become the person she was through a combination of heredity and environment. To lay blame or attach a label was an exercise in futility. Undeniably it was heredity that accounted for Marnie and Callie having Ashleigh's brown eyes and Conrad's smile, but the genetic waters got a bit cloudier when it came to behavior, intelligence, and personality. When Marnie's moodiness first became apparent, Conrad had blamed her early years away from the family. Her personality, he pointed out, often mirrored that of Erica Christonelli, who confessed to having been diagnosed as bipolar, while Callie's even temper and optimistic outlook tended to be more like her parents'. Conrad glossed over the fact that Marnie seldom had to be reminded to wash her dishes and pick up after herself—while Callie typically needed to be told more than once. Ashleigh knew that even identical twins brought up in the same household since birth developed different traits and personalities. *So why waste time analyzing?* she scolded herself. *We just have to deal with whatever comes our way.*

CHAPTER

3

The last strains of Sinatra's "Come Dance with Me" faded, and Callie and Juliana slipped into their ending pose.

"Awesome! Bravo! Bravo!" Marnie clapped her hands and then struggled to her feet from the floor, where she'd been sitting cross-legged. Thanks to her ankle injury, this was no longer a simple task, but she managed and, once standing, threw her arms around Juliana. "Didn't think you had it in you, Midget." Turning to Callie, she said, "I guess you really should open your own dance studio."

Throughout the duet Ashleigh's attention had been more focused on Marnie than on the dancers. Her heart lifted now as she observed Marnie's enthusiasm—apparently genuine—for her sisters' performance. "Great job, girls," she said. "That was fantastic. If I were one of the judges, I'd be awarding you the platinum."

"Riiiight," Juliana said, a grin spreading across her face. "You're our mom, so that doesn't really count."

"Just because I'm your mom doesn't mean I don't know a great performance when I see one."

"Yeah, but you're prejudiced."

"Guilty as charged," Ashleigh admitted, "but I'm no dummy in the world of dance. I've been observing since . . ." Her voice trailed off as visions of four-year-old Callie, all decked out in her pink swan's leotard and tutu, appeared in her head. Although Erica and Mike had given Ashleigh scores of pictures of Marnie from the years before she turned eight, Ashleigh's brain had blocked those images of Marnie all alone, never knowing how much she was loved and missed.

Ashleigh felt Marnie's eyes on her now. "Since forever," she said, as if she hadn't drifted off. Although she knew it was irrational, she felt guilty that Marnie had not shared those early years and was not part of those first memories. Maybe that's why Ashleigh couldn't say no when she had been nominated for chairman of the dance team's parent group. It had drawn her even closer to the girls, as she'd hoped it would. But in the past few years Marnie had begun to drift away.

"Mom," Callie said, "is it okay if I have Sam spend the night?" Samantha and Callie had been fast friends from the first day the Taylors had moved into their Greenwich home seven years ago.

"After you clean your room," Ashleigh replied. She hadn't missed the roll of Marnie's eyes when Callie asked about Sam spending the night. The dynamics between the twins and their friends were a constant source of both amusement and concern. When the sisters first came together, they had disassembled their separate bedrooms, creating one sleeping area for the two of them to share and turning the other into a separate computer and study room. But by the time they were in middle school, they had wanted their own rooms, their own space and privacy.

When Marnie turned to follow Callie and the others out of the studio, Ashleigh called out to her. "Marnie, wait. We need to talk. Let's get some hot chocolate and go into the living room."

"I don't want any hot chocolate."

"Okay. Well, do you want anything before we—"

"I don't want anything. And I don't want to talk." Biting down on her lip, she quickly added, "I said I was sorry. Can't we just forget it?"

"No, Marnie, we can't just forget it. I'm not angry, but I need to know why you are so unhappy."

Heaving a heavy sigh, Marnie said, "Please, Mom. School starts tomorrow, and I need to do some stuff on the computer."

She hasn't called me Mom since coming back from her trip to Chicago to visit the Christonellis. "Sorry," Ashleigh said, heading to the studio doorway. "First we need to clear the air about a few things."

"Whatever," Marnie grumbled, reluctantly following a few steps behind.

———

On the coffee table in the family room, Elizabeth had placed a tray with two mugs, a pot of steaming hot chocolate, and a plate filled with Marnie's favorite sugar cookies. It looked pretty darn good.

Marnie watched as Ashleigh filled one mug. She was sorry now that she'd said she didn't want any . . . . But without even asking, Ashleigh handed her the mug.

"Thanks," she mumbled, reluctantly taking the cup.

"Marnie, I love you with all my heart," said Ashleigh again. "You *do* belong here with all of us. What can we do to make you feel that you belong?"

"But I *don't*. You and Dad tell me you love me because you're my parents and you think you have to. 'I love you with all my heart,'" she parroted. "Isn't that called a platitude? Something you just say but don't really mean?"

Ashleigh's face fell. She looked as if Marnie had actually slapped her. *Obviously she doesn't know what to say. Maybe she's tired of pretending she loves me.* Building up steam, Marnie said aloud, "Let's face it. I was born second. I am number two." Following a dramatic pause, she continued, "And number two spells *loser*." She'd read that somewhere and practiced it. It felt really good to say it out loud.

"Marnie," Ashleigh said, "tell me everything you feel. I'll just listen until you're finished. I promise not to interrupt, but then I want you to listen to me." She looked deep into Marnie's eyes. "Deal?"

Marnie stared back at her. After a few awkward moments she said, "There isn't that much to say that we haven't said a hundred times before. But now I know for sure that I want to live in Chicago with my mom and Uncle Mike and Bill."

Ashleigh leaned forward; she looked as if she were ready to say something, but instead she sank back in the chair, not uttering a single syllable.

This was great. Marnie was feeling in control—something she had not felt for a very long time. But suddenly her stomach felt as though it were a meat grinder churning away. She knew how hard Ashleigh tried to make her feel loved. *It's really not her fault that she can't love me.*

It's my *fault. I look like Callie, but inside I'm not* at all *like her. Callie is perfect. She's a better dancer, she has more friends, she gets better grades . . . She likes everyone, and everyone likes her.* "Let's face it, Mom. I'm an outsider in this family. I'm even on the outside with Callie's friends and the dance team . . ."

Holding her tongue was getting more difficult by the moment, but Ashleigh knew she must not interrupt. She had promised. Besides, if she wasn't willing to listen to her daughter, how could she expect to be heard? It took all her willpower not to contradict what Marnie was saying, even though she was one hundred percent wrong.

Finally, Marnie slumped into the cushions of the couch. "Okay, now you can tell me how wrong I am."

"Darling, feelings are neither right nor wrong. They are what you feel deep inside, but sometimes they come about through wrong assumptions." Shifting away from the psychological and back to what Marnie had actually said, Ashleigh repeated her daughter's words. "You're telling me that you feel less important to us and less loved than your sisters."

Marnie nodded, but she looked skeptical.

"Marnie. I know words don't mean a thing when it comes to expressing feelings. I'll most likely repeat a lot of what you've heard before. But I listened to you without butting in, and I hope you can do the same for me. You have been a part of me since before you were born. Number one, two, or three. There are no losers. You are my daughter, and I love you with all my heart. No, you are not like Callie. You are not like Juliana. You are exactly like you. I might not always like the choices you make, but there is nothing you could ever do to make me stop loving you.

"When you tell me you feel like an outsider, is it because we sometimes talk about things that happened before you were returned to us?"

Marnie shrugged.

"I don't know if you remember or not, but we talked about this while you were still in elementary school."

Another shrug. But before Ashleigh had an opportunity to continue—to start working on solutions that might help her daughter—Marnie blurted out, "You have two daughters here that you are always proud of. Why can't I just go to Chicago?" Marnie set the hot chocolate on the table. Then, without meeting Ashleigh's eyes, she said, "Either today or maybe tomorrow, Mom and Uncle Mike should get the letter about my wanting to live with them. I wrote it on the airplane and mailed it from the airport when I got here."

Paige Toddman stood in the doorway of the master bedroom in the converted guesthouse, watching her mother and mentally shaking her head. A puzzled expression crossed Helen's brow as she placed another lightweight dress on the bed. She stepped back, cocking her head one way and then the other.

Although Helen had been diagnosed with early-onset Alzheimer's nearly fifteen years before, she was still functioning well beyond expectation—though she forgot things, of course, and she did tend to say whatever popped into her head. In fact, since the death of her husband, Rupert, any trace of her former ladylike inhibitions seemed to have departed with him.

"Mom," Paige said, "we aren't leaving for another couple of days, and it's very cold in Greenwich."

Helen with a blank expression on her face. *Has she forgotten that we will be staying with Ashleigh and her family?* thought Paige.

"Wilma has most of the things you will need laid out in the blue guest room."

Helen looked up and gave her a sly grin. "I know, dear, but Wilma put a bunch of clothes together with necklines up to my eyebrows." She paused, biting down on her bottom lip. "I know she and I are about the same age, but I don't want to look like an old lady."

"I agree. At seventy-four, there's no reason for you to dress like an old lady. But it's below freezing in New York, and those dresses"—Paige pointed with a nod of her head—"are far too lightweight."

"Well, how can I be sexy with suits and dresses covering up my feminine curves?"

Paige laughed. "So, now you want to be sexy?"

"Well, dear, just because there's snow on the roof," she said, patting her beautifully coiffed hair and sliding her fingertips down the length of her torso, "doesn't mean there's no fire in the furnace."

Shaking her head, Paige said, "Don't worry, Mom. Your wardrobe is very stylish: Chanel suits, Ferré, Valentino, Ralph Lauren. And you'll knock 'em dead in the big city with your fitted sable fur coat too."

Her mother's face brightened. "I remember. The coat will be perfect, but if I'm going to be a panther, I need something eye-catching underneath."

"A panther?"

"Yes. I want to attract a nice young man like that sexy lady at the Christmas party did." Her eyes twinkled. "You know, the one with the lovely shop on Fifth Avenue."

Paige could hardly suppress the giggle threatening to surface. Her mother meant Viviana and her boyfriend, who was at least twenty years her junior. Maybe more. "Mom, I think you mean you'd like to become a *cougar.*" She smiled, trying to imagine her mother as an older version of Demi Moore or Viviana De Mornay. The image did not materialize.

Conrad Taylor charged up the broad staircase of Trump International Hotel and Tower and dashed through the sparkling, clear-glass doorway toward Jean Georges. It took only a quick glace around the tastefully decorated restaurant to find Mark Toddman seated at a window table overlooking Central Park. He slowed his pace as he approached the table.

With a smile spreading across his tanned face, Mark rose and stretched out his hand. In the next moment, he slowly cocked a thick brow and said, "Appears you could use a time-out."

Conrad laughed. "Isn't that the truth? But your timing couldn't be better."

After a hearty handshake, both men took their seats. *The timing couldn't be better, indeed,* thought Conrad. There were so many ideas he wanted to bounce off his friend. Mark, the most respected icon in the world of retail, had been his mentor throughout his years in the business and remained a trusted sounding board.

Looking around the elegant restaurant, Conrad flashed back to the first time he and Ashleigh had joined the Toddmans here with their girls. It was shortly after they had been reunited with their kidnapped daughter. Having discovered that Marnie liked little more than pasta, peanut butter and jelly sandwiches, and chicken strips, Ashleigh had worried about the menu.

Now, as if reading his mind, Mark said, "I think I'll pass on Jean Georges's special sandwich on a stick."

Conrad laughed out loud. The head chef had concocted a special sandwich dipped in chocolate and served on a stick. And to top it off was Jean Georges's cherry soda, with that explosive fizzle inside. For parents of younger children, it remained the answer to their prayers.

"How are Paige and the family?" Conrad asked.

A neatly attired waiter in black trousers and a crisp white shirt appeared and then quickly departed with their drinks order. Mark smiled, and as if there had been no interruption, he said, "Well, as I mentioned, Paige couldn't get away this morning, but she and Helen will arrive on Tuesday."

"Paige certainly has no shortage of worthwhile causes to fill her days. She's on the boards of—how many charities, museums, community outreach programs . . . ?" Conrad grinned.

"Yes, and she's this year's chairperson for the Save the Children fund-raiser—it's the first of next month, by the way." Mark paused. "Assume you received your invite?"

"On our calendar." Then, after a slight hesitation, Conrad winked. "In ink."

Mark smiled and continued his update. "Since Rupert passed away last year, Helen has become somewhat of a loose cannon."

Conrad chuckled. Ashleigh had kept him pretty much up-to-date on Paige's challenges with her unpredictable mother and had told him about several of Helen's recent shenanigans. "I understand she's become quite the outrageous flirt."

"To put it mildly." Mark shook his head, but there was a tender sparkle in his hazel eyes. "Absolutely no filter." He shrugged. "Thank God, it doesn't seem to faze Wilma." Wilma and her husband, Terrence, had worked for the Toddmans since the mid-eighties and were devoted to them as well as to Paige's mother, who had come into their lives and their household twelve years before. The warm, caring couple were more like family than staff to the Toddmans. But, as Conrad recalled, they were close to Helen in age—no longer spring chickens.

While waiting for their lunch to be served, the two men continued to catch up on personal news. Since the Toddmans' move to Texas, where Mark had signed on to restructure the ailing J. J. Clark's department store chain, the old friends had fallen behind on day-to-day communications, but they had managed to keep up with all the major news and events in their families' lives. He, Ashleigh, the twins, and Juliana had joined the Toddmans in Los Angeles last year to celebrate April's graduation from UCLA with a master's in communications, which had helped her land the coveted internship at JJQ news channel in Chicago. As for the Taylors, Mark knew the latest news—that Ashleigh was no longer heading human resources for John Stewart's—but he and Conrad had never discussed the real reasons behind her resignation. Conrad knew this was no time to go into it. He had other priorities for today's meeting.

The waiter discreetly vanished after setting the plates of pecan-encrusted red snapper on the pristine white-on-white tablecloth. Mark took a bite of his fish, leaned forward, and in a matter-of-fact tone said, "With all that's going on in your life just now, it's clear you didn't arrange this meeting for idle chitchat. What's on your mind?"

"That obvious, eh?"

Mark took another bite. He didn't respond. He didn't need to.

Since Mark was up-to-date with the retail landscape, Conrad had no need to mention the merger with the Hay's Company that had turned Consolidated Department Stores into one of the largest retailers in the world. It was Mark who had started that ball rolling in the early nineties with his successful bid for the debt-ridden Jordon's Department Stores. He had followed up by engineering the 1996 acquisition of the financially troubled Mainway Department Store chain, which operated eighty-two stores in California. Although Consolidated had been left with a hefty debt of about $5 billion as a result of those deals, the acquisitions significantly raised the company's profile, making it the nation's largest retailer, with over eight hundred U.S. department stores and close to $25 billion in annual sales volume.

"We're confident that the merger with the Hay's Company was the right move at the right time." Conrad took a quick sip of water. "But in these uncertain times, the debt factor is of major concern."

Mark nodded. "I hear you. It's a whole new ball game. Three years ago, the U.S. economy was on a roll, with retail rocketing at its fastest pace in more than *nineteen years*. Now that the industry is headed for a slump, we have to take a different approach."

"We've managed to chip away a great deal of past debt," Conrad began, "and we've reduced expenses in the noncritical areas. That's a given. But that's not what I wanted to talk about. I have some other ideas I'd like to bounce off you."

Mark interjected, "If I'm to believe what I read in *Women's Wear Daily,* you're now the king of private-label merchandising, branding, and localization."

A wide smile crept across Conrad's face. "Learned from the master."

Mark waved off the compliment. "But you hadn't anticipated the outrage from the fans of John Stewart's?"

"Bingo. Nothing much slips past you."

"Not exactly new to the game," Mark reminded him.

"We weren't oblivious to the potential for backlash, but the magnitude is mind-boggling. The name change from John Stewart's to Jordon's won't take place until September, but the moment it was announced, an enormous groundswell of protest began." Conrad swallowed hard. "Grassroots groups formed practically overnight."

"I'm afraid the negative reaction we encountered with Bentleys Royale in L.A. will pale in comparison to what's in store for Jordon's. John Stewart's is a tourist destination as well as a Chicago icon. Its fans have gathered worldwide support. You're in for a rough ride."

Conrad turned defensive. "Granted, Chicago is proving to be one hell of a challenge. But our focus must be on the overall benefit to the organization and to our customers."

"I'm not suggesting you alter your vision, Conrad—just make sure all your ducks are in order. Excuse the cliché. I know you've studied all the obstacles as well as the opportunities. It's a tough call."

Conrad followed Mark's thoughtful gaze, which seemed to linger on the activities outside, in Central Park. A full minute lapsed before Conrad continued. "Even with the support of the mayor, taking on the Windy City, with this number of strong mind-sets—customers, community leaders, the media, and in some cases even the staff—it's going to take a goddamned miracle to pull off the win-win scenario we're hoping for. Or anything close to it."

Meeting his friend's eyes confidently, Conrad spoke the thoughts hammering against his skull. "Mergers and name changes happen. Even in Chicago there was barely a murmur when the White Sox's Comiskey Park became U.S. Cellular Field." But as he voiced his rationale out loud, he realized there was really no comparison. In sports, fan loyalty was all about the team; the location was not what had captured their hearts.

Still, Mark, of all people, would realize why regional store names had to go. After all, he was the *pioneer* of branding in the world of department stores—the first to have recognized the value of a broadly recognizable trademark. Jordon's was known from coast to coast, while John Stewart's recognition was limited to the Midwest and East Coast residents and tourists. It was a no-brainer. The money they could save in advertising alone was tremendous, and just think of the clout that the national brand brought to the bargaining table.

Loyal John Stewart's customers, however, demonstrated no desire to understand that those savings would ultimately be passed on to them. *And as CEO, I've been depicted as the devil himself.*

"On a more positive note," Conrad said, "Chicago's mayor is well aware of our mission and has voiced his support." Assembling his thoughts, he paraphrased the mayor's quote from Sunday's *Chicago Tribune.* "He said something like, 'If you aren't willing to accept change, then you stay in the past, and we're never going to stay in the past in this city.' He also stated that he was really in favor of our commitment to showcase Jordon's, housed in the John Stewart's building, as a tourist destination in Chicago, as it had long been in New York."

"So how huge is this groundswell of resistance that you mentioned?"

"We've already received petitions with tens of thousands of signatures, asking us to retain the John Stewart's name. There have also been threats of boycotts in the Chicago area." Conrad reached into the inside pocket of his Armani suit jacket and withdrew a folded piece of paper. Laying the paper flat on the table, he smoothed it out and slid it over to Mark. "I received a mountain of these less than a week after the official announcement of the pending name change."

Mark's eyes widened as he spotted the name on the third line of the petition. "Erica Christonelli?" His tone was incredulous. "After all you've done for her?"

Conrad himself had done a double take when he had first seen Erica's signature on the petition. The trite old saying *No good deed goes unpunished* shot though his mind. He could think of no way to put a positive spin on this revelation.

Consequently, he had not yet shared this new wrinkle with Ashleigh.

CHAPTER

6

The moment the delicious Versace rep wheeled his sample trunk out the front door of De Mornay's and onto the snow-covered Chicago streets, Viviana sighed and kicked off her Maud Frizon pumps. The image of the young man was emblazoned in her memory; those broad shoulders and that well-tapered frame beneath his expertly tailored suit gave her a rush. But while standing flat-footed, flexing her toes and rolling on the balls of her feet, reality hit. *He's the epitome of stylish perfection. There's little chance that young man is straight.*

Viviana padded on stockinged feet across the plush carpet to the door of her new boutique. As she turned the key in the stiff lock, a glow of contentment radiated through her. This shop on Oak Street was the perfect location for her one-of-a-kind fashion boutique. When her partner, Glenn Nelson, had bowed out and the rents on Fifth Avenue had skyrocketed, downsizing and moving away from New York had been exactly the right solution.

For a few silent moments, Viviana stood peering out the double-paned windows, watching the light snow flurries. Her condo was only three doors away, but the thought of venturing out into the cold night air caused a shiver to slide down her arms.

The musical tones of her cell phone's ring broke the stillness.

Dashing to where her handbag sat on the antique French brocade chair, she checked the glass-domed clock on the counter. It was only five thirty, but all signs of daylight had vanished. She fumbled with the catch on the small clutch bag and snatched the phone.

"Viviana?" the caller said before she could mutter a breathless greeting.

She recognized the deep baritone. *Mitchell Wainwright.*

"It's another three months before my grand opening, Mitchell. Tell me you're not calling to say you won't be able to make it."

"Of course not, my dear." Wainwright chuckled. "I just landed at O'Hare, and. . ."

"And you're expecting to come visit the shop right *now?*"

Mitchell chuckled again. "Believe it or not, Viviana, as spectacular as De Mornay's might be, it's not Chicago's only attraction on a Saturday night."

The unflappable Viviana was momentarily caught off guard. Although their affair had run its course, she and Mitchell remained good friends. Without his expertise, she might not have brought a sufficient number of investors on board for her new venture. But she wondered why he hadn't called in advance. Surely he didn't think he could just pop in on her whenever he chose.

Wainwright quickly set the record straight. "Don't worry, Viviana. I know you're up to your pretty arched eyebrows with the boutique. I don't expect to be entertained. But thought I might entice you to join me for dinner."

"Tonight?"

"Heavens, no. I haven't completely taken leave of my senses. However, if you could squeeze me in sometime later this week, there are some things I'd like to run by you." There was a slight pause before he added, "Or does Toy Boy still have that outrageous jealous streak?"

Viviana gulped in a steadying breath and through gritted teeth said, "As I believe you are well aware, Patrick and I parted a month or so before I relocated to the Windy City."

The background noise cut off Wainwright's response.

"Where are you?" Viviana asked.

"Baggage claim. It's noisy as hell, so let's cut this short. But to satisfy your curiosity, Tony moved to Chicago a month ago, and I'm here to see him."

Tony? Tony? The name hammered through her head. *Oh my God.* She'd tried to talk Mitchell into reconciling with his son, Anthony, who had served ten years in prison. He had been out now for just about as long. In the past, her pleading with Mitchell to reunite with his son had fallen on deaf ears. She'd been convinced that no one could make a dent in Mitchell's self-righteous armor. But apparently she had been wrong. He'd even used the nickname his son preferred.

There was a chink in that armor after all.

CHAPTER

7

Erica Christonelli felt the blood leave her face as she read the last line of her daughter's one-page letter.

If you really love me, you will not say no.

On boneless legs, she sank down onto the seat in front of the bay window. Her heart gave a dull kick and then settled into a rapid rhythm. She could hardly breathe. *This can't be happening,* she thought. *It's what I want most in the whole world, but I'm not ready.* The sick feeling inside her seemed to expand. *Maybe I'll never be ready.*

"What's wrong?" Mike asked. "You look as if you've been visited by the Ghost of Christmas Past."

With tears spilling down her cheeks, Erica glanced down at the single sheet of paper she still clutched in her hand. She ran the page between her index and middle fingers in an effort to smooth it, and then handed it to her brother-in-law. The envelope tumbled to the floor.

Quickly scanning the letter, Mike looked up, a grin spreading across his entire face. "Hallelujah," he said. "Marnie didn't say so when she was here, but I saw how much she wanted and needed to come back to us."

Too stunned at first to react, Erica stared up at him. Searching for the words to convey what was in her heart, but unable to pull them together, she blurted out, "You can't be serious?"

"Never been more serious in my life. Marnie belongs with us."

Mike—the voice of reason, the rock who had stood by her through so many troubled times. Mike—the one person she'd relied on to keep her from going off the deep end. Had he suddenly taken leave of his senses? "There's no way—"

"Erica, you're not actually considering telling Marnie she can't—"

Bolting to her feet, Erica stood for a moment on wobbly legs. "Stop, Mike. Please stop. You know that can't happen."

"But it can," he countered without hesitation. "Marnie will be sixteen in August. She can choose where she wants to live—and who she wants to live with."

Wiping away her tears with the back of her hand, Erica said, "No, Mike. There's nothing we can do. The Taylors are Marnie's birth parents. Even if that were not true, we can't offer her the kind of life she's—"

Mike shot forward and gripped her by the shoulders. "Marnie doesn't give a damn about the things gobs of money can buy. She's unhappy. She wants to live with us. Don't you want that too?"

"Of course I do, but Mike—"

"But nothing. Just listen to yourself. The Taylors lack the emotional bond we've had with Marnie since the day she was born. Of course Marnie feels like an outsider with her sisters and all of their shared memories. The Taylors' wealth can't buy what Marnie needs most. What our girl longs for is exactly what we have to give."

Throwing up her hands in utter frustration, Erica cried out, "Stop it. Please, please stop. You know how hard it's been. I've tried to pretend that I haven't been in unbearable pain since the day I decided I could no longer hide Marnie from her biological mother and father. You, of all people, know how miserably I've failed. I still feel she belongs to us every bit as much as she does to them. We've gone over this a thousand times, but under the law, she belongs to them. And no matter how much we'd like Marnie to be with us, we have no justification for fighting the Taylors. Far beyond their financial means, they have proved themselves to be loving, caring parents."

"Then why is Marnie so unhappy? Why did she seem so depressed when she was here? Why is she crying out for us to rescue her?"

"My God, Mike. She's a teenager. That comes with the territory. No matter what they have, they always want more. Corny as it might sound, they always think the grass is greener—"

"Bullshit. Marnie is clearly reaching out to us. Are you going to tell her you aren't willing to fight for her?" He paused before broaching what he knew was a sensitive topic. "Is it Nelson Kennedy? Are you afraid Marnie would threaten your relationship?"

"Of course not." Erica glared at her brother-in-law. But upon seeing the pain in his eyes she took a step back from her anger. *His love for Marnie is clouding his judgment.* "If Nelson hadn't hit it off with Marnie, he'd no longer be a part of my life. Besides, Nelson's younger son lives with him, and he's just a few months older than Marnie, so my having a teenager would hardly be an issue."

If only Nelson were here now, she thought.

With her mind in overdrive, Erica swallowed back her panic. "Marnie has two sisters in Greenwich, and changing schools in the middle of high school . . ." Her voice faded like a trail of vapor. An image of Marnie's face flashed before her—the guilty look just a few days ago as she'd instantly closed the Myspace screen on her laptop the moment Erica had stepped into the room. It wasn't just the teenager's sisters or the school. *I have no idea how to discipline a teenage daughter,* she thought. *How can I keep her safe without losing her love?*

CHAPTER

8

Tuesday morning, before Erica had even crawled out of bed, she called in sick to John Stewart's. Her eyes were nearly swollen shut. She didn't dare face the mirror before splashing cold water on her face.

If she'd slept at all, it had been only in short snatches. *What was I thinking? Of course I want Marnie to be with us. That's all I've ever wanted. And now that she's made the first move, I can't let her down.* Since receiving Marnie's cry for help, all the possibilities—along with the multitude of obstacles—had kept her troubled mind active and sleep at bay. On top of that, Nelson had not picked up his phone, nor had he returned her calls. She hoped he was feeling alright.

A loud knocking at her bedroom door jolted her back to the here and now.

"Erica. Do you know what time it is?" Mike's voice was tinged with frustration.

"Give me five minutes. I'm not going in to work today. If you'll hit the start button on the coffee machine, I'll join you as soon as I throw on some clothes."

She looked into the mirror and cringed at the sight of the dark circles beneath her eyes. She ran a brush through her tangled curls. Not bothering with makeup, she pulled on a pair of jeans and a sweatshirt and made her way to the kitchen.

Mike looked up from the paper when Erica slipped onto a stool beside him at the high counter. *She looks like holy hell*, he thought. *And with no more than a couple hours' sleep, I'm desperately in need of coffee myself.* "Rough night?" he said aloud while pouring the aromatic brew into two mugs.

"The worst," she said.

Her eyes, bloodshot and puffy, left no doubt that her night had been as rotten as his.

"And don't say it. I know I look like shit."

Mike made no attempt to fill the silence. Erica eventually composed her thoughts and addressed the eight-hundred-pound gorilla in the room. "I'm sorry about last night. Of course I want Marnie to live with us. Her letter just threw me off balance. Of course I can't let her down—and yet I fear the Taylors will never let her go."

"You're not alone, Erica." Mike spoke the words he'd rehearsed throughout the night. "We are a team: you, Bill, and yours truly. Maybe even Nelson. We can provide for Marnie. She will want for nothing."

"I know that. My fear has nothing to do with money."

"Then what?" He knew what her answer would be, but he didn't want to dwell on the obvious. Instead he hurried ahead, offering a word of encouragement. "We might have to wait a few months, but any court of law will allow a sixteen-year-old to choose."

Erica took a sip of her coffee. Then, setting the mug on the table, she said, "That's what you said last night. I'd never heard that before. I hope you're right." When he opened his mouth to start speaking again, she held up her palm. "Let me finish. There's a lot to be considered, and I don't want to make any mistakes. There's more to it than just Marnie's biological parents. She has two sisters in New York and—"

"Holy mother of God—"

"Hold on, Mike. I am not saying we can't make this work. I think we can, but it's going to take planning. Marnie won't be sixteen until August, and even if she already were of age, I wouldn't think of taking her out of school until the end of her sophomore year."

"Understood."

"First we need to talk with Marnie, then with Conrad and Ashleigh Taylor. If possible I'd like to avoid a court battle."

"Dream on, cupcake." Mike was a realist. The Taylors were not going to turn over their daughter without a fight. And they had the resources to wage one hell of a war.

"When the time is right, I will talk with Ashleigh, mother to mother. We've shared our concerns in the past over what is best for Marnie. Now I will have to confront her with Marnie's desires and what would be in her best interest at this time."

Mike didn't see much hope in that approach. *And of course Ashleigh Taylor will realize that it's in Marnie's best interest to give custody to the wife of the man who kidnapped her as an infant. Erica is delusional.*

Erica was still speaking. "We'll talk in April, when they come to Chicago for the De Mornay's opening. But I want to wait until after that event to approach the Taylors."

"Sorry. My mind wandered. I didn't hear the first part of what you said."

"I said we'd talk in depth with Marnie in April. I plan to call her this afternoon, after she gets home from school, to let her know that we received her letter and that we will work things out. I don't plan to say too much at this time. I just want to get a sense of how strongly she feels about living here."

Mike sighed and shook his head. "I understand you not wanting to bring the Taylors into the picture any sooner than necessary, but what about Marnie? She's not likely to keep quiet about her desire to live with us."

"If Marnie has already talked to the Taylors, we won't have a choice. We'll have to have that conversation sooner than I'd like. But we'll worry about that later."

"Ah. The Scarlet O'Hara solution?"

Erica smiled, but that smile wasn't reflected in her bloodshot eyes. "Not exactly. I have no Tara to run to, but I will do whatever it takes to get my daughter back." Seeking his eyes, she added, "I'm going to need all the help I can get, Mike. I haven't the slightest idea how to raise a teenager—especially one who has a second family."

"You have as good an idea as anyone raising a teenager for the first time. Bill and I will be with you all the way, and Nelson, although he has boys, is sure to be—" Mike broke off and shook his head. "No special credentials are issued to biological parents, you know. When it comes to knowing how to be a good parent, we're on an even playing field with the Taylors. However, the advantage is ours, since this is where Marnie wants to be."

He didn't mention one important thing: the petition opposing the Jordon's plan to place its insignia on John Stewart's. Erica's signature there would do little to smooth negotiations with Conrad Taylor. *No matter which way we slice it,* he thought, *negotiating with Marnie's biological parents will be "mission impossible."*

Sending David, their new limo driver, to JFK to pick up Paige and Helen gave Ashleigh the perfect opportunity to drive the girls to school. Even Marnie appeared to be in a good mood. Nothing more had been said about her letter or her desire to move to Chicago since Monday night, when Ashleigh and Conrad had taken her aside following dinner for a heart-to-heart talk about her desire to live with the Christonellis. They had done their best to express just how much she was a part of their family and how much they loved her.

But it was clear that Marnie still clung to her misconceptions. When Conrad asked, "What can we do to make you feel like the vital part of our family that you are?" she had remained stoic and silent for a very long time, her eyes focused on the living room carpet. Finally, her eyes blazing with contempt, she'd said, "Words, words, words! I'm so sick of words"—a near-perfect Eliza Doolittle imitation.

At that outburst, Conrad, who had done his level best to rein in his temper and remain supportive of their daughter's feelings, had lost it. "Whether you buy it or not, you are our daughter, a member of this family," he had said firmly. "There is nothing you could ever do to change that. Our love for you is unconditional." Without missing a beat—his voice low and controlled—Conrad told Marnie in no uncertain terms that when she turned eighteen she would have the right to choose where she wanted to live. Until that time, however, she would remain right where she belonged. "You will not be moving to Chicago or anywhere else. And you will not be disrespectful to your mother."

Marnie's eyes had rolled, but she had not spoken. Conrad's no-nonsense tone had left little room for debate.

Although Conrad had wanted to call and confront Erica Christonelli immediately after learning the details of Marnie's request, Ashleigh had suggested they take a step back. He hadn't given her a chance to mention the letter she'd composed to Erica earlier that afternoon.

"My God, Ashleigh," Conrad had said when she told him about it that night. "We've allowed them such liberal visitation. The Christonellis have become the proverbial weekend father figure luring our daughter with . . . with . . . I don't know what. Are you proposing we allow this woman to kidnap our daughter a second time?"

This morning, as Ashleigh's mind returned to the moment, she slowly braked at the corner of Mooreland Road and Round Hill Road. Hitting black ice, the Lincoln Continental fishtailed. She ignored the instinct to stomp on the brake, instead turning into the spin and gently pumping the pedal. Thoughts of all else vanished. The chatter in the backseat ceased. Fortunately there was no oncoming traffic.

With the car now under control, Ashleigh released the breath that had caught in her throat.

"Way to go, Mom," Juliana cried out, slipping one of the straps of her backpack over her shoulder, ready to hop out.

Ashleigh pulled into the semicircular driveway of Parkway Elementary School, wished her precocious daughter a good day, and then headed for the high school. She attempted to tune in to the twins' chatter, but their voices were too low to hear above the hum of the asphalt beneath the car. She could only hope they were enjoying their private chit-chat— rekindling their former closeness.

Back home again, Ashleigh heaved a sigh of relief when she saw there were no tire tracks in the light layer of snow on their driveway. She'd feared that Paige and her mother might have arrived before her return.

Inside, Ashleigh pulled off her boots and hung her coat in the foyer closet. A moment later, as if on cue, the front door burst open, heralding Paige and Helen's arrival.

Paige wore a bemused grin on her face. "Sorry," she said. "You told us to let ourselves in. Afraid Mom was a bit overly enthusiastic."

Helen glanced across at her daughter. "I'm right here, you know. You don't need to apologize for me." She let out a tiny giggle. "I guess I don't know my own strength." Then, without taking a full breath, she asked, "How is Elizabeth?"

"Much better," Ashleigh said. "It's nothing serious. I suggested she take it easy for a day or so, but you know Elizabeth. She says it will take more than a pesky cold to keep her down. She didn't take the Airborne quickly enough. I'm afraid she takes a lot better care of the rest of us than she does of herself."

"So you're an Airborne addict as well?" Paige chuckled. "That stuff has saved us from a lot of colds this winter. But it's not much good after the cold sets in."

"Paige, dear," Helen said, looking down at her snow-crusted shoes, "we didn't come here to talk about how to prevent colds. Where are the girls?"

Paige rolled her eyes, but spoke patiently as she told her mother that the girls were at school.

Ashleigh asked if she could take their coats, and when Helen slipped off her fur to reveal a beautiful St. John dress with matching jacket, Ashleigh was again taken aback by how much the woman looked like her daughter. *Well,* she thought, *it's really the other way around.* Both women were petite, with well-proportioned figures, and had been gifted with those startling green eyes. "Helen, you look amazing, as always," she said.

"Thank you, dear. That's very kind," Helen replied. "Are the girls upstairs?"

Ashleigh quickly repeated what Paige had said earlier and added, "They should be home around three thirty." As she hung their coats in the closet, she saw Helen in front of the gold-framed oval mirror, a frown wrinkling her otherwise smooth brow.

Paige must have noticed as well. "What is it?" she asked.

"I was just thinking about my hair."

"It's beautiful," Ashleigh said, with utter sincerity. "My grandmother dreamed of having shiny, snow-white hair rather than her salt-and-pepper 'do."

"Well," Helen said, "those are old-lady hair colors. I'm sure she wouldn't have wanted them at my age."

Exchanging glances with Paige, Ashleigh turned away from the closet and said, "Let's go into the living room. . ." Feeling a tug on her arm, she turned back to see Helen staring up to meet her eyes.

"Well, do you think I should look like an old lady?"

"Of course not, Helen. And you don't look one bit old-ladyish."

"You know your actor friend? The one who had his ninetieth birthday at the Long Beach Yacht Club?"

"Buddy Ebsen?"

She nodded. "Well, after he did his performance and marched all of us in a circle while playing the saxophone, I asked him how he did it at his age." She paused, making sure she had their attention before she continued. "He said that old age was always fifteen years older than he was. So I've got a long way to go."

"No doubt about it, Mom," Paige said.

Speaking almost simultaneously, Ashleigh said, "You are an extremely attractive woman, Helen. And I just read an article that stated today's seventy is yesterday's forty."

Helen grinned, patting down her hair. "Well, in that case, what would you think of my trading this in for a nice shade of red?"

"My God, Ashleigh, I don't know how you do it." Paige sank down onto the couch in the living room. "It's nearly ten, and we haven't had a moment to ourselves all evening."

"And so the world turns." Ashleigh laughed. "How about some coffee . . . Oops, lost my head. Apparently I'm the only one who's able to down a pot of coffee in the evening and still drift off to sleep the moment my head hits the pillow. Herbal tea, right?"

By the time Ashleigh had arranged the cups on a tray, Elizabeth was showing Helen to her room. The house was peaceful and still, with only the crackling from the fireplace to break the silence. Setting the tray on the coffee table, Ashleigh said, "Alone at last."

Her friend seemed momentarily lost in thought. But at the clank of the tea tray on the table, Paige shifted her gaze from the dancing flames and spoke. "With just one daughter to watch, I was always doing a juggling act. But having three girls going in all directions, along with all your community organizations, it's a wonder you can put a rational sentence together."

"What makes you think I can?" Ashleigh joked. "Unlike you, I couldn't wait to be a mother. I had such great role models—but I need an instruction manual now. My intuition is on the blink when it comes to raising teens. I just can't seem to get it right on my own."

"I don't know of any mom or dad who hasn't felt the same way."

"I never should have continued at John Stewart's after Marnie was returned to us. It may be possible for some women to be a supermom and wife while maintaining a successful career, but I just couldn't do it all. It's been months since I resigned, and there still aren't enough hours in the day." Meeting her friend's attentive eyes, she said, "I know how many challenges you've encountered over the past few years, Paige, but no matter what, you've come out on top. You never seem at a loss." *Like I am sometimes,* she thought. "You've held everything together. April adores you, and no one could ask for a more perfect daughter."

Ashleigh paused and took a sip of coffee, recalling how happy Paige's daughter had seemed with Kyle, the nice young man she had brought to the Christmas party. "By the way, how is her internship going at JJQ? And how does she like Chicago?"

"Great and so-so," Paige replied. "But we'll talk about April later. You've got more pressing issues to discuss—I can feel it. And since there's no telling when Mark and Conrad will be back from the Sotheby's board meeting, let's talk about what's eating you while we have a few minutes' peace."

Just having her friend there to talk to, already Ashleigh felt some of her tension begin to slowly evaporate, like helium escaping from an oversized party balloon. She took another sip of her coffee and put the cup back on the tray. "You know our concern over Marnie's mood swings, so I won't take you step-by-step through what I think might be behind them—" She paused, saw that she had Paige's undivided attention, and went on. "Yesterday she announced that she wants to live in Chicago. With her 'mother.'"

Paige froze, her teacup halfway to her mouth. Then she put the teacup back on the tray. "I'm so sorry, Ashleigh. That must have been terrible to hear. *You* are Marnie's mother. But you don't need me to state the obvious."

"You've just voiced what shoots through my head each time she refers to Erica as her 'mother.' And yet I can't fight it. If that's how she feels . . ." Ashleigh's voice trailed off.

Paige wanted to object, yet how could she? She knew Ashleigh had a great deal of empathy for Erica and for her losses—first her husband, then the daughter she felt was her own. But that empathy only went so far; her friend had made Erica a part of their extended family for Marnie's sake alone.

Paige could relate to Erica's pain over the loss of the child she had raised as her own. Although Paige had not given birth, April was her daughter nonetheless. So in a way she understood why Ashleigh had made the tough decision to make Erica a part of their family. But Paige cursed the day Mario Christonelli was born. *How could so many people be convinced that Erica's late husband had been a good, religious man?* she thought angrily. *That out of love and desperation, he had committed a heinous crime and taken one of Ashleigh's twins?*

"I don't know what to say to her—to my own daughter," Ashleigh went on, taking Paige's silence as an invitation.

At hearing this, Paige was alarmed. "You're not thinking of letting her go, are you?"

"Of course not. Marnie belongs with us—with her father—with her sisters—with me. The problem is, she's so desperately unhappy. I don't know how to fix that."

"Ashleigh, you're a great mother. But face it: Your daughter is a teenager. That's a tough time for any family, much less one like yours that has been through so much." She reached over and touched her friend's hand. "Life is full of drama, and you've said from the get-go that Marnie's highs and lows tend to hit extremes. Although we all want to have superpowers, moms aren't equipped to fix *all* the real or imagined problems of their children. We can only support our kids and help them find their own solutions."

Ashleigh sighed. "Did you ever encounter a period of ongoing rebellion with April?"

"I was pretty lucky," Paige confessed. "I didn't have the uphill battle you do. Mark and I had no other 'parents' vying for April's love and affection. You once asked me what I would have done if I discovered that April's biological mother had lived—that she had not been killed by that bullet." After taking a quick sip of tea, she continued. "I know I'd have fought with everything at my disposal to keep April. I also know that the law favors the biological parent, and I could have lost her. With you, that's not the case. The law is on your side."

Ashleigh rose and crossed in front of Paige to stand by the fire. "While the law may be on our side, it has no control over feelings. It can't dictate that Marnie must feel and believe in our love."

"I'm sure Marnie knows you love her."

"Maybe, but Conrad was right when he said we're like divorced parents trying to deal with what is right for their child. And since Erica represents the parent with visitation rights, she does not have to be the disciplinarian—she just provides the perks."

"What on earth can she provide that you can't?" Whatever it was, Paige knew, it certainly wasn't anything money could buy. At one time Erica Christonelli had been a talented dress designer. Working at De Mornay's, she had started to make a name for herself—but not a fantastic amount of money. But Erica had been forced to abandon her career after learning that the daughter she was raising as her own was actually Callie's kidnapped twin, and while in hiding, she'd become an alcoholic. As far as Paige knew, Erica had been sober for the past eight years. She was now working as the personal shopper at John Stewart's—a terrific job, but most likely one that did not offer an especially high salary.

Interrupting her thoughts, Ashleigh replied, "What she provides is a great deal more freedom than we can afford to give." She returned to her spot on the sofa. "Recently, Marnie has become very secretive. She's spending more and more time on the Internet. She instantly shrinks the window whenever I come into her room."

Paige raised her eyebrow. "Typical teenage behavior."

"Really? I know very little about the online hangouts for teens, but I plan to bring myself up to speed." She paused. "What do you know about Myspace, Paige?"

The kitchen door creaked loudly enough to be heard in the living room, cutting off Paige's response.

"I thought this door had been taken care of."

"To be continued," Ashleigh said to her friend at the sound of Conrad's voice. The two women headed for the kitchen.

Giving Conrad a quick kiss on the lips, Ashleigh said, "The workmen have been focused on the garage. I'll remind them of that squeaking door."

After giving his wife a kiss and a playful squeeze, Mark drew Ashleigh into a brotherly hug, and the four of them headed for the breakfast room table. The men ate the remains of the German chocolate cake while filling their wives in on news of Sotheby's upcoming fund-raiser.

Twenty minutes later, perhaps sensing that Ashleigh and Paige needed more time to themselves, Conrad caught Mark's eye and asked, "Up for a round of pool?" The two men excused themselves and headed for the game room.

Returning to the living room sofa, Paige picked up where she and Ashleigh had left off.

"When April was around the twins' age, there was no Myspace. April's obsession was nonstop telephone chats."

Ashleigh sighed. "I guess in one respect, I'm just feeling my way around. I do understand that teenagers need privacy. As fantastic as Gran and Charles were, I know I didn't want them listening in on my phone conversations, which I suppose is pretty much like today's online conversations. But how do you allow your child total privacy and at the same time keep her safe?"

"The question of the century, my friend. If you don't ask yourself that a hundred times a day, you're not a mother."

Isn't that the truth. "Maybe I'm just becoming paranoid, but since Marnie has not been able to participate in dance, she spends far too much time online. She seems to have withdrawn from the other girls on her dance team. She's spending a lot of time with a newer friend, Lindsey, who comes from a broken home—" She stopped herself. "Of course, in and of itself that doesn't make her a poor choice—"

"But you fear the lack of supervision," Paige cut in. "As the kids say, I know where you're coming from. That's a tough call. How soon will Marnie be able to get back into practice?"

"Her ankle was weak even before the sprain, so Dr. Scott has given her exercises for strengthening it. But it's become a no-win situation—she's not happy about not dancing, but she's not doing her part to get back into it." Noticing Paige's puzzled expression, Ashleigh explained, "The more I push her to do those exercises, the more resistant she becomes. It's like extracting wisdom teeth with no Sodium Pentothal."

Paige smiled and clapped her hands together like a small child after winning a game of pin the tail on the donkey.

Puzzled, Ashleigh waited for Paige to give her some good news.

"Well, that part is a snap," Paige exclaimed. "I imagined you had some unsolvable conundrum, but I just may have the solution. Number one, call Dr. Rockenmacher. I'll give you his number. He's a sports medicine doctor who helped April get through many dance performances, even with injuries."

"I don't want to take any chances . . ."

"Neither did we. Neither did the doctor. He's a miracle man. Even with a sprained ankle, April was able to perform her solo, which included an elliptical, and she was in eleven other numbers. Dr. Rock taped her ankle in a way that both made it tolerable and prevented further injury. He did the same thing when she dislocated her knee." Paige paused. "Number two, you need a personal trainer."

Knowing that Sonny, Paige's redheaded Irish trainer, had moved back to Hollywood, Ashleigh asked, "Any suggestions?"

"Sure do." Paige picked up her handbag from the arm of the couch, dug around inside, and extracted a glossy gold card that she handed to Ashleigh. "He's Irish, he possesses Sonny's quick wit, and he has worked with a ton of Dr. Rock's temporarily broken dancers. His name's Clancy. You'll love him."

"Thank you, thank you, thank you," Ashleigh cried. "If he's even half as lovable as Sonny, he just might get through to my rebellious daughter." She prayed for a miracle, fearing nothing short of that was needed to break through Marnie's defensiveness.

CHAPTER
12

The following morning, before the household awakened, Conrad and Ashleigh slipped into the breakfast nook for coffee and a bowl of granola. They'd had little time alone to discuss how they planned to handle the bombshell Marnie had dropped earlier in the week.

"So, sweetheart, you want to talk about it?" Conrad asked.

He knows me so well. "I know you're not a fan of letter writing, love," Ashleigh began. "But in lieu of a head-on confrontation—"

"Marnie is our child," he cut in without raising his voice. "She belongs here with us. Erica and Mike must be told immediately, in no uncertain terms. There's no room for negotiation of any kind."

"I'm with you all the way." Ashleigh laced her fingers through her husband's and met his penetrating blue eyes. "I do *not* wish to negotiate." Although her voice was soft, it was filled with conviction. "However, since we have no idea what, if any, influence Erica or Mike had on Marnie's desire to live with them . . . Actually, now that I think of it, I'm almost certain there was no conversation about it last week when Marnie was in Chicago."

"How did you come to that conclusion?"

Although Conrad's voice remained low and unemotional, Ashleigh knew only too well the price he was paying. "Marnie mailed the letter from JFK. She wrote it on her way back from Chicago."

"So you believe there was no prior discussion between Marnie and Erica?" There was a tone of incredulity in his voice. His eyes remained locked on hers.

"Yes. And Conrad, before you take any action," Ashleigh said, "please allow me to address the situation by mail first. That way there will be no misunderstanding and the Christonellis will know exactly where we stand. For all we know, they may not even *want* Marnie to come and live with them."

"Fat chance." Conrad rose to his full six foot three, pulling his wife to her feet. "You are far too trusting." He gazed up at the ceiling. Silence permeated the room. After clearing his throat, Conrad said, "Against my better judgment, I'll delay the confrontation. Send your letter by FedEx this morning. However, if we haven't heard from Erica by Saturday, all bets are off. She and Mike will be hearing from *me*."

Ashleigh felt lightheaded with relief. "I'd like to read the letter to you before I send it."

Conrad shook his head.

Ashleigh did not push him. "OK, Conrad. And I want you to know that if either Erica or Mike takes any role in enticing Marnie to come live with them, it's no holds barred. We'll get a restraining order against the entire household," she announced in an unmistakably determined tone.

An expression of surprise and gratitude spread across her husband's face. "Thank God," he said, wrapping his arms around her. "That's my girl."

Ashleigh was glad that her husband was pleased with her approach. But just moments later, the reality of what she had said hit her full on. Her insides felt shredded as she thought of what could happen if they had to file a restraining order against the Christonellis. *Did I really say those words?* When she considered the possible damage that such an outcome might have on their daughter's already fragile psyche, she almost wished she could take them back.

CHAPTER

13

At the sound of the doorbell, Mike squinted at the red digits on his bedside clock as they came into focus: 9:05. It had been well after five o'clock that very morning when he'd crawled into bed. Now, in his darkened bedroom, it felt like the middle of the night rather than well after dawn.

"Coming, coming," he hollered. Pushing his feet into well-worn slippers and shrugging into his robe, he hustled toward the door. Through the mudroom window, he saw a FedEx truck in the driveway. His heart took a nosedive. *Are we expecting a delivery?* He didn't think so. It was unlikely to be good news.

Pulling open the door, he was hit by a blast of cold Chicago air and the incredibly broad smile of a gangly young man wearing a navy blue uniform with the company's distinctive purple stripe and logo.

"For Erica Christonelli?" the messenger said.

"She's at work, but I'm Michael Christonelli. I'd be glad to sign for her," Mike replied, not mentioning that he was Erica's brother-in-law, not her husband. He often found that approach to be more convenient. *Why make it complicated?*

For a long moment after the FedEx truck pulled away, he stood in front of the closed door, staring down at the cardboard envelope and the return address. Today of all days, with all the upheaval of Erica giving her notice at John Stewart's, he dreaded having to hand this envelope over to her when she came home. But that is exactly what he knew he must do.

The instant Erica stepped inside the home she shared with Mike and Bill, she slipped out of her shoes and hung her coat on one of the hooks in the mudroom. Padding toward the aroma of stew wafting down the hall, she experienced a brief sense of well-being and relaxation in her taut muscles. But it quickly dissipated. Her horrendous day had been on continuous replay in her head all the way home, and the reel picked up again as she made her way into the kitchen. Today she had followed through on her heart-wrenching decision—she had picked her battle. Since her prayers for the future of John Stewart's were in direct conflict with those of Marnie's father, she was stepping aside. Marnie's future was her priority.

With a heavy heart, she had contacted Wainwright, who had been instrumental in landing her a freelance job last year, moonlighting at a company under the Wainwright Enterprises umbrella. For the past year she'd been able to make use of her design talents at Medley Originals. Wainwright's recommendation had been a godsend. And she now had a full-time position waiting for her in Medley's design department—but still, handing in her two weeks' notice at John Stewart's hurt like hell.

Mike looked up from across the room. His eyes only fleetingly met hers as he greeted her with a quick "Hi," and then instantly looked back down to the pot on the stove.

Erica knew him too well to ignore that response. "What's wrong?"

"No point in putting off the inevitable. You received a letter by FedEx this morning." Without taking a single breath he went on. "The return address was Greenwich."

Greenwich? The word screamed in her head, robbed her of speech. Erica felt the blood drain from her face. *I'm not ready for this. I'm really not ready for this.* "Where is it?" she finally managed to ask.

Mike nodded his head toward the kitchen counter.

Erica stared at the envelope. Stared at the return address. Her hand shook. She wished Nelson were here beside her.

"Well?" Mike said.

Bill strode into the kitchen. "Well, what?" he repeated before wrapping his arm around Mike and peering into the open pot.

"A FedEx letter. From Greenwich," Mike explained. Then he turned to Erica. "Aren't you going to open it?"

Erica nodded. "But first I want to call Nelson and see if he's up to coming over this evening."

Mike exchanged a glance with Bill, but they both remained silent as Erica walked into the den to use the phone. To Mike, Nelson seemed to be a nice guy who genuinely cared for Erica. He treated her like a princess when he was around. But he stood her up all too often, feigning illness—or so it seemed to Mike. He kept meaning to find out more about fibromyalgia. *I'll google it tonight,* he promised himself.

"How are you feeling?" he heard Erica ask. "Terrific," she said, and then she began to explain about the FedEx envelope. "It has Ashleigh's name on it . . . I don't know . . . No, I haven't opened it. I'm sort of unstrung. . . Have you had dinner? . . . Why don't you come by, then? . . . Wonderful," she said before hanging up the phone.

As Erica walked back into the kitchen, Mike saw a faint smile curl her lips. An overwhelming sense of relief washed over him. *Nelson, buddy boy, you'd better come through. If she ever needed you, she needs you now.*

Nelson Kennedy was feeling far better this evening and had looked forward wholeheartedly to diving back into proofreading the galleys on his desk. He and his architectural team had been working on this megabook for the past several years. It was a long-overdue tribute to architects and their masterpieces from the late nineteenth to the mid-twentieth century. But the project would have to be delayed a little longer. The tightness in Erica's voice left no doubt: She needed him now.

Standing in the doorway between the dining room and the living room, he heard the beat of some not-so-soothing music filtering through the earphones of his son's iPod. Neil sat slumped down on the sofa, his nose in a textbook. *How can he possibly concentrate with that godawful music blaring in his ears?* thought Nelson. "Neil," he called, hoping his voice rose above the volume of the music.

As the copper-headed boy looked up from his history book, his glasses slid down his nose and his eyes filled with concern. "Where are you going, Dad?" he asked.

"I'm going over to Erica's." He paused before adding, "I'd really like you to get to know her better. Maybe—"

Neil rolled his eyes. "Not tonight; I've got a midterm tomorrow." Instantly changing focus, he shifted roles and asked his familiar question: "You won't be out too late tonight, will you?"

"Not to worry," Nelson said. "I feel great. This is a work night for Erica, so I'll be home early." He hadn't meant to imply that he wanted Neil to join him tonight. Erica needed his undivided attention, and it was a school night. But having his son worry about him felt like hell. It should be the other way around. It just wasn't fair. "Annie said she'd be glad to come over for a while so you wouldn't be alone."

Neil rolled his eyes. "Give me a break, Dad. I'm almost sixteen. I don't need any babysitter."

"I know you don't. Give me a call if you need anything. Erica's number is programmed on the landline and I have my cell."

"Later," Neil said, his eyes falling back onto the pages of his book.

Nelson headed for the door and then turned back. "Your brother said he might drop by to pick up his DVD player. If he does, have him give me a call."

"Will do," Neil said without looking up.

Nelson grabbed the keys to his Toyota Highlander, shrugged into a heavy winter coat, and pulled a wool knit beanie over his nearly bald pate. The prognosis on his chronic pain and limited energy level had been less than encouraging, but he refused to give in. *Medical breakthroughs happen for all types of conditions. The answer is out there . . . somewhere.* As Nelson heard the *click* of the SUV's locks opening, he felt the vibration of his cell phone. Slipping behind the steering wheel, he flipped open his Razr and glanced at the caller ID. He smiled and pressed a button, and then held the phone to his ear. "Hi, Alan. What's up?"

After asking Nelson how he was feeling, Alan Grey—the key motivator and organizer of the powerful grassroots group Fans of John Stewart's— said, "We had a terrific wrap-up meeting last night. Gayle took notes and will e-mail them to you, if she hasn't already done so. We want everyone up to speed. But I suspect you know that's not why I called."

Nelson didn't rise to the bait.

Alan himself broke the tension. "Just wondering about your . . . significant other. I heard she resigned from John Stewart's."

"That's right." *My, how quickly news travels,* Nelson thought. But he wasn't actually surprised. Alan seemed to have an ear in every corner of the city. He knew everything, often before it actually happened.

"Was her resignation voluntary?"

Obviously Alan wanted to know whether Erica had been under any pressure from Jordon's to resign. He was well aware that she had not kept her views under wraps; in fact, she'd been blatantly vocal in stating that changing the name of the historic store was an absolute travesty. Just the other night, during the Fans of John Stewart's midnight rally, she had even carried a sign that read CHICAGO WANTS JOHN STEWART'S, NOT ANOTHER COOKIE-CUTTER JORDON'S.

Nelson knew, however, that the pressure propelling Erica to resign had nothing to do with her open participation in those protests. But was he at liberty to tell Alan the real reason for her departure?

CHAPTER
15

Neil Kennedy slammed his history book closed. He would ace tomorrow's midterm. *History's no sweat,* he thought. *If only I could say the same about geometry.* Glancing across the room at the dining room table, he shook his head. The table was piled high with page after page of the whopper of a book that seemed to be sapping every ounce of his dad's energy. Neil wished his dad's partners were equally dedicated to this lifelong dream.

About to head for the shower, he heard the *whoosh* of tires as a car pulled up in front of the house. Neil glanced at the clock on the dining room wall. It was only six forty-five. *Can't be Dad already,* he thought as he strode though the living room and peered out the bay window. Recognizing the silver van, he unlatched the front door.

Rick, his tall, rail-thin half-brother, was hurrying up the walkway. The heel of one of his boots slipped, and he almost fell. Quickly righting himself, he hollered, "Why doesn't someone clear the goddamn sidewalk?"

"Cool it, Rick," Neil shouted back, not bothering to point out it had been only a few hours since he'd shoveled the path to the front steps. *Who is Rick to criticize? He's given Dad nothing but problems—even before Mom's accident. He has no reason to blame her death on Dad.*

Rick opened the front door and charged through the living room, heading straight for his old bedroom. Then he stopped dead.

What is he looking at? "If you're after your DVD player, it's on top of the piano," Neil said.

Not taking another step, Rick frowned down at the dining room table and shook his head. "My God. Is there any end in sight?"

"Sure. That's the final set of galleys."

Rick gave a derisive sneer. "Other than 'Dad' and his freaky old building cronies, who gives a fuck? I mean, this book has been your dad's obsession for years, but I can't see that it has any potential to pay off."

"You know he's never been in it for the money," Neil said, knowing he needn't bother explaining. *He just resents the fact that Dad's not more interested in material things.* Rick blamed his stepfather for driving their mother away, for failing to give her what she needed in life, but Neil knew he was dead wrong.

It had become Neil's habit over the years to avoid certain conversations with his big brother—what was the point?—but there was something he did want to share. He'd heard some things about his dad's girlfriend, and not liking some of it, he'd begun an Internet search. There were a ton of news stories about Erica Christonelli and a kidnapped twin. Neil was blown away when he discovered the twins were the daughters of the Jordon's CEO.

What began as a search to protect his dad, however, had turned into a very different type of quest. It turned out that Erica was not really a kidnapper, and he'd decided she was most likely an okay person. But something else had him instantly hooked: Marnie and all the stories that must be locked up inside her. So he'd found her on Myspace, and they'd formed an online friendship thanks to his pal Brad Adams, who had let him contact Marnie from his computer, under his name. He wasn't quite sure how, but he knew he had to meet Marnie Christonelli in person. She was bound to be a great source for his school newspaper and his English project.

Though Rick seldom went out of his way to lend a hand, Neil had no one else to turn to, so maybe if he formulated a plan . . .

CHAPTER
16

Nelson eased his Highlander alongside the three-foot-high wall of hard-packed snow in front of the Christonellis' home. Throwing the car door open wide, he felt the sting of snow crystals biting at his cheek as his feet slid to the ground.

Rounding the back of his car, he heard the *thud* of the front door echo through the stillness of the quiet suburban neighborhood. A small figure stood on the front porch. As he drew near, he heard muffled sobs and saw the fluorescent white of Erica's parka illuminated in the glow of the porch light.

Mindless of the snow and ice, Nelson dashed forward. "Erica," he called out as he bounded up the steps.

She turned toward him, but her eyes remained focused on the floor.

Taking her into his arms, he held her tight and for several long moments said nothing. He sensed that her trembling had little to do with the cold. It *was* cold as hell, however, and staying there on the porch was not a good option. He wanted to ask why she had stormed out of the house, but he set his need to know aside and instead asked, "How about a cappuccino?" Their favorite Starbucks was a short drive away.

Erica stiffened and took a step back. Still not meeting his eyes, she said, "Oh, Nelson, I've made such a mess of things. When it comes to Marnie, I can't do anything right."

Not sure how to respond, he pulled off a glove, reached into his jacket pocket, and took out a folded handkerchief. He handed it to her, saying, "Come on. Tonight, I'm pretty sure we'll have the coffee shop to ourselves." Taking her by her mittened right hand, he led her to his SUV.

In the shelter of the Highlander's comfortable interior, the dam broke. One word tumbled over the next as Erica said, "I didn't know what to do. As soon we got Marnie's letter, Mike and Bill said I should tell her not to talk to Ashleigh and Conrad about wanting to live with us—at least, not until we retain an attorney and have everything in order. But I didn't think that was right. I can't ask her to be dishonest or sneaky. But now . . . but now . . ."

Listening to Erica weep, Nelson felt a wave of impotence sweep over him. He wished he could find the words to comfort her, but what could he possibly say?

When Erica emerged from the restroom at Starbucks, her eyes were dry, but splashing cold water on her face had done little to fade their redness.

Looking about the nearly deserted space, she spotted Nelson on the sofa beside the fireplace. His grande caramel apple cider and her grande cappuccino sat on the oblong table between the sofa and the flickering firelight. Now somewhat in control of her emotions, she held her chin high. "I'm so sorry you had to see me so unstrung. I'm okay now, and I won't let that happen again."

Taking her hands in his, Nelson waited until their eyes locked. "Don't ever apologize for showing your feelings. At least, not to me. I'm here for you."

Erica swallowed hard. "I know you are. Don't know what I'd have done if you couldn't be here tonight." She stopped herself. *Oh no—there I go again. All Nelson needs right now is some damsel in distress.* "Sorry. Erase that last statement. You have enough on your plate without—"

Nelson dropped her hands. His shot up, palms out. "Please, Erica. We promised that we would be totally candid with one another. Don't shut me out now . . ."

As Nelson spoke, Erica mentally replayed portions of what he'd told her of his past, especially aspects of his previous marriage. Nelson was a man she could trust—she knew that—but what was more, he truly wanted to share every challenge as well as every triumph that came their way. Pulling herself from her inner thoughts, she returned to what he was saying.

"... and I have a feeling you started somewhere in the middle. Please bring me up to date." He placed his warm hands over hers once more. "When you called, you said you had gotten a letter from Marnie's biological mother. Start at the beginning."

Erica closed her eyes for a moment, and then began. "Even though I said I wanted you with me when I opened the FedEx envelope, I found I couldn't wait. This has been a day from hell. I've been filled with roller-coaster emotions, even before I arrived home."

She and Nelson had discussed her decision to resign from John Stewart's, and she knew he understood and supported her. Leaving the company had been inevitable, even before Marnie's letter had made it imperative.

Nelson nodded, his sea-green eyes filled with a gentle concern.

"Evidently, Marnie told her . . . she told Ashleigh about the letter. Ashleigh knew about it before I even received it."

Slowly shaking his head, Nelson spoke in a voice that was less than a decibel above a whisper. "Oh boy."

"Well, as you might imagine, that did not go well."

Erica took a sip of her cappuccino, wishing she had the actual letter with her. She tried to get her thoughts in chronological order. Her brain shut down. Mike and Bill's accusations blocked all rational thought. She'd already told Nelson how angry Mike and Bill were with her, and how they felt she was responsible for their current dilemma. They had wanted her to advise Marnie against telling her parents how unhappy she was. *But if Marnie feels she is being treated as only part of a pair and not as an individual in her own right, shouldn't her family—her entire family—know about it?*

It's possible that all this might just be the usual teenage drama. The thought had occurred to Erica before. *If so, I pray that Marnie will have a change of heart. Or if the problems are real, I hope the Taylors will recognize it and take action.* Marnie may just have been acting out, she knew. But one thing was for sure: Everyone—Erica, her brother-in-law, the Taylors—wanted what was best for their beloved girl.

Tears burned in her eyes, threatening to spill, but she would not allow herself to break down again. She must be strong. Though she longed for just one glass of wine to give her that strength, she shook off the very thought. *I am an alcoholic. Even a single drink can lead me down the road to hell.*

Instead, Erica lifted the Starbucks cup to her lips, took another sip, and then looked into Nelson's empathetic eyes. "To get straight to the point, Ashleigh wrote that if either Mike or I lifted a finger to aid Marnie's desire to leave their family, they would take out a restraining order before we took our next breath, preventing us not only from seeing Marnie but also from talking to her on the phone."

Nelson blinked, an expression of shock registering on his pale face. "Could she do that?"

Erica wasn't entirely sure—and she didn't want to find out.

CHAPTER
17

Marnie sucked in a deep breath as her fingers flew across the keyboard. HOW CUM U NO SO MUCH ABOUT ME? she wrote. Then she hit SEND.

Her attention was suddenly diverted by the *bang!* of her bedroom door as it crashed into the wall. She looked up to see Callie surveying the room. "Have you seen my black parka?" Callie asked.

Marnie shrunk the Myspace screen, turned from her computer, and shook her head, returning the question with one of her own: "Did you check the floor beside your dresser?"

Callie rolled her eyes. "Okay, so I'm not a neatnik like you. But I've checked everywhere, and I can't find it." She paused. "Can I borrow yours?"

"Sure," Marnie said, "I'll get it for you." She sprang to her feet before her sister had a chance to snoop around.

Callie's gaze drifted to the computer. "Were you talking to that guy in Chicago again?"

"No," Marnie lied. *Subject change, please,* she thought. "You going out with Derek again?"

"You know I am. A bunch of us are going over to Sam's." Callie's tone was defensive, daring her sister to say anything derogatory about her on-again, off-again boyfriend.

This time, though, Marnie held her tongue. "Have a great time," she said. She sincerely hoped Callie didn't let that smooth-talking jerk hurt her again.

As soon as Callie left her room, Marnie got back onto Myspace, hoping that Brad had responded . . . He hadn't. Shutting down the computer, she headed for the kitchen.

Ashleigh flipped up the back of her hair and held it so Conrad could hook the emerald necklace he'd given her for their anniversary the month before. She was delighted to finally have an occasion to don this special gift.

She caught a glimpse of her handsome husband in the mirror. At forty-six, wearing his pleated tuxedo shirt and cummerbund, he still possessed the power to make her heart skip a beat. But with all that was going on in his business life and their personal lives, there hadn't been much time for just the two of them. It was up to her, she decided then and there, to find a way to bring more romantic moments back into their lives. *I will not allow life to keep getting in our way,* she promised herself.

Feeling Conrad's lips at the nape of her neck, Ashleigh turned, her arms wrapping around him. But from the corner of her eye, she saw Marnie pass by the open door to their bedroom. Her thoughts flew to the fact that, other than Elizabeth, Marnie might be home alone this evening.

"Marnie," she called out.

"Yeah?" Marnie said, halting midstride in the open doorway. Her parents had stepped out of their embrace, and her dad was shrugging into his tuxedo jacket. Beside him, her mom—well, Ashleigh—looked amazing. She wore a long, strapless evening gown, and her blonde hair, which fell just past her shoulders, was super shiny. *They look like movie stars.*

"Is Lindsey able to spend the night?" Ashleigh asked.

"No, she's with her dad this weekend." Seeing her mother's frown, Marnie quickly added, "Don't worry. Elizabeth rented the new version of *Cheaper by the Dozen.* We're going to make some popcorn and watch it after I finish some of my homework."

Ashleigh arched an eyebrow. "I thought you said you'd rather die than be forced to watch another Hilary Duff movie."

"Not me. That was Callie," said Marnie, unable to take the sarcasm from her tone. "Juliana and I think Hilary is sort of cool." Noticing that the look of concern had left neither of her parents' faces, she stiffened.

"Look, I'm almost sixteen. I hardly need a house full of people to help me make it through the night."

"Of course you don't," Conrad said before giving her a hug and a kiss on the forehead.

"Besides, I sort of like having time to myself," Marnie assured them.

Ashleigh also stepped forward to give her a hug. "Enjoy your movie, darling, and please don't spend a lot of time online."

What's the big deal with spending time online? thought Marnie. But rather than answer her mother she said only, "Have a good time."

Armed with hot chocolate and several Oreo cookies, Marnie glanced at the clock before heading to the kitchen door. She had another twenty minutes before Elizabeth would join her in the family room. She dashed back upstairs to her room, shut the door, and pushed in the lock at the center of the knob.

When she checked the computer screen, she saw an instant message: I HAVE WAYS OF FINDING OUT THINGS ABOUT PEOPLE I'M INTERESTED IN.

Marnie moved her cursor over to her buddy list. She centered it on Brad07 and saw that it said, I AM ONLINE BUT MAY BE AWAY FROM AOL RIGHT NOW.

She recalled the first message she'd received from Brad last week, the day after her return to Greenwich. He'd told her that he lived catty-corner from her mom's place, that he'd seen her several times from his bedroom window. He'd asked around about her, he said, and he wanted to get to know her. He had explained that he'd been stuck in bed with the flu over the holidays—and that sounded reasonable, right?

But the first time Brad had mentioned her dad, Marnie's antennae had gone up. With all the passion for John Stewart's in the Windy City, the name of the Jordon's CEO was frequently bandied about, but information about his family was not something the company advertised. How could Brad know that she was his daughter—and that she had another family in Chicago? She wondered how much of her concern was sensible and how much was just plain paranoia.

Marnie typed, R U THERE?

U BET, came the instant reply.

Brad had told her that he had met her mom at John Stewart's Sunday night, at a midnight rally where he'd been in charge of passing out flyers.

WAS ANYONE WITH MY MOM AT THE RALLY? Marnie tapped on the keyboard. The screen indicated that Brad was typing. She waited.

Finally, the next message came through: SHE WAS WITH SOME GUY WHO WORE A BEANIE.

Marnie did not think her uncle Mike would be at the protest—after all, he had been working on the Jordon's website—and Uncle Bill wanted to keep his job, so he wouldn't be protesting either. Maybe it was Nelson, the bald guy she'd met at the house over Christmas vacation. He and her mom seemed real uptight over the fact that John Stewart's was going to be called Jordon's. WHAT DID HE LOOK LIKE? Marnie typed.

SORT OF AVERAGE LOOKING.

She was about to ask what that meant, but when she saw he was still typing, she waited.

NOT TOO TALL. UNDER SIX FOOT, appeared on her screen, followed by, BUT I DON'T WANT TO TALK ABOUT THEM OR THE STUPID OLD STORE.

WHAT DO YOU WANT TO TALK ABOUT? she fired back. She knew that her mom and Nelson thought her dad was going to destroy the old landmark store. *But that has nothing to do with me or Brad.*

Brad's reply was instant. WHAT I'D REALLY LIKE TO DO IS WRITE A STORY ABOUT YOU.

Y? WHAT DO YOU KNOW ABOUT ME? HOW DID YOU FIRST FIND ME? She'd asked the question before, and this time she wanted an answer.

DUH. YOUR DAD IS ALL OVER THE MEDIA. THE WHOLE FAMILY IS A CINCH TO LOOK UP ONLINE. I HAVE AN ASSIGNMENT IN CREATIVE WRITING CLASS. I WAS GOOGLING TO FIND SOMETHING INTERESTING TO WRITE ABOUT. AND THERE YOU WERE.

WHAT DO YOU MEAN? she asked, her hand shaking as she typed, although she was sure she already knew. *I bet he wants me to tell him about being kidnapped when I was a baby.* She closed her eyes and shook her head once, twice. *My parents—all three of them—would kill me. Besides, that was so long ago, and there's so much I don't know.*

When Marnie looked up again, Brad's response was on the screen: WHEN I CHECKED U OUT ON MYSPACE, I LIKED WHAT I SAW.

That wasn't what she'd expected. But she saw that he was still typing.

Brrrring! Another message popped up: AND I WAS THINKING . . . WITH THE KIND OF STORY YOU HAVE TO TELL, YOU COULD MAKE SOME SERIOUS MONEY.

Standing on a ladder in the dressing room, Viviana grabbed the molding along the doorjamb. The thunderous pounding at the boutique's front door had startled her and sent her heart racing. She collected her breath and quickly checked her watch before swiftly alighting from the stepladder. *Oh my God, it's already eight o'clock.*

She dashed across the newly laid plush carpeting, unlocked the door, and pulled it open, letting in a frigid gust of wind. On the verge of apologizing for not being ready to walk out the door, she noticed Mitchell's gaze drop to her stockinged feet and—God forbid!—her thick ankles. Instinctively, she rose on tiptoe.

After stamping his boots on the welcome mat and brushing the snow from the sleeves of his overcoat, Wainwright stepped inside, planted a kiss on her cheek, and grinned. "Time sure does fly when you're having fun," he quipped.

"I'm so sorry, Mitchell," Viviana replied. "There's still so much to do before the opening. I just hadn't noticed the time." She pushed her feet into her Cole Haan pumps. "It seems there's one darn thing after another. But I'll be ready in a shake." She headed for her office and, pausing at the foot of the stairs, asked, "Do you have any idea where I can get a recommendation for an electrician?"

Wainwright's eyes swept around the store, and a puzzled expression came to rest on his brow. "You don't have an electrician?"

"I did. But he works for my contractor." She didn't want to bring Mitchell into her squabble with the contractor. He might point out that her expectations were out of line—something she definitely didn't want to hear. "Let's just say that he and I didn't see eye to eye on a few things.

What I need is an electrician to work on adjusting the lighting in the dressing room. There's a dimmer switch, but it doesn't—"

"So you want to emulate lighting for various times of day," Wainwright said with a knowing look. "I think I might know someone who knows someone."

"Here in Chicago?" she asked.

"One of Tony's roommates is in some sort of construction. If he can't do it, he's bound to be able to find someone who can."

"Great. Wait a moment while I get my coat and boots." As she dashed upstairs, Viviana let herself wonder what this evening would bring. Back when she and Mitchell were hot and heavily involved, his older son had been in prison still. Would she finally meet that notorious son tonight? This whole reunion between Mitchell and his long-estranged son piqued her curiosity. It seemed her former beau had come to terms with certain aspects of Tony's previous life. If she was not mistaken, he even seemed somewhat proud of the intelligence behind the embezzlement scam that had landed Tony in jail. He had conveniently forgotten about the chaos that followed—Tony's "master plan." Still, she couldn't quite envision Mitchell completely transforming from a card-carrying homophobe to an acceptance of Tony's so-called alternative lifestyle. That was just too broad a stretch.

Perhaps she would find out more at dinner tonight. And anyway, who was she to judge? If Mitchell wanted to make a change in his life, so be it. The words of "Que Sera, Sera" rang in her head. *Whatever will be, will be—indeed.*

Wainwright took hold of Viviana's elbow as she gingerly stepped onto the sidewalk in front of her boutique. In consideration of the snow-encrusted streets, she had changed out of her stiletto pumps into boots. High-heeled boots, that is.

"Heaven forbid that fashion take a backseat to practicality," Wainwright teased, giving her hand a squeeze. "Nor should it." He walked around the car and slipped behind the wheel of the rented Lexus. Without skipping a beat, he asked, "So how's your love life here in the Windy City?"

"No time for anything but getting—"

"Doesn't sound like the foxy lady I—"

"Really, with so much to be done before the grand opening . . . ," she cut in. She didn't even want to think about the monumental task of selecting an impeccable sales staff for her couture boutique in a strange city. "All my energy has gone into De Mornay's." That was true—for the most part. During most of her short tenure in Chicago, she *had* been forced to put her libido on hold. Of course, Mitchell didn't need to know about Patrick's brief visit over the past weekend. *Time to change the subject.* "So, tell me about your reunion with Anth—I mean, Tony."

"Where to begin?" Strumming his fingers on the steering wheel, Wainwright fleetingly slid his gaze across to hers, then instantly back to the road ahead. "Actually, I'm as baffled as you are. All these years, I never thought there was any place in my life for my rogue son. But I was dead wrong."

For a few seconds, silence hung heavily between them. Viviana did not jump in to fill it.

"About six months ago, I received another letter from Tony," Wainwright continued. "On the back of the envelope, he wrote, 'Please do not discard before reading. I googled your name today and discovered you'd had another son. I share your pain over his loss.'" His voice caught in his throat.

Viviana panicked slightly. *Where is he going with this?* His reunion with Tony might not be such a good thing after all—not if it meant the unrelenting depression that had followed the death of his second son would resurface. *Almost fifteen years ago now—can that be right?* Mitchell had been as closed about the tragedy of young Mitch's death at the tender age of nine as he always was about his relationship, or lack thereof, with Tony, who must be at least forty by now.

"To make a long story short," Wainwright said, "I finally read one of his letters. Tony didn't ask for anything. He said he just wanted me to know he was turning his life around—making a living using his computer skills. On the right side of the law this time. Don't understand exactly what his job entails, but he mentioned he and a friend were moving to Chicago."

At the corner of North State and East Randolph, the light turned red. Wainwright slammed on the brakes, and the unfamiliar car fishtailed. He turned into the skid and quickly had it under control. "Sorry," he grumbled.

He remained silent for a few long seconds, as if collecting his thoughts. When the light turned green, he again turned to Viviana. "To tell you the truth, I crumbled up that letter and tossed it in the trash. But that night, as if someone had waved some sort of magic wand over me, my memories of little Mitch were precious and good. They'd lost the power to make me morose. They made me smile. Hundreds of images of Mitch swam through my head. I remembered how amazing he was—talking in complete sentences before the age of two, and that proud, happy smile he always wore. Time after time he beat the leukemia odds, and then—" Shaking his head from side to side, he said, "No point in revisiting what might have been."

Viviana's heart beat erratically. She was relieved when Mitchell did not verbally relive his son's tragic death. Although his wife had been driving the car when the accident occurred, he'd felt responsible.

"Later that same night I retrieved the letter, read it, and reread it," he continued. "The next day I got in touch with Tony. Eventually we got together. First time since—" With a rueful laugh, he said, "No need to mention since when."

No need at all. She was sure that until recently, Mitchell hadn't laid eyes on his son since the day in court when Tony was sentenced, some two decades ago.

"Tony is pretty damn intelligent, and thank God, he has nothing going on in his love life. He claims he has a strictly platonic relationship with his two roommates. Since meeting them, I'm inclined to believe it."

"So it's fair to say that indeed, miracles still exist here on planet Earth?"

Turning onto I-90, Wainwright's eyes flashed with amusement. "Okay, you win. Good, bad, or indifferent, Tony is my son—the only family I've got. For now, we're just taking it one meeting at a time."

As Mitchell brought her up to date on his recent visits with Tony, she sat back and enjoyed the ride to Arlington Heights. She wondered how much, if anything, Tony and his former lover, Jeff Bradley, had actually gotten away with after their embezzlement from the Bentley's/Bentleys Royale organization—that elaborate scheme all those years ago.

". . . so I talked to Mike Christonelli about—"

Viviana started. "Erica Christonelli's brother-in-law?"

"None other," he replied. "Look, Viviana, this has nothing to do with Erica. Mike has a website business that's a good match for Tony's skills. Surely that's not a problem . . . ?"

20

"Of course not," Viviana said, her posture rigid. "It just took me by surprise."

Wainwright took the exit ramp toward Arlington Heights. "Viviana, I don't want to go down that road again."

"What road?" She knew exactly what he meant, and not talking about it would not make it go away.

"Will Erica Christonelli forever be a bone of contention between us?"

"I didn't say anything about Erica. I was merely asking for clarification," she said, forming her face into an expression of uncomprehending innocence.

"Your body language speaks volumes."

"You know I gave that woman a second chance and tried to set my own feelings aside. It just didn't work out." She pursed her lips thoughtfully and then continued. "While you—and even the Taylors, it seems—cling to the image of Erica as a poor innocent victim, I see her differently. Enough said." Viviana folded her arms in front of her.

Pulling the car abruptly into the driveway of his son's small house, Wainwright switched off the engine and turned to face his former lover. "Not so, my dear. We've skirted this issue for far too long. You made it crystal clear quite recently that you resented my part in introducing Erica to the management of Medley Originals."

"Okay, you want it all out in the open?" Viviana responded. "You know that I offered to look at Erica's dress designs, but my own sense—"

"Drop the platitudes, Viviana. Number one," he said, flipping up an index finger. "You had no further need for Erica's talents." He unfolded a second finger. "Number two, all these years later she still possesses talent and a burning desire to continue designing. Number three, Medley Originals had a need to develop some of their own brands. The timing was right. Erica Christonelli fit the bill. End of story."

Erica's past was not the real issue. Viviana was not a woman without empathy. But she was a damn shrewd businesswoman. To attract her kind of clientele, she recognized that she must sprinkle her own couture designs in with the big-name designers. She had made her mark in the fashion industry and had no need for an unknown designer—no need to give away the valuable space in her boutique. No need to share the spotlight, in other words.

Viviana shrugged. "You asked earlier if Erica Christonelli would continue to be a thorn in our sides, or an issue between us, or whatever cliché you used. The answer is a resounding *no*. I'm over it." She cocked her head and met his gaze. "And you are correct: I have no need for Erica at De Mornay's, and Medley Originals is not one of my competitors. However, I have no respect for that woman. If not for the good graces of Conrad and Ashleigh Taylor, she would be behind bars."

The tension between them was suddenly broken by a dull pounding on the driver's-side window. Startled, Viviana shot forward and attempted to peer around Wainwright. The car windows had fogged over, though, and she was unable to see clearly. The hazy silhouette of a stocky figure came into focus as Wainwright thrust open the door and said, "Cut it out."

"Sorry," the stocky young man replied. "Couldn't get your attention. Why in the—why are you sitting out here in the cold? I'd like you to meet Gino before he has to take off."

Wainwright stepped out and came around the car, opening the passenger door and extending his hand to help Viviana, who looked down at the slick driveway before joining him. Wainwright guided her by the elbow up the walkway. The man, who she realized must be his son, greeted her warmly. Noting his thinning crop of salt-and-pepper hair, she recalled that he might be older than she had first surmised.

"Tony Wainwright," he said as he grasped her hand. While he lacked Mitchell's height, she noticed, he bore his father's penetrating hazel eyes and square jawline. There was no denying that the two men were related.

Tony's introduction echoed in her head. *Wainwright?* Apparently Tony's rebellion over the family name had come to an end.

Viviana stepped onto the polished hardwood floor and immediately noticed the tasteful decor. A gorgeous plush area rug sat beneath a leather sectional and matching armchairs circling the crackling fireplace. A cherrywood coffee table and two end tables, though not of the highest quality, lent cozy warmth to the living room of Tony Wainwright's small, single-story home.

"Be back in a shake," Tony said before heading toward the hallway. "Gino. They're here," he hollered down the corridor.

A tall, well-built man hustled into the room, pulling a royal blue sweatshirt over his head. His dark black hair appeared wet as if from a recent shower and fell rakishly above his left brow. His eyes seemed to be appraising Viviana from head to toe as she slipped out of her sable coat. Even the bulky sweatshirt did little to conceal his bulging biceps, she noticed.

Not waiting for an introduction, the young man said, "Gino Cabello."

Viviana felt Gino's eyes on her as Mitchell completed the introduction. When she held out her hand and said, "Viviana De Mornay," Gino took it in his for a lingering moment.

"Understand you're in need of some electrical work," he said, his liquid brown eyes intent on hers.

As she explained her lighting needs in detail, Gino's penetrating gaze never wavered, and for a few breathless moments, Viviana felt her heart beat faster. *What on earth am I thinking?* She instantly pulled herself together, reached into the side pocket of her Judith Leiber handbag, and handed Gino a business card from the sterling silver card holder. "I have some business in Manhattan next week, but if you can work on my electrical fiasco, please give me a call the following week."

Gino pulled out his wallet and tucked the card inside. "Will do," he replied. Then he turned to Tony. "Gotta run. Tell Renzo that April from JJQ News called earlier this afternoon. Meant to jot it down, but the pen and paper by the phone have vanished. Again," he added, pulling on a jacket and heading for the door.

"April Toddman?" Wainwright and Viviana asked simultaneously.

"That's right," Gino confirmed, giving them a strange look. "You know her?" Then he shrugged and, without pausing for a response, disappeared out the front door and jogged down the driveway to the blue Chevy Avalanche parked in front of the house.

"Small world," Tony said, ushering them over to the leather sofa. "Gino's brother Renzo—our other roommate—is a cameraman for JJQ's news department. I'd forgotten about the Toddman girl. She's apprenticing with them."

Small world indeed. But Viviana wasn't nearly as interested in April Toddman as she was in that beautiful Italian boy—and in how this new father–son relationship was going to play out.

Wainwright sank back on the leather sofa beside Viviana, his eyes fixed on the mesmerizing flames reflected in the living room floor.

Tony set the drinks tray down on the coffee table in front of them before dropping into the armchair across from the couch. "Met with Christonelli again this morning."

"Again? And . . . ?" Wainwright picked up his Glenlivet on the rocks.

"Soon as I wind up the web work I started on the NASCAR site for Bloomfield, I'm giving my two weeks' notice. I've agreed to climb on board with Christonelli by the first of March."

"He has enough work to employ you full-time?"

"He's created more than two dozen retail websites. He's maintaining those and a few others that he's taken over. They're good and solid. But Jordon's is by far his largest account—and he mentioned that he and his sister-in-law were at odds over that one."

Viviana's blue eyes flashed. "I told you Erica was stirring up trouble, Mitchell. She has the unmitigated gall to side with Fans of John Stewart's in the protest against Jordon's." She arched a brow. "Apparently her lack of loyalty to Conrad Taylor and his mission is endangering her own brother-in-law's business as well."

Taylor's decision to replace the John Stewart's logo with the Jordon's insignia had rocked Viviana to the core too. The landmark store was a treasured Chicago icon, no less revered in this city than the Bentleys Royale store had been in Los Angeles. But unlike Erica, Viviana was forced to keep her mouth sealed. She could not risk falling out of favor with Jordon's management.

CHAPTER
22

No, no, no! Marnie wanted to scream. She balled her hands into fists. *Not another marathon talkathon.* With her stomach in free fall, she closed her bedroom door and slowly descended the stairs, one hand trailing down the banister.

Hearing an unfamiliar voice from the living room, she stopped short. Elizabeth had said her parents wanted to talk to her . . . *again.* But the man's voice she heard was not her dad's. *Who could* that *be? If only I could just disappear.*

"Marnie," her dad called out.

"I'm here," she said, taking one tentative step after another into the living room. Her eyes flashed between her parents, sitting side by side on the sofa, and the burly man who sat in the matching armchair, his legs crossed, a beefy ankle resting on one knee. Her mind reeled. *Why is Mr. Pocino here? Do they need a private investigator to make sure I don't talk with Mom and Uncle Mike?*

Finding her voice, and praying it sounded normal, she said, "Hi, Mr. Pocino," and flopped down on the other sofa, directly across from her parents.

Her mother looked uncomfortable as her dad began to speak. "No point in beating around the bush, Marnie. Until you graduate from high school, you must stop entertaining any thought of moving to Chicago."

Inadvertently, Marnie let out an audible moan. They'd already told her this, but that didn't make it right. She wasn't going to stick around for another two years. *Mom and Uncle Mike will do whatever they have to do so I can go live with them. I just* know *they will. I can't* wait until *I turn eighteen to go be with them—I just can't.*

She saw her dad's jaw tighten. *Can he read my mind?* she thought.

Ashleigh placed a hand on Conrad's arm and then turned her focus on Marnie. In a voice as soft as the falling snow, she said, "Sweetheart, I know you miss your family in Chicago. We did as much as we could to make Erica and Mike a part of our family—"

Marnie stiffened so her posture was ramrod straight. "Yeah, and you got her a job . . . *in Chicago.*"

Silence permeated the room for a few brief seconds. Marnie was aware of the ticking of the clock over the mantel and the rustle of the private detective's trousers as he recrossed his legs. She sat very still and stared at Ashleigh. *There,* she thought. *I finally said it. And I'm glad.*

Ashleigh waited a beat as she collected her thoughts. It was true that she had facilitated Erica's landing of the personal shopper position in Chicago. What she had never discussed with Marnie was Erica's needs prior to that move to Chicago. As an alcoholic, Erica had feared living on her own in New York. After slipping last year for the first time, she had come to Ashleigh and confided in her. Erica did not want to be away from Marnie, but she felt that her brother-in-law could help her.

Ashleigh had assured Erica that she would have very liberal visitation privileges and that Marnie would be allowed to spend part of her school vacations with them in Chicago. And she had kept her end of the bargain, but now things were spinning out of control.

"That's true, Marnie," she said at last. "When I was head of human resources for John Stewart's, I did tell Erica about that job opening. She was lonely in New York when you were not with her, and she missed your Uncle Mike and Bill."

"So you're telling me she wanted to be with *them* more than with *me.*" Marnie's voice rose to a shrill, and she looked as if she were ready to burst into tears.

"Of course not, darling. She didn't *want* to be far away from you, but during the school year, you were here with us for the most part. She was lonely." Before Marnie could interject, Ashleigh continued. "The job in Chicago was a wonderful opportunity for her. However, before she made up her mind, we worked out—"

"Big deal," Marnie shouted. "A week at Christmas, a few weeks in the summer, and—"

"Whoa," Conrad interrupted, holding up the palm of his hand.

But there was no point in stating that the Christonellis and Bill had been included in all of the Taylors' important celebrations for the past eight years—or that this year, since Erica no longer had an apartment in New York, they had stayed in the Taylors' guest rooms so that they could be a part of the family's Christmas Eve and Christmas Day celebrations before whisking Marnie away with them to Chicago.

"Marnie, that's not what we're here to discuss right now." Ashleigh glanced from Conrad to Pocino, swallowed hard, and at last launched into the reason for this meeting. "Your announcement that you had written a letter to—"

"Mom and Uncle Mike," Marnie filled in.

Ashleigh nodded. Her daughter's eyes, though damp, were filled with defiance, so Ashleigh got straight to what needed to be said. "I have also written a letter—"

Marnie jumped to her feet. "About me?"

"Sit down, Marnie," Conrad said firmly. "Yes, your mother's letter to Erica was about you—about the fact that you belong here with your family. With your sisters, your mother, and me." Raising his palm again to stop his daughter from interrupting, he continued, "Your mom and I are going to Chicago on Monday to visit with Erica and Mike—even Bill, if he wants to join us."

Marnie's eyes widened in alarm, and she glared across at Pocino. "Well, there must be some reason *you're* here. What are you going to do? Arrest me? Or my mom?"

Pocino laughed. "I'm not a policeman. Just here to help out."

"Like how?"

"Marnie," Ashleigh said, her brow furrowing, "you owe Mr. Pocino an apology."

"Sorry," Marnie said.

The apology sounded anything but sincere. Ashleigh would have to talk to her daughter later about her behavior. For now, she returned to the subject at hand. "The next few days will not be easy for any of us. I wish I knew how to avoid this, but until we sit down and talk with the Christonellis, we must ask you not to contact your . . . other family."

"No way. You can't keep me from talking to my mom and Uncle Mike." Marnie's eyes filled with tears, and she bolted from the room.

"Marnie," Conrad shouted after her. He had shot to his feet and was halfway across the room when Ashleigh reached him.

"Please, love," she said, placing her hand on his arm, "give her some time."

He shook his head. "We can't just allow her to fly out of here like . . ." Then, with an exaggerated shrug, he said, "Guess you're right. There's nothing to be gained right now."

"Holy shit," Pocino said, rising to his full six feet. "Got no cotton-pickin' precedent for something like this."

Conrad gestured for Pocino to take a seat, and Ashleigh took hold of her husband's hand as they lowered themselves back down on the sofa. *Every time I think things can't get more unpredictable, I'm proven wrong.* This had been the way of things for the past week, ever since Marnie had told her about her letter to Erica.

"So, just exactly how does this work?" she asked, feeling as if she'd been left out of the loop. Although she didn't understand the plan Conrad had worked out with Pocino, she knew they would be tracing all of Marnie's incoming and outgoing calls and tracking her Internet use. To Ashleigh, taking this precaution seemed like both too much and not enough. *How will they monitor what she does when she's out with her friends?*

CHAPTER

23

Ross Pocino kept the motor running while he loaded the trunk. No use letting the car get cold; out here, his breath was visible a good two feet in front of him. *Colder than a witch's tit,* he mused as he waited for Ashleigh, who in her haste had forgotten the charger for her cell phone and had dashed back into the house to get it.

He'd told the Taylors from the get-go that the Christonelli woman was trouble. It burned his ass that the woman had gotten off scot-free after the kidnapping, and now she was pulling a stunt like this? He had no doubt she was behind the girl's sudden desire to leave her real family. If he had his way, that Christonelli broad would have served a good fat sentence in the slammer for what she'd done.

Giving his head a shake, Pocino thought about how Ashleigh had taken pity on the woman—had actually treated her as if she were a member of their family. And what had she gotten for all her kindness and understanding? "Goddamned son of a bitch," he muttered to himself as he shoved the last suitcase into the wide trunk of the Lincoln. "Ashleigh sure as hell doesn't deserve this bullshit."

His thoughts reeled back in time. Maybe, just maybe, it was true that the Christonelli dame had been an unknowing victim. But only at first. She sure as hell was no fair-haired innocent after Callie's friend had spotted Marnie at Carlingdon's back in '94. But did she do the decent thing—the moral thing? Hell, no. She had taken the child, whom she knew to be the Taylors' kidnapped daughter, and spirited her away. *And kept me on the run,* he grumbled inwardly. *For the next four goddamned years.*

Charger in hand, Ashleigh checked her bedroom for the last time and hustled downstairs, hoping she wasn't forgetting anything and praying that Conrad would be at the hotel in Chicago when she arrived.

While there was still plenty of snow on the ground, it hadn't actually snowed for the past few days, so the roads were clear. At 10:45 AM, well after the workday commuter traffic, they should have no trouble getting to JFK for their 1:45 PM flight.

Seeing the driver's-side door swing open, Ashleigh motioned for Pocino to stay put, opened the passenger door herself, and slid in.

"Got everything?" Pocino asked.

"I sure hope so," she said, giving him an apologetic smile. "Sorry to keep you waiting, Ross."

He shrugged. "No biggie." Strumming his fingers on the steering wheel, he cleared his throat. "Look, Ashleigh. The plans are all in place. Nothing has been left to chance. The Christonellis don't have a leg to stand on. And if they make any threats, we will have them recorded. After I set up the recording apparatus, I'll be in my room—out of sight. You just need to remember to leave the adjoining door unlocked in case I need to bust in."

Ashleigh nodded, knowing that she could trust him. She and Ross Pocino had gone through a lot together. She loved this burly, cliché-addicted private investigator and was thankful that he had her back. *Oh my God, now I'm starting to think in clichés.*

Anyway, she wasn't worried about physical violence. Her mind rolled back nearly eight years, to the first time they had met the Christonellis in a hotel room—to negotiate Marnie's return. "Conrad is in Chicago on business already. He should be at the Sheraton when we arrive. I can't imagine that Erica would actually go after custody, but—"

Pocino let out a derisive laugh. "So why didn't she just tell you that and put it in writing as you asked?"

His words mirrored her own thoughts. *Why indeed?*

CHAPTER

24

Ashleigh wavered, only half listening as the hotel manager said something about her husband having called at three o'clock.

"Mr. Taylor asked that you be given this message the moment you arrived," the manager added.

Taking the message from his outstretched hand, she stared down at the folded paper. *Conrad can't possibly allow Jordon's business to take priority. Not today.* Taking a deep breath, she slowly unfolded the note while Pocino collected their room keys.

Reaching the end of the note, she felt a wave of relief and smiled up at the pudgy investigator. "Conrad says his meeting lasted longer than expected, but he's on his way."

Once inside her suite, Ashleigh shrugged her coat from her shoulders and kicked off her pumps. While Pocino went about setting up his recording devices, she pulled out her cell phone and called Elizabeth to check on the girls.

Marnie's increasingly sullen demeanor following their meeting with Pocino on Saturday had been unsettling. Their daughter had been even less willing than usual to tell them what was on her mind. She had said nothing yesterday when Conrad had reminded her that they were meeting with the Christonellis this evening. "Whatever" had been her only response. Ashleigh was thankful that her husband had not pressed for more at that moment. As it was, Marnie had appeared ready to bolt from the room. She had stayed put, but only because she knew her dad wouldn't have tolerated her leaving.

This morning, however, when Ashleigh had attempted a parting hug, she hadn't been surprised when Marnie had stepped back, her eyes flashing. "No matter what you say, my mom will fight for my rights," she had growled.

Ashleigh had given no rebuttal. She wasn't sure what Erica would do or try to do. She'd merely given her daughter a loving look and responded, "And so will we."

Conrad arrived at their Sheraton suite determined to leave all thoughts of Jordon's behind. Despite the swell of negativity coming from the Fans of John Stewart's group, he had no doubt that he and his team were moving in the right direction. Change was not only inevitable but necessary to move forward in today's world. A world that no longer resembled the one he'd grown up in.

The door clicked shut behind him. Now enveloped in his own private world, Conrad called to Ashleigh. Not a single business thought intruded. His family, and what it was going to take to keep it together, was paramount in his mind.

Ashleigh appeared in the doorway of their bedroom, clad in a white wool skirt and matching cashmere sweater. Her hair hung loose, and the amused expression upon her face reassured him.

She wrapped her arms around his neck, giving him a sexy smile along with a light kiss on his lips. And then, gesturing toward the door to the adjoining room, she said, "Ross finished setting up a little while ago." She hesitated before continuing. "Listening devices seem so . . . cloak-and-dagger."

"Hope we won't need them, but I guess it's better to be prepared. If either of the Christonellis gives the slightest indication that they might encourage Marnie's current rebellion, it's no holds barred." He paused. *There's no way in hell we're going to let Marnie go live with her kidnapper's family.* "So how's the big guy taking all this?"

Ashleigh grinned. "Trying his darnedest not to tell me, 'I told you she was trouble.'"

"No point in looking back," Conrad said. "We did what we thought was right for Marnie. As it turns out, Erica Christonelli is not the woman we gave her credit for being. Whether we were right or wrong, the priority is to move forward." His voice grew firmer as he spoke. "She must not be allowed to undermine what is best for *our* daughter."

When Nelson Kennedy turned onto University Drive, he checked his watch. *Already past four thirty. Where has the time gone?* He was pleased with all he'd accomplished on the galleys, but now he was afraid he might have missed his best friend—and his opportunity to get an update on the momentum of their grassroots preservation group.

Rounding the semicircular drive, however, he spotted Alan Grey's burgundy Ford Ranger and pulled up beside it, parking between the barely visible white lines. Though unable to see Alan's office from the front of the architecture building, he was fairly certain that was where he'd find him.

Few students could be seen on campus as Nelson trudged down the snowy pathway to Alan's ground-floor office—the second one on the left-hand side. He flung open the door.

Alan looked up from the stack of papers on his desk and smiled.

Nelson noted the dark circles below his friend's red-rimmed eyes.

But when Alan spoke, he appeared more enthusiastic than exhausted. "Hallelujah." He gestured toward the stack of boxes piled beside his desk. His smile was warm and contagious. "When I came back from lunch, I found these outside my door."

Peering inside one of the boxes, Nelson saw the colorful John Stewart's brochures. It was amazing how the donations flowed in. Some fans gave money, some bought supplies, and some even supplied their credit card number to cover the cost of printing flyers, purchasing campaign buttons, what have you.

"Another fan?"

Alan nodded. "Before you ask . . . I haven't a clue who this benefactor is."

For business reasons, a number of strong supporters opted to remain anonymous. Nelson understood this. Celebrities and other public figures were unwilling to offend the opposition.

What he couldn't wrap his mind around was why the "powers that be" at Jordon's failed to take a step back and recognize how deep-seated the love of John Stewart's was in the hearts of the store's fans. Support came from far beyond the city boundaries—from other American cities as well as Europe, Japan, Australia . . . The list went on. Many had signed petitions and sent donations. How could the Jordon's executives turn their backs on this kind of love and loyalty? If they would just set their bloody egos aside, they could even capitalize on it. An announcement that they would not replace the John Stewart's name with Jordon's could bring hordes of boycotting customers back to their stores, and particularly to the landmark store. That move might even reverse the company's plummeting profits in the Chicago area.

Alan leaned back in his chair, his feet resting on the open bottom drawer of his walnut desk. "I sure as blazes hope you feel as good as you look. Not as much pain today?" He frowned and added, "But I get the feeling this meeting is going to be brief anyway."

"You've got that right. I'm feeling a whole lot better, though—thanks." Nelson was relieved that others did not see through his façade. Even his best friend had a hard time really understanding the devastating reality of his illness. "It's Erica. I promised to be with her this evening. She's going through a lot right now, and she needs me."

"She sent an e-mail informing me that she'd resigned from John Stewart's—but of course, I already knew that. Anyway, she said not to count on her at any future protest rallies."

"That's right," Nelson confirmed. "It's not what she wants, Alan. You know how she feels. Her heart and prayers are with us. She supports our efforts with every fiber of her being. But she has a lot going on right now. She simply can't afford to . . ." Nelson's heart shifted in his chest as his words trailed away to nothing.

Alan held up his hand. "No need to explain. If she's pulling out for personal reasons, that's her business."

Nelson felt a wave of relief. He didn't feel right rehashing the depth of Erica's current challenges, and anyway there was no point. Quite honestly, even if it was what Marnie truly wanted, he didn't actually believe Erica had the slightest hope of gaining custody of her daughter. The odds were against her, Nelson realized. *John Stewart's has a far better chance of retaining its name . . .*

CHAPTER

26

Erica followed Mike into the Taylors' suite. All her well-rehearsed words flew from her head, and she felt like some sort of automaton on the other side of a thick, impenetrable glass wall. She saw Conrad's lips move, and a wave of panic washed over her. *What did he say?*

Sucking in a breath of air, Erica swallowed hard. Fleetingly, her eyes sought those of her brother-in-law, hoping to find a degree of reassurance. But it appeared that Mike had none to give; he looked as nervous as she felt. The pounding of her heart thundered in her ears. Swallowing again, she avoided Conrad's penetrating gaze and focused on Ashleigh. But now the warm, caring woman who had welcomed her into the Taylor family eight years before, and with whom she'd shared so much, appeared cool and unapproachable. *What was I thinking? There are no words that will make Ashleigh understand how unhappy Marnie has become—how much she needs us.*

The words she wanted to say were stuck in her throat. Was Conrad still speaking? Without knowing whether she was interrupting or not, Erica blurted out, "If there are any right words to begin with, I don't have them. I know you have been wonderful parents, but the fact is that Marnie is unhappy. Her roots are with—"

"Hold on." Conrad's expression was unchanged, but his face had reddened. "Please have a seat." It wasn't a request. He gestured to the chairs around the oblong walnut table beside the windowed wall.

Mike pulled out a chair for Erica, his eyes pinned on Conrad.

Once everyone was seated around the table, again Erica looked to Ashleigh. Surely she would want what was best for Marnie. Then a rush of logic consumed her. *Even Ashleigh, kind as she is, will not buy into the fact that Marnie would be happy with us. She'll never believe that moving away from them is in Marnie's best interest.*

Conrad seated himself in the armchair at the head of the table. In a calm, steady voice, he said, "We arranged for this meeting in the hope of avoiding unnecessary unpleasantness or legal proceedings."

"*Unpleasantness?*" Mike's response was neither calm nor controlled. "What would you call cutting off all communication between Marnie and her mom?"

"We considered the disruption of phone contact between Marnie and Erica to be a temporary measure, but apparently—"

A cacophony of voices filled the room: Everyone talking. No one listening.

Conrad slammed his fist on the table, but it was Ashleigh who shot to her feet at last. All eyes turned toward her, and the room fell silent. Her dark eyes flashed and seemed to blaze straight through to her soul.

Erica had never seen her daughter's biological mother like this.

"How *dare* you bring up *our* daughter's roots?" she said through gritted teeth. "Had you not kept Marnie away from us when you discovered that she was not yours to raise, the bonding would have been with us—her blood relations. Her *two-parent* family and her twin sister. She would have known her grandfather and been with us when Juliana was born. She would not have been living in a trailer park with an alcoholic."

Ashleigh's words came in a rush. She had not raised her voice. She didn't need to. As intended, her words stung. But it wasn't until the mention of the restraining order that Erica's world turned black.

CHAPTER
27

Again this evening, Gino Cabello left the job site early to drive by De Mornay's in hopes of getting a glimpse of the gorgeous entrepreneur he had met more than a week ago. She had said she would be away for a few days, but she should have returned from New York by now. Listening to the low, seductive voice on her answering machine still gave him a rush. He had called periodically since the day she had given him her card, but not wanting to appear too anxious, he'd left not a single message.

Now, praying for a sign that the auburn-haired beauty had returned to Chicago, he nosed the Avalanche into the loading zone in front of the classy boutique. The rhythm of his heart quickened as he spotted a dim radiance through the arched windows. The light had not been there on his previous drive-bys. Gino switched off the motor, climbed down from the truck, and alighted into the brisk air. He peered through the elegant, beveled-glass front windows and noticed that more light shone from what appeared to be a mezzanine. *Most likely the lovely lady's office,* Gino figured. *She has returned.*

He slipped his cell phone from the holder hooked through his belt loop and hit redial.

Viviana pored over the figures. The remodeling costs for turning De Mornay's into an unforgettable shopping destination for the crème de la crème of Chicago society had far exceeded her original estimates—in Viviana's hands, these sorts of costs invariably did.

But now that she was investing a good deal of her own money, she must be particularly circumspect. Mitchell had insisted that she discover creative ways to cut a few corners. He had brought investors to the table for this venture, but he could not ask them for more capital, he'd informed her. She knew he was right and had mulled over every possibility until her head ached. For her clientele, there was no room for cost-cutting in patron areas, and the sales staff must be the ultimate in professionalism. All that cost money, of course.

Viviana rose from her desk chair and, reluctantly, spread out the carpet samples on the floor of her office. Carpeting for her office was the only area where she could possibly afford to cut some corners.

The unexpected blare of the phone on her desk jarred her from the depths of her thoughts. Glancing at the clock, she saw that it was getting late. She continued to appraise the carpet selection while ignoring the insistent ringing.

"Ms. De Mornay," came the deep, masculine voice emanating from the speaker of her answering machine, "this is Gino Cabello . . ."

As he unnecessarily explained who he was and how they had met, Viviana lunged for the phone and picked it up. A recurring dream, one that featured visions of this young man—his hard body, thick black lashes, and velvety brown eyes—had been replaying in her head since the night at Tony Wainwright's. She'd wanted to ask Mitchell what he knew about Gino, but hadn't. She knew one important detail already, though: The way Gino had scanned her from head to toe telegraphed his unquestionable sexual preference. It was all in his eyes. The man was straight. She'd bet her life on it.

Replacing the receiver in the cradle, Viviana flew into the small powder room adjoining her office to freshen her makeup. Knowing Gino was in the neighborhood and would arrive at any moment had lit a fire inside her—one that she hoped would be quenched as the evening progressed.

She smiled, recalling that the awesome Adonis was well over six feet tall. With confidence, she slipped back into her stilettos and took a quick spin in front of the full-length mirror. Quickly checking to make sure her hose were run-free, she wondered why so many young women had abandoned stockings for the bare leg look. It was beyond her. Legs were so much more appealing with a silky glimmer.

Breezing down the staircase, she saw a tall shadow of a man in front of the entrance. Her hand trembled as she pushed the key into the lock. *Calm down,* she told herself. *This is not a date.*

As he waited for Viviana to pull open the door, Gino didn't even notice the icy breeze in the air. *God, she is stunning.*

"Hi," he said, feeling like a country schoolboy as he met her gaze. "Been meaning to call. Have you been back in town long?" He hoped his attempt to sound casual was having the intended effect. He wasn't quite sure how to play it with this elegant woman a few years his senior.

"Just got back this afternoon. My business in New York took longer than expected." She gave him a dazzling smile, showing her straight white teeth, and then began to explain that she had a shop on Fifth Avenue.

"So you'll be traveling between the two stores?"

"Not a chance. My home will be here in Chicago. The closing day for De Mornay's in New York is March twenty-fifth. I'm opening here the week before Easter." She locked the door behind him.

"Glad to see you're security conscious," he said, feeling his brow crease into what he feared might be a series of unattractive grooves. "But I don't like to think of you leaving this area alone after dark. Not much going on here after shop hours."

Her blue eyes sparkled. "My condo is just three doors down, but I must admit I'm not crazy about venturing out after nightfall. And it gets dark so early at this time of year."

"You ever thought about getting a dog?"

"Not real seriously," she said. "And certainly not one of those big ferocious ones. The only type of dog that appeals to me, that could be a good match, would be a toy poodle. But I guess that wasn't what you had in mind."

Gino laughed. "Can't see some little toy being much protection, but it could be good company. And it sure would look good with your lovely hand on its leash." Impulsively he reached out and took her hand. "Now show me the electrical job you have in mind."

Gino listened as Viviana told him of her vision for the lighting in the dressing rooms. He realized that the work she had in mind could take just a few hours. *I'll see to it that it takes me a whole lot longer,* he thought. *I can find a jillion other projects to keep me coming back.* Not that he intended to rob Viviana of her money. *What I intend to steal is this lovely lady's heart.*

CHAPTER
28

"Rick." Sarah-Jayne dabbed around his swollen eyes with a cotton ball saturated in hydrogen peroxide. "You're going to get yourself killed. Please," she pleaded, placing her hand over his, "at least think about it. If we move far enough away, no one—"

"There's nowhere on this planet they can't find me." Rick winced and reached for the bag of frozen peas to cover the left side of his face. *How could I have been so goddamned stupid?* He knew plenty about addiction—firsthand, up close, and oh-so-personal. *So what made me think I was different? Drug dependency, debt—that special kind of hell is so predictable, a sure thing. So why—*

Sarah-Jayne's voice filtered in, interrupting his self-recrimination.

"What? What did you say?" he snapped.

Backlit against the window, with her arms folded in front of her ample chest, she did not speak again for what seemed a long time. Rick was unable to see the expression on her pale face, but he detected the tremble in her body. Finally, between sobs, the words came in torrents: "I'm so damn scared . . . I can't do this anymore . . . I can't live like this. I can't sit in this apartment, not knowing . . . not knowing if you'll get dumped here like a pulverized piece of meat, or if maybe you won't come back at all."

God, he hated drama. "Cut the histrionics." *Damn.* His voice had come across as more menacing than he'd intended.

So he rose gingerly from the folding chair and took the two short steps to the window, pulling Sarah-Jayne into his arms while doing his damnedest to ignore the pain that shot through his rib cage. "Sorry," he said, and this time he meant it. *Sarah-Jayne deserves better.* "I know this is no kind of life for you. No life for either of us. Don't worry. I've got a plan."

As he uttered the words to calm down his lover, a vague plan did begin to jell. Before, it had been only a fleeting thought—no form, no substance. But why not take advantage of what could be right at his fingertips? *Even if those fingertips are actually attached to my baby half-brother . . .*

CHAPTER
29

Ashleigh stood back as Marnie sprinted to the front door and ushered Clancy inside. After a brief greeting, he and Marnie headed upstairs to the dance studio.

Having the trainer focus on Marnie alone for the first half-hour was working out even better than Ashleigh had figured it might. Clancy had introduced all three girls to the wobble board and the agility ladder. Not only had Marnie stopped resisting the strengthening exercises, she appeared to revel in being a step ahead of her sisters.

Callie had not yet returned from school. Ashleigh sighed. *Ever since Callie's boyfriend got his driver's license . . . What am I thinking?* And yet she knew this was only the beginning. *The twins already have their learner's permits . . .*

The doorbell chimes brought her abruptly back to the here and now. Marnie was at work in the studio with Clancy, and Elizabeth had gone to pick Juliana up from Kelly's for her session with the trainer, so Ashleigh was the one to answer it.

Flinging open the door, she was greeted with Pocino's customary "Ciao." She caught him wiping the remains of a glazed doughnut from his chin and crumpling the napkin. Then she noticed the disorderly stack of printouts in the crook of his arm.

"This isn't my bailiwick," he confessed as they headed to the kitchen, "but I've learned a hell of a lot over the past couple weeks since our rendezvous in Chicago. Also found a damned clever hacker who can dig into the deleted files—as well as these." He gestured to the printouts.

Since Pocino never said no to a cup of coffee, Ashleigh filled two mugs and set them on the kitchen counter while he filled her in on what he'd learned since leaving Chicago.

Pulling out a stool for herself, Ashleigh peered down at the papers now spread across the counter and frowned. "What is this?" she asked. There were words and strange-looking codes and a lot of marks that looked like the signs for *greater than* and *less than* that the girls used in their math homework. "You know I don't read computerese," she joked.

The sound of the house phone intruded before Pocino had a chance to respond. Ashleigh glanced at him apologetically. The big man nodded and took another swig of coffee.

Picking up the phone and listening to the initial greeting, Ashleigh smiled. The Toddmans were back from Switzerland. Covering the mouthpiece, she said, "It's Paige." She hadn't spoken to her friend since the day before her meeting with Erica and Mike Christonelli. "I want to hear all about your trip, and I have so much to tell you about our unfolding drama here. But I'm meeting with Ross Pocino right now, so I'll have to call you back. Say, in half an hour?"

"Sure, Ashleigh. The trivia about our ski trip can wait," Paige said. "I just wanted to check on how you're holding up."

Ashleigh paused, her mind spinning ahead. "OK—well then, if you don't mind, I can put you on the speaker and bring both you and Ross up to date at the same time."

Pocino nodded, and the moment Ashleigh hit the speaker button, he gave Paige a hearty "Ciao."

Pocino refilled his coffee cup while Ashleigh described the meeting she and Conrad had had the previous week with James Sutton, their attorney. "I know the restraining order is necessary, but we'd hoped to avoid it. Clearly, Erica is rattled. She says she wants to do what's in Marnie's best interest . . ." The minute the words left her mouth, her eyes shot across to Pocino, and she regretted them.

Paige's response was immediate. "Where is her head? How could she—" Paige paused. "So how is Marnie taking it?"

"I'm not sure how to answer that. We knew we were in for a rough ride, but Marnie is hard to read. Even more so than usual. While her mood swings are nothing new, she's no longer so outspoken. She's more withdrawn. But not all the time." *Not when she's in drama queen mode.*

Pocino strummed his fingers on the countertop; the thin, maplike lines above his brows seemed to deepen. But he did not interject.

Ashleigh searched her mind for the right words to describe her daughter's acting out. "When we told Marnie that we had been forced to take out a restraining order, and that until everything was put to rest she would be unable to communicate with her . . . her other family, it went over like the proverbial lead balloon. Her reaction was hardly unexpected—she flew into a rage, telling us we couldn't do that, it wasn't fair, we're the meanest parents in the world, yada, yada, yada. Then she threatened to run away." Fearing Ross's reaction, she hardly took a breath. "Since our initial go-around, she's back to giving us the silent treatment. She even avoids eye contact with us most of the time."

"How about with her sisters?" Paige asked.

"She and Callie seem to be getting along now, and she's never shown any hostility toward Juliana. Having Clancy work with all three girls has been a godsend." A trace of unease trickled up Ashleigh's spine. Not knowing what was really going on behind Marnie's dark, haunted eyes had her worried. "But she's so secretive, and not knowing what Erica's up to . . ."

"What a nightmare," Paige broke in. "And after all you've done for that woman."

Ashleigh felt Pocino's eyes on her. He said nothing, but his posture spoke volumes. *How much is it costing him to keep everything inside?* Had the situation not been so threatening, his uncustomary restraint might have amused her. However, it was hard to find the humor at this moment. Still, she decided to take the sting out of his self-imposed silence. "I can see that Ross is about to bust," she said, "but he hasn't said a word about us ignoring his advice."

Tossing his hands in the air, Pocino spoke at last. "What's the point? You did what you thought best for Marnie. The fact that I thought the dame and her brother-in-law should be behind bars is water under the bridge." Gnawing on his lower lip, he fell silent for a fraction of a second, and then with utter sincerity rather than sarcasm, he said, "I'm just sorry your kindness has come back to bite you in the ass." His face reddened. "Sorry," he said again.

His apology, Ashleigh knew, was for the language and not the sentiment. Maybe he had been right, and she and Conrad had been wrong. Right now, if truth be told, she wished Erica and Mike Christonelli would vanish from the face of the earth. But even if she had it all to do over, she would not have handled things differently—she would still choose to keep Marnie's other "mother" in her daughter's life. *It's what was best for Marnie.* But was that still the case?

After Ashleigh said good-bye to Paige and hung up, Pocino attempted to update her on the monitoring of Marnie's cell phone and computer.

Ashleigh was still unclear on one thing: "What if she uses a friend's phone or computer?"

"I don't know all the ins and outs of the Internet, but unless your daughter sets up a bogus e-mail account, I think our man can pretty much handle that. The phone is a whole other bag of worms. It could be a problem. At this point, we have no access to the Christonellis' phone lines, nor any probable cause to get a wiretap. Afraid you're going to have to keep an eye on your daughter."

Ashleigh sighed. *I must remain positive. We are going to get through this.* Then she sent up a prayer—something she'd found herself doing more often lately. *Please, God, let Marnie feel our love.*

CHAPTER
30

At the *click* of her mother's heels on the tile floors outside her room, Marnie pulled the covers up high, over her face, so only the top of her head and ears were visible. Her eyes were closed; she lay very still and pretended to be asleep. She heard the faint *clink* of the water glass on her bedside table and felt a kiss as it was planted on her forehead. She moaned faintly but did not open her eyes.

Earlier, before Elizabeth had taken her temperature, Marnie had run the thermometer under the hot water faucet. Ashleigh had checked in on her then to make sure Marnie didn't want anything to eat and had even brought her a glass of 7UP. But now, as Ashleigh's smooth hand swept across her forehead, Marnie feared that her mother was wise to her act.

Ashleigh said softly, "We'll be back before noon, darling. I'll have my phone on vibrate while we're in church, so send me a text if there's anything you need me to stop and pick up on the way home."

Marnie turned over, still pretending to be more than half asleep. She was relieved to hear her mother's retreating footfalls in the corridor outside her bedroom. *Why does she have to be so nice? Why does she act as if nothing is wrong—like we're a normal family? Like she really cares about what I need? Like she isn't ruining my life?*

Elizabeth came in again too, hovering over her and asking if there was anything she could bring before she departed with the rest of the family for church.

"No, thank you," Marnie said, no longer faking sleep. "I think I just need to rest."

Elizabeth leaned down to give her a kiss and then said, "Take care, angel."

Marnie was surprised—Elizabeth hadn't called her that for a long time. *Why now? I'm no angel.* She turned over and buried her face in the pillow. *Not by a long shot.*

Even after hearing the roar of the engine as the Lincoln pulled out of the garage, Marnie did not yet dare to venture from her bed. She remained wrapped in the blankets for several long moments before creeping over to the window to peer out. As the car's taillights faded from view at the end of the long driveway, Marnie let out the breath that was lodged in her throat.

Her hand shook as she pulled Callie's cell phone from her bedside table. It wasn't fair. She'd had to sneak into Callie's room the night before and switch phones. She didn't like the idea of Callie having access to her cell, but it was the only way. So she'd slipped her phone into Callie's jeweled cover. What else could she do? Her parents were being such jerks. She hadn't talked to her mom in weeks. She had to do something.

Callie would quickly discover the switch, of course—as soon as she opened her case and flipped open the identical pink Razr—and there would be hell to pay. But by then it would be too late.

Marnie flipped open Callie's phone now. There were already three text messages from Derek and one from Samantha. Marnie tried not to think about Callie flipping open *her* phone, which she was most likely doing right now. *Please, please, please, Callie, keep your mouth shut. Give me a break,* she prayed.

Her heart beat wildly as she gazed up at the ceiling, sending a silent request to the Man Upstairs, pleading with Him to forgive her for not going to church today. Surely He would understand how much she needed to hear her mom's voice.

CHAPTER
31

Marnie stood close to the window, where she knew she would get the best reception, and punched in the number to her mom's house phone in Chicago. On the fifth ring, just as she was about to hang up and try her mom's cell, her call was picked up.

It was so good to hear her uncle's cheerful greeting. *Please be glad I called*, she prayed. "Hi, Uncle Mike," she said tentatively.

"Marnie?"

"Yes, it's me. Don't be mad," she said without giving him a chance to respond. "I just had to talk to you and Mom."

"Are your parents there?" His voice didn't sound right. He didn't sound as if he were glad she called.

She shook her head before it dawned on her that he couldn't see her response. "No," she said, defiance surfacing in her tone. "They never would have let me call. Anyway, I can't talk to you guys with them standing right beside me, listening to every word."

"I understand, precious, but—"

"Uncle Mike," she interrupted, "don't you want to talk to me?" She felt hot tears burning behind her eyes.

"Of course I do. But as much as we want to be able to talk to you now, we can't take the chance of being caught in violation of the restraining order. We need to follow the law so we have the best shot at guardianship for the long run."

"But I'm not using my own phone. I borrowed Callie's—"

"Numbers can be traced on any phone, precious. As far as your mom and I know, our phones might even . . ." He hesitated, letting his unfinished sentence hang in the air. "Precious, I know how hard this is for you. It's hard for all of us. But we can't take any chances. If we are found in violation—"

"It's not fair." Marnie couldn't believe what her uncle was saying. *Why isn't he standing up for me?* "I need to talk to Mom," she said curtly. "Is she there? Does *she* want to talk to me?"

There was only dead air between them for a very long moment; then her uncle sighed. "Sure," he said. "Hold on, I'll get her."

As she waited, Marnie pictured her uncle pushing back his desk chair from the computer and going in search of her mom. She heard him call, "Erica," and then there was silence, followed by some muffled talking on the other end of the line. Next she heard her uncle say, "I know . . . already on the line . . . can't be undone . . . may as well take the call . . . Marnie needs . . . your voice. But . . . needs to . . . hard we're working . . . permanent part of the family . . . can't afford to jeopardize . . ." His voice faded then, and she couldn't make out her mother's words in response.

Goosebumps rose on the skin of her upper arms as she waited on the other end of the phone. *I have to make her understand.*

Finally Erica's voice came on the line. "Darling, I miss you more than you'll ever know, but for now we can't violate the restraining order."

"That's *so* not fair. They don't care about me. They just want to control my life."

"Oh, Marnie, I don't think that's true. While they may not understand how you feel, I'm sure they love you very much."

"Whose side are you on? Don't you and Uncle Mike and Bill want me to live with you?"

"Of course we do. That's why it's so important that you try to be patient. Our chances of getting the court to rule in our favor are much better if we follow the rules—if we abide by the restraining order and delay the actual hearings until after the end of the school year, when you turn sixteen—"

Marnie's blood turned icy cold. *But it's more than six months till my birthday.*

Erica ended the call a moment later, professing her love, and Marnie wished she could just lie down and disappear. *I never should have called. Mom and Uncle Mike don't understand either. They're cowards.* A wave of despair engulfed her as she thought about what lay ahead, knowing now that there was no one to come to her rescue.

It's up to me to find the way.

Viviana reached over to the pillow beside her and slowly opened one eye. Bright streaks of sunlight filtered through the blinds. The impression of her lover's head was clearly visible on the satin pillowcase, but she was alone. She rose up on an elbow, and the aroma of fresh coffee greeted her.

A smile curved her lips. Slipping out from under the covers, she grabbed a green silk robe from the velvet settee at the foot of the bed and headed straight for the bathroom. She flipped on the light and went over to the mirror. She dabbed a bit of concealer under her eyes before applying her usual foundation. Then she brushed some color on her cheeks, gave them a gentle pinch, and applied a burgundy shade of lipstick, wiping most of it off. As a final touch, she brushed her hair and then ran her fingers through it to make it appear fresh from bed. She looked damn good for her age, but getting that fresh, natural look took far more time than it had in the past.

"Gino," she called out as she slowly glided down the hallway toward the kitchen.

There was no answer.

In the kitchen, the coffee was perking. A mug, a cup and saucer, and two glasses of orange juice sat on a silver tray beside the Toshiba all-in-one coffee machine. There was an empty frying pan on the stove and a carton of eggs and a rasher of bacon on the countertop. She glanced across the kitchen and saw that the breakfast room table had been set, complete with her new linen napkins. But Gino was not there.

Where can he be? And what's he up to?

"Gino," she called out again as she made her way through the dining room to the living room.

No answer.

Feeling off balance, she dashed into the guest bedroom. It was empty.

She returned to her own bedroom and threw open the closet door. Gino's robe, a couple pairs of jeans, and a few odd shirts hung neatly in place in his section of the closet.

How odd, she thought as she returned to the kitchen. She wasn't worried, just perplexed. Obviously, he didn't plan to be gone for long— he had just stepped out in the middle of making breakfast. *But why?*

Hearing the final gurgle of the coffee pot, Viviana filled Gino's mug and her cup, and as she was setting them on the table, she heard Gino's key in the lock. She dashed to the door to meet him.

When the door swung open, her mouth did likewise. "Oh my God. Oh my God," she repeated, and she reached out for the fluffy ball of fur he cradled in one of his powerful arms. In his other hand was an elaborate, gold-framed bed with a royal-blue velvet cushion. Gino's dark eyes sparkled with amusement as he set the bed on the living room floor, beside an end table.

"When . . . ? Where . . . ? How . . . ?" Viviana was so delighted, she couldn't get the words out. Gino had teased her about her desire for a toy poodle—painting a picture of an adorably fluffy but nonmenacing guardian—but she knew he really did want her to have a dog. He continually told her he didn't like it when she was alone in the shop or even here in her condo. And despite his banter, a toy poodle was exactly what she was now holding. "She's adorable . . . ," Viviana gushed. "It *is* a she, isn't it?"

"You bet," Gino confirmed. "Not about to be sharing my lady with another male." He winked and asked, "Do you like her?"

"She's perfect. And she's sure to be a hit with all my 'hoity-toity' clientele," she said, mimicking his description of her future Chicago patrons.

"Not only your patrons," Gino said. "I was also thinking that your son would like her." He paused, watching as Viviana stroked her new pet with her manicured fingers. "Don't you think it's time we met?"

Viviana froze.

Before the Lincoln had even pulled away from the house, Callie had slipped her cell from her pocket to check for messages. She would have to set it to vibrate before they arrived at church. She saw there was one text message and discreetly clicked on it. *Why is Lindsey texting me? How did she even get my number?* Suspicion began to rise from the pit of her stomach. *Obviously this is for Marnie.*

Callie scrolled through the menu. The contact list that popped up was not hers. She wanted to scream, "Marnie's taken my phone," but she remained silent, realizing that this was no accident. *Marnie put my cover on her phone.*

Never one to miss a thing, Juliana asked, "What's wrong?"

"Nothing," Callie lied. "Just setting the phone to vibrate now so I won't forget."

As they rounded the corner of Maple and Putnam, Ashleigh looked over her shoulder. Callie knew her mother didn't miss much either, but this time she was merely checking that both girls had silenced their cell phones.

Callie reassured her with a composed smile and a nod, but thinking about the implication of the switch—*Marnie has my cell*—she shook inside. She wanted her parents to know what was going on, yet she couldn't be the one to betray Marnie. At least not until she knew what her twin was up to.

Then her mind flashed to Derek, and she felt a flood of white-hot anger. *Thank God, Derek is probably still in bed. But Marnie better not be reading any of his text messages to me . . .*

Turning sideways so Juliana couldn't see the screen, Callie's fingers flew across the keyboard: WHAT R U UP 2? BETTER NOT OPEN ANY OF MY TEXTS.

Her father had pulled into the parking lot of the Second Congregational Church and turned off the ignition. He glanced back at her, saying, "Maybe you'd better leave that phone in the car."

"I'll just put it in my pocket?" Her pleading gaze shot from parent to parent.

"Okay," Conrad said, "as long as it stays on vibrate and inside your pocket."

Callie headed straight for the church's teen center, wishing desperately that she could return home, retrieve her own phone, and find out just what her unpredictable sister was up to. She waited until her parents had disappeared into the church crowd before pulling out the phone. Inconceivably, she couldn't remember Derek's number.

When Samantha dashed up, Callie quickly told her friend about the latest Marnie drama. Sam read off Derek's number from her phone, and Callie sent him a message: DON'T SEND TEXT TO MY PHONE UNTIL I GET HOME AND MURDER MY SISTER. But she didn't hit SEND. Instead, she deleted the last four words and added simply MARNIE HAS MY CELL. After all, she was at church.

After hitting SEND, she slipped the phone back into her pocket.

"What are you going to do?" Sam asked. "Are you going to tell your parents she took your phone?"

"I don't think so. Not, yet anyway." Callie wasn't sure just what she would do. Sometimes she thought it *would* be best if Marnie went to live in Chicago. She was tired of all the drama. She loved her twin, but sometimes she resented her. Why should Marnie get all the attention now? She thought about how things had been before Marnie came into their lives . . . Then, of course, Callie felt ashamed about feeling that way. She felt guilty when she thought about all those years Marnie hadn't known her real parents, about how much more love and attention she'd had than her poor, lost sister. So, rather than focus on the not-so-good parts, Callie tried to think of how cool it was to have a twin.

Sam was still pestering her with questions. "Do you think she took it to call those people who kidnapped her?"

Callie shuddered. She knew that Erica and Mike weren't the villains others thought them to be. But right now she had no desire to defend either of them. If they were out of the picture, her life—all their lives—wouldn't be so topsy-turvy all the time. And her sister wouldn't need to be restricted from using her phone or spending time with her friends. *Just because Marnie isn't allowed to spend the night at a friend's shouldn't mean that I should get punished too.* But apparently, it did.

CHAPTER
34

Erica dropped the phone receiver back into the cradle. "Mike," she called out. When she got no answer, she wavered momentarily, knowing there was a bottle of chardonnay in the fridge, left from Mike and Bill's early Valentine's Day party the other night. *Could I . . . ?*

She strode purposefully to the refrigerator and swallowed hard. Her hand shook as she bypassed the chardonnay and reached for the chilled bottle of Evian. *This is no time to give in to temptation.*

She looked up to see Mike standing beside the kitchen counter, his dark hair tousled and a mug of coffee in his large hand. He looked at her as if he were fully aware of the demons that continued to haunt her.

"Would you please ask Bill to join us in the family room in about ten minutes?" she asked.

"Sure thing," he said without question.

Erica felt warm inside just thinking about her *brother-in-law's* unconditional love. It was such a blessing. *We might have our differences, but we are a truly united family unit.*

Running her fingers through her unruly curls, she trudged off to her bedroom to exchange her old, beat-up bathrobe for a fresh pair of jeans and her new DKNY T-shirt. She dabbed on a bit of foundation and ran a brush through her hair.

At the sound of the doorbell, she paused, knowing that her brother-in-law was closer and would get it. Hearing the deep tones of Nelson's voice, Erica began to relax, but only marginally. Leaning her hip against her dresser, her bottom lip quivering, she momentarily closed her eyes. *Dear Lord, help me,* she prayed. *Make me strong. Help my daughter through this time of need. Help her to feel our love.*

She shook off her malaise, squared her shoulders, and hustled into the family room, where the three men greeted her with puzzled expectation.

"Please, sit down," Erica said as she sank to the couch. Her gaze shifted from Nelson to Bill. "Did Mike tell you that Marnie called this morning?"

Bill nodded.

When Nelson looked at her expectantly, she told him about the call. "I don't have to tell any of you how much I love Marnie and want her to be a part of our daily lives. But what we are doing—what we are encouraging her to do—is all wrong. We are turning her into a sneak and a liar."

She looked directly at Mike, expecting a rebuttal. She got none. No one said a single word. All eyes were on her, waiting for her to go on, so she did.

"When Marnie told me she had stolen her sister's phone, played sick, and waited for everyone to go to church so she could call us . . ." She couldn't control the tremor in her voice but forced herself to continue. *I'm so ashamed. We were wrong, and we've—I've—been so selfish.* "I was wrong not to discourage her—to turn her against her biological parents. It's not like the Taylors are bad or uncaring parents. They aren't. They love her as much as we do. And they have the law and maybe even Marnie's best interests on their side.

"Yet we've made the job of raising a teenager even harder for them, and we're doing Marnie a disservice." She paused. *This is so damn hard.*

Nelson came over and sat down on the sofa beside Erica, slipping his arm around her shoulders. He was fully aware of the price she was paying as she tried to do what was in her daughter's best interests.

"Damn it, Erica," Mike was saying, "I hate to admit it, but you're right. Before Marnie's call, I couldn't see it. All I thought about was having our girl back and how terrific it would be to see her every morning. To take her to school, to watch her enjoy her dancing and other activities, to see her with her friends."

Erica had leaned forward and dropped her head into her hands.

"But as I tried to articulate the situation to Marnie this morning," Mike went on, "I got a sick feeling in the pit of my stomach." He shook his head sadly. "So what are we going to do now?"

Nelson felt Erica's silent sobs and rubbed her shoulders lightly, trying to find words of comfort. But his well of compassion was dry. The reality of the restraining order against the Christonellis hit him square in the gut. *What can I possibly say to make this hell any better?*

Nelson took hold of Erica's hand as they trudged through the wrought iron gate and up the steep steps to the front door of his Victorian home. No light shone through the upper-story windows, nor through the Tiffany windows where the cellar cut away from the ground. With only faint illumination from the bay window to light their way, they proceeded cautiously.

As the door creaked open, Nelson was relieved to see Neil sitting cross-legged on the floor in the dining room. Several boxes were stacked neatly beside him, and he was folding the latest batch of John Stewart's flyers.

Neil looked up and greeted them, looking his father in the eye.

"Glad to find you home this evening," Nelson said.

Neil glanced toward the old grandfather clock. "Actually, I've got to run. Brad will be here any minute. We're going to his house, and he's helping me study for the big geometry test on Monday." Having skipped a grade, Neil would be one of the last in his class to get his driver's license. His blossoming independence was inevitable, and yet Nelson was thankful his son still had a couple months left before he could start driving on his own.

At the blast of a horn, Neil shot to his feet and grabbed his geometry book. "Nice to see you, Erica," he said, eyes downturned, as he hurried to the door. Before darting outside, Neil turned back to his father. "I got a good start on the flyers. Sorry I couldn't do more."

Nelson waved off his son's concern. "I appreciate you plunging in." He resisted asking when to expect him home that evening. *I have to loosen the strings.* Neil was a good kid. *But why does he always seem to want to avoid Erica?*

"What's wrong?" Erica asked as the door closed.

"Nothing, really." But he couldn't shake the feeling that Neil had some problem with his new relationship. "I just wish he'd spend more time at home."

Erica laughed. "My God, Nelson. Your son is nearly sixteen. You should be thanking your lucky stars he's going out to study on a Friday night."

Nelson pulled off his cap and smiled. "You're right, of course. I guess it just worries me that he's been spending so much time with Rick lately."

Erica frowned. "Rick is quite a bit older, isn't he?"

He took Erica's jacket. "Twenty-five." Nelson hung both their jackets in the hall closet. "Out of the blue, Rick just started hanging around the past couple of weeks. I don't want to come right out and say that I don't trust him, but . . ."

Erica pulled out one of the dining-room chairs beside the box of flyers. "But he has a steady job now, right?"

"So he tells me. Maybe he's finally tuning into family values. Maybe I'm just borrowing trouble." Even as the words rolled out, he didn't really buy it. Rick had been nothing but trouble long before he'd even reached his teens.

Erica took his hand. "You're just trying to do what's best for your son," she said. "That's all you *can* do. And I can see how the thought of your stepson as a role model for Neil is frightening."

She's hit that nail on the head, Nelson thought.

Wainwright was about to flip his cell phone shut when at last he heard Viviana's husky "De Mornay's?" on the other end of the line.

"How are the closing sales going?" he asked.

"Hello, Mitchell. Even better than expected," she said, sounding bright and optimistic. "If tomorrow goes even half as well as what's been happening in the early part of this week, there won't be a lot to transfer to the Chicago store." Wainwright heard her draw in a breath and imagined the excitement that no doubt was written all over her face.

"Tomorrow night's party is going to be one Manhattan will be talking about for a very long time. It's going to be sensational. Governor Pataki, Mayor Bloomberg . . ."

He waited patiently as Viviana went through her impressive guest list, which would top any Who's Who. She ended by asking, "How about Tony? I sent him an invitation but haven't heard from him. Gino said he hadn't mentioned coming to New York." *So, this Gino is on the Fifth Avenue guest list.* An image of Tony's brawny roommate shot to mind, bringing a smile to his lips. *My God, the young man can't be any older than Viviana's son.*

His mind returning to her inquiry, Wainwright said, "Come on, Viviana. I assume the Taylors are on your 'A' list." It wasn't a question.

There was a gasp on the other end of the line, and then a moment's silence. "How stupid of me," she said. "But I'm trying to look forward, not backward. We've got to do something for the future. Everyone has been so impressed with our new website design. Tony just *has* to be at the Chicago opening."

Wainwright wanted opportunities for his son, but all he could think of was the awkwardness. As always with Tony, it was a festering predicament. "I'll talk with Ashleigh and Conrad before the Chicago soiree." *Ashleigh is the most forgiving person I know.* "I'll pull Ashleigh aside at your Fifth Avenue closing and speak to her. I'll do my best. We'll make it work."

But he knew there would be at least one obstacle. *Conrad might be a tough sell.*

CHAPTER
36

Ashleigh was struggling with the zipper of her shimmery beige Versace gown when Conrad reached the bedroom door. "Wow," he said as he crossed the threshold. "I should have made it home a half hour earlier."

"That would have been nice. But this shouldn't be a terribly late night," Ashleigh added as she gave him a seductive smile. Dropping her arm from behind the back of her cocktail dress, Ashleigh reached up and wrapped both arms around his neck. Following an extra-long embrace, she lifted the back of her hair and turned so Conrad could pull the zipper past that difficult-to-reach area.

As he kissed the nape of her slender neck, she began filling him in on the plans for next month's trip to Chicago. The Toddmans were in town again—both for the weekend's festivities and, in Mark's case, for business reasons—and she had worked out spring break arrangements with Paige earlier in the day, on their ride from JFK to the Taylors' Greenwich home.

"Viviana's grand opening is April ninth, but I've booked the penthouse at the Palmer House to accommodate our small army throughout the girls' entire spring break." Ashleigh was really looking forward to a luxury getaway. *Even with the renovation going on at the Palmer House, I can't think of anywhere I'd rather stay.* "April reserved the presidential suite for Paige and Mark—and Helen, of course. We'll just have to help them make sure she doesn't go wandering off in an unfamiliar city." *It wouldn't be the first time . . .*

"Terrific," Conrad said. "I'll have to work during that time, you know. But it'll be a real treat—having us all together again, with April to show us around her new hometown."

Ashleigh bit her bottom lip. "Conrad, there's something else we'll have to consider. Now that we've lifted the restraining order, Marnie is bound to want to spend time with the Christonellis . . ."

Conrad frowned. "Marnie's old enough now that she'll have to understand. Sometimes we don't get what we want—we get what we need."

But at this point Ashleigh wasn't even sure what Marnie might need. *What is the right course?* Forbidding her daughter to see the Christonellis would only cause further rebellion, but how could she allow Marnie to go back down that same path . . .

Conrad, as usual, was quick to pick up her unspoken concern. He took her hand. "You have nothing to feel guilty about. Anyway, we have a couple weeks before the trip. Plenty of time to work things out."

Ashleigh gave a heavy sigh. "I don't know what I feel. It's not guilt, but it sure doesn't feel like a win."

Now Ashleigh had to tell him what she'd learned of Tony Wainwright. He shook his head slowly. "If it's not one thing, it's a boatload more." He hesitated, remembering just what that bastard had done. The embezzlement alone was an atrocious crime, but kidnapping Ashleigh and that young buyer was not something he would ever forgive or forget. "I'm not crazy about Tony Wainwright resurfacing, as you can imagine. I had hoped to avoid any chance of our paths crossing."

Ashleigh turned toward him, her dark eyes widening as if to say, *Fat chance.* "But Mike Christonelli created and is maintaining the Jordon's retail website," she said.

"As far as I know, he has nothing to do with the financial end—Christonelli's just a graphics guy. No access to Jordon's funds." He'd already decided to have Pocino dig deeper into what the younger Wainwright might be up to, other than the website business. *You never can tell . . .*

"I wonder if Mitchell has finally come to terms with the type of man his son has become," Ashleigh mused.

"The takeover king?" Conrad scoffed. "Who knows. For now, though, there's no cause for worry. Okay, love?"

He headed for the shower, the dynamics of the Wainwrights running through his head. Tony Wainwright weaving his way back into their world was somewhat unsettling. Conrad knew too much about that bastard's scheming mind not to wonder: *Is there a hidden agenda?*

Upstairs the house was abuzz with activity. The catering staff had handled the place settings and retrieved chairs from the storage room, and were now busying themselves in the kitchen. The Taylor girls had set up the dance studio, theater-style as promised, and the three of them had retreated to their rooms to get dressed for the evening's dinner party.

Now that Marnie's ankle was stronger and she was again able to dance with her sisters, Ashleigh had hoped that there would be less friction between them. But other than those moments when they were immersed in planning or practicing their dance routines, there remained an uneasy undercurrent between the twins. Juliana, while not oblivious to Marnie's dark moods, ignored them and had an uncanny ability to lead her sister into fits of laughter. With Ashleigh and Conrad, however, Marnie seldom smiled. She was still giving them the cold shoulder.

A faint scent of roses drifted through the air as Ashleigh descended the winding staircase. She made her way to check on the dining area and saw that Elizabeth had arranged a centerpiece. The candles had been lit, and the soothing tones of Sinatra's voice crooned in the background.

The door chimes startled her, and she checked the tiny face of her Pavé watch. It was nearly six thirty. *Where has the time gone?*

She hurried to the door and was delighted to see the girls' dance teacher, Miss Daryl, who had agreed to choreograph and oversee tonight's performance—a preview for De Mornay's closing party tomorrow evening. A step behind her was Clancy, their trainer. Together they stepped into the foyer, where Ashleigh took note that Miss Daryl was decked out in a simple black cocktail dress with pearl earrings—her only accessory. Meanwhile, Clancy looked quite dapper in a neatly tailored charcoal suit.

"We decided to get here a bit early to check on Marnie's ankle," he said. "I brought my kit in case we needed to retape it."

The door chimes sounded again. Flinging open the door once more, Ashleigh was greeted by a cool, early spring breeze—and the smiling Glenn Nelson, as usual looking as if he'd stepped off the front cover of *GQ*.

"I'm so glad you could make it, Glenn," Ashleigh greeted her old friend.

"Wouldn't have missed it for the world," Glenn said, giving Ashleigh a strong hug that nearly lifted her off her feet, before stepping back to appraise her from head to toe. "How ever do you manage it, Ashleigh? No one would ever guess you're the mother of three." His grin was contagious.

Reaching for his overcoat, she said, "I heard you were moving back to California."

"I am indeed," he said, turning toward the sound of footsteps above him.

She followed his gaze and saw Elizabeth descending the stairs, followed by Paige, who was looking every bit as sensational as Glenn. But something was wrong. The worried expression on her friend's face brought Ashleigh to full alert. "What's wrong?" she asked.

Paige's face had taken on a pale hue. "Have you seen Mom?"

Ashleigh searched her memory. "Not since we went up to see the girls' rehearsal about an hour ago."

"We can't find her anywhere," Elizabeth said, concern clouding her expression. "When I went in to check on her, the bathwater was cold, and the outfit I laid out on the bed hasn't been touched."

Ashleigh straightened and stood at the alert. "Have you looked outside?"

"I just told Mark a few minutes ago—I think he's searching the grounds." Paige's voice crackled with panic. "He hadn't even finished dressing yet. He just threw on a pair of slacks and took off to search for her."

"We should join the search," Ashleigh said quickly, and the others didn't wait for instructions. Clancy, Miss Daryl, and Glenn took off out the front door, nearly colliding with Gino and Viviana, who had been just about to ring the bell.

"Please, come inside. We'll be right with you," Ashleigh called out before turning to dash up the stairs. She shouted out to the girls while heading toward her own room to alert Conrad.

Soon the entire household, along with their guests, was looking for Helen—all except Viviana, who stood frozen in place in the foyer, holding Dolly protectively and looking altogether confused about what was going on.

When it seemed there was nowhere left inside to search, Ashleigh turned to Elizabeth and said, "Would you please call the police department? And wait inside, in case Helen returns? I'll join the search party outdoors."

"Of course," answered Elizabeth, worry lines wrinkling her forehead. "I don't understand. Helen seemed fine earlier. She was so excited."

Ashleigh gave a quick nod. "Be right back," she said, running for the front door.

Just as she threw it open, the porch light blinked out, leaving her in darkness. Undeterred, she barreled toward the familiar porch steps—a very bad idea, considering her four-inch heels. Her ankle twisted, and Ashleigh fell headlong down the six steps to the still-frozen ground below.

Viviana and Dolly sat alone in the living room, a Sinatra ballad playing softly in the background. There was no point in her joining the madness. *Why doesn't everyone just wait for the police?*

From the corner of her eye, Viviana saw the flicker of candles from the dining room and sighed. Slowly rising, she picked up Dolly and headed into the next room. *Utter perfection,* she thought, as she took in the beautiful Belgian lace tablecloth and elegant table settings. Spotting a candlesnuffer on the server, she strode over and picked it up. *If this train wreck of a party ever comes together, at least the candles won't be burned down to a nub.*

Just as Viviana extinguished the last candle, she saw someone gliding down the staircase in a figure-hugging vintage Coco Chanel dress. *Helen.*

The elegant woman appeared as if she hadn't a care in the world. "Hi," she said to Viviana. "Where is that yummy young man of yours?" Then, spotting the puppy, Helen headed straight toward her, reaching out to grasp the squirming ball of pure white fur.

Viviana was speechless. Just then, Elizabeth descended the stairs with the Taylor girls trailing after her. They had slipped out of their dance shoes and were ready to join the search.

"Helen!" Elizabeth exclaimed, relief spilling across her face. "Where were you?"

Helen gave her a confused look. "Getting dressed for the party. I thought Wilma would have told you."

Wilma? thought Viviana. Of course—the Toddmans' help back in Texas.

"Helen," Elizabeth repeated, her usually pleasant, round face now turning beet red. "Everyone is out looking for you."

Sounding perplexed, Helen asked, "Why? I told Paige I could dress myself." She grinned. "I know I get confused sometimes, but after Wilma laid all my things out, I—"

"Where were you," Elizabeth repeated, "*before* you got dressed?"

Police sirens suddenly filled the air, and Marnie ran to the front door and flung it open. Then Viviana heard her give a sharp cry.

"Mom!"

As two police cars swept up the circular drive, the motion sensors lit up the grounds. Marnie hit the steps at breakneck speed, reaching the spot where her mother lay in a pool of shimmery beige, the side of her face in the flower bed. Marnie's heart pounded fiercely. When she looked down and saw the blood on the pathway at the base of the steps, she thought her heart might burst.

She heard a moan and, finding she was able to breathe again, reached out to touch her mother's forehead—a familiar gesture that her mom had soothed her with so many times before. "Mom, are you hurt?" *Of course she's hurt, dork.*

Pounding footfalls caused Marnie to look up from her mother. Two policemen were quickly beside her. The hefty one, who reminded her of Ross Pocino, grasped Marnie's forearm. "Step aside," he ordered. Then, turning to his partner, a short, trim man who was not more than a couple yards from them, he shouted, "Call the paramedics."

Ashleigh was faintly aware of her daughter's voice drifting in and out of the fog before her eyes, but she couldn't make out any words. Her head felt as if it were about to split in half, and she was so cold.

What happened?

She seemed to be surrounded by running feet; they were thundering through her muddled brain. She tried to sit up but felt a rough, callused hand restraining her. Her elbow hurt. Her ribs hurt. Everything hurt.

Reaching up to her damp cheek, she brushed off clumps of cold dirt. A sense of déjà vu washed over her, and she struggled to pull away from the restraining hand. "Please," she said, "help me up."

"Just try to relax. An ambulance is on the way," the officer said.

"I don't need an ambulance. I just need some help to sit up," she insisted. "You need to find—"

Elizabeth had scurried up beside the two police officers, her rubber-soled heels emitting a squeak on the stone path. "Oh my. Ashleigh dear, are you alright?" She pushed the police officer's hand aside and knelt beside her employer and friend.

"Just help me up, Elizabeth," Ashleigh said weakly, "and tell the policemen to stop fussing with me. Tell them to look for Helen."

Now the firm hand restraining her was exchanged for a soft one. Elizabeth said, "Ashleigh, Helen has been found. We're not even sure she was actually lost."

"Wh—what?"

"I'll explain in a few minutes. Right now, you just stay still until the paramedics arrive."

Straining against the not-so-gentle pressure of Elizabeth's hand, Ashleigh said, "I don't need the paramedics. I'm fine." Then, realizing how ridiculous that sounded, she added, "Well, maybe not fine, but not . . . not broken."

More sirens could be heard in the distance. Ashleigh moaned again, "Please—"

"Ashleigh," she heard Paige's voice cry out. "Oh my God. What happened?"

A bunch of voices meshed together, but Ashleigh couldn't sort them out. That was her last thought before everything turned black.

CHAPTER

38

"Thanks, Mr. Adams," Neil said as his friend's father pulled up to the curb. It had been necessary to get dropped off three blocks from the protest rally. Jogging around the gridlocked traffic toward the department store, Neil clutched a bag that was chock-full of the John Stewart's buttons his father had asked him to bring. *Great turnout,* he observed. *The mucky-mucks at Jordon's would have to be blind to ignore this—or just plain stupid.* He saw hundreds of protesters marching in front of the store and around the corner, most carrying signs with sayings like STEWART'S IS CHICAGO ~ BOYCOTT JORDON'S and WE WANT JOHN STEWART'S and JORDON'S GO HOME, while others were passing out leaflets to all who passed by.

Stretching up on tiptoe, Neil peered through the throng in an attempt to locate his father. He smiled at the group of ladies wearing nineteenth-century costumes in honor of the early days at John Stewart's. At last he spotted Alan Grey with a large sign, standing under the landmark clock, but it took him another few minutes to find his father, who leaned against the grand old store beside his own protest sign. Nelson's face was as ashen as the walls beside him.

Oh shit. Why does he have to do this?

Weaving his way through the crowd, Neil reached his father's side.

"Thanks, son," Nelson said, a faint smile coming to his lips. "I knew I could count on you."

Holding up the huge sack so his father could see the full stash, Neil said, "Let me give these to Alan and get you home."

Nelson shook his head. "No, no. I just need to catch my breath. I'll be fine." His voice was whisper-soft, and weak. "Isn't this a fantastic turnout? Even better than expected. Alan worked his butt off, and it's sure paid off." Neil knew how important the preservation of the building was to his dad and the other members of the grassroots group. But the fact that it had been designed by renowned architect Daniel Burnham didn't seem to matter to Jordon's management. "It's bound to be low on the profit-oriented corporation's hit list," he'd overheard Alan say more than once.

"Dad, please," Neil said now. "You've done enough."

Nelson gave him another weak smile and asked to see the buttons.

Neil opened the bag and pulled one out.

"This is beyond terrific," his father said, seeming to get a second wind.

Neil rolled his eyes. "I'll help for the next hour, Dad, if you just let me call a cab for you now."

Nelson shook his head again. "A whole herd of *Oprah* fans showed up earlier, and we handed out a ton of flyers. They're going to go nuts for these."

Ross Pocino pulled into the Motel 6 parking lot and selected a spot in front of his room. Since he had no reason to go into the city, he'd chosen a location close to O'Hare. His belly was rumbling after the ham dinner special he'd eaten at that greasy spoon nearby, but that wasn't the real problem. In his gut he had this gnawing feeling that he just couldn't dispel.

Maybe it's all just a wild goose chase, he thought, playing his own devil's advocate. Maybe Tony Wainwright had seen the light and was on the straight and narrow—but maybe not. Pocino wasn't a fan of coincidence. And right now, as he began adding up the seemingly unrelated ones, it seemed there were just too damn many coincidences. Even the far fetched ones seemed more and more plausible.

The schmuck was still a computer whiz. He'd managed to wangle a job with Christonelli, who had recently been a party to raising havoc with the Taylors. *Again.* And Christonelli had a contract for designing the Jordon's retail website. Plus, Tony's roommate was dating Viviana De

Mornay. And to top it all off, thanks to the Internet monitoring setup, Pocino had found out that Marnie had some secret online admirer—one who claimed he lived in the Chicago area. *Coincidence . . . or conspiracy?* This could all add up to a big fat zero, but if there *were* trouble afoot and Pocino ignored it, he'd never forgive himself.

Slipping his key card into the door, he realized that he might be connecting the dots in a web of intrigue and deception—or he might be just acting like the guy from that damn musical *The Man of La Mancha.* The one who was always out chasing windmills.

Ashleigh awoke with a start. The blinds were wide open and the sun was streaming in. Odd-shaped shadows danced across the floor. *Is there a tree outside my window?* Fighting to pull her thoughts together, she glanced at the clock on the opposite wall. *A wall clock?* Squinting and shading her eyes, she read the time: nine twenty. Suddenly she knew where she was, and she remembered how she'd gotten there. She just hoped it was Saturday morning and not Sunday—or later. Surely she hadn't slept more than one night—or been in a drug-induced sleep for God knows how long . . .

Pushing herself up on her good elbow, she winced as a sharp pain shot through her rib cage.

"Good morning, sleepyhead." Conrad stepped into view. "How do you feel?"

Ashleigh felt as though she'd been run over by a ten-ton truck, but she responded, "I'm fine, and I've got to get out of here." She noticed that Conrad was dressed in a pair of Levi's and a crewneck sweater. *Did he miss his morning meeting?*

"Not so fast, love. You had quite a tumble last night." Conrad's gaze was tender. "There's no internal bleeding, thank God, but you may have a mild concussion, and there's a lot of bruising."

"I understand, but Viviana's closing is tonight. After last night's calamity, I can't just not show up. This is Marnie's first show since her injury. Besides, I need to be there for all the girls."

Conrad gave her a dubious look, but she didn't wait for him to offer another protest. Gritting her teeth, she pushed herself fully upright and gently swung her legs to the side of the bed.

Her husband reached out to steady her, but said nothing.

"Do I look frightening?" she asked, lifting a hand to her burning cheek.

"Well," he said with a grin, "you've looked better."

She let out a groan. "That's not real encouraging, but I guess it's better than telling me I look like hell—which I probably do," she said, forcing a sarcastic smile. "Thanks for reining in your usual candor."

"Well, I can't see how you're going to make it to the party tonight, but I will check on getting you released." Then, taking in the determined set of her jaw, he hastily added, "When we get home, we'll see how you feel and take it from there. Okay?"

The tone of Conrad's cell cut off further discussion. He flipped open the cover and lifted it to his ear, and she saw a smile spreading across her husband's unshaven face. "No, love. Not now . . . No need to worry . . . Yes, she's a little beat up, but she's fine . . . I'm just going to check with her doctor . . ."

As she listened to Conrad's side of the conversation, Ashleigh realized it must be one of the girls. *Probably Juliana, my little worrywart.*

Still smiling when he slipped the phone back into his pocket, he said, "That was Marnie. She had a fit when I wouldn't let her come with us in the ambulance last night."

"Marnie?" Ashleigh's brain was still foggy, but the events from the night before, which had been fading in and out, were beginning to clear. *It* was *Marnie beside me after I fell.* A warm feeling spread throughout her aching limbs. *She called me Mom.*

As Conrad went in search of the doctor, Ashleigh slipped her feet to the floor and mentally counted to ten. She saw no slippers, so in bare feet, she trod gingerly to the small cupboard in search of her clothes. *Terrific.* There hung her torn Versace along with some undergarments and the treacherous four-inch heels. She made an instant decision: She'd wait until she got home to take a shower and get dressed. In the meantime, she would have Conrad go to the hospital shop and buy her some slippers and a decent robe to cover her hospital gown.

She made her way to the sink to splash some water on her face. That's when she saw what Conrad had tried to warn her about: The whites of her eyes were red, and beneath a lump of bandages, the side of her face was swollen, black and blue. *I don't own enough concealer to hide this,* she thought.

At the sound of the Lincoln pulling up the drive, Paige flew down the stone steps in front of the Taylors' home—the same steps Ashleigh had toppled down the night before in search of Paige's mother. Paige had been berating herself for hours. Ashleigh's fall, and the subsequent dismantling of her well-planned party, was all her fault. *Why didn't I just keep my mouth shut?*

As horrible as Paige had felt throughout her sleepless night, when she saw Ashleigh as Conrad helped her out of the limo—her right arm in a splint and her hair hanging loosely around her battered cheek—she felt a thousand times worse.

Oh my God, she silently cried.

Ashleigh's eyes met Paige's. With a stifled peal of laughter, she asked, "That bad?"

"Well, you could use some makeup. And a snazzier outfit," Paige joked. But her wan smile disappeared as she said, "Ashleigh, I am so very, very sorry. Your accident—"

Waving off her apology, Ashleigh asked, "What about Helen? Conrad said she'd been found inside the house?"

Paige shook her head, reproaching herself. "I guess she was never actually lost."

Conrad, who was supporting Ashleigh on her good left side, said, "Ladies, you can talk in a few minutes, but first let's get my wife into the house."

He got no resistance, but once inside, Ashleigh pushed her shoulders back and straightened her posture as best she could. "Thank you, love," she said. "I need to do as much as possible on my own." She lifted her splinted arm slightly and stifled a wince. "So, what did I miss?"

Before Paige had an opportunity to fill Ashleigh in, they were greeted by Elizabeth and the girls, and the foyer echoed with a cacophony of rapid-fire questions.

"Chill, everyone." Marnie's voice rose as she stepped closer to her mother. With eyes flecked with concern, she said, "Can't you see that Mom isn't up to all this? She needs to rest."

Ashleigh, a bit disoriented, felt Conrad take hold of her good elbow once more. She desperately needed to sit down. "Thanks, love," she said, reveling in Marnie's uncharacteristic protectiveness. "No need to worry, but I think I should get settled in the living room."

For the next few moments, Ashleigh allowed Marnie to fuss over her, plumping up a pillow behind her back, while the others continued to pepper her with questions.

Helen burst into the room, breathless. "Ashleigh," she cried out. "Paige told me about your accident." She stopped in her tracks. "Oh my." She sank down on the couch beside Ashleigh, concern mirrored in her vibrant green eyes. "They said you'd gone out looking for me, but I never went outside."

"Apparently," Paige interjected, "we must have been doing one of those Abbott and Costello routines, popping in and out of rooms and just missing each other. Our timing must have been off. If only—"

"I'm just glad it turned out that you were safe," Ashleigh said, resting her right hand on Helen's. "No harm done." She looked up to see quizzical frowns on the faces surrounding her, and the total absurdity of Ashleigh's statement hit them, bringing with it a stream of uncontrollable laughter. Although her body ached, she knew in her heart that she'd been lucky. It could have been a lot worse. *And bringing Marnie a bit closer is worth the pain.* "Well, nothing that won't heal."

As the words left Ashleigh's mouth, she noticed Helen's cockeyed brows, which she'd drawn on with an auburn eyebrow pencil. Amused, she caught Paige's eye and glanced at Helen again. Her friend's eyes widened as she also took in her mother's haphazard brows.

"Mom," Paige began, "tonight, for Viviana's party, let's help each other get dressed for our grand entrance."

"Oh yes," Helen said with enthusiasm. "Tonight will be such fun. I'm looking forward to meeting some of Gino's friends."

CHAPTER
41

Still in her robe, Erica was busily folding Fans of John Stewart's flyers when she heard the chirp of the doorbell. Mike was in the shower, and Bill was on a buying trip, so she heaved herself to her feet, brushing off a scattering of cookie crumbs. *Oh my God*, she thought, noticing that she'd eaten the entire bag of Mrs. Fields.

She hadn't given in to her urge to drink, but overeating was a different matter altogether. She'd gained nearly twenty-five pounds since coming to live with Mike and Bill last year, and she knew she really must get serious about that diet she kept promising herself to begin. *Today,* she silently vowed, making a mental note to shop for the right foods so she could start that seven-day diet featured in *Cosmopolitan*—the same diet that flight attendants swore by.

She stepped to the door and looked out the peephole. Her heart nearly stopped beating. Why had Pocino landed on her doorstep? There was no longer a restraining order. After coming to her senses and calling the Taylors to nervously announce their heart-wrenching decision, she and Mike had apologized and made it clear that they had no intention of uprooting Marnie. Erica had expressed her gratefulness that Marnie had a loving family and sisters to support her. The relationship between the Christonellis and the Taylors, Erica knew, would never be as it once was. But at least she and Mike would no longer be excluded from Marnie's life.

Running her fingers through her unruly curls, Erica sucked in her breath and pulled open the door.

"Good morning, Mrs. Christonelli," the overweight investigator said. "Is your brother-in-law in?" He attempted to look beyond her, into the house.

"What is it that you want, Mr. Pocino?" she asked, keeping the door only partially open.

"I'd like to speak to Mike Christonelli."

"Who is it?" Mike called out as he appeared a few feet behind her in the living room, his hair still damp from the shower.

"May I come in?" Pocino asked.

Easing the door open, Erica felt her heart thundering in her chest. *Why is he here? And without any advance warning?*

She stepped back to let him pass. Pocino's lack of trust in her—his pure hatred—was revealed in his narrowed eyes. *The Taylors must have sent him. But why now?* She closed her eyes. *What now?*

Mike was instantly at Erica's side. His sister-in-law's mood swings had escalated in the past month. She'd been deeply depressed following her last conversation with Marnie, but in the past couple of days she seemed to be pulling herself together. *She sure as hell doesn't need this now,* he thought.

The two men exchanged cautious greetings. Mike looked the bulky man up and down. *How dare he show up without calling ahead?* Rather than confront Pocino in front of Erica, though, Mike reluctantly led him back to his office. Mike sat at the desk in the center of the room, his back to the windows. Below the glass panes there was a long counter on which three computer screens sat, all turned on. Gesturing to a chair on the other side of his desk, Mike noticed that Erica had chosen not to join them. *Can't blame her.* Then it occurred to him that she'd most likely gone to conceal any evidence of her involvement with the John Stewart's group. *As if the intrusive investigator gives a damn.*

Pocino spoke first. "What can you tell me about Anthony Wainwright?"

Thrown off balance, Mike asked, "Tony?" *Of course that's who he means.*

"Anthony, Tony, whatever he calls himself. I understand he's working for you."

"That's right. No complaints. I'm aware of Tony's past—he and Mitchell filled me in on the details before I hired him. He knows his way around computers and has proven himself to be a hard worker." When Pocino did not respond, Mike asked, "Do you have any reason to believe that Tony's been in any sort of trouble since serving his sentence?"

Ignoring his question, Pocino asked his own: "Can you give me a rundown, sort of a job description, of what . . . ?" He paused, but when Mike's answer was not forthcoming, he rephrased the question. "What exactly is it that Tony does for you?"

Sensing the investigator's hostility, Mike spoke in no uncertain terms. "I have no intention of giving you the rundown on any of my employees," he said firmly. "If you have something specific to ask, you'd better spit it out."

"Got something to hide?" Pocino countered.

Mike leaned closer and glared. Through gritted teeth, he said in slow, measured syllables, "You are without a doubt the most unforgiving bastard I've ever had the misfortune of running across. Time for you to take your leave." He hesitated, then added, "If you have any legit reason for your bullshit questions, get a warrant."

Pocino stood, chuckling, and gave a snide grin. "Just might do that. In the meantime, I'd suggest you watch your back." He spun on his heel and charged from the office.

Mike followed at his heels, concerned that he might head into the other room to interrogate Erica rather than head for the front door. *Watch your back.* The phrase echoed in his head. *Was that a threat? Watch out for Tony Wainwright, or watch out for him?* He brushed it off. *Tony deserves another chance. I trust him, and we've got nothing to hide from Pocino.*

Pocino was the first to reach the front door, and he flung it open. "Well, speak of the devil," he growled.

Tony Wainwright stood on the top step, his mouth agape.

Leaning back against the wall of the shower for support, Ashleigh did her best to ignore the dizzy sensation that had come over her and concentrated instead on the piping hot water pelting her aching ribs and shoulders. Enjoying the degree of comfort it brought, she gently rubbed a bit of Ralph Lauren bath gel across her skin. Taking in the gentle fragrance of Blue, she began to relax and her mind began to drift toward the upcoming evening's events. *This clumsy tumble down the steps is not going to keep me from my girls' performance.* Thanks to Miss Daryl's terrific choreography, each of her daughters would have her moment in the spotlight.

"How are you doing?" Conrad was trying to keep his tone steady, but she detected a note of concern wafting through the steam of the shower. "Could you use some assistance?"

"Thanks, love. I'm doing okay," she lied. *I'm sure this dizziness will subside. It just has to.* She reached for a towel and then slipped into her terry-cloth robe.

Conrad stood in the doorway to the master bedroom, ready to give her a hand. *I must give him no cause for concern. This is an important night, for Conrad and for the rest of us. He can't be hovering around me.*

As good as the hot water felt on her aching muscles, the heat had taken its toll. *If only I could lie down for a moment . . .* "It sure is warm in here," she said aloud as she dried her face and made her way to the dressing table in their bedroom.

There was a light tap on the door of the bedroom before Marnie stepped inside. She was already in her solo costume, Ashleigh saw, and she held a handful of hairpins. "Mom," she said, looking Ashleigh up and down, not bothering with subtlety, "do you think it will be okay for me to wear my hair down for my solo?"

The warmth spreading through Ashleigh's body had little to do with being overheated just a moment before. At the uncharacteristic request for approval from her ultra-independent daughter, Ashleigh asked, "What do *you* think?" When Marnie did not immediately respond, Ashleigh prodded, "You're dancing to Mariah Carey's track, 'Can't Let Go,' right?"

Marnie nodded.

"Well, if you want my vote, for this type of romantic ballad, I'd say leave your hair down and let it flow."

Marnie's smile spread from ear to ear. "That's what I told Callie, but she thought I should do a half ponytail." She paused. "Mom, if you aren't up to going out tonight, we all understand."

Ashleigh looked into the mirror. "You're ashamed to be seen—"

"No way," Marnie cut in. "We just thought—"

Ashleigh shook her head. "I wouldn't miss your performance for the world, darling," she said. "Tell your sisters it will take more than a little fall to put their clumsy mother out of commission." Then, glancing at the time, she continued, "But since I'll need a bit more time than usual to become presentable, I'll rely on you to make sure everyone is ready to leave the house at five thirty."

Ashleigh and Conrad were the last to slide into the large white limousine they had rented for the evening.

Everyone seemed to be talking at once. Elizabeth and the girls were seated closest to Mark, Paige, and Helen. April sat on the opposite side of the limo beside a skinny kid with dark, curly hair and a gold hoop in his left ear. Wearing a double-breasted tux, the pale young man awkwardly joked as he straddled a black case—the shape and size could easily accommodate a violin. But, taking in the two cameras hanging loosely around his neck, Ashleigh surmised he must be the JJQ cameraman whom April had enlisted to photograph this evening's event. If Conrad and Ross

Pocino were correct, this Renzo Cabello was also Tony Wainwright's roommate—and the brother of Viviana's latest beau. *Small world*, she thought.

April, decked out in a sophisticated black-and-white Valentino gown, made eye contact and smiled. With a twinkle in her dark eyes, Paige's gorgeous daughter rose and, straightening as far as the low headroom would allow, carefully made her way toward Ashleigh. The other passengers scooted over a fraction to make room for her to sit down.

"Aunt Ashleigh," she said, taking Ashleigh's right hand, "Mom told me about the accident. What a story. I'm so sorry." She bobbed her head in her grandmother's direction, with a glance that held no reproach but was filled with indulgent affection. "But you look fantastic."

Ashleigh laughed. "Always the diplomat." She knew she must look dreadful, but she refused to dwell on it. In fact, considering everything, she felt pretty good. "Toppling down those steps was a result of nothing but my own awkwardness in four-inch heels." Glancing down at the gold ankle straps she now wore, she added, "They weren't really suitable for a sprint."

April gave an amused nod. "It's a miracle you didn't sprain your ankle," she commented.

"And where is your fiancé?" Ashleigh asked.

"Kyle had to work," April replied, then quickly added, "but he's promised to get the time off for Viviana's opening party in Chicago next month." With a devilish grin, she said, "This weekend, Renzo is my date."

Throughout the hour-long drive, champagne, wine, sodas, and sparkling water were served. The conversations, whether of the getting-to-know-you or the catch-up variety, never let up—not for a single moment.

Conrad and Mark exchanged glances, a nonverbal communication. Both men knew it would be impossible to conduct any intelligent one-on-one conversation amid the chaos, so they took advantage of a little time to just sit back and relax as they made their way into the city.

Klieg lights and motion spotlights lit up the Manhattan sky in front of De Mornay's on Fifth Avenue. Temporarily blinded as they pulled up behind a Lamborghini and a long string of limousines, Conrad waited behind the limo's tinted windows for David to come around and open the door for him. After stepping out, he extended his hand to assist Ashleigh. The others filed out behind her and made their way into the boutique, the three Taylor girls leading the way.

Gino greeted them at the door. He had donned a well-tailored tuxedo that did little to disguise his muscular physique. Conrad suspected that the young man was feeling a bit out of place, but doing his level best to conceal his unease.

Once inside, Conrad recognized the strains of "Some Enchanted Evening" coming from the elegantly attired eight-piece orchestra seated on a riser that had been set up in front of the windows. The ambiance of De Mornay's, transformed from a posh boutique into a luxurious dining area, easily rivaled that of the most prestigious Manhattan restaurants.

Viviana and Glenn smiled as they chatted with guests coming through the reception line. As Conrad made his way across the room to greet them, he heard a familiar voice addressing Ashleigh. He turned to see Mitchell Wainwright approaching at a rapid pace.

"I need to talk with you," Wainwright said, before doing a double take. Without a word, he looked from Ashleigh's battered cheek and black eye to Conrad, raising a thick brow before adding, "Tomorrow morning if possible."

As Wainwright walked away, Conrad said, "That's a first for the man who wants everything yesterday. Wonder what he has on his mind."

Battling the overwhelming fatigue that threatened her, Ashleigh sipped her coffee and tuned into the activity surrounding her. Across the room Viviana seamlessly floated from one table to the next, weaving in and out of tuxedoed waiters serving dessert. Gino followed her step for step, as if he were attached to her hip.

At the first notes of "Dark Eyes," Ashleigh's gaze traveled across the room to the Toddmans' table. She knew that Paige and Mark would be the first to grace the gathering with one of their breathtaking performances of the tango, and she wasn't disappointed. In seconds, Mark was sweeping Paige onto the small dance floor. *What an exquisite couple,* she thought, once again enchanted by their flawless execution. For several moments they owned the tiny floor, before another couple joined them. Ashleigh strained to get a better view and then smiled as she recognized the back of April's elegant gown and the flamboyant Renzo gliding her across the floor.

Viviana and Gino breezed up to the table, interrupting her thoughts. Viviana was dazzling, and her companion was equally eye-catching. Even more eye-catching was Gino's undisguised adoration of the fashion maven.

Here we go again, Ashleigh mused.

"And how are your girls feeling tonight?" Viviana asked, leaning slightly on her lover's arm. She laughed nervously. "I hope everyone is in tip-top shape. This evening's closing ceremony must be pure *perfection.*"

Earlier in the evening, Viviana had let the Taylors know that the girls' performance would follow dessert. Although she knew no one was at fault, Viviana was unable to conceal her disappointment about the previous evening's canceled dress rehearsal. She had seen the twins perform in the past and knew they were extremely talented; plus, their dance teacher was widely admired for her outstanding choreography. *But the younger sister was only eleven. I sure hope Juliana is as good as I've been told . . .*

Ashleigh had offered to have the girls come earlier in the day in order to perform a dress rehearsal, but Viviana had been able to spare no time for that; there was far too much she had to oversee. As it was, she'd hardly had enough time to take care of her hair and nails. The amount of time it had taken the beautician to fill in her not-so-permanent individual eyelashes had totally thrown her off schedule.

It was almost performance time now, and the dance instructor had not yet arrived, yet Ashleigh seemed unfazed.

"Miss Daryl might have been caught up in traffic," Ashleigh explained.

Viviana knew her discomfort must be written all over her face, because Ashleigh added, "Don't worry. The girls have their numbers down pat. They don't actually need the teacher tonight; they just want her to see her choreography in costume."

Which was why we came all the way out to Greenwich last night. But there was no use discussing intentions. Viviana said a silent prayer that the performance would be perfect. *It just has to be.*

Despite the heavy traffic, the petite, blonde dance instructor arrived just in time. She'd called ahead, so Clancy was there to usher her in through the stockroom door and lead her straight to the area where the girls were busily limbering up, performing a series of stretch exercises.

"Miss Daryl," Callie called out, "Marnie and I practiced our duet with that extra spin you suggested. We'll show you how well it fits with the music."

"You were right," Marnie agreed. "It looks *waaayyy* better."

"Wonderful, girls. Now, where did Derek go?" Miss Daryl asked.

Callie wished she knew the answer to that question. Her boyfriend was supposed to be taking care of the lighting for this evening's performance, but Callie knew he was pissed off. Miss Daryl hadn't taken his suggestion about working him into one of the numbers. Although Callie would have liked that, she knew he wasn't up to Viviana's standards. Even in the backup numbers at school, he was not outstanding. *I'm not sure he's really meant to be a dancer.* He was on the lighting team for all the school performances, though, and had become a real pro. Callie was proud of him, and she felt confident recommending him for the De Mornay's show.

Marnie rolled her eyes in answer to the dance instructor's question. "I think he went out the back door. *Again.*"

Callie pursed her lips and turned to glare at her twin. "I'm really getting fed up with all your snide remarks," she said. *Why does she have to put Derek down, especially in front of Miss Daryl?* She couldn't let Marnie get away with it. "At least *my* boyfriend goes to the same high school as we do." *And at least he hangs with the in-crowd.* "He's not some faceless creep in another state."

Callie couldn't understand why her sister kept sending messages to this Brad character in Chicago. She'd never even laid eyes on what Samantha called the "mad messenger." *Probably because he's hideous— or fifty years old.* "For all you know, this Brad character could be a total nerd."

Juliana stamped her soft-soled jazz shoe on the tiled floor, barely making a sound. "Chill, you two," she said, her voice rising above the others'. "Come on, we need to practice the finale."

Miss Daryl stepped in, resting her hand on each girl's shoulder in turn. All the bickering came to an abrupt stop. But as the girls went through their routine one last time, Callie's mind was not focused one hundred percent. Derek had been acting weird, she had to admit. *He keeps disappearing.* He had even left the high-intensity discharge lamps and following spotlight on and unattended, which he knew was a fire hazard. *And his breath.* That was her biggest concern: Was he going outside to smoke pot?

Please, please, please don't mess up, Callie prayed. *Not tonight . . .*

Conrad had arranged to be picked up immediately following the girls' performance. He knew his wife was a real trouper, but he'd noticed that her face had become quite pale earlier in the evening. Fortunately, she did not refuse leaving ahead of the crowd. The others in their party would return to Greenwich a bit later in the same white stretch limo that had delivered them.

After the Taylors said their good-byes, Ashleigh silently slipped into their own Lincoln limo with Conrad close behind. Though her natural beauty was marred only slightly by her battered cheek, she looked more fragile than usual, and Conrad sensed that she had something on her mind. If it was something urgent, he was sure she'd let him know. For the moment, he preferred that she just relax. "Our girls were sensational as always," he said with considerable pride.

Ashleigh leaned back against the plush leather and smiled. "The show went off without a hitch—other than Viviana nearly going into cardiac arrest when the orchestra had to play the intro twice while waiting for the opening spotlights." She squeezed his arm. "It never ceases to amaze me. No matter what clashes take place before a show, the girls seem to pull it together."

"You know that old cliché: 'Bad rehearsal, good show.'"

Ashleigh nodded. "They even managed to make their synchronized ellipticals appear seamless."

"And why not?" Conrad grinned. "They've been practicing night and day for eons."

Ashleigh watched the city lights flash by the Lincoln's window. She couldn't put her finger on it, but she'd picked up an undercurrent between the twins. Yet, after the show, all three sisters had shared big hugs and seemed pleased with their own performances—and with one another's as well.

"What is it?" Conrad asked.

"Just thinking about Callie and—"

"That boy was out smoking pot," Conrad said through gritted teeth.

"Are you sure?" Ashleigh's heart sank.

Conrad nodded. "Absolutely. Would have confronted him on the spot, but couldn't risk creating a scene. However, Callie is to have nothing more to do with Derek Stanton."

They were silent for the rest of the drive home. Ashleigh wished Callie had not suggested that Derek handle the lights. *That boy is so self-absorbed.* Time after time she had found Callie in a bundle of tears over Derek's unkind or thoughtless words or actions. The young man could be attentive one moment, building up Callie's expectations, and the next he would break her heart by announcing that he needed some space.

Ashleigh was well aware of the roller-coaster emotions of teens, especially when encountering their first love, and hopefully this was just that—a *first* love. Callie was far too young for a long-term relationship. *I try so hard not to be overprotective . . .* But Ashleigh often had to bite her tongue to avoid saying anything negative to Callie about that boy. She didn't want to put her daughter on the defensive. And yet Conrad was right: Somehow, this unhealthy relationship would have to be dealt with.

CHAPTER

45

The morning after her Manhattan closing, still foggy with sleep, Viviana rolled over. From across the bed, she felt before she saw—peering through her long, perfectly spaced lashes—that dark, adoring eyes were trained on her. Her mouth widened into a seductive smile. Gino's ebony hair fell rakishly over one eye. He was propped up on his elbows. *My God, he's gorgeous,* she thought as she took in his strong, hard body. *And he's all mine.*

He grinned down at her before pulling her roughly to him. His large, callused hands traveled the length of her body, exploring every inch. Again. Those magnificent hands were all over her, and it felt incredible. He wanted her, that was crystal clear, and—as if he were a drug—she found she couldn't get enough of him.

She ran her fingertips across his hard belly and smiled as Glenn's comment replayed in her head: *Good God, Viviana. Gino is young enough to be your son.*

Her response had stopped her former business partner cold. "Jealous?" she'd asked. And then, widening her eyes, she had mockingly continued, "You know perfectly well that my son is *much* older than Gino."

Her thoughts faded now, and every grain of tension evaporated as Gino's arms wrapped around her. Lost in the intensity of his gaze, she smelled the faint scent of his aftershave and felt a red-hot fire burning inside. The feel of him was so overwhelming, and their lovemaking was so intense, that in just moments he was driving her out of her mind. "Now, now," she cried out. "Don't hold back—I want you now."

"Just give me a few minutes and I'll take you there again," he said, running his finger along her jawline. "This time, slow and easy."

"Hey, cowboy," she challenged, "don't offer what you can't deliver."

"With you, I have no trouble with the delivery."

The man is as insatiable as I am. That thought bubbled to the surface. *Lucky, lucky me.* Beneath it, however, she sensed that Gino had something he wanted to say but wasn't able to find the words. "What is it, handsome?"

"Umm . . . ," he uttered, his dark eyes intense and locked on hers.

Her stomach roiled, and she felt a lump in her throat. *What does he have on his mind?*

Finally he spit it out. "Tell me again about your *present* relationship with Wainwright."

"Mitchell?" Not waiting for him to confirm, she asked, "What do you want to know that I haven't already told you?" It was no secret to Gino that she and Mitchell had once been lovers. She had thought he understood: In that realm, Wainwright was history.

"Okay. Let me give it to you straight. I don't understand why he was a part of last night's closing celebration."

Taking his strong jaw between her hands, Viviana felt her heart swell. Instead of being upset over his jealously, she reveled in it. "Mitchell is the go-between with my investors," she patiently reassured him. "Some of last night's guests are currently investing in my Chicago venture. It's Mitchell's job to reassure them that De Mornay's will continue to be a good investment."

Gino nodded. "Sorry," he said. "I don't much like the man, and I don't quite buy in to the whole situation—a former lover transforming into a platonic, business-only relationship." His eyes traveled across her naked body.

"Well, that is *exactly* the case here." She paused, a little troubled. "I'm sorry his presence makes you uncomfortable. I need his expertise and his connections. He won't be around very much. But," she added, "he *will* be at our Chicago opening. Other than that, most of our business will be conducted by phone. Believe me, Mitchell Wainwright is history." Ruffling Gino's hair, she smiled. "On his best day, he'd be no competition for you."

Her young lover gave her a dazzling smile. "I'm probably overreacting. I don't know much about the man, but . . ." He paused as a scowl darkened his face. "I don't like the condescending way he looks at Renzo, as if he were something disgusting he found on the sole of his Italian loafer. I mean, look at the way he treats his own son."

Viviana wasn't surprised. Gino's brother was so obviously gay that she was sure Gino was not exaggerating Mitchell's disdain. "Give him time," she said. "It's taken him ages to accept Tony."

"I don't see acceptance, only a reluctant tolerance."

Time to change the subject. Running her fingers through Gino's thick hair, in her husky early-morning voice she whispered in his ear. "Now, or in the shower?"

"Yes," he said with a grin as he pulled her tight against him. "How about now, and again in the shower?"

Viviana had no regrets about the life she'd lived. She'd had it all— money, power, prestige. She wouldn't have changed a thing, even if she could. Her life's choices had led her here. *And now I can afford to indulge my inner child.* That was her last rational thought—her last thought, period—before Gino filled her with his manhood.

CHAPTER
46

Paige and April said their good-byes to the Taylor family a good five hours ahead of their scheduled flights from JFK, allowing plenty of time for lunch in one of their favorite Chelsea restaurants. The trendy Colicchio & Sons was just as Paige remembered it. She knew April loved the more laid-back vibe of the Tap Room, which seemed just the right place for them to play catch-up before heading home to their separate destinations. Mark had left at the crack of dawn for a board meeting at the Dallas Museum of Art, and Elizabeth had taken Helen under her wing to spend a few more days in Greenwich—and give Paige a much-needed break.

Paige and her daughter chatted nonstop, pausing only when the waiter arrived with their order—the signature taleggio and prosciutto pizza. After the waiter refilled their water glasses and departed, April bit into the mouthwatering soft crust and smiled. Then a serious expression crossed her brow. "Mom," she said, "I managed to spend some time with Marnie this morning."

"Did she open up to you?"

"Sort of," April said with a nod.

"I didn't detect anything particularly off-key this weekend," Paige said. "Her concern over Ashleigh's tumble down the steps seemed genuine. That was reassuring, but I sense there are still some unresolved problems." She hoped she was wrong.

But April agreed. "It's tough on Marnie. She still thinks of Erica as another mother. But I actually think she's more relieved than upset about the custody case being dropped. Although I doubt she'd admit it, I think the idea of living with the Christonellis will soon be a faded memory. There *is* something that does concern me, though."

Paige listened as April relayed her conversation with Marnie about the boy she'd met online, who said he was the Christonellis' neighbor in Chicago. Paige was well aware of the dangers of predators lurking in cyberspace. Recalling Ashleigh's questions about Myspace and how the Toddmans had dealt with April's online time, she asked her daughter, "What's the attraction? Does she even know the boy's real name?"

April shrugged. "He calls himself Brad. My guess is that he makes her feel important. She said he already knew a lot about her, and he wants to know more. He told her he's a reporter for his high school newspaper and he thinks her life would make a great story."

Paige's stomach did a little flip. "That sounds creepy, even dangerous. Why would she want to tell someone about herself when she doesn't even know him?"

"I'm no shrink, but I think Marnie is flattered. I mean, here's someone who wants to know all about her. She's the focus, not just one of the twins." April paused. "You've got to remember, Mom, Marnie was already eight when she learned she was a twin, and her entire life was turned upside down."

"But in a good way," Paige interjected. "She'd been living in a mobile home in the mountains, and her so-called mom was an alcoholic."

"We know that, but it's not necessarily how Marnie views it. At first she thought it was really cool to be a twin. But being an adored only child, rather than part of a package, became appealing. As time went by, it seems she forgot all the negatives of her past life. Especially in contrast to living with a popular identical twin and a vivacious, savvy little sister." April sighed. "I think Marnie feels like the least important member of the family—the number two twin, the middle child. Most of her friends, on and off the dance team, were Callie's friends first. They have history and shared memories that she's not a part of. She feels left out." April stopped and smiled. "Actually, I can remember feeling left out as a teenager for no reason at all. And in Marnie's case, she has a spare set of parents, so she's always going to be physically left out of one family or the other."

That makes a lot of sense, thought Paige. *April's only seven years older than the twins. When did she become so insightful?* "But what about this Brad?"

"Along with showing a lot of interest in Marnie herself, Brad claims to know the man who's dating Erica. Apparently Brad is one of the John Stewart's protesters."

"What kind of high school kid would get involved in the protest?"

April shrugged. "Actually, at the last protest rally, I saw quite a few young people holding up signs and passing out buttons and flyers. Renzo was the cameraman assigned to a segment for JJQ, and I went with him. I think most of the young people had come along with parents who were involved. Maybe that was the case with this Brad character."

Paige knew that Erica had worked for John Stewart's until the whole custody affair had happened this past winter. According to Mark, she had signed one of the petitions to stop the name change to Jordon's. But he'd also told her that Erica had resigned from the store and was no longer involved with the protest rallies. She could just imagine the reaction from the press if the daughter of the Jordon's CEO were linked with the protest. *With the current boycott of Jordon's Chicago stores and falling profits in the area, a sensational story in some high school newspaper is all Conrad needs.*

Breaking into her thoughts, April said, "Mom, Marnie says she knows better than to meet up with a stranger she's met online. But I think she might have said that only because she thought it was what I wanted to hear." She leaned across the table, her expression serious. "Next month, when you all come to Chicago for the opening of De Mornay's, I think someone should keep an eye on her."

Conrad popped two Advils into his mouth, washed them down with water, and set the glass on his étagère. A quick glance into the mirror confirmed his lack of a good night's sleep. In fact, he couldn't recall a single morning of feeling well rested in the past few months. *Good thing this string of around-the-clock strategy meetings will soon be coming to an end.*

Reaching for the Visine, he tilted his head back. While the liquid did little to erase the redness of his eyes, it was the best he could do. Then, turning his attention to the aspects of his appearance that were within his control, he straightened his tie, buttoned the bottom two buttons on his suit jacket, and threw back his shoulders before heading for the conference room.

Geri, his assistant, caught him just outside the conference room door and handed him the folder he'd requested. "Alex Arnold's assistant just called," she said quickly. "Alex has a family emergency and won't be able to make today's meeting."

Conrad groaned inwardly. Today of all days, Alex shouldn't be out of the loop. While he had an overview of Jordon's community involvement and corporate giving in the Chicago area, he had been counting on his regional vice president of cause marketing to fill in the details and give everyone some insight. "What kind of family emergency?" he asked.

Geri, who had darted back toward the reception room, stopped in her tracks. When she turned to face her boss, her face registered curiosity. "Her father had a stroke. The paramedics have taken him to New York–Presbyterian Hospital."

Conrad knew his uncharacteristic questioning of one of his executives had thrown her, and he suddenly felt foolish. "Sorry to hear that," he said. "To miss today's meeting, Alex obviously had a good reason." With his hand poised on the knob of the conference room door, he turned back and said, "Please arrange for flowers to be sent to the hospital."

All the other members of his management team and the regional vice presidents for Jordon's North appeared to be assembled around the long, mahogany conference table. In the midst of Conrad's mental roll call, William Uniack, general manager for Jordon's Chicago locations, slipped through the door and took a seat at the far end of the table. Uniack had been the John Stewart's CEO for many years, and his office was located in the landmark John Stewart's building—site of the many recent protests.

As Conrad gazed around the table, he took in the phenomenal power Jordon's had on board and at his disposal. His spirits lifted. Without a shred of doubt, within these walls were some of the brightest, most savvy merchants and financial executives on the planet. The combined intelligence and proven track records of the men and women surrounding him gave him a renewed sense of confidence. *We're on the right track. We'll overcome all our present roadblocks.*

Dumping his folder on the table, he pulled out his customary chair, midway down the table rather than at either end. He preferred to conduct meetings with his team around him rather than at a distance.

Not bothering to open the folder, he shot a glance at the information packets in front of each executive. They were topped with a detailed agenda that Geri had distributed earlier. Conrad cleared his throat. "Before we begin, does anyone have anything to add to the agenda?"

Roger Williams, the chief marketing officer, spoke up. "I'd like to discuss our private branding goals for the Chicago area."

Conrad nodded, jotting down PB on his agenda. Since jumping ship from Neiman Marcus to join their team, Williams had assembled an awesome stable of private brand designers who were now working exclusively for Jordon's.

Conrad's eyes quickly scanned the room. In view of the full agenda and known priorities of this meeting, it was no surprise that no one else spoke up. So he plunged straight into what was central to all of their concerns. "No one could have anticipated the strength or the longevity of the opposition to our national branding goals in Chicago. Our mission is to form a concrete plan for damage control and set it in motion posthaste." Heads around the table nodded their agreement. "The campaign being waged under the Fans of John Stewart's banner has been devastating. There is no denying the remarkable groundswell behind this group nor that their boycott has been costly. To date, the profit loss in the former John Stewart's location in Chicago is . . ." His eyes shot straight to CFO Rob Welter.

"Thirty percent," Welter confirmed without the aid of his notes, indicating that the information packet included spreadsheets with the actual dollar losses per store.

"We must not be deterred," Conrad said firmly. "These losses are temporary. We must not lose sight of our vision." He poured water from a pitcher into the glass in front of him and took a long swig. "Our goal is clearly defined. Our strategy and long-term plan were clear at the time we acquired the debt necessary for the purchase of the Hay's Company. They remain crystal clear today. To be a national brand, we cannot run under different names. The imprint of Jordon's must blanket the country."

In his peripheral vision, Conrad saw Lloyd Wilcox lean forward. His head of advertising appeared eager to share his analysis. Conrad gestured for him to go ahead. "Lloyd."

"If you will turn to page three in your packet," Wilcox said, "you will see detailed estimates of the cost of running advertising under various regional banners across the nation versus running all eight hundred department stores with the Jordon's brand, coast to coast." He picked up his glass of water and took a swallow. "You have the figures at your fingertips. This is a no-brainer. The cost savings as a result of national versus regional advertising are staggering."

"Couldn't agree more." Uniack's voice echoed off the walls. "We will prevail," he added with certainty, "but Chicagoans don't like change. Brand loyalty has not skipped a beat in our fair city. The Fans of John Stewart's cling to their regional brand, and they don't seem inclined to give in anytime soon."

"My God, this is the twenty-first century," Roger Williams cut in. "Corporate branding is a reality. When are they going to wake up and move on?"

Uniack held up his hand, palm out. "Hold on, Roger. I agree—one hundred percent. But let me give you my take on the mind-set of the people we're dealing with." He paused thoughtfully. "Chicagoans are fiercely loyal to those brands they consider uniquely theirs. John Stewart's is as much a Chicago icon as is the city's Sears Tower, the tallest building in the nation. But guess what? The Sears naming rights expired three years ago, so that name could change." He paused again, groping for another example. "Chicagoans often refer to U.S. Cellular Field as 'Old Comiskey Park' even though that name changed in 2003. The people of Chicago are not likely to walk away from the battle to preserve the John Stewart's brand."

"Are you saying that we're fighting a losing battle?" Williams countered.

"Not at all. I'm just saying we need to know what we're dealing with. It's a tough nut to crack, but we are making headway. The boycotters are beginning to fade. Even a good many of the protesters, though at first reluctant, are now shopping at Jordon's. Some never will." Uniack shrugged. "That's the breaks. But in the long run . . ."

When Uniack concluded, Conrad thanked him for his insights and then glanced down at his agenda. As the various members of the management team contributed their ideas for a winning strategy for the future, Conrad began to relax. *Within these walls, we have what it takes to overcome the obstacles—to make our vision a reality.*

Shirley Nyquist, vice president of sales promotion, was the last to report. "We had scheduled this summer's Joffrey Ballet fund-raiser in our flagship store. Due to the ongoing protests at John Stewart's, the fund-raiser's chairman has expressed concern. It seems they'll most likely switch to another location for their black-tie extravaganza."

The hairs on the back of Conrad's neck stood up, and outrage shot up his spine.

"Better make that call today," Renzo called out as he brushed past Tony. "Less than a week till opening."

"Get off my case," Tony growled. "I said I'd make the call."

Renzo did a pirouette in the entryway. Now face-to-face with Tony, he looked up and said, "Sorry. I realize it's no piece of pie, but you said your father and Viviana De Mornay had paved the way with the Taylors. She's expecting your call."

Tony jammed his arms into the sleeves of his jacket, snapped up his keys from the entryway table, and headed for the door. Then he stopped suddenly, realizing his friend didn't know his history with Ashleigh, and amended his tone. "Okay. You win. I'll do it now."

Renzo grinned. "Way to go," he said, and went on his way out the door.

Tossing his keys back on the table, Tony returned to the kitchen. Erica Christonelli's comments about Ashleigh's forgiving nature might have been more reassuring if he hadn't overheard Erica's recent conversation with her brother-in-law, in which she expressed her anxiety about the planned meeting with the Taylors during their upcoming visit to Chicago.

With his shaking hand, he plucked up the receiver of the landline; with the other hand, he dialed the number written on the crumpled sheet of paper. Shifting his weight from one foot to the other, he thought, *Now or never.* He pushed his unease aside and prayed that the former Ashleigh McDowell—and not her formidable husband—would pick up the phone.

————

Standing in front of the open doorway, Ashleigh bent down to pick up the newspaper before waving good-bye to the girls. She watched them pile into the car, a smile playing on her lips as she thought about Callie's resilience. Just the week before she had been uncharacteristically angry and uncommunicative, telling her parents she was mortified and would never forgive them. What had brought her to the boiling point was Conrad's insistence that they meet with Derek Stanton and his parents the day following the De Mornay closing festivities. Ashleigh hadn't thought it was necessary, but Conrad had overruled her.

"Derek's parents have a right to know about their son's drug use from the get-go," he'd said. "Even if it is 'only pot,' the time to bring it to an end is now. No pussyfooting around. Callie may spend absolutely no time alone with the boy. If she must see him, it will be at our house or during supervised activities."

The meeting at the Stantons' home had not gone well. Derek had lied, and his parents had chosen to believe their son. They were defensive, insisting that Conrad must be mistaken. The meeting ended with Derek hissing through clenched teeth, "Callie, you are nothing but a spoiled brat, a troublemaker, and a liar."

Callie had held her head high. "You're the liar, Derek. Don't bother calling me, ever again." But the instant the three Taylors had descended the front steps, she made a beeline for the car and dissolved into tears. She had not wanted talk about it, nor had she wanted to go to school the next day. Her parents did not push for a discussion, but she was not allowed to miss school.

Miraculously, though, by the end of week, Callie was all smiles. As Ashleigh eventually found out, upon hearing that Callie and Derek had broken up, Eddie Noice had asked Callie to be his date for the junior prom. The only thing Ashleigh knew about the young man was that he was vice president of the student body and very active in the community. Although Callie had yet to say anything negative about Derek, Ashleigh was sure she would soon wonder what she'd ever seen in him.

The shrill ringing of the phone tore Ashleigh away from thoughts of Callie and what the future might bring. She dashed inside and called to Elizabeth, "I'll get it."

She snapped up the phone before the third ring and heard a familiar voice. Although it sounded almost exactly like Mitchell Wainwright, she knew it was not. Mitchell's son, Tony, had deceived her in the past, but not this time. She'd been expecting his call.

She isn't going to hang up on me. Tony felt the tension drain from his shoulders and the back of his neck the moment Ashleigh informed him that she'd been expecting his call.

"Did you receive my letter?" he asked.

There was a long silence, and he feared she wasn't going to answer. Maybe she *would* hang up after all.

"The one you sent when you were still—"

"Yes. When I was serving my time."

"Yes, I did," she said without elaboration.

"Then you know how much I regret what I did. It had nothing to do with—"

"Tony," she cut in, "I accept the fact that you were going through a difficult time, and I'm willing to close the door on the past." There was a brief silence, which he was about to fill, but she beat him to it. "I'm glad to hear that you and your father have put your differences behind you. I will be attending Viviana's opening, but I have no objection to your being there . . ."

As the soft-spoken woman continued, Tony's head was filled with images of his father. He wasn't certain that they had actually put their differences behind them or that his father ever could. However, they were no longer at war. Tony had come to respect Mitchell Wainwright for the man he was—to accept him with all his flaws. And he knew his father was incapable of ever understanding sexual preferences that did not mirror his own. His father's tacit acceptance of his homosexuality was only because Tony had no domestic partner to "tarnish" his image.

Nor is there any real danger of disrupting that image, he thought as he thanked Ashleigh for her time and hung up the phone. It was unlikely,

Tony felt certain, that he would ever find someone who could fill the void Jeff Bradley had left when he'd died.

But Tony no longer blamed his father for his inability to give love. Mitchell carried an excess of emotional baggage too. He had never managed to gain his own father's approval or that elusive gift of unconditional love. It was funny how that worked: No matter what the son did, it was never enough, never exactly right in the eyes of the father.

49

Marnie was thankful for Monday's day off from school—it was a teachers' day—and had gone straight to her computer before breakfast, in hopes of catching Brad before he went to school. After a little back-and-forth, their plan seemed to be coming together. She just prayed nothing would go wrong.

OK C U THIS WEEKEND. Marnie hit SEND on the instant message screen. Her heart pounded wildly, and a shiver of anticipation slid down her spine. She could hardly wait to meet Brad. A bond of friendship had been growing between them over the months, and she felt she could trust him. She'd shared thoughts with him that she'd shared with no one else. He wasn't like any of the guys at her school.

She was no dummy; she knew better than to meet any online friend on her own. What if it turned out she was wrong about him? If her parents found out what she was planning, they'd go ballistic. Although Callie was leery of Brad's intentions and had tried to talk Marnie into dropping their cyber-relationship, Marnie could count on her twin keeping her mouth shut. *Now I've just got to talk her into coming with me to meet Brad on Saturday.*

Shifting that concern to the back of her mind, Marnie focused on the exclusive story she had promised to share with Brad for his school newspaper. Although she knew quite a lot about her own twisted history, there were some pretty big holes. She needed to know more. It seemed the whole world knew a lot about what had happened on the day of her birth, but no one knew the whole story. No one but Mario, the man who kidnapped her, and he was dead.

Ever since she was a little girl, she'd wanted to know more about Mario. She'd asked her mom about him, back when Marnie thought he was her real dad, but talking about her late husband had always seemed to make Erica sad. *Now that she has Nelson in her life, maybe she won't be so sad about Mario.* Besides, there was a lot even Erica didn't know. *She didn't even know I was the abducted twin until I was four.*

Her heart racing, Marnie swallowed hard. She flipped open her phone and scrolled down to her mom's number.

"Is this what you're looking for?" Mike called out, dangling Erica's car keys from an outstretched finger.

Erica pushed herself to her feet and gave her brother-in-law a spontaneous squeeze. "Thank you soooo much." Although she could have sworn she'd hung them on the key rack above the kitchen counter, when she'd returned for them, Mike's had been the only keys swinging from one of the hooks. "Where did you find them?"

Mike's expression was that of an indulgent parent. "Right where you left them. On your desk. Next to the phone."

"Bless you." She shook her head. "Guess I've got more on my mind than usual these days, what with Marnie's visit just around the corner."

Moments later, when Erica turned the key in the ignition and backed her green Chevy Caprice out of the driveway, her thoughts once again shifted to Marnie and the upcoming Easter holiday. Everything had been arranged: Erica would sleep on the couch in the family room so the twins could share her room. Mike would temporarily move his computers into his and Bill's bedroom and turn his office into a bedroom to accommodate Elizabeth.

Erica had thanked God that Marnie was being allowed to spend part of her vacation with them. And while she couldn't blame the Taylors for insisting that Elizabeth and Callie be a part of the package, it was an unsettling arrangement. Fear of the unknown loomed dark, dominating her every waking hour. What other measures would the Taylors be taking to reassure themselves that their daughter was safe? Elizabeth was a warm, generous woman, and they had enjoyed a wonderful relationship in the past. Erica knew she would do her best to ease the uncomfortable situation. She always did. *But what about Pocino?* Erica wondered if he would be sticking his ugly nose in. Despite the unseasonably warm morning, the thought gave her shivers.

As she pulled into one of the many parking spots in front of the manufacturing office building of Medley's Originals on North Austin Avenue, Erica's spirits rose. In spite of her misgivings and the frantic morning routine, she had arrived half an hour early for her first day. The sting of leaving John Stewart's began to ease as she considered the advantage of this remote location. She would no longer need to drive into the city and contend with the nightmare and expense of parking in downtown Chicago.

Throwing open the car door, she slung her handbag over her shoulder and stepped out. The musical tones of her cell phone cut her short. She quickly pulled it out and flipped it open. A smile blossomed on her lips when she heard Marnie's excited voice on the other end.

At Marnie's first question, however, Erica's hand began to tremble. She stumbled into the driver's-side door, then pulled her legs inside the car as she sank back into the seat. And there she froze, listening intently.

When she finally forced words past the lump in her throat, Erica asked her daughter to repeat what she'd just said. She'd heard every word—they continued to pound in her head—but she needed a moment to regroup. She wasn't as well armed for Marnie's nonstop questions about her early life as she'd thought.

She could almost feel the goose bumps rise on her arms at the sound of Marnie's voice speaking Mario's name. *If only she had known him. Known what a good man he really was.* Over the years, a multitude of stories had circulated about the kidnapping. Many of the articles written at the time, and a lot more written since then, could be pulled up with a simple Google search. Erica shuddered at the image the media frenzy had painted. There were the undisputable facts, of course, but a whole lot more out there was pure fiction.

As Marnie peppered her with one question after another, Erica gripped the cell phone and nodded, unable to squeeze a single syllable from her dry mouth. Her thoughts spun back to that fateful day.

Marnie was only four years old, and I was late getting home. In Erica's absence, Mike had been forced to take Marnie with him for a meeting about the website he was designing for Carlingdon's. While in the landmark store, Marnie was mistaken by the Toddmans' daughter for Callie—and the truth of her kidnapping was revealed. Erica and Mike were confronted with the undeniable fact that Marnie was not the child of an unwed mother who had wanted a better life for her daughter, as Mario had told them. *Mario would have told me everything in time, I'm sure . . .* But her husband had been in a fatal accident shortly after placing Marnie in Erica's arms for the first time. He'd gone to his grave revealing nothing about the events that took place on the night of the twins' birth.

The only living soul who had been privy to Mario's actual plan and how it had come unglued had been Erica's brother, Ian. But after seeing Marnie in Erica's arms, his lips had remained sealed. When the truth finally came out, and she'd been forced to accept that her daughter had been kidnapped, Ian had told her that the unwed mother who had wanted them to raise her daughter was not a lie. Mario had indeed arranged to pick up the newborn from the unwed mother he'd told them about, but when he arrived, he found them gone. Erica had clung to that fact, proof that Mario had not plotted it all from the start. *That person, at least, had been real.*

Shaking the images away, Erica finally said, "Yes, darling, I have that bag in the cedar chest. Tell me what this is all about."

Marnie's next words almost sent her into cardiac arrest: "I have a friend who knows a lot about publishing. He said my story is a darn good one. He can help me get a lot of money for it."

Marnie waited. All she heard was her mom's breathing. It sounded sort of raspy. *Is she hyperventilating?* "Mom?" She waited. Still nothing. "Mom, are you there?"

"Yes," the unsteady voice wafted over the airwaves. "Just give me a second."

"Mom, you're scaring me. Why are you acting all weird?"

"Sorry. You just caught me by surprise. Let's back up a second." Finally, Erica went on, "First, tell me: Did you read about the bag somewhere?"

"Yes." Marnie shifted the phone, pressing it closer to her ear. "Could you send me a picture so I can describe it? And explain how Mario made it and got away with sneaking me out of the hospital in it?" She heard another intake of breath.

"Darling," came her mother's voice, "we'll talk this weekend when you get here. I'll tell you anything you want to know. But Marnie, please don't even think of writing that story for publication. Your father has enough on his plate without having that kind of publicity."

Erica flipped her phone closed and slipped out of the car. Though weak in the knees, she forced herself to put one foot in front of the other. As she made her way to the office, the cell phone clutched in her hand, she checked her watch. *Still time to make a quick call to Nelson.*

He picked up on the first ring. "Is everything alright?" he asked.

"Not really," she said. "Marnie has some bee in her bonnet about becoming the next best-selling author."

"Oh," he said, his voice gentle as ever, "I was afraid it might be something serious. That's wonderful. Judging from her recent letters to you, the girl has a way with words."

Beads of perspiration broke out on Erica's forehead, and she did not immediately respond.

"So what kind of book does she intend to write?"

An awkward silence hung in the air before Erica spoke. "She wants to write the story about how she was kidnapped."

By the time she reached her office door, she was feeling a bit better. Just picturing the wide grin brightening Nelson's pale face as he talked her down from the proverbial ledge, she felt a tug on her heartstrings and wondered whether this kind, passionate man could shatter her notion that she needed no man in her life.

At first she had questioned her growing need to share every concern as well as every triumph with Nelson. She wasn't sure she had space in her messy life for a new love, especially when he had his own issues to contend with. But now—not for the first time—the saying *It's better to have loved and lost than never to have loved at all* drummed through her head.

After losing Mario, Erica had been certain she would never love again. Love had been an all-encompassing emotion, at least for her, and it had left a gaping hole in her heart. Marnie had filled that void, but once again love had ripped her heart out. She was still bleeding. If Nelson were to leave her, could she survive another loss? She'd loved Mario and Marnie and losing them had shattered her heart, turning her into an empty shell. Mario was gone forever, and Marnie was . . .

I can't think about that now, she said to herself as she opened the office door.

CHAPTER
51

At the first bleep of Rick's cell phone, Sarah-Jayne heaved herself from the sofa to retrieve it from the kitchen counter. Rick's eyes remained glued on her. This was the call they had been waiting for. Sarah-Jayne handed him the phone without flipping it open.

"Whoa, slow down, dude," Rick said when he put the phone to his ear. His baby brother was talking a mile a minute. Neil sounded nervous. And with good reason, Rick felt more than a little uneasy. But he held his tongue until Neil was finished. "I said I'd help you out. You can count on me. Everything is under control. That hoity-toity boutique party starts at 6:00 PM on Saturday. Right?"

When Neil confirmed the time, Rick said, "Well, since you say your online dream queen is a bit skittish and wants to meet in a public place, arrange to meet her at Starbucks on North State Street—the one that's close to the Palmer House. Sarah-Jayne and I will come to the house early and drop you off there at whatever time you arrange. Then we'll pick you up again when you call."

He paused, looking for words that wouldn't put his half-brother on the defensive. "And Neil, I hate to bring this up again, but we need to know for sure that Dad is out of the loop. That e-mail address you've been using—it can't be traced back to you, right?" Neil's only answer was to ask why he was so paranoid.

For chrissakes, he's even willing to give her his real e-mail address. Doesn't see any need to keep secrets from his puppy love. But Rick had made him swear he'd never used his own e-mail address or computer— too easy to trace. When he'd first found Marnie Taylor online, he was at a friend's house and using his computer. *Brad.* The girl had assumed that was his name. At first Neil had just wanted to get to know her, but he didn't want his dad to know he'd connected with the daughter of Nelson's girlfriend. So he'd let her think his name was Brad. *And it was the beginning of a beautiful romance . . . Ugh.*

Rick wanted to scream, but he couldn't afford to get his half-brother rattled. *Who's this Brad character? This could seriously screw everything up.* Even though Neil had then set up a Hotmail account for "Brad1834" at a cybercafé, registering it with phony information, Rick still felt that the involvement of the real Brad was a complication they couldn't afford. His baby brother, of course, thought they were going to a lot of trouble for nothing. His only concern was disappointing his precious, uptight dad, who wasn't at all computer savvy anyway, and his new online girlfriend, with whom he just *knew* there would be a real connection when they met in person. *What a sap.*

The wimpy kid was getting on his nerves, but Rick had to string him along. Right now he was their only hope. "Don't worry, Neil," he said reassuringly. "We'll leave you and the girl alone for as long as you want, and get you both back home before anyone's the wiser." Finally Neil seemed to accept Rick's guidance and terminated the call.

Rick stood still for a moment, clenching the phone in his hand.

"Nobody's going to get hurt, right?" Sarah-Jayne asked, her voice several decibels above normal.

Rick nodded. He had everything in place. He knew how to arrange for the ransom. He had a foolproof plan for getting away without being caught. *The only problem is Neil.* Rick's mind filled with all the possible fuckups. Maybe if he let his baby brother in on their plan . . . ? *No way.* Yet Neil was the key to getting their hands on the girl.

Sarah-Jayne popped her gum as she passed back and forth in front of the window. Shadows streamed across the carpet as she paced through the area lit by the streetlamp below.

Holy shit, she can't be losing her nerve. That's all I need, Rick said to himself. "Please trust me on this, baby. I have everything worked out. I don't like keeping Neil out of the loop any more than you do, but he's too much of a goody-goody. He could seriously screw up our plan." He paused. "Baby, this is our only way out."

Sarah-Jayne stopped pacing. "I do trust you, but—"

"Look. I have the magnet panels I told you about, for the doors of the van. I also found a roll of those clear plastic strips that look like rust." He gave her a pleading look.

Her eyes bored into his, but they carried no challenge—only fear.

When he noticed how her body trembled, he hurried on. "I was also able to lay my hands on a couple of license plates: one out-of-state and one Illinois. Just in case."

Rolling the wad of gum along the roof of her mouth, Sarah-Jayne said at last, "I know we have to get far away from here, and to do that, we need the money. I just wish there was some other way."

Rick sighed but said nothing.

"Okay," Sarah-Jayne said. "I still don't like the idea of staying overnight on the boat, but if that's the only way . . . Tell me exactly what I have to do."

"That's my girl," Rick said, pulling her close. *She's coming around. Thank God.* But when he stepped back and began to fill her in on the details, Sarah-Jayne's gaze slipped to the floor. His heart plummeted when he saw the color on her round face drain as she asked a simple question, her voice wavering.

"How long will we have to keep the girl?"

Tony's fingers drummed on the desktop. This last upload for the De Mornay's website was moving at glacial speed. Realizing he hadn't a prayer of getting out of the office by four thirty, Tony found it damned near impossible to concentrate. *Four thirty? Hell, at this rate I'll be lucky to get out of here before Easter.*

His stomach was in knots over being less than candid with Christonelli about moonlighting for Viviana, but she'd been adamant that both Erica and Mike be kept out of the loop. *Why the woman is so paranoid is beyond me,* he thought. Taking a deep breath, he willed himself to relax. *This is no conflict of interest. I'm working my ass off in my spare time and not short-changing Mike a single second.*

It had been no big deal, until now. But he'd promised Christonelli that he'd be at the Frontera Grill on North Clark Street by five o'clock on the dot. The blowout celebration for the landing of the Honda account was important to the boss. Now there was no way in hell he could make it on time. Should have been no problem, but time and time again . . . *This fucking computer.* It kept shutting down seconds before the end of the upload. The uploads were taking ten times longer than they should. *Viviana sure as hell didn't make upgrading the system a priority.*

Just as that thought ambled through his mind, the stunning entrepreneur drifted on high heels across the threshold of the office, her white pants and expensive-looking sweater pristine despite a full day of weaving her way through a gauntlet of construction projects and workmen.

"Oh, Tony," she said, surprise written across her brow. "I thought you'd left hours ago. Didn't you say you had a dinner engagement?"

"Sorry, Miss De Mornay, it's taking a lot longer than expected. But I'm almost finished. I'll soon be on my way." Since she was paying him for the end result rather than by the hour, he knew she wasn't worried about being billed for additional time. But the fact that she remembered and showed concern over his personal schedule pleased him. It pleased him a lot.

With an exaggerated lift of a perfectly arched brow, she repeated, "*Miss De Mornay?* Puh-leese. You know I prefer—"

"Sorry, Viviana," he said, looking up from the computer screen.

She flashed him a winning smile. "I need to check on the caterer. See you tomorrow night," she said, and in a flash, as quickly as she'd appeared, she had turned to resume overseeing each and every detail for her grand opening celebration.

Tony was startled by a shout. Gino was barking orders to various workmen while he tightened a loose screw on the doorplate. Just then, the electricity blinked off—for the third time. Exasperated, Tony did some shouting of his own. "Goddamnit Gino, give me a break. I'll be here all night if you don't stop shutting off the effing electricity."

Gino poked his head around the office doorjamb. "Sorry. Didn't know you were still here. How much longer you gonna be?"

"About ten minutes, if you stop shutting me down."

"Hey, bro, lighten up. Like I said, we didn't know you were still here." His voice boomed above the racket of tables being brought in for the gala. "Think you can come an hour or so early tomorrow with Renzo to help set up the indoor photo background?"

Tony nodded. "No problemo. But your brother will need his own set of wheels." Ashleigh Taylor had said she had no problem with his being at the opening—but Tony planned to make this appearance a brief one.

Tony had just left for the evening when Gino checked in on Viviana. She was no longer in the salon area, but roaming the back of the store, busy with the modeling coordinator.

"No, no," she said, her voice projecting across the salon. "You can't set up the stairs to the ramp here. That would destroy the entire setting."

Gino's glance shot across to the reception table. He had been trying his best to conceal his jealousy, but having Mitchell Wainwright anywhere near his lover made his skin crawl. No man who'd been intimate with a woman like Viviana De Mornay would ever be satisfied to remain merely a friend and business associate. She was just too damn sexy, too desirable.

He headed straight to the reception table to check the seating chart. If need be, he was prepared to make some changes.

CHAPTER
53

As the taxi pulled up in front of the Palmer House early Saturday morning, April leaned forward to view the meter, then rummaged in her oversized handbag for her wallet.

At the curb, the doorman opened the passenger door. "Nice to see you again, Miss Toddman," he said with his usual warmth.

She returned his greeting and confirmed that her parents and the Taylors had checked in. Then she glanced down at her wristwatch. She had just enough time to stop off for a short visit with Ashleigh and the girls before joining her grandmother.

Stepping inside the lobby, April savored the ambiance of the awesome, turn-of-the-twentieth-century architecture. The hotel, she knew, had been built as a gift for Chicago's pioneer businesswoman and socialite, Bertha Palmer, so it made sense that a strong woman like Mary Ann Cronin should lead its historic $150 million restoration and renovation. The budding journalist in April would have longed to interview the well-respected real estate consultant known as "Mac." She was impressed by the masterful way the contractor was managing to conduct the makeover in stages—maintaining the historical integrity while also creating something strikingly new.

Her Manolo Blahnik pumps tapping a brisk tattoo as she crossed the gleaming marble floor, April felt the vibration of her cell phone and paused to pluck it from her handbag. A few feet short of the registration desk, she smiled at the sound of Juliana's effervescent voice and courteously stepped out of the pathway leading to the desk clerks.

"Yes, I'm here," she said into the phone. "Can't wait to see you either. I was just going to check in to ask about your room number and . . . The penthouse? Okay, great . . . Whoa, slow down, princess. I'll be right up."

April snaked her way through a group of Asian tourists and several luggage dollies to the set of elevators that led to the penthouse suite. She loved seeing the girls, of course, but more important, she hoped for a few moments alone with their mother. Aunt Ashleigh was such a good sounding board.

As great as April's relationship was with her mom, she needed an unemotional listener. That person was her aunt. Though not truly related to the Toddmans, Ashleigh had always been there for Paige and Mark's adopted daughter whenever she needed advice on the best way to approach a sensitive issue. It wasn't just that Ashleigh knew all of them so well. She also intuitively seemed to grasp the heart of a problem, and she was always ready with practical suggestions on ways to avoid the hot buttons.

I'm not really worried about Mom, thought April as she waited for the elevator. *She'll come around. But Dad . . .*

CHAPTER
54

Distracted at the sound of Juliana's rapid footfalls pounding across the room, Ashleigh looked up from *Architectural Digest* in time to see her youngest daughter race to the entry of their suite and fling open the door. She closed the pages of the article she'd been reading on the Palmer House restoration. "What's up?" she asked.

"April," Juliana said, her voice bubbling with excitement. "She's on her way up."

Ashleigh smiled. It was clear that Juliana knew something was going on with the twins and that she felt left out. Callie and Marnie had been excluding their younger sister since the family had arrived in Chicago, and Ashleigh intended to talk with them about it. But that could wait, now that April was here. She could see that Juliana was determined to get to April before her sisters barged in.

In moments, April arrived. She was dressed in white from head to toe, set off by her shiny dark hair pulled back in a ponytail. If Ashleigh wasn't mistaken, her outfit was the Ralph Lauren ensemble featured on the cover of this month's *In Style* magazine. In the fitted white wool jacket, straight-legged pants, and sky-high platform pumps, April looked so grown up.

With Juliana babbling nonstop, it took Ashleigh a moment to give April a welcoming hug. By then the twins, who had been behind closed doors most of the morning, burst into the room, vying for April's attention.

"Girls," Ashleigh said, "give April a chance to come inside and take off her jacket."

April met her eyes and smiled. As usual, Ashleigh admired April's maturity as well as her overall patience and kindness. She had a way of making each of Ashleigh's three daughters feel special. April was as beautiful on the inside as she was on the outside. *Paige and Mark have a daughter to be extremely proud of.*

Ashleigh's mind snapped back to the present when she heard April ask, "I know the opening party is tonight, but would you mind if I took the girls for about an hour? Nana would love it."

"It's fine with me," Ashleigh said, knowing it would be easier for April to have the girls with her to help entertain Helen.

April turned to the girls. "How about coming with me when I take Nana to Millennium Park? There's a small platform near the area where they have the ice rink in the winter. We can sit there."

"Could we go ice skating?" Juliana asked.

"Sorry, princess," April said, "but the rink closed last month. Besides, I think Miss De Mornay would have kittens if she heard that one of her performers had taken to the ice."

Juliana giggled.

"Besides, we can't be gone too long. You need to get ready for tonight. How about giving me ten minutes with your mom? Then we'll all go get Nana."

As the girls dashed off, Ashleigh strode to the kitchen counter and asked, "Would you like some coffee, April? Or something else to drink?"

April shook her head, tapping her fingertip against the counter. "I just finished breakfast about a half hour ago."

Ashleigh refilled her cup and noticed April's eyes scan the suite. "Where is Elizabeth?" the younger woman asked, biting her lip.

"She's visiting with your parents and Helen. She's been looking forward to seeing you. In fact, I bet she'd love to join you on your stroll over to Millennium Park."

"Terrific," April said, nodding absentmindedly. "I suppose Uncle Conrad is at John Stewart's, trying to put out all the new brushfires?"

Ashleigh nodded, pondering April's fidgety behavior. *There's something she really wants to bounce off me.* But uncharacteristically, April was not getting straight to the point.

Ashleigh took a sip of her hot coffee and said, "Let's go into the living room, where we can talk. If I'm not mistaken, you have something more important on your mind than the location of various family members."

With a light peal of laughter, April said, "Busted." She gestured to an empty cup and saucer beside the coffeepot. "On second thought, I think I could use some coffee."

Once they were seated, April set her cup on the coffee table and plunged in. "Before I talk to my parents today, I'd like to get your reaction to . . . my news." She paused, noted Ashleigh's nearly imperceptible nod, and continued. "It's about Kyle and me. Even though we haven't been engaged long, we've been in a relationship for a little over a year now."

Meeting April's expectant eyes, Ashleigh took another sip of her steaming coffee and set it on the end table, but remained silent.

With a shrug, April said, "Well, if Dad were here, he'd tell me to get to the bottom line, so here goes: Kyle and I are both really busy at the station, and neither of us has much spare time. His apartment isn't far from mine, but it's really become a big hassle since we'd like to spend as much time together as possible. My lease is up at the end of the month, and although my roommate still has another year at the university, she plans to move back home with her parents so she can save some money. So . . . Kyle and I decided that we would like to share an apartment."

She paused, met Ashleigh's eyes, and then hurried on. "It doesn't really make sense for us to waste so much time going between apartments, and finding a parking space is a nightmare at either location. Bottom line is, we found a perfect one-bedroom close to the news studio. And luckily Kyle was able to find another guy to take his place in the apartment he's sharing with two of his buddies." Taking the briefest of breaths, April said, "He moved in last weekend, and I'm moving in at the end of the month."

Ashleigh nodded expectantly. She was a little puzzled. *Surely April isn't worried over talking with her parents about this?* Mark and Paige had always been there for April. They had done their very best to instill their values; the rest was up to April. Neither tried to run their daughter's life, nor were they old-fashioned and likely to be easily shocked by an engaged couple living together.

As she let April's news sink in, Ashleigh realized April had more to say.

"Aunt Ashleigh, you know how they say hindsight is twenty-twenty?"

Ashleigh nodded, noticing that April's dark eyes had widened with apprehension.

"My parents like Kyle a lot, but I'm afraid they'll flip when they find out about his past. Especially Dad." She sucked in her bottom lip. "I know I should have told them everything a long time ago. I really wanted to, but the timing was never right, at least that's what I kept telling myself. And now . . . it's really awkward." Her voice had dropped to just above a whisper and she seemed to be studying the pattern of the rug beneath her feet.

Ashleigh waited until April was ready to push on.

At last, the nervous young woman said, "Kyle has a six-month-old daughter."

CHAPTER
55

Viviana scooped Dolly into her arms as the workmen scurried in and out of De Mornay's. Gino and a burly man in coveralls began to roll up the plastic sheeting that stretched from wall to wall across the freshly carpeted showroom and beneath the round tables delivered the night before. She'd originally considered hosting the celebration at Spiaggia. That might have been easier. But here, unlike at the prestigious restaurant, she would have *complete* control over the ambiance.

The public opening of De Mornay's was in just two days—the Monday before Easter. A handful of the impressive cast on her distinguished guest list, which included sixty of the most influential personalities in Chicago and the world of retail, had attended her farewell shindig recently in New York. Even so, this celebration would be no carbon copy. The shades of purple and lavender selected for the tablecloths and napkins, as well as the menu selections, set a completely different mood. The Taylor sisters, with the aid of April Toddman, had choreographed a new show around Viviana's chosen theme: Easter in Chicago.

Dolly licked Viviana's cheek and began to squirm in her arms. "I'm not about to set you down in the midst of all this," she whispered in the puppy's ear, and she headed for the office. Having a party preceding opening day presented more challenges than a closing did, but Viviana wasn't deterred. She was the boss, and she had everything under control.

Hunched over her laptop in the bedroom she was sharing with Callie, Marnie felt a flood of adrenaline surge through her body. *Oh my God.*

"Close the door," she said to her sister. "It's Brad. He wants to meet me tonight."

"Meet you?" Callie repeated, a warning written all over her face.

Marnie clucked her tongue. "Don't worry, I told you I wouldn't go alone. But I didn't tell him *you* were coming." She hesitated before adding, "I didn't want him to think I was afraid."

"Well, you darn well should be afraid. I wish I could talk you into just forgetting the whole thing." Then, running her fingers through her hair, Callie asked, "Didn't you tell him we were busy tonight?"

"Duh. Yeah, but we'll get back early."

With all the excitement of traveling—not to mention the time change—Juliana was running a slight fever, but their parents had agreed to allow her to perform as long as she came straight back to the hotel afterward and got right to bed. Elizabeth would return to the hotel to look after Juliana. This had given Marnie and Callie a perfect opportunity to bow out early too. They really didn't want to sit through another formal dinner, making polite conversation and answering the same dumb questions about school and whatnot. If Marnie heard *My, how much you've grown* or *You girls must have to beat the boys away with a stick* one more time . . .

"I still don't like it," Callie said.

Marnie let out an exaggerated sigh. *Not again. Why can't she just give it a rest?* "Cut it out, Callie. Don't ask me to start back at square one. And please tell me you aren't going to back out now."

"I didn't say I wouldn't do it. I just want you to know how I feel."

"You've made that crystal clear."

"I'd feel a lot better if you asked Brad to meet us here in the lobby."

"That's really lame." Marnie had dismissed that idea without a second thought. Brad had said they should get to know each other before letting their parents put in their two cents. She glanced at the screen and then back up at her sister. "Like you said, we need to meet in a public place. Brad suggested Starbucks."

Callie hesitated. "I know there's one right around the corner, but I still don't like the idea of sneaking out to meet some strange guy. And it won't be easy to get past Elizabeth."

"No sweat," Marnie countered. "We'll leave with Elizabeth and Juliana right after the performance. We'll need to have dinner, but we'll tell her we don't want room service. I'm sure she'll let us go down to the Corner Bakery Café since it's attached to the hotel."

Marnie began typing, and then waited for Brad to message back. "He said to let him know when we got back to the hotel." She couldn't believe it. *This is really happening.*

Callie tossed two Tylenols into her mouth and washed them down with the glass of water. Her head pounded with the intensity of a jackhammer.

Flopping down on the bed, she winced. She hardly ever got a headache, but this one not only pounded, it also seemed to dim her vision. Tiny bubbles appeared to be floating in the air before her.

Out of the corner of her eye, she noticed Marnie slip into the bathroom to take the first shower. *I'll just grab a short nap if I can.* Gently placing her aching head on the pillow, she tried to let her mind go blank. She remembered what her psychology teacher had said about self-hypnosis and tried to imagine herself beside a babbling brook.

After what seemed like a long time but was probably just a few minutes, she decided that didn't work any better now than it had the first time she'd tried the technique. The queasy sensation in her stomach was unsettling, but the pounding in her head was worse. And she knew it didn't have anything to do with jitters about the performance.

Might as well focus on how I'm going to get through this night. Betraying Marnie's confidence was not an option, and yet if anything happened to her sister because of her silence, she'd never forgive herself. Marnie was being such an idiot. *If only I could talk her out of this stupid meeting.* Her sister hadn't listened to her warnings. *I mean, this guy might be a geek . . . or even something worse.* Sneaking around behind their parents' backs was wrong, and betraying Elizabeth was just as bad.

Her stomach felt as if a flock of birds were fighting for release. She had to make a decision. *What decision?* she asked herself. *Who am I kidding? I can't let Marnie meet this stranger by herself.* Callie knew she had no choice. *I have to go with her.*

56

As the door of the Toddmans' suite clicked shut, Helen threw her arms around her granddaughter. "That was lovely, dear. Thank you so much," she said, and then gave April a wink. "Who'd have thought I could enjoy the best of both worlds—a grandmother by day and a foxy lady at night?"

Suppressing a grin, April reached up and wiped a smudge of chocolate from her grandmother's cheek—the remnant of their nostalgic Millennium Park splurge, ice cream on a stick—and returned her hug. "Nana," she said, "why don't you get some rest before the party?"

Helen seemed to consider this for a moment, but after checking the glass-domed anniversary clock on the mantel, she said, "Oh my, it's already after two, and I have a lot to do before this evening."

The party isn't until six. What can she possibly need to do that will take so much time? "Show me your dress for tonight, then," she said, and they headed toward Helen's bedroom.

Hanging on the hook of the open closet door was a slinky green velvet Versace gown. On the floor beside the dressing table were matching green shoes with sensible heels. The perfect jewelry had been laid out atop the table along with Helen's makeup.

"Oh my God, Nana," April said, removing the dress from the hook and holding it in front of her grandmother. "This is perfect. It's the same shade as your eyes. You'll be the hit of the party." She hung the gown back in place. "It looks like everything is ready for tonight's soiree. Mom will help you with your makeup and hair and make sure you look smashing. You have plenty of time for a bit of a nap."

Helen shook her head emphatically and reached for the large white box on the dresser. On the front of the box was a picture of a woman whose face was covered in a purple mud mask.

Doing her best not to giggle, April said, "Nana. You have gorgeous skin. You don't need this."

Helen's fingers moved to the corners of her eyes and then down to the outer curves of her mouth. "Well, how about these? *You* don't have these lines around your mouth."

April searched for a response but found none. She was rescued when her grandmother asked, "Is that young man you work with going to be at the party?"

"Kyle?"

"No. Not your boyfriend. The one who was with you in New York. The one who danced the tango with you and took pictures."

Her grandmother smiled like a Cheshire cat, picked up a pillow, and began gliding across the carpeted floor, a faraway look in her eyes.

This time April couldn't hold back her grin. "Yes, Renzo will be there. He's been hired to take pictures again, so he won't have a lot of spare time. But if they have dancing, I'm sure he won't be able to resist taking a short break for a turn on the floor with you."

It was after five when April dashed through the door of the apartment that she and Kyle would soon share. "Kyle," she shouted as she raced to the bedroom. There was no answer. She stopped and listened. That's when she heard the shower turn off.

As if on cue, Kyle walked out of the steaming bathroom, a towel wrapped around his well-toned body. Drying his thick, dark hair with a second towel, he closed the space between them in two long strides and pulled her to him. He kissed her gently, then pulled her closer and kissed her long and hard.

"Well," he said, "how did it go?"

CHAPTER
57

Tony shifted from one foot to the other as the earsplitting applause filled the crowded salon. The performance was over, and he could tell that the crème de la crème set had enjoyed the emotion and energy of it. It seemed that the Taylors were engrossed in some heavy-duty conversation, probably congratulating themselves on their daughters' achievements, but if he didn't get this out of the way soon, he was sure he'd begin to hyperventilate. At the first pause in the couple's conversation, he cleared his throat loudly.

Conrad and Ashleigh glanced up from their tête-à-tête, and Ashleigh was the first to speak. Following a polite "Hello," she turned to her husband. "Conrad. You remember Tony Wainwright."

Tony tried to interpret the slight tremor in her voice. *Is she concerned about her husband's reaction, or just uncomfortable in my presence?* It was hard to tell. Either way, though, how could he blame them?

After a few blinks of his eyes, Conrad gave a nod, rose, and extended his hand.

"Your daughters are real pros," Tony said. "You must be very proud of them." He was no damn good at this polite, bullshit kind of conversation, but he had to say something.

Conrad's voice was wary as he murmured a thank-you, and Ashleigh's smile seemed frozen on her face, but at least it was done. Tony was about to take his leave when the three Taylor sisters, still in costume, dashed up to the table. They stopped inches from where he stood. Three sets of big brown eyes looked from him to their parents and back again.

Ashleigh quickly introduced the girls to "Mr. Wainwright's son, Tony." She looked as if she wanted this moment to pass. And Tony noted the flash in Conrad Taylor's ice-blue eyes.

Suddenly the temperature in the room seemed to drop several degrees.

Tony wanted to thunder out of the fancy boutique, but he knew that wouldn't be cool. Without looking back in the direction of the Taylor family, he headed straight to Viviana's table, intent on offering an excuse for leaving early.

The mayor and his wife were seated next to Viviana, along with two other couples. He didn't know them but had seen all four on the society page of the *Chicago Tribune* on several occasions. Tony was about to mumble some lie about ducking out early because of the work piled up at home—but in front of these high society figures, how could he? He sighed and turned away, realizing that he must remain through dinner.

His father and another exquisitely clad man were seated at the next table, beside Paige and Mark Toddman. The man in the Armani tuxedo looked familiar, but Tony couldn't place him. As Tony made eye contact with him, he stood and, extending his hand, said politely, "It's been a long time."

Tony shook his hand, still unable to attach a name to the face.

"Glenn Nelson," the man said. "We were never formally introduced."

"Tony," his father cut in, "Glenn was a former buyer for Bentleys Royale, and more recently Viviana's partner in the New York De Mornay's."

Tony remembered now why Glenn looked familiar. He had seen him in the courtroom during the Bentleys Royale embezzlement trial. He swallowed hard. "Nice to meet you," he managed. "Will you be part of the Chicago operation?"

Glenn shook his head and sank back into the lavender satin–draped chair where he'd been seated. "I'm moving back to California. I need a break from this rat race. I've invested in several properties in the desert, and I'm just going to work part-time until I get my head cleared."

He seems like an okay guy, thought Tony. Not the pretentious prick he might seem to be at first glance. "Palm Springs?" he asked.

"Exactly," Glenn said with a nod. "Taking a job with a men's store in Palm Desert, though."

His father gestured to the seat beside him, and Mark Toddman began introducing his daughter and her fiancé. Then, turning to his left, Toddman said, "And this is my mother-in-law, Helen Sheldon."

"So nice to meet you, Tony," said an elegant older woman with flashing emerald eyes that did not waver from his for a second. Then, without an ounce of subtlety, she batted her long, false lashes and asked, "Do you like to dance?"

Relieved not to see his stepdad's car in front of the old Victorian house, Rick honked the horn.

Neil was out the door and barreling down the steps in a heartbeat, but he slowed as he approached the van, his face devoid of color. Rather than getting into the van, he stood stock-still beside the driver's-side window.

Rick rolled down the window. "What's wrong, bro?"

"Lots of stuff," Neil said. "I didn't want to lie to Dad, but I did. Then Marnie sent me an IM saying that she couldn't be away from the hotel for more than half an hour." Then, in a rapid cadence, he said, "I really appreciate you coming here and trying to help me, but it just all seems . . . wrong." Neil's eyes sought Rick's for understanding. "Besides, if Dad finds out . . . Well, he has enough to worry about. I've just got to find a better way—"

Rick's stomach lurched. From the get-go he'd known the kid was skittish and bound to be trouble, but he hadn't anticipated this. Not at the last moment. *Jesus, Mary, and Joseph*. He sighed. "Lighten up, kid, and climb in. How many times have I gotta tell you? Nobody's gonna get hurt. Your dad will never be the wiser. Since your little princess can only be away for a half hour, you'll be home way before him." He was doing his best to sound reassuring. *Tonight is the night. I can't let baby bro weasel out now.* "It'll be a lot easier to figure out your next step after you meet her. But you gotta calm down."

Reluctantly, Neil nodded his agreement and moved toward the rear of the van, opening the doors.

Rick glanced over at Sarah-Jayne and gestured toward the thermos. It was filled with hot chocolate and laced with enough Rohypnol to put his nerdy half-brother out for the duration of the evening.

Sarah-Jayne's hand shook, but she reached for the thermos, her dark brown eyes large as salad plates—eyes that asked, *Do we really have to do this?*

Rick took the thermos from Sarah-Jayne's trembling hand, slid from behind the wheel, and jogged over to Neil. "Change of plan." He gave Neil an understanding look. "You look like shit. Sarah-Jayne can drive, and I'll sit back here with you so we can talk." He took hold of Neil's elbow, steadying him as he climbed through the van's rear doors. Then, pulling out a wet wipe, he scrubbed his hands with rapid motions until they were nearly raw, and inspected them for any remaining speck of dirt.

As Neil sat on one of the narrow benches lining the van's side walls, his eyes darted from his brother to Sarah-Jayne, who was edging her heavy frame between the front seats and squeezing behind the steering wheel.

Rick eyed Neil skeptically. "Relax, we have everything under control." Nodding toward the thermos, he said, "Here, have some of Sarah-Jayne's soothing hot chocolate. It will settle your nerves." Unscrewing the lid, he poured some of the hot liquid into it.

"I don't know. For the past couple of days, I've barely managed to choke anything down . . ."

Rick handed him the cup. *Let's get these roofies pumping through baby brother's bloodstream.* "Mom used to give us this for stomachaches, remember? Just what the doctor ordered."

Neil smiled for a moment, and then said, "Thanks." And like a lamb led to slaughter, he took the cup and sipped from it.

Callie slid the key into the slot and unlocked the door to their suite. She knew that Marnie could hardly wait to check her computer. But glancing at her twin, she saw that Marnie looked calm, as if everything were normal.

Inside, after catching her sister's eye, Marnie turned to Elizabeth and asked, "We really don't want room service tonight. After we change out of our costumes, can we go downstairs to the Corner Bakery Café for dinner?"

"Yes, you *may,*" Elizabeth said. "But don't leave the hotel."

Callie immediately felt guilty about lying to Elizabeth. She could hardly believe she was going to be a part of Marnie's wacky plan.

After giving their little sister good-night hugs, Marnie raced straight to the computer for news from Brad. Callie headed to the bathroom, where she shed her costume and quickly pulled on some jeans and a sweatshirt. She was about to remove her stage makeup when, through the bathroom door, she heard her sister holler.

"Why did you shut the computer down?" Marnie's frustrated shout was loud enough to echo through the entire suite.

"Not guilty," Callie called out.

"Well, *I* sure didn't," Marnie shouted back, and then she flipped the laptop back on. "Hurry up. I've got to pee."

"Hold on." Callie finished removing the last traces of stage makeup and reapplied her lip gloss. "All yours," she said. "Marnie, please hurry. We've got to be back here when Mom and Dad get back."

"Sure thing. As soon as my laptop is booted up, I'll see if there's a message from Brad, and then we can leave right away." Marnie pulled a clean pair of jeans and a sweatshirt from the dresser drawer and whirled around, nearly colliding with Callie in the bathroom doorway.

The computer finished booting up, Callie noticed, just as the bathroom door clicked shut behind her twin. Callie glanced at the screen. There was only one new e-mail in Marnie's mailbox. It was from Brad1834@ hotmail.com.

After pausing for the briefest of moments, she clicked on it and read:

STARBUCKS IS A MINUTE FROM YOUR HOTEL. GO UP N. STATE STREET TOWARD JORDON'S. LEFT SIDE OF THE STREET. YOU WON'T SAY ANYTHING TO ANYONE ABOUT OUR MEETING TILL WE GET TO KNOW EACH OTHER BETTER, RIGHT? YOU KNOW HOW PARENTS ARE. THEY DIDN'T GROW UP WITH COMPUTERS, SO THEY DON'T UNDERSTAND. THEY REALLY JUST DON'T GET IT. BUT I BET WE KNOW EACH OTHER BETTER THAN THEY DID BEFORE THEIR FIRST DATE.

Callie felt her temperature rise a notch. *How can Marnie fall for such stupid lines?* She didn't know what annoyed her more—Marnie's stupidity or this "Brad" for making her sister lie to her family. Suddenly it seemed like it was all just too much. *I have to put an end to this.*

Glancing again at the closed bathroom door, she tiptoed out of the room.

Juliana was already in bed, and Elizabeth, who had changed into her nightclothes, was crossing the living room and heading toward the twins' bedroom. "I was just coming in to tell you girls good night," she said. "Please come straight back after your dinner."

"We will," Callie said, forcing the words through the lump in her throat. "I'm going on down now. If you see Marnie, tell her I'll get a table and see her downstairs."

The minute Rick was sure that Neil was in la-la land, he asked Sarah-Jayne to pull over. They were on a deserted side street, a couple blocks from the Loop—close enough to hear the roar of the "L" and feel the vibrations. After checking to make sure no one was around, she cut the engine.

"Give me a hand," he called out to Sarah-Jayne as he opened the rear doors of the van and hopped out. He gave her one of the door magnets and told her to put it on the driver's side, right where a company logo would be. He'd ordered the two large magnets from Vista Print a few weeks before, under the name Jim Armor. He'd taken that name from one of the stolen credit cards. The magnets had been delivered to the post office box he'd set up under that same name. In bold, red-and-blue lettering was the fictitious name Tasty Baked Goods. "I'll get the passenger's side," he said. "Then I'll need your help with the rust strips."

These strips were phenomenal—the perfect disguise for his minivan, in case anyone was around when they made their move. The adhesive strips would make the van appear to be dented and rusted. After they had the girl in the van and had pulled into another deserted side street, they could easily pull off the laminated strips, remove the door magnets, attach the second stolen license plate, and be good to go. "You drive," he said. "I'll stay back here and keep an eye on my saintly half-sib."

Rick had to pat himself on the back. Everything was falling into place.

CHAPTER
59

Callie closed the door to the suite, doing her best not to make a sound. Hardly daring to breathe, she swallowed hard and then made a mad dash down the carpeted hallway. At the elevator she began punching the button repeatedly as if that might shorten the wait.

Was Marnie on her heels? Callie looked over her shoulder, her stomach roiling. No, the door to their suite had not swung open.

She didn't have to wait long. The elevator doors slid open and she stepped inside and pressed the button marked L for *lobby*. She silently prayed that she could get to Starbucks and talk to this Brad character before Marnie showed up. *What will I say?* She didn't know exactly, and no matter what she found out, Marnie wouldn't be happy about it. But most of her feelings of guilt and betrayal were washed away by the feeling deep in her heart that she was doing the right thing. *This is the only way.* If it turned out that Brad was a decent sort of guy, then he'd come back to the hotel with them and meet their parents. If he refused, he wasn't the kind of person Marnie should be getting involved with.

As Callie stepped through the doors onto State Street, a cold breeze hit her cheeks and chills shot up her arms. She wished she'd worn a heavier sweatshirt or a jacket. *Nothing I can do about that now,* she thought. Pulling her lightweight hood up, she tucked in her chin and did her best to ignore the stiff breeze as she set off toward Jordon's.

Balancing a silver tray filled with delicate white bowls of crème brûlée, each waiter skirted the ramps that snaked between the dining tables and wound around the perimeter of the salon, scurrying to deliver the desserts before the start of the De Mornay's special pre-Easter fashion show.

Conrad skimmed the crowd with the eyes of an astute observer, noting that Mitchell Wainwright had taken his coffee to the next table and appeared engrossed in conversation with the mayor. Taking in the dynamics, he couldn't help but be amused: Viviana's new beau had twisted his chair so his back was turned to Wainwright, effectively cutting off eye contact and conversation between Viviana and her former lover.

Then Conrad's glance rested on the Toddmans' table. He saw Tony Wainwright push back his chair and take the few steps to Viviana's table, where he leaned in close. Although he could not hear a single word of the conversation, he had no doubt of its nature. Tony was making his apologies for leaving before her spectacular fashion extravaganza.

Moments later he saw Tony wind his way through the tables and elevated platforms to the front door and disappear. He felt a wash of relief, until it occurred to him just how obviously uncomfortable Wainwright's son had been all evening. Ashleigh, he noted, had seemed largely unfazed by the younger Wainwright. *If Ashleigh can forgive Tony Wainwright and believes he deserves a second chance, why can't I?* he thought. He vowed to keep an open mind going forward.

Lifting their desserts from the table, he said to Ashleigh, "Let's join the Toddmans before the fashion show begins."

"Your timing couldn't be better, love," Ashleigh agreed, reaching under her chair to retrieve her Judith Leiber minaudière. Her mind was filled with thoughts of her earlier conversation with April, and she'd been eager for a quiet moment to discuss with Paige and Mark the news about Kyle. April's fiancé was bright and had a lot going for him, she knew, and best of all, he treated April as if she were a rare and precious gift. But a baby, even one who won't be living with them, was bound to add complications to his and April's lives. Ashleigh couldn't help but feel some concern. *How will this impact their relationship?*

She slipped into Tony's vacated chair beside Paige. Conrad took the other empty spot, seating himself between Mark and Glenn. Surrounded by such dear old friends, Ashleigh felt a rush of warmth. "But where is Helen?" she asked.

April turned to her mother and said, "I think I'd better check on her." They both looked over to the far corner, where Helen hovered beside Renzo and his array of cameras.

"Thank you so much," said Paige. "I was just about to venture over to see if Renzo was in need of rescue."

Kyle stood and pulled April's chair from the table. "Yes," he said with an amused grin, "let's go see how our cameraman and his foxy assistant are getting along."

Ashleigh and Paige were silent for a few moments as they observed the young couple weave their way across the room. Paige was the first to speak. "Whatever would I have done if they hadn't come into my life?" Her voice broke, and an uncharacteristic tear rolled down her cheek.

Ashleigh was momentarily thrown until she realized that Paige was talking not about April and Kyle, but about April and Helen. She reached out and squeezed Paige's hand, her gaze drifting toward the ceiling. "Well, the Man Upstairs seems to know what we need to make our lives complete, even when we don't," she said. "April and Helen have brought a lot of joy into all of our lives."

"Oh my God," Paige said, "where did all this sentimentality come from? I must be getting old."

Ashleigh grinned. "Not a cha—"

Cutting her off, Paige said, "So I guess you were the first to know about Kyle's little indiscretion."

Ashleigh blinked.

"Sorry." Paige sighed. "I didn't mean to come off as such a prude. And I don't think any less of Kyle. I guess I was just hurt that April didn't share this with us until after they announced their engagement."

A wave of relief washed over Ashleigh. Paige was not upset that April had confided in her, only that the girl had kept her mother and father in the dark. "I believe she was quite concerned about Mark's reaction . . ."

Paige nodded. "Not that we have much of a choice, but Mark seems relatively unfazed. Obviously, this does not change our feelings for Kyle." She paused. "I'm not sure how much April told you about the mother of the child."

"We only spoke briefly. She didn't give details."

"To make a long story short," Paige said, "Kyle said he met the baby's mother at a fraternity party when he was visiting his alma mater, Penn State—a month or so before he and April met here in Chicago. He told April that he and the girl had quite a bit to drink, and she asked him to drive her home. When she came on to him in the car, he didn't say no. Apparently, he never talked to her again—until she called to tell him she was pregnant.

"He wasn't convinced the child was his, so he asked for a paternity test. Kyle told her if she expected any financial help from him, she would have to do a test at a qualified DNA diagnostic center immediately. Within two days it was confirmed that Kyle was the father. The rest is history."

"What rotten luck." Ashleigh didn't know what else to say.

"Rotten luck, indeed," Paige said, shaking her head. "Kyle wants to do what he can, but hadn't even seen his daughter until recently, after the grandmother contacted him."

"The grandmother?"

"The child is living with her grandparents in New York—Queens, I think. Evidently, the mother is none too stable. She left when the baby was about two months old, but came back. Kyle isn't sure how many times she was back and forth, but her parents have no idea where she is now."

"So why did they decide to contact Kyle?"

"Kyle was sending the mother money each month. There was nothing legal or binding, since she never took him to court, but Kyle's name and address were on the envelopes." Paige sighed again. "Kyle is a responsible, caring young man, but with this erratic situation, April could be in for more than she's bargained for."

60

As Sarah-Jayne drove the van slowly down State Street past the Palmer House Hotel, Rick spotted what he took to be a young girl walking briskly down the sidewalk. He could not actually see her face, but she walked like a girl. Her hair was pulled back off her face and into the hood of her sweatshirt. Pausing for a second, she tucked in a few errant strands of light-colored hair. Then, jamming her hands into the pouch of the dark sweatshirt, she resumed trudging down the street at a rapid clip. She was headed in the direction of the designated Starbucks. Her height was about right, the time was right, and no one else was making their way down the street with such purpose. Rick figured she had to be their target.

A low moan came from beside him.

Oh, shit. What am I going to do with him? He eased his half-brother down across the bench seat to keep him from toppling forward. Next, he pulled a ski mask over Neil's head, adjusted the holes to clear his brother's glasses and nose, and slipped the duffel bag beneath his head. Neil wasn't completely horizontal, but it would have to do. At least he wasn't likely to roll off the narrow bench. As the sound of light snoring resumed, Rick felt the tension between his shoulder blades begin to ease.

"What are you doing?" Sarah-Jayne asked.

"Just making baby bro more comfortable so he won't give us any trouble. Don't worry, he's fallen back into his stupor." They had reached a loading zone, and he instructed Sarah-Jayne to pull over. With his eye steady on the bobbing dark hood of the target, he pulled on his own flesh-colored ski mask as the van came to a halt. Hitting the PLAY button on the boom box, which was set to full volume beside the rear doors, he hopped from the van and crouched in position just in front of the fender on the passenger side, out of sight of anyone approaching from the rear of the van.

Sarah-Jayne signaled with a nod that the girl had paused as she drew near the van, and Rick held his breath, then slowly let it out. As anticipated, the sound of a crying infant had done the trick. The girl had stopped to listen. As she stepped toward the van and cupped her hands to peer through the back window, he made his move.

Soundlessly, on sneakered feet, he was behind her.

The girl stepped back. In the reflection of the window, he saw eyes the size of dinner plates.

"You think someone abandoned a tiny baby?" His soft, controlled voice was edged with believable concern.

She didn't respond at first. Then, in a flash, she spun around. Her eyes widened as she took in his mask, and she looked as if she were about to take flight. The street was not totally deserted, he knew, but as the commotion began, no one turned in their direction. Everyone was wrapped up in their own world. Before that could change, Rick grabbed the girl around the waist and pressed a damp cloth to her nose. She struggled, flailing her arms and kicking at his shins with her boots. She was a hell of a lot stronger than he'd imagined she'd be. Neil had told him she was into dance—not the martial arts.

And then, as suddenly as it had begun, all the fight vanished from the little tigress, and within seconds she slumped against him.

His shin throbbed from the blow she had delivered with the heel of her boot. *The little bitch.* Ignoring the pain, he scanned the immediate area, scooped her into his arms, and flung open one of the van's rear doors, mentally giving himself a pat on the back for a job well done. If anyone observed them, they had their bases covered.

And someone had observed them.

Hearing a shout, Rick turned and saw that less than half a block up State Street another she-devil in a hooded sweatshirt was dashing toward them hollering at the top of her lungs. *Her damn twin must have followed her.* He couldn't make out the words, but he wasn't about to wait until they became clear. Tossing the girl inside, he jumped into the van and hollered to Sarah-Jayne, "Hit it!" as he pulled the door closed behind him.

Marnie skidded to a stop. Out of breath, her lungs on fire, she watched the silver bakery van pull away from the curb. "Stop . . . Stop . . . Stop," she hollered as loud as she could, so loud that her vocal cords burned. *This can't be happening.*

Reining in her rising panic, she did her best to pull herself together. She must think, and think fast. The van hadn't gone far. It was stuck behind a single car at the red light. *Get the number on the license plate,* she told herself. Dashing forward again, she pulled out her cell phone, focused on the rear plate, and snapped a picture. Though it was splattered with mud, she could make out most of the numbers: 080_ _70.

Marnie was gasping for breath and still several car lengths behind when the light turned green and the van shot forward, passed the car directly in front of it, and disappeared into traffic. She quickly tapped the numbers of the license plate into her phone. Saved it. Then hit 9-1-1. The phone rang once before the light blinked out. Her battery was dead.

Without a second thought she spun around, scanning the block for a phone booth. She was surprised to find a pay phone that had not been removed, but it had been vandalized and was missing its receiver.

She dashed back to their hotel. Pain shot through her ankle, but she didn't slow down until she reached the doorway to the Palmer House.

Nearly colliding with one of the guests, she said, "Sorry," and dashed up to the registration desk. "Call 9-1-1," she said to the desk attendant, expelling what little breath she had left. "My sister has been kidnapped."

"Excuse me," said the man in the dark suit and the shirt with the stiff white collar. "What is your emergency?" he asked, his eyes nervously scanning the line of people she'd burst in front of, all waiting to check in.

Another dark-suited man quickly strode up beside Marnie. "If you will follow me into my office, I will be happy to help you."

She glared at him. "My sister was just kidnapped. The kidnapper is getting away, and you want me to come to your office?" She didn't wait for a response. Instead, she turned on her heel and ran across the pristine floor to the elevators. She couldn't waste another second. She'd call from the suite. She just prayed that the penthouse elevator would be awaiting her. *And please, God, look out for Callie* . . . As if in answer to her prayer, the doors of the right elevator opened, and Marnie slipped in. She pressed the P button for *penthouse* and took out her special key card.

It wasn't until the elevator began its slow rise that she thought about what was really going on. Was it Brad wearing a ski mask who tossed Callie into the van like a rag doll, or was it someone else? Maybe it had nothing to do with Brad. Maybe Brad was waiting for her at Starbucks.

The elevator stopped and the door slipped open. Thoughts of the boy she was so eager to meet melted into thin air. Callie was in trouble, and it was all her fault. *She never would have been alone on State Street after dark if not for me. I got her into this, and it's up to me to get her out.* Sliding the key into the lock and pushing open the door, she was about to shout out to Elizabeth but stopped herself. She didn't have time to explain. She needed to call 9-1-1.

She picked up the first phone in sight—the one on the table in the foyer. The instant the call was answered, Marnie told the operator all she knew. She rattled off the partial license plate, a description of the van, and the approximate time and location.

"May I speak to your parents?" asked the woman on the other end of the line.

"They aren't here. They don't know yet. I wanted to call you first so you could put out an APB."

"An APB?" the woman repeated, a note of amusement in her tone.

"Isn't that what you call it?" *Maybe that's just some stupid mumbo jumbo they use for TV shows and movies.*

"Yes," the operator said. "When we have identifying information on a vehicle used in a crime, an all-points bulletin is issued." There was a brief hesitation, and then she continued, "One moment, please."

Marnie heard a click on the line, and then another voice said, "Officer Irina Kowalski, badge number 0637."

After getting Marnie's location, the officer asked, "Is there any adult there who can speak to me?"

She had to call her parents. Marnie's hand shook on the receiver. "Yes," she said, "but I think she has gone to bed. I will tell her everything before the police get here, but I need to call my mom and dad first. And I need to do that right now."

There was a short silence on the phone, as if Officer Kowalski were considering her request. Then she gave Marnie her direct line and said, "We're on our way. Have one of your parents get in touch with me immediately."

Marnie flipped open her cell and scanned down to Ashleigh's cell number, then quickly punched it in. *Please don't let her be away from her evening bag,* Marnie thought. Her hand gripped the receiver so hard, her fingers felt numb and her knuckles were drained of all color. *Callie has to be okay,* she pleaded to no one. *I should have been with her. If we'd been together and that guy with the ski mask had tried anything, he'd be toast.*

The phone continued to ring. Finally, the voice mail came on. "Mom, this is Marnie. Call right away. It's an emergency." Next, she quickly tapped in her father's number. A couple of seconds passed, and then she heard the distinctive ring of her father's phone. But not through the phone in her hand.

Her dad had left his cell phone on the mantel above the fireplace, right there in the penthouse suite.

CHAPTER

61

Viviana felt Gino's liquid brown eyes on her. At his smile, his handsome face, the breath caught in her throat, but she managed to shift her thoughts from what lay ahead this evening to the here and now.

As the background music for the grand finale began to fill the room, Viviana drank in her success and sank back in her chair to enjoy the conclusion of the show. Then an unexpected sour note wafting from the saxophone jolted her, and her posture turned rigid. *Hopefully I'm the only one that noticed.* Other than that faux pas, the music was perfect. As one after another spectacular ensemble floated down the winding ramps, she was pleased that the background music she'd chosen turned out to be inspiring and filled with emotion.

From the next table, Ashleigh leaned toward her. "Bravo," she said a mere decibel above a whisper. "You have really outdone yourself, Viviana, with your designs for the season."

Viviana smiled. She had good reason to be proud of her latest collection.

Just as she was beginning to relax, a petite young woman from the catering staff crept up beside her. Annoyed, Viviana shot her a glare of impatience. The young woman, dressed in a plain black, knee-length dress beneath a ruffled white apron, did not retreat, but the pale skin on her neck reddened.

"Are you sure this can't wait until after the finale?" Viviana asked in a hushed tone.

The young woman shook her head, her lips moving rapidly. Between her soft voice and the music reaching a crescendo, Viviana could barely make out her words. But when the girl thrust one of the salon's portable phones into her hand, Viviana felt her heartbeat quicken.

Once the message had finally sunk in, Viviana's eyes darted across to Conrad Taylor. Ignoring the models as they glided down the ramp in her haute couture designs, she sprang from her chair. The instant she reached Conrad, she handed him the phone without a word.

Neil woke with a start, unable to breathe or move. He felt as if he'd jumped from the high dive and landed head first at the bottom of a shallow pool. His hands shot up to his face as he tried to gather his thoughts, and he found it covered in scratchy wool. *What the heck?*

"Hey," he heard Rick shout, "leave that on."

Neil tried to sit up but felt disoriented. As he swayed on the narrow bench, he looked across at his brother on the opposite bench. Rick was wearing a ski mask. Fingering the mask on his own face, he said, "What's going on?" and ripped off the mask. That's when he saw her lying on the floor a few feet from him: Marnie. Her hands and feet were bound. *What the . . . ?*

His heart seemed to stop beating as he looked at the girl. The one, presumably, he'd been talking to online. The vulnerable teenager he'd grown to care about. He dropped down to the floor beside her and saw the faint but steady rise and fall of her chest.

"Rick. Are you crazy?" he shouted, his voice quaking. "What have you done?" *How did this happen?* His dad had warned him not to be so trusting, especially when it came to his half-brother.

"Calm down, bro. Everything's gonna be alright. But there's been a change of plans. Now for God's sake, put that mask back on, and don't call me by name."

With his whole world spinning out of control, Neil tried to remain calm and make sense out of all this. *What did Rick plan to do?* "You were supposed to drop me off at Starbucks so I could get to know Marnie." His eyes drifted back to the girl. "My God, Rick. What have you done?"

"It was all your idea. You turned me onto the fact that this little brat is worth big bucks. Now we don't have to talk her into anything. *We're in the driver's seat.*"

Neil's stomach roiled. *What have I done?* "What are you talking about? I asked you to help me so I could *talk with* Marnie. I wanted to get to know her, away from her family—not to steal money from them . . ." He shook his head. "This girl is my friend. I care about her."

Rick jeered at him. "Have you lost your fucking mind? You said you'd never met her. And by God, that better be the truth."

Neil shook his head again. "Not in person. But I've gotten to know her. We . . . we want a lot of the same things. Now please, Rick—please untie her." He glanced over at the girl and saw a tear slide down the curve of her cheek.

CHAPTER
62

Loud voices had pulled Callie from an uneasy slumber. She was scared. No, not scared—it was worse. She was *terrified*. Her heart pounded and her breath came in gasps. Fumbling through her memory, she tried to pull herself out of the nightmare. *What has happened to me?*

She opened her eyes, but not all the way. A faint light dimly illuminated her surroundings. She made out vague shapes and tried to make herself calm. She swallowed, took regular breaths, and attempted to think straight. She was lying on a hard floor. It was moving. She felt the vibrations and heard the sound of the ground moving beneath her. She was in a vehicle—a van. And she could barely move. She had a headache, a dry mouth, and a feeling of nausea. She was cold, but hot needles of pain shot through her left shoulder, and she realized her wrists were tied together. So were her ankles. The slightest movement caused the ropes to bite into her skin.

Slowly, the realization that this was more than a bad dream washed over her, and her throat closed over. *I was right . . .*

Don't panic, she told herself, and she prayed silently for courage. Not daring to let anyone know she was awake, she tried to form a plan. *A plan . . .* The idea reverberated in her head. *What am I thinking? I don't know where I am, I don't know who these people are, I don't know what they want.* And yet doing nothing was not an option. Already she knew she would not allow herself to be defeated. She had watched a lot of movies and TV shows and read novels about kidnappings. That's what this was, right? That's what she would have to draw on.

Callie stretched her mind, trying to conjure up some scenario in which escape would be possible. Peeking through the narrow slit between her upper and lower lashes, she could just make out two male figures. Each was wearing a tan ski mask. The rail-thin guy with his hand on the van's ceiling sounded angry as he stood over the other one, who swayed on the bench that ran the length of the vehicle. The one on the bench said something she couldn't decipher, and then he ripped off his mask, revealing tousled copper hair, a thin Roman nose laced with freckles, and light blue eyes behind horn-rimmed glasses. He was about her age. *Could he be Brad?* Callie wondered.

The skinny man was shouting for the boy to put the mask back on and stop calling him by name. But there had to be more than just the two of them. The steady hum of the tires told Callie they were moving steadily along a smooth, paved road. She couldn't see over the high seat backs, but someone was obviously behind the wheel, and maybe someone else was sitting in the passenger seat. *There could be three or four of them.* Her blood turned to ice. *Relax,* she told herself, but she couldn't loosen the knot of tension lodged between her shoulder blades.

The van rounded a corner. Callie rolled forward slightly, and sharp pains erupted all over her body. As they subsided, she felt two sets of eyes upon her. She moaned groggily, praying they would assume she was still unconscious.

Opening her eyes a fraction, she saw the boy slide off the bench and move to within inches of her face. "What have you done?" he kept saying. "Please untie her." Kneeling beside her, he whispered, "Marnie?" Then he pressed his hand to her forehead and asked, "Are you alright?"

Callie flinched as his fingers crossed her brow, and she felt a tear slide from each eye. She heard the voice of irony play in her head. *Peachy keen. Is he a total idiot?*

"She's not asleep," the skinny creep said. "She's faking it."

She didn't move. She didn't open her eyes.

The boy leaned in close and held his hand up to her nose. "Untie her," he said again, attempting to assert some authority, but his shaky voice betrayed him. There was no question who was in charge, and the creep's next move confirmed that in spades.

He slid his booted foot beneath her left elbow and rolled her onto her back. Involuntarily, she let out a cry. Then he grabbed her by her wrists and yanked her upright, pushing her against the double back doors. She felt cold air seeping in on her neck.

"Stop," the boy cried out. "This is all wrong. You tricked me."

"Shut the fuck up," the man said, and he shoved the boy, who nearly toppled over.

"I'm not Marnie," Callie suddenly shouted.

"Of course you aren't." The man's sneer was chilling.

"What do you mean?" the boy asked.

"Marnie is my twin, you idiots." As the words left her mouth, she knew she'd made a very big mistake—even before the creep slapped her hard across the face.

"Don't do that again," the boy said to the creep through gritted teeth, his anger apparently now stronger than his fear.

Callie wasn't about to give the creep cause. She couldn't retract her words, but she could change her attitude. In the movies, it never went well for the one who stood up to the kidnappers. She'd have to drop the bravado and fake being timid and scared. That was no stretch. She'd never been so scared in her life.

The boy spoke again. "I told you Marnie had a twin." Turning to her with confusion on his face, he asked, "Are you Callie?"

She nodded her head, tears spilling down her cheeks. "Are you Brad?"

He paused, then nodded his head. Then he asked, "Where is Marnie? Why—"

"I told you to shut the fuck up." The man's eyes flashed from Brad to her. "Marnie, Callie—it don't matter. I don't give a flying fuck. When it comes to what we're after, one twin is as good as the other."

Puzzled that Viviana would allow a call to intrude upon the grand finale of her fashion extravaganza, Ashleigh followed with her eyes as their hostess headed in their direction, making a beeline for Conrad. A frown crept across his brow when he looked up at her, but without a word he extended his hand to take the portable phone she proffered.

Ashleigh's heart skipped a beat.

Her husband cupped his hand over the receiver and spoke into it. Thoughts of Juliana popped into her head. Her daughter's forehead had been warm to the touch off and on since their arrival in Chicago. *Has her fever spiked?*

Her unease rose another notch when she observed the color drain from Conrad's face and his grip tighten around the receiver.

"We'll grab a taxi and be right there," she heard him say. "I'll call Officer Kowalski on the way."

Officer Kowalski—the words echoed in Ashleigh's head. This wasn't about any escalating fever. Sensing the urgency, she pushed back her chair, grabbed her minaudière, and followed her husband's lead through the labyrinth of tables and ramps.

Enthralled with the sea of the latest spring fashions, those around the Taylors seemed to take no notice of their abrupt departure.

"I need your phone," Conrad said when they'd almost reached the door.

Ashleigh reached into her evening bag and handed him her cell. They gathered their coats from the hatcheck girl and went outside to hail a cab. Panic rising, she said, "For God's sake, don't keep me in the dark."

Sucking in a shallow breath, he squeezed her hand. His words—a staccato response—set her blood on fire.

———

Pocino glared at the blaring phone and turned up the volume on the TV. Jim Thome had just stepped up to bat for the White Sox, and nothing and no one would intrude on his enjoyment of the game.

Crushing his empty beer can and tossing it in the trash, he reached for another and slammed shut the fridge door. The motel room was small but adequate. The large-screen TV was all he required.

Trying once again to ignore the insistent ringing, Pocino slumped back into the armchair and hefted his feet onto the ottoman. With his fourth can of beer midway to his lips, he heard the answering machine click on, and the deep tones of Conrad Taylor's voice penetrated his slight buzz. Catching the strain in the man's voice, Pocino heaved himself out of the chair and hit the MUTE button on the remote.

He grabbed the receiver. "Pocino," he bellowed, interrupting Conrad's message. Then he just listened. *Holy shit. This is friggin' unbelievable.*

His mind took flight at the news, his suspicions immediately landing on the Christonellis. *Did they really imagine they could get away with a second kidnapping . . . ?* But with Conrad's next words, that unlikely scenario died.

"Hold on," Pocino said. "Are you saying *Callie* is missing? Not Marnie?" His mind raced forward. "The younger Wainwright—was he at the party tonight?" Absorbing Conrad's confirmation, he asked, "Was he still there when you received the call? . . . No shit."

This was no time for further conversation. "I'm on it," he said. While jamming his feet into some loafers, grabbing his car keys and jacket, and heading for the door, he assured Conrad, "I'll run down Tony Wainwright's address and call you en route."

Stopping dead in his tracks, Pocino said, "Come again?" *What the hell?* "Viviana De Mornay's boyfriend lives . . . ? Never mind. Okay, I'll give her a call now and get his address and home phone. Yeah, I'll report back to you at the Palmer as soon as I have something." After a beat, he said, "And Conrad, you know the FBI has got to be called in. If Chicago PD doesn't initiate—"

But Pocino should have saved his breath. The line was already dead.

Elizabeth pulled Marnie into her arms and kissed her on the forehead. But this just made Marnie feel a thousand times worse than if she'd shouted at her. *I bet she wishes it was me who was kidnapped instead of Callie . . . but not as much as Mom and Dad do. And not as much as I do.*

Wrapping her arms around her own waist as if to hold herself together, Marnie was unable to look Elizabeth in the eye. "I am so . . . so sorry. It's all my fault. I have to do something to fix this, but I don't know what to do—"

There was a loud knock, interrupting further self-incrimination.

Marnie shot to the door and flung it open. Two police officers stood on the other side: a tall, dark-haired woman and a rangy male with thick salt-and-pepper hair. Both were in uniform and they extended their badges toward her. The woman took the lead. "I am Officer Irina Kowalski, and this is my partner, Officer John Knight."

As Marnie stepped back to let them inside, she heard the elevator grind to a stop once more, and her parents stepped out. In an instant, both were in the suite's entryway beside her. She felt no bigger than a matchbox when her father said, "Marnie, thank God you're alright . . ."

Ashleigh took her into her arms and squeezed her so tight, Marnie could hardly breathe. Before the officers had a chance to begin their questioning, she reassured her daughter, "Marnie, we *are* going to get Callie back. But we need your help. Please, just start from the beginning. Why was Callie out on State Street? And why was she by herself?"

Damn, Marnie thought. Callie really had no business leaving without her. *That's a good question.*

Helping Paige into her coat, Mark craned his neck to scan the departing guests. "Did Conrad and Ashleigh already leave?"

Paige shrugged. "I didn't see them go, but Ashleigh said they planned to head back to the hotel right after the finale to check on Juliana and Elizabeth." Still, it struck her as odd.

"Right," Mark said, nodding. "Come to think of it, I heard her mention that. Guess we'll have to catch up tomorrow at dinner."

With a bemused smile, Paige said, "Catch up? As if we ever could." Then she added, "I made a reservation at Keefer's. It will just be the four of us. April and Kyle offered to spend some time with Mom."

Overhearing her mother, April nodded. "We thought we'd also get together with Elizabeth and the girls."

"Terrific. Nana will love that," Paige said as they headed for the door, but her mind returned to Ashleigh and Conrad's departure. They'd disappeared without a word. *It's just so unlike them . . .*

Neil gritted his teeth, swallowing back the wave of threatening nausea. *Dad warned me about trusting Rick. If only I . . .* Pushing aside thoughts of what he hadn't a prayer of changing, he concentrated on clearing his throbbing head and figuring out what he could and must do.

He kept his eye on Rick, who leaned forward, close to the driver's seat, and was saying something to that weird girlfriend of his in a voice so low, Neil could not make out the words. He twisted his body slightly toward the back of the van, facing away from his half-brother, and fished in his pocket to pull out his cell phone. Keeping it close to his body, he took a quick glance over his shoulder toward Rick before flicking the cover open with his thumb. The phone emitted a shrill beep that shattered the near-silence inside the van.

"What the fuck?" Rick roared, whirling back around to face Neil on the opposite bench.

Instantly, Neil snapped the cover back in place and slid the phone under his butt. But it was too late.

Rick's face turned a blazing red and seemed to swell with rage. "Give me the goddamn cell," he yelled, glaring at the girl, who looked up in bewilderment.

Pulling his phone out from beneath him, Neil said, "It wasn't her. It was me."

Rick sat frozen in place for a full ten seconds, then stood up, placing one hand on the ceiling of the van, and stretched out his other hand. *Is this dork for real? What is he thinking?* "Give me the fucking phone."

"I—I wanted to call Dad," the little twerp stammered, "so he wouldn't worry if he got home before me."

Shaking his head, Rick said, "You may be a fucking honor student, but you sure ain't too bright. Since you're not with us, you're a goddamn threat. Not a chance in hell you'll be winging your way home anytime tonight."

Rick took the phone and removed the battery, then tossed the useless device over the back of the seat. "Put this in the glove compartment," he ordered Sarah-Jayne, "and hand me a wipe."

Neil straightened his posture. "But you know how Dad—"

"But nothing," Rick shot back. "You're a liability, not an asset. Even if you could convince us you were part of the grand plan, which is damned unlikely now, you've screwed yourself by taking off the motherfuckin' mask."

"Rick, it's not too late—"

"Shut the fuck up." Rick had no patience for this. "Your tiny little world has shrunk. If the girl lives, your life as you know it comes to an end."

"What do you mean?" Neil's voice was trembling like a little old lady's. "You can't hurt her. She's done nothing to you."

Rick unfolded the wipe and scrubbed at his hands until they were blood-red and angry-looking. "It's not what she's *done to me*. It's what she can *do for me*. She cooperates, nobody gets hurt." He chuckled. "Well, I guess you've got a problem either way. We'll be long gone, but if the girl lives, she can identify you."

Callie felt numb. Rolling her lips inward to control the trembling, she concentrated on forcing her mind into gear. The brothers' banter would soon end. She must act now before it was too late.

She shifted to face the back doors of the van. The ropes on her wrists remained tight, but at least they were tied in front and she had full use of her fingers. She slid her hands into the pouch of her sweatshirt and retrieved her cell. The next maneuver was more difficult, but she had to do it. *If I can just slide it inside my bra* . . . With her hands tied together, there was no way to slip it through the neckline. *Keep talking,* she prayed as she slipped her hands up under the bottom of her sweatshirt.

She heard the man called Rick hiss, "If the girl lives . . ." and nearly dropped the phone. But finally she was able to shove the cell upward, between the bottom of her sports bra and her skin, and she lowered her hands back out of her sweatshirt.

She had done it just in time. As if it had just occurred to him, Rick turned from Neil and reached for Callie. He pulled her toward him by her tied wrists. "Give me your cell."

Tingling from head to toe, Callie let her gaze drift up to meet his. In a timid, shaky voice she didn't have to fake, she said, "I forgot it. It's at our hotel."

"A teenager leaves home without a cell? I don't think so." He hunkered down within inches of her face. "Hand it over."

Attempting an expression of wide-eyed innocence, Callie said quietly, "I don't have it."

"Little girl," he said, "you'll find the next few hours a whole lot easier if you cooperate. Now hand it over."

"I . . . I . . . don't have it," Callie sobbed, just as she had when she played one of the orphans in her high school's production of *Annie.*

He shoved his skinny hands into each of her jeans pockets and then pulled her up to a kneeling position.

"Stop that," Neil shouted. "She said she forgot it." He tried to pull his brother away from her. Rick nearly lost his balance, but he instantly righted himself and gave his brother an unrestrained shove. Neil fell to the van's floor beside her. The thin man was a lot stronger than he looked.

When Rick forced his hand into the pouch of Callie's sweatshirt, her breath caught. "My God, the chick's telling the truth. What gives?" He chuckled. "You want the world to leave you alone?" His smirk ran from ear to ear. "Well, little lady, you got your wish."

Neil started to pick himself off the floor, and Rick hoisted him to his feet. "Put your hands together in front of you." When Neil hesitated, Rick backhanded him.

Then he reached for the duct tape.

As the last guest disappeared from the salon, Gino began to unwind. Viviana slipped out of her stilettos and emitted a long, lyrical sigh. Gino leaned over and kissed her cheek. *Alone at last.*

Leaning down, he gently lifted her feet to his lap and began massaging them. During the entire spectacular, star-studded evening, they'd barely had a chance for more than a few words; their focus had been directed solely at making the evening the success that it had turned out to be.

"Happy?" he asked. He hadn't seen her so relaxed since the day they met.

"Never been happier." Viviana grinned and began to hum.

Gino recognized the tune: "You and Me Against the World." A familiar thought flashed in his head: *God, I love this woman.* "Now tell me," he said, "what was so important about that phone call for Conrad Taylor?"

Viviana gasped, and her brows drew together suddenly. She bit down on her lip before responding. "Oh, Gino. I can't believe I allowed that to slip right out of my head. I'm so ashamed. The call was from Callie— or maybe it was Marnie. I'm not sure which one. Those girls sound just alike to me." She paused. "Did you know voices are determined by DNA?"

"Interesting." Gino prompted her back on track. "So what was the call about?"

"Whichever girl it was, she told me she had to talk to her dad. She said her twin had been kidnapped. Someone in a ski mask grabbed her and threw her into a silver bakery van."

Gino clamped his eyes shut and for a long moment said nothing. Finally, his voice just above a whisper, he said, "And you forgot?"

Viviana covered her face with both hands. "You must think I am a terrible, uncaring person. I have no excuse. I can't believe I could have let anything distract me from that kind of disastrous news."

Pulling her hands away from her face, Gino looked at her compassionately. "I don't think any such thing. You had a lot on your plate. Plus, even though I didn't know what had happened, I did hear Taylor ask you not to make a fuss when he and his wife slipped out." He paused. "I know Tony appreciated the lack of fuss when he asked you the same thing."

Gino wasn't sure if she'd registered what he said, but in the next instant her eyes became as large as demitasse saucers. "Oh no," she cried out. "I know he had nothing to do with abducting the twin, but he's sure to be a suspect."

Gino looked at her, uncomprehending. "Who?"

"Tony."

Pocino squinted up at the number barely illuminated by a dim porch light. Without the GPS, he would have been up shit creek. There seemed to be no goddamn rhyme or reason to the layout of this midpriced community.

He nosed the Ford Bronco into the driveway of the address he'd been given for Tony Wainwright. He parked beside the red VW Bug and quickly checked it out. The surface above the engine compartment was cold to the touch.

Pounding his way up the front steps of the modest ranch house, he allowed his mind to race through various scenarios. It appeared that no one was home, but he sure as hell wasn't going to slip away without a sneak preview. *There.* Through the glass at the top of the front door, he saw a light from somewhere at the back of the small house. He pushed the doorbell and waited impatiently, but no sound echoed inside. There was a door knocker in the shape of a dragon, a few inches below the glass. He pounded the knocker against the brass plate. Not once or twice, but repeatedly.

"Hold on," a lilting soprano sang out from inside.

It seemed to take a full minute before the door was flung open.

Before Pocino stood a rather short person, five foot four at the most. The man had curly black hair and was clad in a deep purple, velvet robe. A baby-blue satin sash wound around the man's wisp of a waist.

Holy freaking shit. Pocino sucked in his breath, feeling every single one of his extra forty pounds. He remembered Tony's former partner, Jeff Bradley, and was well aware of the man's lifestyle, but . . . *Holy Toledo.*

Clearing the cobwebs from his mind, Pocino introduced himself, then asked, "Is Tony Wainwright here?"

"I'm Renzo," the delicate young man said. "We cohabitate this home."

Cohabitate? A novel way to put it, Pocino thought. Still, he couldn't imagine this wimpy character as Tony's new lover.

"Just got home about twenty minutes ago," Renzo told him. "I was in the mood to chat, but Tony was already in bed and sound asleep."

"I'll just bet," Pocino said, serving it up with a huge slice of irony. "Tell him I need to speak with him."

"Oh no," Renzo cried out. "Tony's been working full-time and moonlighting for Ms. De Mornay too. Burning a lot of midnight oil, as the saying goes, and he has to be up early tomorrow. I'm afraid you'll have to come at another time."

"Afraid not," Pocino countered. "This can't wait."

"Well," Renzo said, giving an effeminate wave of his wrist, "perhaps you can leave a note, and I'll have him call you first thing tomorrow."

Pocino frowned. "If you aren't willing to get him out of the sack, I will. There's been a kidnapping. And he's a suspect. A *prime* suspect."

"No." Renzo glared at Pocino, and all the friendliness drained from his demeanor. "You wait here. I'll get him. But you're way off base. Tony is *not* your man. He's turned his life around. I can vouch for him one hundred percent. He's *not* your man," he repeated and sashayed down the hallway.

Pocino followed right behind him.

Tony shielded his eyes when the bedroom light flashed on. "What?" His voice was garbled.

When Renzo told him who it was and what he'd said, Tony rolled over. "Tell him to get off my case. I told him everything he wanted to know the other day at Christonelli's office. He has no right coming here unless he has a warrant. Tell him to piss off."

Pocino shoved Renzo out of the doorway. "I think you might wanna change your mind. One of Ashleigh Taylor's twins has been abducted. It happened right after you left the party at De Mornay's. And you just happen to be our suspect *numero uno*."

Tony shot up in the bed. All traces of slumber were gone. "What in the hell are you talking about? I never laid eyes on the twins until tonight."

"And I suppose you never used your computer moxie to strike up an online acquaintance with one of the Taylor twins."

"What in the hell are you accusing me of? Even if I had the spare time, I'm hardly into striking up an online friendship with some kid."

"Strange thing is, right after you meet the girls, one goes missing."

Throwing his legs over the side of the bed, Tony rose and strode over to Pocino and came up to within inches of his barrel chest and big belly, invading his personal space. "So what's my goddamn motive?"

Pocino stepped back. "You tell me."

Above his brother's protestations, the guy in the ski mask barked to the person driving the van, "Turn here." The roar of the L above them nearly drowned out his words.

Thank God, we're still in Chicago, Callie thought as the rumble of the train faded. *Marnie will be mad that I took off without her, but when she discovers I'm not at Starbucks, she'll tell Mom and Dad, and the police will find me.* She would just have to use her head . . . and make sure this creep didn't kill her first.

The continuing verbal exchange between the brothers had set her nerves ablaze. Her heart plummeted to a new low, however, when the creep ripped off his own mask. Straight, dull blond hair fell past his shoulders. Did he no longer care if Callie could recognize him? She knew that should bother her—a lot. And it did.

While the creep was busy wrapping the duct tape around his brother's wrists, she put her fear on the back burner and scooted a few inches across the floor, so she could rest her back against the bench that ran along the driver's side. She had to clear her mind. She wondered where they were taking her. She no longer wondered why.

The creep's name is Rick. When did he stop objecting to his brother calling him by name? She rummaged through her memory. It didn't really matter when. His was the only name she'd heard. He'd never called the younger brother by name. *But I doubt "Brad" is his real name.*

The sound of ripping duct tape short-circuited her thoughts. An instant later, after stepping away from the younger brother, the creep set his pocketknife on the bench seat beside her and hunkered down to check the ropes around her wrists and ankles. "Rick" was far too nice a name for this malevolent creep tugging on her. *He should be called Satan.*

When he rose, ducking so his head did not bump the top of the van, he unwrapped another damp wipe and again cleaned his hands relentlessly. *What's that all about?* Whatever his deal was, it was clear he had never told his brother that he was out for ransom. Callie was sure that was his motivation. The creep had said that one twin was as good as another.

Reining in her random thoughts, she began working out a plan. Conscious of her cell phone wedged inside her bra and pressing into her skin, she wondered if she'd get a chance to use it. *Not if—when.* Her mind kept at it. *Could "Brad" be an ally? I'm not sure.* He seemed not to be a part of this evil plan, but . . .

The van jerked to a stop.

As the creep moved toward the double doors at the back of the van, he hollered over his shoulder to the person behind the wheel. "Get into the passenger seat. I'll drive from now on." Callie heard a muffled, shy voice respond before the creep swung open one of the doors and jumped out into the night. He didn't shut the door, and a stiff breeze instantly whipped Callie's hair into her eyes.

Pushing back the errant strands, she tried to figure out what the creep was up to. He said he would drive, so he must be sending the other person back here. Otherwise he'd have closed the door.

Although Callie couldn't see the driver, now she knew it was a female. Not one who was well educated or at ease with the situation, the voice told her. *Maybe this girl might be the chink in the monster's armor.*

That thought was curtailed by the creep's sudden reappearance. He shoved the bakery signs she'd seen on the side of the van into the back, along with some kind of dirty, transparent strips. The creep rolled them into a crumpled ball and slammed the door before slipping back into the driver's seat.

Unfortunately, the girl stayed up front in the passenger seat.

"Don't worry, Erica," Nelson said, wrapping one arm around her shoulder as they headed toward her front door. "The accommodations you've worked out for the girls and the woman accompanying them are terrific. This house looks warm and welcoming. Besides, upscale living quarters aren't even on a teenager's radar." He chuckled. "As long as they have their laptops and cell phones, they're content."

"I know," Erica said, but her whispered words held no conviction.

If only I could convince her that she doesn't have to compete with the Taylors in material things. Of course, he knew she had a lot more on her mind than the accommodations she could offer the young girl whom she had raised as her daughter.

Erica paused at the closed door. She did not reach for the knob. Instead, she turned to face Nelson, and then melted into his arms. Her silent tremble made him feel helpless. He wanted so badly to protect this good, vulnerable woman. The media had it all wrong. She was no monster. No kidnapper.

Finally, Erica took a step back. Her gaze shot down at her wristwatch. "Oh, Nelson, I'm so sorry. It's past midnight. I didn't realize it was so late. I've kept you up again tonight, and I've been so self-absorbed I haven't even asked how you feel."

"Don't worry, I feel fine," he lied. Although he'd distracted himself from it most of the evening, every joint throbbed in pain, and he looked forward to dropping into bed even knowing that sleep would be a challenge.

"Is that the God's honest truth?"

If I want to take this to the next level, I must be candid. He couldn't pinpoint when it had happened, but he was certain that his caring about Erica had turned to love. "Not totally," he confessed. Taking her hand, he suggested that they talk in her living room for a little while. "You deserve the whole truth."

Dropping into the plump sofa cushions, he began. "When you have fibromyalgia, the pain never goes away. I try not to think about it, and more often than not I'm able to distract myself for periods of time. That was the case for most of this evening." He held her gaze. "So when anyone asks how I feel, I seldom say anything but 'fine.'" He grinned.

"Hey, don't look so glum. I find that if I don't talk about it, I can fill my mind with more pleasant things. This disease can rule my life only if I give it the power to do so. I refuse to do that."

He thrust himself forward onto his feet. "But now, my dear, I must be on my way." He chuckled, more to himself than anything. "Neil will be worried about me." It should be the other way around, he knew, but as he grew older, Neil had become the proverbial mother hen.

Erica smiled. "I hope Neil doesn't have plans for tomorrow," she said. "I would love for him to meet Marnie and her sisters."

Ashleigh crossed and recrossed her legs as Conrad paced back and forth in the living room of their suite. Officer Knight had taken out a small spiral notepad and begun jotting down information as Marnie spoke.

Meanwhile, Officer Kowalski pulled out her cell phone and hit her speed dial. She took several steps away and stood close to the windowed wall overlooking State Street. "Violent Crimes Unit," Ashleigh heard the officer say. Although she was obviously keeping her voice low, the words shot terror up Ashleigh's spine. As Officer Knight and Conrad talked with Marnie about everything she'd seen, Ashleigh strained to hear Officer Kowalski.

"This is a high-priority call," Officer Kowalski said to whoever was on the other end of the line. She gave a brief overview of the situation: that Callie had been seen being thrown into a van, the exact location, a description of the van. "We need detectives dispatched immediately." She gave the suite number and then began nodding her head, but said nothing more for several long seconds. She ended the call with "Copy that."

"Excuse me, officers," Ashleigh said. "It's getting very late. I think Marnie has told you all she knows, and I'm sure Elizabeth must be exhausted." *At least the door chimes haven't awakened Juliana. That child can sleep through anything.*

"It's alright," Elizabeth protested.

Ashleigh looked at Elizabeth, who always gave two hundred percent to their family. Meeting Officer Kowalski's eyes, she asked if her daughter and Elizabeth could be excused.

"Of course," the officers said in unison.

"Mom," Marnie cried out, "I need to help." Her eyes shot down to the laptop beside the police officer's foot.

"You've been a great help, darling," Ashleigh said. "There's nothing more you can do tonight—"

Officer Kowalski broke in. "Marnie, we have computer experts who will follow the trail of all the messages between you and the person who calls himself Brad. As we told you earlier, it's quite possible that this Brad is not a high school student after all."

"But—"

"Marnie," Conrad interrupted. Pulling his daughter to her feet, he hugged her close. "The police department's team of computer pros will get to the bottom of these messages and trace them back to the sender." He kissed her on the forehead. "But now it's time for you to try to get some sleep."

Marnie dropped her head, staring down at the paisley carpet. Tears pooled in her eyes and began to run down her cheeks.

Elizabeth asked the officers to let her know if there was anything she could do. Then, turning to Ashleigh and Conrad, she said, "You are all in my prayers." Quickly she put her arm around Marnie's shoulders.

Marnie shrugged away. Her lip quivered and she began to sob. "I'm so sorry." Covering her face with both hands, she choked out a plea. "Please don't send me away."

Ashleigh and Conrad were beside her in a flash, and the three shared a long hug. An unspoken communication passed between the parents. Conrad gave Marnie another quick kiss on the forehead. "Of course not. Never doubt our love for you, sweetheart," he said. Then he stepped back and let Ashleigh take over leading their daughter back to her bedroom.

Although Marnie insisted she wasn't tired and wouldn't be able to sleep, she had crawled into bed and allowed Ashleigh to remain by her side, rubbing her back. She had quickly fallen into an exhausted slumber, but Ashleigh feared she would not sleep through the night.

Back in the living room Ashleigh listened as Conrad filled in areas of their family history that seemed significant. Officer Kowalski nodded while Officer Knight took notes. What Conrad overlooked, Ashleigh filled in, and vice versa. Reliving all the past history while realizing the worst was not behind them was painful. Ashleigh was alternately feverish and chilled; Conrad continued wearing a path in the plush carpet. Several times he barely missed stepping on his tuxedo jacket, which he'd dropped in a heap on the floor. No one mentioned it or seemed to care.

"Mr. Taylor," Officer Kowalski tried to assure him, "your daughter's quick thinking has given us a good head start. We've got a partial license plate number and a photo of the van. We've issued an APB on it. Units near the scene and on the outskirts of town are covering all avenues of escape. Helicopters have been dispatched and are in the air. They are currently scanning a fifty-mile radius, which will be extended if need be."

"But what can we do? My daughter is not quite sixteen. She's had no experience—"

"Mr. Taylor, you've got to trust the system."

Two plainclothes detectives knocked on the open door to the Taylors' suite but did not wait for anyone to answer. Once inside the entryway, they were introduced by Officer Kowalski as Detectives Bob Senske and Greg Murdock.

Not missing a beat, the tall, white-haired Detective Senske assured Conrad and Ashleigh that the Chicago PD would work hand in hand with the FBI for the safe return of their daughter. The other detective nodded.

"We appreciate that. We've also called in our private investigators," Conrad said.

Senske did not look pleased. "That's not necessary, Mr. Taylor. We'd prefer that you let us do our jobs."

"With all due respect, we already have one man on it."

"Mr. Pocino?" Officer Kowalski asked by way of confirmation.

Conrad nodded.

She quickly filled the detectives in on the Taylors' relationship with the Landes Agency as well as their past history with Tony Wainwright and with the Christonellis. When Kowalski finished, she and Knight rose. After a few parting words to the detective, she turned to Ashleigh and Conrad, saying, "We'll be in touch." Then she and Knight showed themselves out.

Conrad turned back to Detective Senske. "What if I get a call for ransom? When Marnie was abducted from the hospital, strange as it may seem, we *prayed* for a ransom demand. We were devastated when it never came."

"I understand," Detective Senske said. "That's not at all strange. You wanted your baby back."

Conrad nodded. "And now it's Callie. She isn't an infant, after all. She's a teenager. It would be even more devastating if we never . . ."

Ashleigh's mouth dropped open. *What if there is no ransom demand?* She forgot to breathe.

The words were out of his mouth before he'd processed their disturbing effect. Sinking down beside his wife on the sofa, Conrad reached for her hand and rubbed his thumb across her palm. It felt ice cold. His unthinkable words had turned her face ashen. If only he could pull them back. If only the thought had never crossed his mind. *Human trafficking.*

It must have been that damn documentary they'd watched last week. Ashleigh had not stayed to see it through to the conclusion, and now he wished he hadn't either.

"Forgive me, Ashleigh," he began, squeezing her hand. "I don't know why I said that. That's not what this is about. I'm sure of it. We were warned by the board of Jordon's that our family could be a target for this kind of thing." As a high-profile figure and leader of a megacorporation, he and all his family members were potential targets for kidnapping and extortion—especially as the media spotlight had been on him since the takeover had made Jordon's the first national department store with more than eight hundred stores. "The motive is sure to be ransom." His voice was soft and his head filled with self-recrimination. "I should have . . ." He dropped his head into his hands. "My own family, and I can't even protect them."

Squeezing his hand, Ashleigh said, "Conrad, you are not to blame. You had no reason—"

Squeezing back in appreciation for her vote of confidence, he lifted his head and addressed the detectives. "If you have everything you need, I think it's best that we let you focus on finding Callie. We'll wait by the phone for the abductors to call about the ransom." *And when that demand comes, I'll do whatever it takes to get her back.* Neither the police nor the FBI, he vowed, would impede his daughter's safe return.

Seated behind the wheel of the Highlander, Nelson removed the cell phone from his belt loop holder and scrolled down to his home number. When the answering machine clicked on, he checked his watch. He didn't leave a message. Neil had most likely gone to bed wearing earbuds and plugged into his iPod.

Nelson's thoughts turned back to Erica. He'd felt as awkward as a middle school kid the first time he'd asked her to join him for coffee at Starbucks. Until tonight, he'd done his level best not to let himself feel what he could no longer deny. *I love this woman and want to grow old with her.* After she spends Easter break with her daughter, he decided, he would hold nothing back.

At this late hour, he reached home in less than twenty minutes. He was taken aback, however, when he flipped off the ignition and saw that the house was completely dark. He and Neil always left on both the table lamp in front of the window and the porch light if either of them was out for the evening.

Doing his best to keep panic at bay, Nelson sprang from the car, hustled up the front steps, and jammed his key in the lock. Not a single light had been left on downstairs. The only illumination came from the streetlight a few yards from the house. The eerie glow, which spread from the living room to the back of the Victorian house, was unsettling.

Flicking on the stairway light, he took the stairs two at time and raced down the hallway. His footfalls on the hardwood floors echoed off the walls. Neil's door was open. The bed had been made in typical teenage fashion—the quilt simply pulled up over the pillows.

"Neil," he called out as he sprinted back down the stairs. Turning on lights along the way, Nelson arrived in the kitchen and looked to see if Neil had left a note in their usual spot on the fridge. If Neil were planning to be out late or was spending the night at a friend's, he would have left a note. There was none.

He hurriedly called Neil's cell phone. It went directly to voice mail. The kitchen clock announced that it was nearly 1:00 AM. "Call me," he said, and then he stopped to catch his breath and plan his next move. Feeling weak in the knees, he inhaled deeply and asked himself, *Who might he have told about his plans?*

Grabbing his cell, he scrolled down to Brad Adams's home number and punched TALK. The phone rang five times before the recorded message came on. Simultaneously, a sleepy voice answered. Nelson waited a beat for the greeting to click off, then said, "This is Nelson Kennedy, Neil's dad. I apologize for calling so late, but Neil is not home and—"

"Hold on," said Brad's father. He called Brad's name, and Nelson heard the sound of movement followed by an exchange between Brad and his father. He couldn't hear each word, but he got the gist of the conversation. *Something about a girl . . . ?*

"Sorry," Mr. Adams said. "Brad said he hasn't seen Neil since the science club meeting yesterday." He cleared his throat. "I asked him if he knew Neil's plans for this evening, and he said all he knew was that Neil seemed excited over meeting some girl."

What girl? "Does Brad know where they were to meet? Or how he planned to get there?"

Again, he could hear the father's question but not the response.

"Sorry, Brad says he doesn't know."

Nelson apologized again for the lateness of the call and thanked him. His hands shook as he lowered himself into a chair at the kitchen table and reached for the landline. *Neil is a responsible kid. Something has happened. Something beyond his control. He could have been in an accident. Maybe I should call the hospital. But what hospital?* Not knowing where Neil might have gone, he had no idea where to begin. He had to call the police, but he'd read somewhere that with the multitude of domestic squabbles and all the runaways, it was unlikely they'd do anything if a kid had been missing for less than forty-eight hours. Still, he picked up the receiver.

Then another thought struck him: Rick had been hanging around lately. Setting the receiver back down, he scrolled through his cell phone contacts again until he came to Rick's number. It went directly to voice mail too. Neither his son nor his stepson was answering the phone. *Could they be together, or was it merely a coincidence?* He left the same brief message. Rick had no landline, which left Nelson with no choice.

He picked up the landline once more and called information to ask for a number: "Chicago PD, please."

The melodic tones of the penthouse suite's door chimes broke into the detectives' good-byes.

"That's bound to be Pocino," Conrad said. "He dropped in on Tony Wainwright just a while ago. Let's see if he uncovered anything."

Ashleigh sprang to her feet and headed across the foyer. Throwing open the door, she greeted Pocino.

The private investigator's gaze scanned the room. At the sight of the Chicago detectives, his bushy brows inched up toward his receding hairline.

"Ross," Ashleigh said, suppressing a yawn, "this is Detective Bob Senske and Detective Greg Murdock. They're with the Chicago PD."

"Good timing," Pocino said. He ambled across the room to shake their hands and then took over, saying to the detectives, "Take a seat, and I'll fill you in." Then he turned to Conrad and Ashleigh, who had sat back down on the sofa. "The boss managed to grab a seat on the red-eye. Be here first thing in the morning."

Conrad cut in. "Dick Landes was a homicide detective with LAPD before forming his own agency. They have offices in five major cities." Knowing that most police departments frowned on amateurs messing around with their cases, he also filled the detectives in on Pocino's background with the LAPD. "Officer Kowalski has the contact information of ranking officers in four separate police divisions where the credentials of both men can be checked."

Ashleigh had figured that Landes, CEO and founder of the Landes Agency, would fly in to lend his support. After all, he had a long-term relationship with the Taylors. They were almost like family. And since it was imperative to Callie's safe return that there be no friction among those working toward her release, she was relieved that Conrad had laid the groundwork for forming a cohesive team.

Although at first the detectives didn't seem particularly comfortable with Pocino's take-charge manner, neither voiced an objection. They listened attentively and took copious notes.

"That about sums it up," Pocino said.

"What's your gut feeling?" Detective Senske asked.

"Tony Wainwright is the proverbial bad seed, but we discovered long ago that he's nobody's fool. He appears to be alibied up for the time of the abduction." Pocino's hand drifted inside his sports coat to his left shirt pocket, which held a pack of Camels, before he dropped it to his side with a frown. "But I wouldn't rule him out just yet. First I'll check out his friends—all his connections here in the city."

"Mr. Taylor told us that Tony Wainwright works for Mike Christonelli," Senske said. "Do you—"

Vigorously shaking his head, Pocino interrupted. "I know where you're going with that line of thinking, but the wrong twin was snatched. Mike or Erica have no reason to take Callie. Plus, they would have to be nut jobs to plan—"

"I agree totally," Conrad cut in. "Why would they risk such a move? It's safe to rule them out."

Ashleigh nodded and changed the subject. *We have neither the time nor the energy to waste on a wild goose chase.* Instead, she asked, "Detective Senske, how soon will your computer team have some results?"

Marnie bolted upright in the unfamiliar queen-sized bed. Images of the man in the ski mask shoving her sister into the van had jolted her from a restless sleep—the same recurring nightmare that had woken her periodically throughout the night as if on automatic replay. *Except this nightmare is true.*

She rubbed her eyes with the index fingers of her closed fists. Her eyes couldn't have felt worse if someone had pitched a handful of sand into them. When she glanced across the room to Callie's unmade bed, she wanted to put the pillow over her head and just disappear.

Since she kept waking with a start, she knew she must have gotten some sleep, but not much. Throughout the night, when sleep evaded her, she'd heard her parents talking. They couldn't have had much rest either. She couldn't hear what they were saying and had not crept out of bed to listen. She didn't want to hear. They were probably talking about her. How it was all her fault that Callie had been taken. No matter what they said, she knew they wished it had been her who was taken and not Callie.

Don't go there, she told herself. She couldn't blame them, though. Suddenly her anger came full circle; she clenched her fists into tight balls and tried to curb it. *Why did Callie have to take off alone? Who does she think she is? She tells me it's dangerous to go without her, and then she . . .*

Covering her face with both hands, Marnie tried to shut off the voice in her head. But no sooner had she diverted those thoughts than others replaced them. *What about Brad? Who is he? Did he have anything to do with what happened last night?* In her gut, she knew he was a good person. Maybe those people in the van had nothing to do with Brad. She was sure the police were wrong when they'd said Brad might not even be a high school student. He knew too much about that scene to be faking it.

Maybe Brad really was at Starbucks when whoever was in the van took Callie. Maybe he'd waited for her and thought she stood him up. *Maybe he sent me another message last night.* If the police were tracing the messages he sent her, even if he had nothing to do with the people in the van, he would be in hot water.

She glanced at the blinking green light on her cell phone sitting on her bedside table. She guessed it was good that her phone had died last night, or she probably would've tried to call Callie. "If the kidnappers hear the phone, they'll take it from her," the lady police officer had warned.

Marnie prayed her sister was able to hide her phone so she could make a call when the kidnappers weren't around. *Please God, help Callie. I'll do anything. I promise I won't ditch Sunday school ever again. Just bring her home safe.*

Although she didn't feel tired, her eyes still hurt like crazy. But Marnie saw no point in staying in bed. She got up and grabbed the jeans she'd worn the night before, along with a clean tank top, and headed to the bathroom. But when she thought of the day's agenda, she stopped in her tracks. *I can't go and stay with Mom and Uncle Mike. Not until we get Callie back.*

Callie awoke squinting into the bright rays of sunlight filtering through the van's windows. Her whole world was unhinged. How could she have fallen asleep? *This is insane,* she thought.

Sliding her tongue across the roof of her dry mouth, she felt a dull ache in her head, and her stomach let out a low growl. She'd missed dinner the night before, and other than an energy bar right before their performance at De Mornay's, she'd had nothing else to eat since that ice cream at Millennium Park yesterday. She'd had nothing to drink, either—except that hot chocolate from the thermos here in the back of the van.

Clumsily lifting her tied wrists, she covered her eyes as best she could and tried to orient herself. She lay on one of the side benches, opposite the copper-haired boy, who appeared to be sleeping. The van was not moving.

Her heart beat a wild tattoo. It was morning. Her parents must be out of their minds with worry. Struggling to right herself, she looked down and saw that her ankles were no longer bound. *When did that happen?* She leaned forward, craning her neck to see into the front seat. No one.

Where are the creep and his girlfriend?

Pushing herself to her feet, she stretched her sore muscles, and her head grazed the ceiling of the van. She had no idea where she was. Were there any cell towers nearby for reception? She didn't know, but she had to try.

Callie turned her back to the dozing boy and slipped the phone from her bra. She shuffled to the rear of the van and peered out the windows on both sides and those at the top of the double doors. Still she saw no one. Through the passenger-side window, however, she saw an old cabin cruiser. It appeared to have been washed up on the riverbank and was now stuck in the mud.

The kidnappers. They have to be inside. She sucked in her breath, praying that they would stay there and that her cell phone would work. Holding the Razr close to her body to absorb any sound, she flicked open the cover. Nothing. She glanced down at the screen. *Zero bars.* She had no reception, yet she knew her battery was charged.

When she heard Brad yawn, she froze. Her hands trembled; she couldn't let him see that she had a phone. Burying it in the pouch of her sweatshirt, she turned back toward him and asked, "Do you know where we are?"

"What?" He sounded as disoriented as she felt. "Oh shit," he said, pushing himself up on his elbows. When his eyes met hers, he blinked. "Sorry."

Is he apologizing for his language? How lame. "I said—"

"I heard you." Awkwardly pushing himself to his feet, he leaned into the window. "Where are Rick and Sarah-Jayne?"

As if on cue, the van doors flew open. "Nice sleep, kiddies?" the creep asked with an amused grin.

Pure evil, thought Callie.

"So, how are Hansel and Gretel this morning?"

"What do you mean?" Brad asked.

Hansel and Gretel? What kind of game is he playing? Then it hit Callie: The hot chocolate they had drained from the thermos—it must have been drugged.

"Just like a house made of gingerbread, that hot chocolate was just too yummy to resist, wasn't it?" Rick gave a hearty laugh.

"Oh shit." His brother had finally caught on. "What did you put—"

"What's that old cliché your dad's so fond of?" He placed an index finger on his cheek. "Let's see. *Fool me once, shame on you. Fool me twice, I'm one hell of a dumb SOB.*"

"Cut it out. That's not funny. My head feels like it was run over by a six-wheeler."

"So sorry. Will Daddy's precious little straight-A student be okay?" Rick's face changed suddenly. "Now stop your sniffling and haul your ass out of there."

So that's why my feet are untied. Callie followed the boy, almost falling out the rear doors onto the marshlike ground. Without the use of her arms, her balance was off and her movement wobbly. The creep caught her, but not before the damage was done: Her cell had slipped into the mud—and with it, her hope of reaching out for help.

Neil's gaze shot down to his Nikes, where cold, yucky mud seeped in as they sank deeper into the marshy shore beside the boat. His socks were getting soggy, and he was starting to lose his cool.

"Move it," Rick commanded.

But Neil didn't budge. *I'm through being bullied. I got us into this, and it's up to me to get us out.* He'd come to know and care about Marnie. He was sorry that her twin had been caught in his sicko half-brother's web, but he was relieved that Marnie had escaped whatever unpredictable fate might lay ahead. Still, he had to do whatever he could—whatever it took—to keep her twin safe.

Taking in the splintered wooden plank that ran from the old boat to the soggy shore a few feet ahead, he surmised what Rick intended for his victims. The plank wasn't much over three feet wide, and even if Neil actually wanted to climb aboard that poor excuse for a boat, it would be an unreasonable challenge with his hands tied. "I'm not taking another step until you tell me what this is all about," he growled.

"You sure as hell are. And if you know what's good for you, you'd better do it now."

Neil saw the tight grip Rick had on the girl's arm and feared that beneath the sleeve of her sweatshirt she was bound to have a bone-deep bruise. "Let go of her. And untie our hands." This time Neil's voice did not waver.

Rick's glare held a boatload of anger and incredulity. He released Callie so suddenly that she tilted to the left and almost lost her balance. Flinging her bound wrists up and to the right, she saved herself from a tumble into the mud.

Rick's face turned scarlet. "You're not in charge, baby brother, so haul your ass on up that plank."

Neil thrust his hands toward his half-brother. "Cut the tape," he said, "and hers too." He gestured toward the rope that bound the girl's wrists.

"No way, José. And just where did this sudden gumption come from, anyway?" Before Neil could respond, Rick warned, "May turn out to be the death of you, bro." He withdrew a small gun from his pocket.

Neil knew nothing about guns, but this one looked like the close-up of one he'd seen on *CSI: Las Vegas* last week. What had they called it—a Smith & Wesson? That didn't mean much to him, but he was smart enough to know any kind of gun was a dangerous thing in Rick's hands.

"Now, get a move on." Rick gestured with the gun. If there had been even the slightest hint of warmth or openness in his expression before, it was gone now.

Neil was so scared, he thought he might wet his Levi's, but he held his ground. Surely Rick wouldn't shoot him. Still, it was all he could do to keep his knees from buckling. Ignoring the queasiness in his gut, he swallowed past the lump in his throat and concentrated on keeping his voice steady. "What are you planning to do, Rick?"

A voice called down from the rail of the boat. "What's taking so long?" Despite the chill in the air, Rick's girlfriend had changed into a pair of shorts and a shocking-pink top that was tied under her ample breasts, exposing a fair amount of white flesh.

Are they living on the boat? Neil wondered, and then he instantly dismissed the idea. There weren't enough sanitized wipes in the state of Illinois to keep Rick comfortable in this environment.

His eyes darted to Rick when the muzzle of the gun pressed into his ribs. "Cut that out," he said with more bravado than he felt. "You're gonna get caught if you try to collect any sort of ransom, you know. You'll never get away with this." Even to himself, he sounded like a scared teller in a bank robbery movie.

"That's not your concern. Don't worry your brainy little head about our safety. These are things they don't teach in school. Now, for the last time, walk on up that ramp."

Neil held his ground.

And then the gun fired.

The shot shattered the silence, echoing off the hull of the boat.

Callie nearly lost her tenuous balance once again when she saw the mud splash up around the younger boy's feet. "My God," she shouted. "You could have shot him in the foot."

"Could turn out he'll lose a lot worse than a foot if he doesn't trot on up that ramp PDQ," Rick snarled.

"What's wrong with you? He's your brother." Family members *shooting* each other? Callie could barely conceive of such a thing.

Her heart was racing like crazy. It had skipped a beat—or two or three—when her cell phone had fallen into the mud, but she had just bit down on her lip and remained quiet, hoping against hope that the creep wouldn't see it. He hadn't, and they'd kept marching on. She'd clamped her eyes shut and said a silent prayer: *Thank you, Lord.* No point in lamenting the loss; it could have been a lot worse.

Now, as the creep's hand wrapped around her arm just above the elbow in a viselike grip, a cold shiver crept up her spine. "*Half*-brother, dearie, but who the fuck cares?" Turning back to the boy, he said, "Ready to move now? Or do I need to make a real hole in the little lady's classy boots?"

The copper-haired boy bit down on his lip and kept his mouth shut as he pulled one Nike and then the other from the mud and onto the plank. As Callie watched, he held his bound wrists out in front of him and climbed precariously up the ramp. At the top, the girl took hold of his elbow and pulled him forward.

"Your turn," the creep said to Callie, waving the gun in the direction of the plank.

She wanted to resist but knew better. Now was not the time to put her plan in motion. "Okay," she said, making her voice quaver. Her boots had sunk deep into the mud, though, and she had trouble lifting them.

"No more stalling," Rick roared.

Callie had never been this scared before, but she still couldn't seem to bring tears to her eyes. "I'm trying," she whined, hanging her head. "I'm trying real hard, but my boots are stuck." Her voice broke, as if with a sob. She hoped the creep would not see that her eyes were dry.

He shoved his gun into the waistband of his Levi's, leaned down, and tugged at the top of one of Callie's boots until it splashed out of the mud with the sound of a toilet plunger. She placed her foot on a large stone nearby that was just breaking the surface of the water. While the creep pulled on the second boot, her eyes rested on the gun. *If only I had both hands.* Although she'd never held a gun, she would have tried to grab it—if she had a prayer of being successful. She didn't.

When the creep took hold of her elbow again, she wanted to recoil, but without his steadying hand, she'd fall. With her right boot balanced on the stone, she placed her left foot on the plank. And with a boost from her abductor, she was able to bring her right foot onto the plank as well. The rise was gradual, but she didn't dare take a breath or think of anything other than putting one muddy boot in front of the other, all the while praying she didn't slip or lose her balance.

At the opening along the boat rail, the girlfriend pulled her roughly forward. Involuntarily, Callie let out a sharp cry, fearing she was about to lose her balance once again and crash onto the deck.

"Sorry, princess," the girl said in a dull voice without a hint of sincerity. Her eyes drifted down to Callie's muddy boots. Leaning in close, she said, "Nice Uggs. What size do you wear?"

"Holy fucking crap," the thin man spat out. "You couldn't get your big toe in them boots. Now let's get *the children* down below."

The boy had already started down the companionway. Rick's girlfriend followed a few steps behind. Callie stared down at the four narrow steps to the cabin, and then slowly and carefully made her way down, keeping her eyes on the large butterfly tattoo visible at the base of Sarah-Jayne's neck. In the cabin, the stench of mold assaulted her nostrils. But what really repulsed her was looking up to see the look of pure malevolence on the creep's face as he slowly pulled on a large pair of gloves.

Mike Christonelli grabbed the phone with one hand while filling his and Erica's coffee mugs with the other. Hot coffee ran over the top of one of the mugs, over the lip of the counter, and down onto the floor.

"Watch it." Erica grabbed the pot from his hand. When she looked up, she saw that her brother-in-law's face was ashen and the hand holding the phone shook.

"When? . . . Marnie? . . . I don't understand . . . Is she alright? . . . Why the hell was she wandering around in downtown Chicago at night by herself?"

Erica's blood turned icy cold.

"You're not coming in?" Mike shouted. "I don't think so. The deadline for the Honda account is looming over our heads. If you value your job, you'll get over here pronto." Mike slammed down the phone and turned to Erica. "Marnie's fine," he said right away to alleviate her anxiety. "It's Callie. She's been kidnapped."

Erica leaned against the kitchen counter for support. *Oh God, how I could use something a bit stronger than coffee,* she thought as Mike finished filling her in.

Her brother-in-law wrapped his arm around her shoulder. "Thank God, it wasn't Marnie."

With her elbows resting on the tiled counter, Erica dropped her head into her hands. That had been her exact thought. "Why did Tony say he wasn't coming in to work?"

"Some double-talk about having to find Callie." Mike's expression was grim.

"Mike, what can we do? I can't imagine what hell Ashleigh and Conrad must be going through. How could this have happened? They're good people. They sure as hell don't deserve this."

Still, she wondered why the Taylors hadn't called to let them know. Something occurred to her then. "Do you think they will still let Marnie stay with us?" she asked. She felt the blood drain from her face and climbed up on the bar stool, afraid her legs wouldn't hold her. "They couldn't possibly suspect *us*, could they?" Even as that thought floated through her head, though, she knew it was ludicrous. *What motive would* we *have for abducting Callie?*

Mike shook his head. "But Tony is sure to be a suspect. I hope to hell he isn't involved."

Erica picked up the phone, realizing that there was one thing she needed right now, even more than a strong drink: to hear Nelson's reassuring voice.

"You look fantastic, Mom."

Helen grinned from one rosy cheek to the other as she slipped her arm through their limo driver's. "I missed most of your growing up, dear, and even April's baby years, so I'm relishing every celebration with my grown-up granddaughter as she starts a life of her own."

Paige smiled. "We'll meet you down at the car in just a few minutes."

As Helen departed on the limo driver's arm, Paige quickly checked the mantel clock. She had just enough time to give Ashleigh a quick call and confirm their seven thirty reservations at Keefer's that evening.

The phone was answered after the second ring. "Hello. This is Conrad Taylor."

Paige blinked. Conrad's deep baritone was unmistakable, but the unfamiliar formality seemed out of place. She ignored it. *Perhaps he's expecting a business call.* "Well, good morning, I hope," she said with a smile in her voice. "We're just heading off for breakfast with the lovebirds, but I'd like a quick word with Ashleigh if she's nearby."

"She is, Paige. But please call her cell. I'm sorry," he said flatly.

And Paige found herself listening to a dial tone.

Slipping into his blazer, Mark turned toward her. "Ready?" Catching her odd expression, he asked, "What's wrong?"

"I'm not sure, but something sure is out of kilter." She picked up her Coach handbag and began fishing for her cell phone as she headed for the door. She relayed her strange mini-conversation with Conrad.

Mark's brows furrowed. "He just hung up?"

Paige nodded, her ear to the receiver, as she heard Ashleigh's cell phone begin to ring.

Ashleigh picked up immediately.

Although more than a little curious, Paige didn't want to begin their conversation on the wrong foot. "Good morning. We're on our way to see the kids' apartment, but I wanted to update you on our dinner—"

"Paige," Ashleigh cut in, "we won't make it for dinner." There was a drawn-out silence. Ashleigh stammered, as if struggling to find her voice.

Paige waited, not daring to breathe. *Something is very wrong.*

Finally Ashleigh's words tumbled out. "It's Callie. She's been kidnapped."

Paige gasped at the devastating news. She felt as though she were watching footage of the second plane crashing into the World Trade Center all over again.

Nelson sat on the edge of his seat. He had trouble wrapping his mind around the drama playing out in both his life and Erica's, but he waited patiently as Erica poured out her anxiety over the phone. It was all too much. *How can I tell her that Neil is also missing?*

He had yet to hear a word from the Chicago PD. They had made it clear that a teenager missing for less than twenty-four hours could not be high priority, yet Nelson knew something was very wrong. Neil was no runaway, and now learning that Marnie's twin was also missing, he wondered if that could somehow be related.

He immediately dismissed the idea. Neil and Callie didn't even know each other. The only common link was Erica, and she certainly had nothing to do with either the twin's abduction or Neil's going missing. He suspected Rick was behind Neil's failure to come home, but his stepson had no connection to the Taylor twin either.

Nelson had been berating himself since the police had left last night or, more precisely, in the wee hours of the morning. He was well aware they didn't believe him when he said he did not have Rick's address, but that was the God's honest truth. All he had was Rick's cell number. He and his stepson had never been what you might call close. All Nelson could tell the police was that Rick was sharing an apartment somewhere in Cicero with a girl he'd met the last time he'd been released from jail after doing nine months for selling drugs.

The police hadn't even tried to pick up a beat on Neil's cell phone, and Nelson was pretty sure they weren't going to do much of anything to track him down. Not unless Neil failed to show up in the next couple of days. Nelson had no intention of waiting for the police to take action; it would be up to him to find his son.

When at last he was able to tell Erica that Neil hadn't been home when he arrived last night, he heard the intake of her breath through the phone line. "Nelson," she said, her voice high-pitched, "what is going on? The whole damn world is falling apart." She broke into sobs. "I can't take it. I just can't take it." After a few very long moments, she seemed to get a grip on her emotions and said, "What did the police have to say?"

Before Nelson could reply, he heard someone pounding on the front door. Whoever it was hadn't bothered to try the bell. Someone was hammering against the plate of the antique knocker as if his or her life depended on it.

CHAPTER
75

What's with her? Rick wondered. *She's looking at me like I plan to eat her for lunch.* Then he looked down and saw that Callie's eyes, the size of silver dollars, were focused on his gloved hands. *Good. Having that kid scared out of her mind is just where I want her.* Now that the short spark of spirit he'd seen in her earlier had dissipated, he had to admit she was far less interesting. And yet he could do without another kick in the shin. His right leg still smarted from the kick the little bitch had delivered before being thrown inside the van.

Although Sarah-Jayne said she had wiped down the handrails, Rick wasn't about to touch it or any other surface on this decaying old tub. He detested the feel of unclean hands—even for a minute. Now the gloves had an added benefit: They made him seem weird and creepy, thus keeping the cute teenager in line.

The boat stunk to high heaven, but there wasn't a whole lot Rick could do about that right now. Sarah-Jayne had scrubbed down the walls and flat surfaces with Lysol, and they'd gone through three aerosol cans of air freshener, but it still had that foul odor of rot. He decided he'd get a few more cans of air freshener when he went to the store. If only he didn't have to leave those kids with Sarah-Jayne. But it couldn't be helped. She had screwed up his timing by not checking the batteries for the cassette player. He had no choice but to go into the small town, back before the turnoff onto the dirt road that ran alongside the river inlet. Sarah-Jayne had offered to go, but he trusted no one but himself.

He double-checked the latches he'd installed on the doors of the front and rear cabins, and then he turned to Sarah-Jayne. "Keep their hands tied and lock them inside," he ordered. "You'd better separate them too.

I've got to run. I'll be back within the hour. I want this tape in the bag and delivered to Big Daddy before nightfall."

Callie heard the creep mumble something about "Big Daddy" to the girl, who then followed him outside to the main deck. For some reason, Rick's calling the two of them Hansel and Gretel flashed across her mind. If only she and the boy had been able to leave a trail to the boat.

It was a nice thought—until reality seeped in. That was a fairy tale. There was no way to leave a trail of bread crumbs or even stones. And now she didn't have her cell phone either. Even if it hadn't been shorted out in the mud and water, there was no way she could get to it. She remembered what had happened to her first cell phone when she was in middle school. Her parents were baffled as to how she'd managed to drop it into her milk glass, but somehow she had, and the battery had been ruined.

Enough. As if suddenly emerging from a fog, she found her thoughts shifting from fairy tales and silly memories to a plan of escape.

"Oh God, Erica, I hate to cut you off at a time like this, but someone's about to pound my door down. Could be the police about Neil," he said. "Promise I'll call you back right away."

As he hung up the receiver, he heard her say something, but it was a fraction of a second too late. The connection was severed. Dashing across the room, he flung open the door and was greeted by a well-groomed man in gray trousers and a blue blazer, and a tall, portly man looking like an unmade bed.

The first man flashed his badge. "I'm Detective Bob Senske. I work with the forensics lab," he said. "And this is—"

"Forensics?" Nelson said. His heart leaped into his throat.

"Computer forensics," the detective clarified, and then introduced the man beside him as private investigator Ross Pocino. "May we come in?'

Nelson stepped back. *What are "computer forensics"? Why are detectives involved?* he wondered as he recalled the police officers he had spoken to in his living room earlier that morning. "Have you heard anything about my son?"

"Excuse me," Senske said, "we are here to *get* information about your son." He seemed to emphasize the word *get* as he took a small spiral notebook from his shirt pocket. "Neil Kennedy?"

"Yes. When I talked to the police officers last night—"

"Hold on," Detective Senske cut in. "You talked to police officers *last night?*"

The burly PI rocked back on his heels. He appeared to be having a tough time keeping his cool.

Nelson filled them in on his son's disappearance and his conversation with the two Chicago PD officers. "So, if you didn't know about my reporting Neil as missing . . . what are you doing here?"

Nodding in Kennedy's direction, Pocino said, "Bob, you mind?"

The detective nodded his approval.

"What do you know of your son's extracurricular activities, Mr. Kennedy? More to the point, what do you know about his online hookups?"

"What are you getting at? Neil is an honors student. Has a three point nine three average," Kennedy said with pride. "He doesn't have much time for fooling around on the computer, other than for schoolwork. He also has a part-time job and helps a friend of mine at the university. And has been assisting me with research for my book on architecture."

"You're telling us your son has no account on Myspace?"

Kennedy shrugged. "If he does, he sure doesn't spend much time on it." He glared. "Goddamnit, my son, who is as decent as they come, is missing, and you're here wasting our time with his online activities, which I'm sure are ninety-eight percent related to schoolwork and research. What you *should* be doing is using your manpower to *find* him."

Senske gave Pocino a meaningful look. "Hold on, Mr. Kennedy. You are obviously out of the loop, so let me bring you into focus. Our tech squad has been working for the past several hours and was able to trace messages over the past three months from a cyber café to a high school girl in the New York area. They had no lead on the user until they went back to the onset of their communication."

"A girl in New York? What does that have to do with my son?"

"Hold on," Senske repeated. "Do you know a Brad Adams?"

Nelson ran his hand over his nearly bald pate and nodded. "Sure, he's Neil's best friend. I called his house last night when I found that my son wasn't home." He scowled. "Where are you going with this? Brad told his dad that he hadn't seen—"

Pocino could not hold his tongue. "Look, Kennedy. Maybe you know what's going on. Maybe not. But Detective Senske and I just came from the Adams house. We talked to the father and then to Brad about these messages, and he told us *your son* was on his computer when he first connected with the girl. Neil is the one who sent a message from Brad's e-mail account."

Kennedy shrugged. "Okay, so he was sending messages to some girl in New York. So?"

"*So* . . . that girl was abducted on State Street last night," Pocino said. "The plot is thickening. We've not only traced messages from your son to the girl, but now you tell us it just so happens your son didn't come home last night and you have no idea where he is."

Kennedy's face turned the color of porcelain. He sank down onto the armchair, gesturing for the two men to be seated. In a voice barely audible, he asked, "What . . ." He swallowed hard and asked the question he feared he'd already answered in his head. "What . . . is the girl's name?"

CHAPTER
76

Mark noticed that his wife's face had turned ashen and her hand shook as she dropped her cell phone back into her handbag.

As usual, Helen had hopped into the limo in the front seat beside the driver. Mark and Paige no longer objected. As long as the driver didn't mind, there was no harm done, and Helen got such pleasure out of chatting with the young man behind the wheel.

Mark waited until Paige slipped in and fastened her seat belt before he spoke. He'd heard only part of the conversation, but there was no doubt something was terribly wrong. Taking Paige's hand, he asked, "What's going on?" He kept his voice low.

Paige responded in a whisper.

He listened intently without interruption. At last, incredulous, he asked, "Last night?" Not waiting for a response, he continued, "We must keep your mom out of the loop until we know more, but April and Kyle—"

"Mark. Of course we won't say anything to Mom, but April is no longer a child. She would be hurt if she were to find out from anyone other than us."

He nodded. "The thought of keeping this from April hadn't entered my mind. Besides, she has ready access to breaking news now. All hell would break loose if she were to discover that we'd withheld even a scrap of information from her."

Paige reached up and gently touched his right cheek, where the familiar tic in his eyelid signaled his intense agitation.

"But that's beside the point," Mark continued. "What I was thinking is that she and Kyle could facilitate immediate air time." Then he switched gears. "We'll have breakfast, make the appropriate noises about the apartment—"

"I'll keep Mom occupied while you take April and Kyle aside. Mark, I'd like to get back to the hotel as soon as possible to be with Ashleigh." After a thoughtful pause, Paige added, "And since April and Kyle had planned to be with Mom tonight during dinner, they can bring her back to the hotel later. I'm not sure about Elizabeth and Marnie and Juliana. They were supposed to visit with the Christonellis . . ."

As Paige spoke, Mark's thoughts shot ahead. He hadn't heard much of what she'd said; his mind was elsewhere. "I must call Conrad without delay. The FBI and the Chicago PD will already be on board, and Conrad is sure to enlist the expertise of Landes and Pocino, but broadcasting an alert to everyone in the vicinity—"

"Do you think that's what they'll want?"

"Not for sure. Law enforcement might have other ideas. I don't intend to interfere; I just want to let our friends know we'll help in any way we can. That's why I need to call Conrad now."

A decade before, he and Paige had seen the film *Ransom*, with Mel Gibson and Rene Russo, and the outcome—with the kidnapped son home, safe and sound—flashed through his mind now. For a family like the Taylors, there was bound to be a ransom demand. And whether they chose to pay it or not, Mark prayed that the Taylors would have their own happy ending.

Not waiting for the driver to come around to open her door, Helen unbuckled her seat belt, pushed open the door, and scurried out of the limo.

April stood beside Kyle, grinning, and then dashed down the stairs leading to their apartment. She took her grandmother's hand and ushered the three of them in. Paige and Helen followed April into the living room, but Mark excused himself, pulling out his phone as he stepped back toward the front door.

The apartment was small and sparsely furnished, but quite nice. Paige wondered if the young couple would replace some of the furniture with pieces from April's apartment. Fiercely independent since graduating from UCLA, April had prided herself on her ability to live on a budget— within her current means. She had always been drawn to quality over quantity, so she didn't turn down the wholesale prices her parents were privy to for buying home furnishings and clothing. And yet, Paige knew, April wasn't about material things. She valued people, not things, and loved to help the underprivileged. As a child, she had accompanied Paige on monthly and holiday outings to help feed the homeless. While a young newsroom intern did not have much extra cash, she gave generously of the time she could spare.

Paige smiled as she eyed the breakfast table in the tiny kitchen. While the fifth plate setting did not match the others, the five placemats appeared to be new, and Paige noticed that April was making use of the napkins they had brought from Denmark. *She may not have much to call her own just yet, but she will in her own time.* Looking at April and Kyle, no one could miss the special love and respect they had for each other.

Suddenly, it occurred to Paige that she had much to be thankful for.

After his call to Conrad, Mark snapped his cell phone shut; his course of action was clear. Catching his wife's gaze, he nodded before addressing his daughter and her fiancé.

Paige read his gaze, smiled, said a few words to her mother, and then escorted her out onto the small apartment balcony to see the hummingbird fluttering above the flowers.

April wore a puzzled expression. "What is it, Dad?"

He filled them in on the kidnapping and gave them a brief moment to absorb the shocking news. "We'll head to the Taylors' suite later today and do what we can to support them." But the time for action was now, so he didn't wait long before asking, "How quickly can you orchestrate a breaking news segment?"

Nelson forced himself to reach for the phone. For the last ten minutes, he'd rehearsed what he would say. He knew procrastinating wouldn't make this call any easier; he might as well get it behind him, even though it could mark the end of the relationship he'd hoped to build with Erica.

His unsteady hand punched in her number.

"Nelson?" Her tone was hesitant.

Did she know about Neil? If so, he would find out now. "Any news?"

"Only that Marnie has been communicating with some kind of predator online. It's a miracle *she* wasn't the one kidnapped." She gasped. "I can't believe I said that. It's a tragedy either way. Oh, how could all this have happened?"

Nelson's heart crashed against his rib cage. "Erica, I must talk with you." His well-rehearsed words could not be delivered over the phone, he realized. "I'll be right over."

He hung up quickly, not giving her a chance to ask questions or protest. In his heart he knew that what he'd told the investigators was true: Neil had become an innocent pawn in his warped half-brother's scheme, whatever that might be. With a jolt, he suddenly realized Neil's life might be in danger. *Rick's motive for abducting the girl must be ransom, but what are his plans for Neil?*

Sarah-Jayne exhaled a ring of smoke, then set the joint on the rim of the ashtray, eyeing the two kids, who sat stoically with their bound hands resting awkwardly in their laps. She felt good, but she desperately needed a little bit of sleep; her eyes were bloodshot and sore as blazes. She stared at the cushioned bench that surrounded the salon table in a horseshoe shape. *It looks uncomfortable as hell.* There was no way she could stretch out.

Rick had said to separate the two kids, but what did it matter? If she locked them both in the aft cabin, she could sack out in the V berth of the forward cabin. All she had to do was make sure the hook was securely in place on the outside of the door. With their hands tied, neither the spoiled little rich kid nor Rick's nerdy brother would have a chance of getting away. *Besides, where would they go?* she said to herself.

Sarah-Jayne stood, not all that steady on her feet, and snarled, "Stand up, and move to the back of the boat."

"Why are you doing this, Sarah-Jayne?" Neil asked. "It's all wrong. You'll never get away with it."

"Shut up, Neil," Sarah-Jayne said, shortening the distance between them.

The girl's enormous doe eyes bore into hers. "It's about ransom, isn't it?"

"What do *you* think?" Sarah-Jayne wondered what was going on in the girl's head. The little bitch had no fucking idea what the real world was like—a world without Big Daddy's bottomless pit of money. She no longer felt squeamish; if the girl or Neil got hurt in the process, so be it. Rick was right: He and Sarah-Jayne needed this. And if they didn't silence these pampered kids, they took a chance of being ratted out to the police. "If you know what's good for you, you'll start moving."

She pulled the gun from the pocket of her shorts.

Callie leaned forward and rose at once, as did Neil. *That must be his real name.* Confronted with Sarah-Jayne's malevolent glare, all thoughts, other than those of her immediate peril, vanished. In a way, this nutso was more frightening than the creep. He seemed more or less indifferent; his girlfriend, on the other hand, glowered at her with pure hatred. But why? She had seemed nervous earlier; maybe the drug she was smoking had given her false courage. Maybe her hatred was not personal but a result of her own issues. Maybe it was aimed at what Sarah-Jayne perceived as Callie's life of privilege. After all, she had been truly impressed by something as simple as Callie's boots.

Callie followed Neil to the back of the derelict boat and stepped over the raised threshold into the aft cabin. To her left she saw there were bunk beds, but the one on the bottom was a double bed; only the one on top was a single. On her right there was a built-in dresser, and on the floor in front of it, to Callie's horror, a metal chamber pot.

Thinking fast, and using as meek a voice as she could muster, she looked to Sarah-Jayne and said, "Could I please use the bathroom—uh, the head—before you lock us in here?"

Sarah-Jayne's eyes swept the room. "What? You don't like your accommodations, princess?"

After Callie returned to the cabin, Neil was allowed to use the smelly, claustrophobic head. He was quick about it; this was no time to annoy Sarah-Jayne, who had finally given in to their requests.

But evidently he hadn't moved quickly enough. As he stepped over the threshold, Sarah-Jayne grabbed the gun by the barrel and swung it across her body, striking him with the butt of the pistol. It slammed into the flesh just above his right knee. He fell sideways into the cabin, and his glasses slid down to the edge of his nose.

Callie knelt down beside him, awkwardly extending her tied hands. "Are you okay?" she asked. Her eyes traveled up to meet Sarah-Jayne's, but the older girl only shoved Neil further into the cabin with her bare foot.

"I'm okay," he said, pushing himself upright.

The door slammed shut, and he heard metal against metal and knew his brother's girlfriend was latching the door.

Callie sat down on the lower bunk, her posture rigid. "Okay, Neil," she said through clenched teeth. "I have a lot of questions for you."

"You *are* Callie, right?" he asked. His knee felt as if it were on fire, pierced by a thousand hot needles. He clumsily removed his glasses and wiped them with the hem of his sweatshirt.

"Yes." She pursed her lips. "You arranged to have the wrong twin kidnapped. Although maybe that doesn't really matter."

His stomach churned, and he felt heat rise to his neck and face. "I knew nothing about this, I swear."

She rolled her eyes while shifting her body to a more comfortable position. "Are you—were you—Brad?"

He nodded. "I used that name. At first it was by accident. But let me explain."

Callie awkwardly swiped the hair out of her eyes with her hands. "An *accident*? You *accidentally* made up a false name?"

"No. I mean . . . The first time I found Marnie on Myspace, I was at my friend Brad's computer. So when I sent her the first e-mail, I was logged in under his name. She assumed it was mine and called me Brad."

"How convenient. So you just kept calling yourself Brad."

Neil sank down on the lower bunk and opened his mouth to reply. But every explanation that came to mind just made him sound naïve and stupid. So he just sat there, wondering—as he had since this nightmare began—just how he could possibly explain.

Callie tried to get hold of her anger and listen to Neil's lame explanation, but she wasn't sure she could trust him. And yet she couldn't afford to alienate him. Her mind was bent on finding a way to escape, and he might be part of the solution.

". . . so when I found out about Marnie, I wanted to know more about her adoptive mom."

"Hold on, Neil. Erica Christonelli is *not* Marnie's adoptive mom. If it weren't for my parents—I mean *our parents*—Erica would have gone to jail for—"

"I know," Neil cut in. "That's why I wanted to find out as much about her as I could."

Callie's head was spinning. "Let me get this straight. You said your dad is in a relationship with Erica, and it's getting serious."

Neil nodded. "I wanted—"

"Hang on. You also said your dad has serious health issues, so when you heard of Erica's background, you were worried she would cause him too much stress. But just how did getting to know Marnie fit in?"

Neil tried to explain that at first he only wanted to find out what kind of woman Erica was.

Callie cut in. "Well, it's true that Erica didn't know that her husband—"

"I know. The whole story is splashed in the news—it's all over the Internet. Marnie and I didn't talk much about that, but I know how she feels about her . . ." Abruptly changing the subject, he said, "What I found out about Marnie is, we have a lot in common."

"Such as?" Then, answering her own question, Callie said, "Oh, the writing thing?" Knowing why Neil had reached out to Marnie, she felt some of the tension slip away. *He seems to really care about my sister,* she thought, but aware of precious time slipping by, she forced herself to cut to the chase. "So you're telling me you had no idea what your brother was planning when you asked Marnie to sneak out and meet you last night?"

Flinging his taped wrists in the air, Neil said, "What do you think?"

"If you weren't a partner in your brother's plan, how did he—"

"I was stupid. Okay? I should have known I couldn't trust Rick. He never took any interest in anything I did before—only made fun of me. For as long as I can remember. He started calling me 'Four Eyes' while I was still in preschool." He paused, a thoughtful expression on his face. When he spoke again, his voice was just a whisper. "Mom didn't think it was any big deal, but—"

Not knowing how much more time they might have, Callie interrupted his trip back to childhood. "So how did he know my sister was planning to meet you last night?"

At first Neil seemed to be ignoring her question. "I thought Rick had changed," he went on. "He was finally taking an interest in what I was doing. He started acting more like a . . . a big brother. Asking how I was doing on the story for the competition. But now I . . . It wasn't the story that interested him. After I told him about finding Marnie online—"

"He knew who Marnie was?"

"Well, I told him. And here in Chicago, your dad often makes the headlines. Your family history is not exactly hard to come by."

Callie's mouth went dry.

"Rick began coming over more often. I have a learner's permit, but I still have another month to go before I get a driver's—"

"Please just tell—"

Neil frowned and continued his explanation. "Rick started letting me practice driving his car. He would drive me to my friends' when Dad was busy. When I found out Marnie was coming to Chicago, I told Rick I wanted to meet her in person before telling Dad we'd hooked up online. Rick said that was smart. He told me to arrange a time and he'd take me. He was supposed to drop me off at Starbucks and come back for me in an hour." He took off his glasses and rubbed his right eye. "I can't believe I was so gullible. I should've known better." Shaking his head, he murmured, "He's given my dad a hard time since he was a kid. Once he even shot a man."

Callie opened her mouth to speak, but no words formed. The boat had given a sudden lurch, and she heard a *thud* on the deck, close to the cabin window. Springing to her feet and peering out the window, she saw nothing but bright sunlight. But in the next instant she heard the heavy tread of feet and Rick's voice hollering, "Sarah-Jayne. Sarah-Jayne."

There was no answer.

Rick stopped dead in his tracks when he found the salon empty. *Where is she?*

He felt a knot in his chest and called her name again. When he saw that the forward cabin door was unlocked, his heart began to race. He dashed across the salon to the partially closed door and flung it open with more force than he'd intended. The door banged off the wall and the boat rocked.

His temper rose to boiling when he spotted Sarah-Jayne in the forward cabin and heard her soft snores. Jerking her to a sitting position, he said through tight lips, "What the fuck are you thinking?"

Looking confused, she began pulling her arm away from his grip. "Huh?" Then her bloodshot eyes widened. "Rick," she said. "Sorry, baby. Guess I fell asleep."

He wanted to strangle her. *After all this planning . . .*

He turned her loose. "Where are the kids?"

"Don't worry. They're aft. I locked the door."

His heart rate slowed a tick, but his temper failed to follow. "I told you to separate them."

"But Rick, I don't feel so hot. I had to lay down. They can't get away."

"But they *can* put their heads together and cook up some cockeyed escape plan," he said, although he knew that was damn near impossible. *Even if they could figure out where they are, there's nowhere to* go—*especially without a car.* "Now you've given them enough time to—"

"Ah, baby," Sarah-Jayne said as she pushed herself to her feet and moved toward him. "I didn't take any chances, I swear. Even if they could use their hands, there's no way they could unlock the door from the inside."

Taking a step back, he reached for a wipe and repeated, "I told you to keep them separated." His eyes were like a laser on hers. "You ever hear the phrase 'divide and conquer'?" He paused. "Forget it. Let's get the girl. I want to deliver the tape this afternoon."

Neil heard anger in his brother's booming voice. *That's good,* he thought. He couldn't make out every word, but he sensed there was trouble brewing. *Rick is so bullheaded, he won't listen to reason. But if he pisses off Sarah-Jayne* . . .

Callie sat down stiffly on the edge of the double bed, her dark eyes intense as she stared at the locked door.

Beside her, Neil whispered, "I think I have a plan."

"If your plan includes making an ally of Sarah-Jayne," she said, as if reading his mind, "that may work for you, but it won't for me. She hates my guts."

He wanted to argue—to tell her she was wrong—but he could not. Every word Rick's strung-out girlfriend spoke to Callie had been venomous, her jealousy undisguised.

Neil glanced down at Callie's wrists. They looked raw, and a trickle of blood ran from her right wrist to the ribbed cuff of her sweatshirt sleeve. A thought hit him suddenly, squarely, where it hurt the most: *She doesn't trust me.*

Heavy footfalls were making their way to the cabin door, cutting off further contemplation. He fell back onto the mattress and rolled onto his side. He needed time to clear his mind. It would be best if he appeared to be asleep.

Noting Neil's ploy, Callie considered following suit, but she immediately dismissed the idea. She had to act—and soon. *I must find a way to escape.*

A phrase drifted into her thoughts, one she'd often heard her dad say: *Information is power.* She had to find out exactly what her captors had in mind. Her parents were no doubt searching for her, with the help of Pocino and others—the police and maybe even the FBI. But they might never find her here. At least, not in time. The only helping hands she could rely on were her own.

She'd had only a few minutes to look around the area, but she'd memorized everything she'd seen between being marched from the van and taken aboard the rotting old tub. All she'd been able to see was that the boat had settled against a steep embankment along a marshy shore, surrounded by dirt, tall grass, and shrubbery. The embankment would not be easy to climb, but she had strong legs and did not intend to linger here a moment longer than she had to. Once she got free, she would not be defeated.

The rattle of the door lock brought her back to the present, sending a shiver of ice up her spine. But she was prepared.

The door flew open and the creep stepped inside. His girlfriend was on his heels.

Callie waited.

Rick crossed the aft cabin to the bunk bed and shook his brother. "I know you're not asleep. Don't try any bullshit on me." Then, turning to Sarah-Jayne, he said, "Take him to the V berth."

Neil rubbed his eyes as if he'd actually been asleep, but he didn't say a single word as he rolled to his side and off the bunk. When he tried to stand, he winced and clutched his knee.

The creep gave specific orders to his girlfriend. "Lock him up in the bow, and haul yourself back here ASAP so I know you've done it."

Callie saw that he held a plastic bag and a sheet of paper in one hand; in the other was a small tape recorder. She knew exactly what was coming next. As he dumped the batteries from the bag onto the dresser, then loaded them into the cassette player, her mind spun. *If only there was a way I could let Mom and Dad know where I am.* But even if *she* knew where they were, how could she get that information across to them in the recorded message? She'd seen enough movies and TV shows to know that kidnappers never allowed their victims that kind of opportunity. The creep would have her read a prepared statement. About the only way law enforcement got a break was if there were some sort of identifying sound—a foghorn, the sound of a train rumbling down the tracks . . . But there was nothing here. It was deadly quiet.

The creep sat down on the bottom bunk, unwrapped another towelette, and scrubbed his hands. Then he wiped off the tape recorder and began talking into it: "Testing: one, two, three." He stopped the tape, rewound it, and played it back: *Testing: one, two, three.* He rewound it again and looked down as if scanning the sheet of paper.

Callie wondered what was on the paper. *What is he going to make me say?* If there was any way to send her parents a message, she'd have to find it.

"What kept you?" Rick said, his tone filled with suspicion and irritation.

"What?" Sarah-Jayne said as she tripped over the threshold. She reached out and caught hold of the doorjamb in time to right herself.

"I said . . . Shit, you know what I said."

"I was just . . . I just locked your brother in the front cabin."

"And had a little chat," he sneered. The last thing he needed was for Sarah-Jayne to go soft on him.

"No." Her pale face turned an ugly shade of red.

She's lying through her teeth. "Don't try to play me, bitch."

Sarah-Jayne looked startled. "No, Rick, I . . . I just locked him in and came back here, like you said." Then her pale eyes met his, and she bit down on her bottom lip and set her jaw. "Hey, don't talk to me like that."

"Okay, okay." He raised his hand in the air, palm out. The last thing he needed was a mutiny. Anyway, she might be a bit soft on his nerdy brother, but there was no chance of her easing up on the little rich girl. Still, the whole package had to be kept intact. His brother could seriously screw things up. Just having him here was a liability. The instant his stepfather discovered Neil had not come home the night before, he was sure to call the police. *And dear old stepdad will point the finger straight at me.*

If only there had been a way to get the girl without involving Neil. But there had been no way around it, so now it was imperative that this go down quickly. There was just this small window of time. The payoff had to be tomorrow.

Callie had not uttered a single syllable since the creep and his girlfriend entered the cabin, but she'd been tuned in to every sound, every word they'd uttered. Her mind was on full alert. Sarah-Jayne's loathing for her was raw and unconcealed, but now it seemed that she and the creep were falling out. Maybe she could coax him to drop his guard and untie her wrists.

Curb your temper, she told herself, fully aware that her best chance was to continue playing the meek, scared little girl. *No problem there.* As much as she longed to give these lowlifes a piece of her mind, that wouldn't be smart. Her captors could care less that they'd turned her world upside down, that they were terrorizing all the people who loved her. But expressing her true feelings now could get her seriously hurt. It could even get her killed.

"Wait in the salon till we're done," the creep said to his girlfriend. "And shut the door behind you."

"But—" Sarah-Jayne started to object, but the look on his face seemed to change her mind. The boat rocked again as she retreated into the main cabin, slamming the door behind her.

Rick turned to lock eyes with Callie. It was a few long seconds before he spoke. "You haven't said one fucking word since I walked in. Well, baby, you're gonna talk now. It's showtime." He handed her the paper he'd been studying.

It would do no good to protest, so she steeled herself and tried to sound subservient. "Okay, Rick. But first, would you please untie my hands? I really have to use the bathroom and—"

"Shit," he said, throwing up his hands. "Can't you wait?"

"I'm sorry, but I really can't."

"Okay. But make it fast."

She held out her hands. "Please," she said, her voice soft and trembling.

He frowned. "Go ahead. There's no need to untie your hands."

Callie did not move. *I've got to get these ropes off.* "Please, Rick," she pleaded. "They really hurt and—"

"Now ain't that too bad. The ropes are hurting the little princess's wrists." He paused to take in the raw, bloody skin around the ropes. "Well, I'll be damned. You've been trying to wiggle out of them bracelets." He gave an awful grin. "No such luck. When I tie a knot, it's tied to stay tied."

She didn't want him to lose his cool, but she had to try again. "Please," she moaned. "You don't need to keep my hands tied up. We're in the middle of nowhere, and this door is locked." She stopped a beat. "I really have to pee, and with these ropes—"

"Enough. Sniveling brat." He pulled a Swiss Army knife from his pocket and flicked it open.

At the sight of the knife, Callie gulped and gave a silent prayer. When he roughly pulled her to her feet, she teetered. Regaining her balance, she thrust out her throbbing wrists. Rick eyed her suspiciously but cut the rope that held her hands together—not the ones that circled her wrists.

Callie didn't press her luck.

The girl came back from the head and went straight to the edge of the double bed, picking up the sheet of paper. What a little mouse—not a tigress at all. Still, as she looked up from reading, Rick spotted intelligence behind those wide, dark eyes and wondered what she was thinking. Was she trying to put together some sort of escape plan?

What does it matter? He had everything worked out. There's nowhere she and Neil could go. *By this time tomorrow, I'll be out of here with a million and a half large.* He smiled with satisfaction, thinking of his brilliant ransom plan. *Practically risk free . . .*

"Rick," Callie said, "I don't understand. Why is this message just for my mother?"

"Just read it. Every single word—and don't change a thing."

Callie began. "Mommy, please listen. The man who kidnapped me wants one and a half million dollars and said that only you can bring it to him. He said if you don't deliver it by the time he tells you, he will send you my . . ." She paused, looking as if she were about to cry. ". . . right thumb. Please, Mommy, don't call the police. If you do, the man will kill me piece by piece. He said he would do it slowly. I'm so scared. He said he'd chop . . ."

Her eyes widened with horror. The paper fluttered to the floor and tears ran down her cheeks.

Rick pressed STOP on the recorder. "Pull yourself together. Your parents have plenty of money. As long as they follow directions, you'll be returned. *With* all your body parts."

"I . . . I don't think I can."

"Think again." He pulled out his pocketknife and snapped it open.

Callie quickly picked up the paper and nodded. When he pressed PLAY, she continued from where she had left off.

"He said he'd chop off one body part at a time. He means it. He is big and strong, and he doesn't care if I live or die. If you've already called the police, he said to tell them that you've heard from me and I'm alright, and that you don't need their help. He said to notify the bank by fax, and to do it as soon as you receive this tape. If you want to see me again, tell them to have the cash ready no later than noon tomorrow. He will call you at twelve thirty. Make sure there are no police or FBI at the hotel, and no police helicopters. Make sure they're not tapping your phone and there are no tracers in the bag with the money. He says his men will be watching you and will know if you don't follow his instructions exactly. I love you, Mommy. Please don't let him hurt me."

When she looked up, he turned off the recorder. "Good job," he said. He patted her on the shoulder and grinned when she shrank away from his touch.

Following the exit of her carpet cleaners, Viviana locked the elegant boutique door and headed home. Her mind turned to the Taylors' missing twin. Elizabeth had returned the call she'd made to Ashleigh a few hours ago, explaining that they knew little more than they had the night before.

As Viviana approached the door to her condo, she heard Dolly's pint-sized bark. *Uh-oh. I sure don't need another complaint about Dolly's barking,* she thought, and she hurriedly threw open the door.

As she stepped inside, Dolly danced around Viviana's feet, her tail wagging. She scooped her up and drifted toward the kitchen. "Gino," she called.

"Should be done in a shake, angel," Gino said from under the sink. She hoped he could get that leak taken care of before there was any real damage. Throwing him a noisy kiss, she headed back to the living room, took a seat near the telephone on the end table, and placed Dolly beside her.

Wainwright picked up on the first ring.

Before she could say more than a few words about her indignation over Tony's being considered a suspect, Wainwright cut her off.

"I appreciate your support. Tony had nothing to do with the abduction, but to be fair, Pocino was hired to find Callie Taylor, and he had to follow any lead, no matter how remote. And it sure didn't help that Tony left the opening party early." Wainwright paused and, with a sigh, said, "For what it's worth, Tony's determined to help find the guilty party. He was in a hell of a hurry when we spoke, and he hung up before I could offer to assist with my resources here in Chicago. Nevertheless, I plan to keep on top of this."

Viviana heard some mumbling in the background. Then Wainwright said into the phone, "I'll keep you in the loop."

She was left with the dial tone buzzing in her ear.

Rick locked the door to the aft cabin and hastened to the salon. Sarah-Jayne sat on the curved bench, her elbows resting on the warped mahogany table. Her mind seemed elsewhere as she sipped from an oversized mug. *Better be coffee—and not spiked.*

As Rick slid in beside her, he caught a whiff of marijuana on her hair and clothing. His gut tightened. He couldn't have her all strung out. This was too important. But as he moved closer, he was relieved to catch nothing more than the aroma of strong black coffee on her breath. *Thank God.*

He touched her tattooed arm. "Sugar," he began, as gently as possible, "until this is behind us . . . about this time tomorrow . . . we have to have all our faculties in gear. Both of us have got to cut down on the weed and booze. These next twenty-four hours are too damned important for us. Hell, one wrong step can mean the difference in our entire future. We can't screw up."

"I know. I know, baby. I'm doing my best. I just had one joint today. No meth. No booze. Not even a beer." She squeezed closer, resting her hand on his thigh and looking up at him through unfocused eyes. "Are you mad at me, baby?"

Can I really depend on her? he thought, knowing he had no choice. *Well, she's all I've got. I'll make it work.* "No," he lied. "Sarah-Jayne, you know, it's just that we've got to be sure nothing goes wrong. I need you at your best." He leaned over and gave her a peck on the cheek. "Now go in and splash some water on your face while I get us some more coffee. Then we've got to rock and roll."

He handed her a couple of his wet wipes and rose from the horseshoe seat. While she went to clean up, he mentally reviewed his plan, ambling across the creaking floor of the salon to the bow. The door to the forward cabin was secure; the hook-and-eye latch attached to the outside of it was triple-strength. Still, he'd better try it again. He threw all his weight against the door. Yes, it would hold. Even if little Neil, with his uncharacteristic bravado, tried to escape, he'd get nowhere.

When Sarah-Jayne returned from the head, she was considerably improved. Although her eyes were still pretty bloodshot, she looked more alert. She'd changed into some torn denim jeans and a sweatshirt, and she'd combed her hair and clipped it into a somewhat neat ponytail. "How about the snooty rich girl?" she asked. "Shouldn't you retie her hands?"

He shrugged. "She's got nowhere to go. No way is she going to get that door open." He stuffed a couple of wipes in his pocket. "Now let's get a move on."

He helped steady Sarah-Jayne as she mounted the wide plank leading down to the shore. Once he was sure she had her balance, he followed behind her.

When they reached the van, he quickly slid behind the wheel. Once the passenger door banged shut, he put the van in gear and maneuvered it back onto the dirt road. Then he began to go over the plan. "You remember exactly where you're supposed to meet me?"

"Of course," she whimpered. "I'm not stupid."

Take it easy on her. Rick knew he couldn't afford to have her freak out now. "I know you aren't, sugar, but I know this area like the back of my hand, and still it can be confusing. You've got to park the car exactly where I showed you."

"I got it, I got it. Jeez, baby, you took me there twice."

He grinned and patted her hand.

At last they reached the main road. About a mile down, he pulled off into the wooded area just beyond the rest stop and parked beside two vehicles, both stolen, each beneath a faded canvas cover. The plates had been changed, and he'd done a crude paint job. The Toyota Sienna minivan, which he'd taken to a locksmith's the week before, was what he would drive into the city that afternoon. It would take the two of them on to Alaska tomorrow. The valet key to the Honda Civic coupe, which he'd found in its console, he handed to Sarah-Jayne. As long as the girl's mom did what she was told, there would be no need for the trunk key. Everything was good to go.

After they'd rolled up the canvas covers and dumped them in the back of the van, Rick pulled out the waterproof duffel and the throwaway cell phone he had purchased.

"You sure it's safe to drive this car?" Sarah-Jayne whined as they approached the Honda.

"Absolutely. It's been a good two months since the owner would have reported it missing. It's off the police radar by now. New color, new plates." He pulled her into his arms and squeezed her tight. She wasn't the brightest bulb in the all-night factory, but she'd given him something he'd never had before: unconditional love and admiration. For now, that's all he could ask for. *Once we have the money . . .*

He opened the driver's-side door. The fuzzy slippers were on the floor of the passenger seat, as he'd instructed. He grinned. The pretty mama was sure to need these. Then with one of his wet wipes he scrubbed the outside of the plastic bag that held another throwaway cell phone and the outside of the duffel bag. Leaning across the driver's seat, he put the duffel on the floor beside the slippers and placed the cell phone on the passenger's seat.

He backed out of the car and straightened up, then reached into his pocket and pulled out his iPod. "Here," he said, handing it to Sarah-Jayne. "This should keep you entertained until I get back." He glanced at his watch. "It won't take long to deliver the tape and this here mind-blowing box." He slipped the slim box into the envelope with the cassette player. "But I'll most likely run into traffic on my way out of the city. You know where to go. Pick you up in about two hours. Two and a half at the most."

"But what if you're seen dropping off the tape?"

"Got that covered. Gotta run," he said over his shoulder as he headed toward the burgundy minivan. He made a mental note to change the silver van's plates in the morning before showing up at work. He intended to stay just long enough to fake a sudden onset of the flu.

Ashleigh rinsed her hair a second time. It felt good to get away from all the voices, even if only for a short while. Although the FBI special agents and the Chicago PD detectives had agreed that a public appeal should go out as soon as possible, neither she nor Conrad was sure. And yet they felt they had no choice but to cooperate with law enforcement. They were out of their depth in the drama that was unfolding around them, and if the TV alert and appeal would help bring Callie home safely . . .

April and Kyle had dropped everything and managed to arrange for Cliff Fowler to host the special news alert. The charismatic TV personality was JJQ's most sought-after on-the-spot news interviewer.

An image of Callie, alone and frightened, drifted through the steam of the spacious hotel shower. But that image vanished as quickly as it had appeared. Far more frightening thoughts crossed Ashleigh's mind— images where she was not alone but threatened by her captor. *Who took my Callie? Had he meant to take Marnie? Stop . . . Stop . . . Stop,* she screamed in her head. What did it matter which twin was the intended victim? The fact that someone had abducted any one of her daughters shredded her insides. *Please, God, protect Callie. Keep her safe. And bring her back to us unharmed.* Ashleigh tried again to clear her head, but all she could think of was that Callie was gone and they had heard nothing from her abductor.

In spite of the TV host's recommendation that Marnie and Juliana be a part of their appeal, she was adamant that their girls not be exploited on TV, and she was thankful that Conrad supported her wholeheartedly. Marnie was already buried in a tsunami of guilt, and Juliana, usually the voice of reason, couldn't seem to stop crying. Her poor girls had enough on their plate already.

As the steaming-hot water reddened her skin, Ashleigh wondered if she'd done the right thing by allowing Marnie to cancel her week with the Christonellis. Ironically, as apprehensive as she'd been over the visit, it would be less stressful now if the girls were elsewhere during the nonstop chaos of law enforcement in their suite, not to mention the TV crew who were now setting up in the living room. And yet she couldn't bring herself to let them out of her sight, and anyway, she wasn't about to force Marnie against her will. Especially now.

A hard knot tightened in her chest. *I must be strong. Callie will soon be back with us.* Holding on to that thought, she hoped, would transmit that positive energy to her girls.

A few minutes later, after she'd slipped into her terry-cloth robe and begun drying her hair, Conrad charged in, his face flushed with anger. Under his arm was a large manila envelope, and one hand was wrapped around a small rectangular object. The other was clenched in such a tight fist, his knuckles had turned white.

Ashleigh flipped off the dryer and set it down beside her hairbrush. "What is it?"

Conrad saw fear flash in her liquid brown eyes and cursed himself for bolting into the bedroom Pocino-style, with the grace of a toddler. "I'm so sorry," he said. "I don't want to frighten you." Mystified by the small box, which was sealed shut with a slender gold lock with the longest row of combination cylinders he'd ever seen, he'd stuffed it back into the envelope. He'd worry about that later. The tape he'd just listened to had set his blood on fire even as it sent a blade of ice straight to his soul.

But his dramatics were only making matters worse. He sank down on the chaise longue beside their bed and held out his arms. "Please, love, come over here." He patted the space beside him and drew in a quick breath. "We have been contacted by Callie's kidnapper."

"Thank God," Ashleigh cried out. Her eyes dropped to the cassette player in his hand. "Is she alright?" Then without a pause she asked, "What do we have to do to get her back?" She reached for the cassette player in his hand.

He did not immediately release it. "This was delivered when you were in the shower. I listened to it only once. I have told no one about this." He paused and gestured to the envelope. "I asked the bellman if he knew who had delivered this envelope. He wasn't on duty when it arrived, but he contacted the receptionist and was told it was delivered by a young boy. When the receptionist asked the boy who had given him the envelope, he pointed to the Washburn entrance and said a man had given him ten dollars to bring it inside. The man had been parked there in a dark red SUV. But when she looked, he was no longer there."

Conrad wished he had the power to protect Ashleigh from what she was about to hear, but she must listen to the tape. The relief he had expected to feel when they were finally contacted had been short-lived. Now he had far more questions than answers. And there was a multitude of decisions to be made. *I'll pay the ransom, no matter what any branch of law enforcement has to say. But Ashleigh cannot be involved in the delivery. If that's what the kidnapper has in mind, he'd better think again.*

Briefly closing her eyes, Ashleigh took in two slow, deep breaths, battling for control. Her temples throbbed and a wave of dizziness washed over her. Since her fall, she had been plagued by intermittent headaches, but she would not allow them to clog her mind. She willed herself to close the door to everything in her mind, everything other than getting her daughter home safely.

"The tape said that we were not to inform the police or FBI." It wasn't a question. Although she had no personal experience with ransom demands, she had seen plenty of movies and read many a book where that was the case. *Isn't that what kidnappers always demand?*

"Naturally," Conrad confirmed, "but we can't go along with that. Even if I were foolish enough to want to go it without the pros, I'm afraid we couldn't pull it off."

Ashleigh bit her lip. "That was definitely Callie's voice on the tape, don't you agree?"

Conrad nodded. "It's Callie's voice, but not her words. She's reading from a prepared script—I'd bet my life on it. That sicko's threats are pretty darn graphic."

"You're right. Those weren't Callie's words. She hasn't called me 'Mommy' since preschool. And listen closely. She's crinkling the paper." Steeling herself, she hit PLAY again. And terror ripped through her body once more. "What should we do?"

"Until we have a chance to think this through, we need to call off the TV segment. Let's run the options through our minds. Meanwhile, I'll get a fax sent to the Chicago Branch of Citibank, and then we'll call Landes in to bounce—"

There was a light tap on the bedroom door.

For several long seconds, neither Ashleigh nor Conrad moved, and then both rose as if one.

"Just a moment," she called out.

Conrad strode across the room and threw open the door.

April stood in the doorway with a pot of coffee and a tray of sandwiches. She raised a well-shaped eyebrow when she saw that Ashleigh's hair was still damp, but said only, "Take your time. The camera crew is still setting up."

"April," Conrad said, "we need some more time. Something has come up, and I'm not at all sure we should go through with this TV segment. We need to talk the situation over with the detectives and the FBI agents. Are you prepared to run filler?"

Callie listened intently. At the roar of a motor, she sucked in her breath. Her heartbeat pounded in her ears, nearly drowning out the grinding of the van's gears. The boat sat wedged into the marshy shore, limiting her view to only a few feet up the dirt hillside. But in seconds, as if in slow motion, the sound grew softer. She strained to determine the direction. It grew absolutely still. *At least one of my prayers has been answered.* The creep had left, and he'd taken Sarah-Jayne with him.

Since she'd first awakened in the smelly van the night before, she'd thought of little other than a plan of escape. Tied hand and foot, she'd felt the horror, the powerlessness of being unable to stop whatever was happening to her. But now, with both her feet and her hands free, she felt hopeful.

Suddenly she felt angry too, and she took advantage of being alone to speak her thoughts aloud: "I could strangle Marnie for being so gullible. How could she trust a total stranger?" Then instantly she chided herself. "What am I saying? It wasn't *totally* her fault. I played right into their hands." Biting down on her bottom lip, she willed herself not to lay blame—on her sister or herself. She had to focus all her energy on finding a way out of the cabin and off the boat.

If only she hadn't been knocked out on the way to this godforsaken location. She didn't know where she was or which way to go—but that didn't matter at the moment. *My priority is to get out of this cabin. Then I'll figure out the rest.* She could just see daylight through a crack between the cabin door and the doorjamb. But the creep had been diligent in removing anything that could be used as a tool to flip the heavy hook that locked the door on the outside. Other than the chamber pot, the bed, and the small table, the room was bare.

Callie had already figured out that her only chance at unlocking the door was to release one of the mattress springs. She had been lying on the bottom bunk for some time now, staring up at the rows of exposed springs supporting the mattress of the top bunk. The thumb and forefinger of her right hand were already red and throbbing from her efforts to free one of them. She was confident she could then straighten it by stepping on it with all her weight. It wouldn't have to be completely straight—just straight enough to slip through the crack in the door so she could lift the latch.

It was so cold in the cabin that misty clouds formed every time she exhaled. She must find something to wrap around her raw thumb and forefinger, but there were no sheets on the beds, and the blankets were too bulky. The drawers beneath the bunk were sealed shut, impossible to budge. Unable to think of anything else, Callie pulled her sweatshirt over her head. Goose bumps rose on her arms. She clenched her jaw and ignored her discomfort as she wrapped her index finger and then her thumb in a single layer of the soft cotton.

The sky was darkening, and she had no idea when her captors would return. As much as it hurt, she kept working on the bedspring, oblivious to the cold. It was nearly free when she lost her grip once more, and it snapped back to where it had long been lodged. She tried flexing her hands. They felt like they were being stuck by hundreds of straight pins. She was tempted to give up, to just lie down on the bed and go to sleep. *Don't go there,* she told herself. *That kind of thinking is for losers—losers whose bodies are found on stinky old boats.*

Callie wished that the creep had left some of his wipes behind, but there were none. So she rewrapped her index finger in her sweatshirt and began tugging on the spring again.

———————

The phone on the entryway table began a not-so-melodic *brrring*.

Ashleigh stood frozen in place.

"I'll get it," Conrad said. A moment later he turned toward her and said, "It's Pocino," and with the phone pressed to his ear, he disappeared out of her sight.

Thank God for Pocino. And of course Dick Landes, whose calm, cool manner and finesse kept everything running as smoothly as possible under the circumstances. Ashleigh returned to the living room, thinking again how impressed she was at the response and the attention that Callie's abduction had been given from all areas of law enforcement. Chicago PD had willingly partnered up with the FBI, and fortunately they hadn't encountered any jurisdictional problems—at least, not so far.

During the long delay as Ashleigh and Conrad made their final decision, cameraman Renzo had flitted around, making sure that Fowler and the rest of the TV crew were comfortable. He'd taken on the role of a cruise director, making the best of the situation. He'd ordered food and drink from room service and arranged it on the dining room table that seated twenty. The TV crew was amiable yet respectful, given the subject matter of the segment they were planning to record.

Ashleigh felt as if a swarm of bees were buzzing around inside the middle region of her body. *Pocino must have news.* For Conrad to be gone so long, the call had to be very important. Ashleigh thought of going in search of her husband, but realized she must be the one to tell the TV crew they had decided to cancel the special segment.

Ashleigh took a deep breath and attempted to ignore the lump in her throat. She made eye contact with Dick Landes, who gave her a reassuring nod. He'd been in full agreement with the Taylors' decision, which they'd arrived at after discussing it for the better part of the last two hours. She forced herself forward, weaving her way around the several cameras and white-hot lights that filled a good portion of the suite's large living room. Again she prayed that they were doing the right thing.

She shot another glance around the suite for Conrad, but he was still out of sight. Curling her hands into fists, she steeled herself to meet

Cliff Fowler's eyes. "I am so sorry, Cliff. We've received some news that prevents us from filming this news alert."

Fowler asked no questions, but his eyes conveyed his empathy. "Renzo," he called out, sweeping his arm toward the equipment, "the segment is canceled. Let's tear it down."

Praying Pocino had some good news, Ashleigh went in search of Conrad.

"Does Ross have any leads?"

Seeing the anxiety on his wife's face, Conrad felt his heart sink. "He's got more than a lead," he said gently. Taking her hand, he led her to the loveseat in their master bedroom suite, where they both sat down. "The identity of Marnie's online acquaintance has been discovered." Conrad did his best to keep his emotions and bewilderment in check.

She leaned closer, her eyes seeking his.

"His name is Neil Kennedy." Knowing the name would mean nothing to her, he went on. "He is the son of Nelson Kennedy."

"Nelson Kennedy?" she repeated. Then her brown eyes flashed and widened. "The architect?"

Conrad nodded.

"Oh no," Ashleigh said. "The man who Erica has been seeing, the one who is helping with the protest rallies and boycotts." It wasn't a question.

"None other."

A perplexed expression distorted her beautiful features. "But why would he—"

Troubled by the same implications, Conrad interrupted her. "I have no idea how or even if the father is involved. However, I don't believe in coincidence any more than Pocino or law enforcement does. Pocino says that when he and Detective Senske arrived at Kennedy's door earlier today, the man appeared genuinely blown away. His son is about the same age as the twins. Kennedy claims he's a good kid, an excellent student. Never given him an ounce of trouble. When Kennedy discovered his son hadn't come home last night, he expected foul play and immediately reported his disappearance to Chicago PD."

"So the boy who befriended Marnie online just happens to also be missing?"

Wrapping his arm around her shoulder, he said, "Love, I can't make the pieces fit. It's all twisted up, a conundrum—to say the least." He extended a finger, then another. "Number one: Kennedy is dating Erica, which makes a rather slim connection to Marnie. Number two: From what I understand, he is a vehement architectural preservationist with a well-publicized link to the John Stewart's protesters." He paused. "That said, I can find no rational reason why abducting one of our daughters would bring him any closer to his goals. If Jordon's were a privately held company I owned outright, there might be some rationale. But anyone with an ounce of common sense would know I report to a board of directors. Even if I voted with the loyal customers, the name-changing train has already left the station. Abducting my daughter to curtail that plan would be an exercise in futility."

A tired, helpless look crossed Ashleigh's lovely face but was gone almost before he registered it. "So what does it all mean?"

Conrad shook his head. "I don't know, but I've come full circle. The purpose of this kidnapping is now clear. It's money they're after. It has nothing to do with human trafficking—and that's a relief."

Ashleigh swallowed hard. "Is that what you thought?" Gripping her hands tightly together, she said, "And yet you told me you were sure—"

Conrad pulled her close. "I didn't really think so. I couldn't. But I can't deny that, after watching that documentary last month, it crossed my mind. It was the worst-case scenario. The very thought terrified me, Ashleigh. To share it with you was . . . unthinkable."

"What about the Kennedy kid? How does he fit in?"

"According to Pocino, Kennedy has a stepson who has been nothing but trouble since he was a kid. They were pretty much estranged, but recently the stepson started coming around to visit Neil, and Kennedy said he's been concerned over these sudden brotherly overtures."

"What kind of trouble?" Ashleigh asked.

"All kinds: extortion, theft, drugs, you name it."

"But why did Kennedy allow his son—"

"Love," he said, pulling her closer, "I don't know. Pocino will fill us in when he gets here, which"—he glanced down at his watch—"should be in less than half an hour."

Once again, Conrad realized, they would have to play the waiting game.

Ashleigh sank deeper into the loveseat as her husband stood and crossed the room.

"This is bound to be a long night," Conrad said. "Mind if I hop in for a quick shower?" He was still clad in the Armani suit and tie he'd chosen for the TV segment.

Ashleigh, too, was dressed for the segment, wearing a Chanel suit, accessories and all. Shaking her head as she kicked off her high heels, she said, "Go ahead. I'll freshen up in the guest bathroom. But first I'd like to check on Marnie."

Conrad raised a thick brow. "Want me to come with you?"

She shook her head. "Not now, love. Go ahead and take your shower. Pocino will be here before we know it. Mark and Paige will be here soon too."

Ashleigh headed for her daughter's room, then tapped softly on the door. There was no answer, so she tapped a little louder. Nothing. She slowly pushed the door open and called Marnie's name. Silence was her only answer. Noticing that the bathroom door was shut, she crossed the room and tapped on the door.

"Just a minute," Marnie called through the closed door.

Ashleigh heard no running water and was about to say she'd come back when Marnie opened the door.

"What's up?" she said, feigning nonchalance, but her words fell flat. Her face was the color of the porcelain sink, and there was a spot of fresh blood on her sleeve, surrounded by a large wet stain where she'd tried to wash it off.

Ashleigh's heart filled with sorrow, and for a moment she almost forgot to breathe. This wasn't the first time Marnie had been caught cutting herself. The first time had been months ago. Both parents had talked to her about it, but their talk had not gone well. Marnie had been sullen, mumbling again and again, "It's my body." Remembering what her daughter had said—"Why should you care?"—Ashleigh felt another wave of sadness wash through her. She had recognized it as a cry for help and understanding, but she was at a loss. They'd done their best to try to raise her self-esteem, and Marnie promised it wouldn't happen again.

Ashleigh had been so sure the cuttings were a thing of the past— that Marnie had worked through the urge to hurt herself. But now, she supposed, the burden of guilt for Callie's disappearance was more than she could take. Marnie had taken a step back in time.

Like a creature of the wild caught in a trap, Marnie's eyes widened and then filled with tears. She made no attempt to cover up what had happened. "I'm sorry, Mom. I'm really, really sorry."

Sidestepping Marnie through the open doorway, Ashleigh made her way across the tiled floor to the small wastebasket. Inside she found bloody tissues and a plastic razor that was broken to pieces, the blades removed. *Why, why, why?* She just couldn't wrap her mind around it. She had no idea how to handle this, other than total candor. "Marnie, I don't know what to say."

"I know, Mom. I really am sorry. I know you don't understand." Her gaze fell to the marble floor. "I guess I can't do anything right. I should have been the one thrown into the van, not Callie. I don't know why she went out by herself. She was the one who told *me* not to do it. But that's no excuse. She wouldn't have gone if I hadn't made the plan to meet Brad." She lifted her chin. "And now I've made you cry."

Ashleigh wiped away the tears that spilled down her cheek. "Darling, no one is blaming you."

"But it's all my fault. Callie wouldn't have—"

Ashleigh raised her hand to halt further recrimination and wrapped her arm around Marnie's shoulder, leading her to the upholstered bench at the end of one of the queen-sized beds.

"Darling, we've talked about this before. When you cut yourself, you're using physical pain to take away the sting of emotional pain. That's a strong urge that you'll always have to fight."

Marnie sucked in her lips and stared down at the toes of her sneakers. The boy who called himself Brad had made her feel good about herself. She thought that he had really understood her and liked her—for herself. She hadn't had any urge to cut herself in a long time, but last night when she'd watched helplessly as Callie was thrown into the van, she had felt as though her own life were over. "I can't really explain, but maybe that's it. When I cut myself, I don't think about anything but that little bit of pain. For a few minutes, I didn't think about Callie or what they might do to her, but . . . but . . . Oh, Mom, Callie's *gone*, and I've made you cry. I'm so sorry," she repeated. "I promise. I'll never do anything like this again."

"Ashleigh," Conrad's voice rung out. "You better get dressed—" He stopped abruptly just outside the open doorway. "What's wrong?" he asked.

"You mean besides *everything*," Marnie mumbled.

Ashleigh squeezed her hand, saying, "We'll talk about this later. Right now, I'd better finish getting dressed." Right now, she knew, they had to focus on getting Callie back.

CHAPTER

85

The muffled voices of Conrad and Ross drifted toward the hallway, halting just as Ashleigh entered the living room. She had caught a few whispered words but couldn't be sure. *Did Ross say . . . ?* Panic mounted in her chest, but she did her best to stifle it.

When he saw her, Pocino heaved himself out of the library armchair and yawned. "Sorry," he said, patting the doughnut roll around his middle. "Mind if I nab a cup of java—and maybe something to eat for the road?"

Ashleigh pulled herself together and nodded. "Certainly, Ross."

"Be our guest," Conrad said. The investigator had obviously eyed the food that had not yet been cleared from the dining room table. "I'll grab a jacket and meet you at the front door. Toddman is supposed to be here any minute."

As Pocino headed to the dining room, Marnie dashed in and stopped short of her parents. "I need to talk to you," she said, taking them in with a single penetrating gaze. "Both of you."

Ashleigh caught the sadness and apprehension in her daughter's brown eyes. She was still shocked and heartbroken to discover that her daughter had been cutting herself again, and she didn't intend to discuss it with Conrad—not until Callie was home safe. There was no need to distract him. Not now, anyway. But she would have to keep a close eye on Marnie.

"What happened? Why did you put a stop to the TV alert? Is it because you think my other mother and her boyfriend have something to do with taking Callie?"

Ashleigh exchanged a sharp look with her husband. "No, darling, we don't think that. Why do you—"

"I was at the door a few minutes ago, listening to what Mr. Pocino told you." Marnie held both hands up. "I know I shouldn't eavesdrop. But I had to." Her gaze dropped to the floor. "It's my fault Callie got kidnapped, and I need to help get her back. Mom even said you needed my help."

"Sweetheart," Conrad started, "I appreciate you wanting to help, but we're going to be up very late—"

"Dad, you didn't let me finish."

Conrad reached for her, but she stepped back.

"Mr. Pocino told you that Brad's dad—I mean, the boy who called himself Brad—is Nelson's son. I know you're going over to talk to him, Dad, and I need to go with you."

Conrad's eyebrows shot up.

"I'm the only one who knows everything his son and I talked about," Marnie continued. "I really need to be there." Her hands were shaking, but in spite of that, Ashleigh saw the firm set of her daughter's chin.

Conrad blinked and started to speak. "Marnie, my little love—"

Ashleigh cut in, giving her husband a knowing look. "Love, she's right. What Marnie knows about Neil Kennedy and his plans could be important." And it was just as important, she knew, for her daughter to feel that she was a part of her twin's rescue. *I hope he can see that.*

"Well, little love, run and get a warm jacket."

"Thanks, Dad," Marnie said, with relief in her tone. "You're the best. You too, Mom."

Ashleigh reached out to give her daughter a hug, and there was no resistance. But when Marnie hugged her back, Ashleigh felt her daughter's body tremble.

"Mom . . . Mom," she repeated with a catch in her voice. "I love you. I'm so . . . so sorry for everything. I really, really meant it when I said I wish it was me who was taken."

Ashleigh pulled her in tighter. "I don't. And that's the truth." Having Marnie taken would have been every bit as devastating.

"Your mother and I are glad you are here with us, safe and sound," Conrad said. "We have no such wish. Never have, never will. Now," he continued, feigning insult, "how about my hug?"

"Love you too, Dad," Marnie said, reaching out to bring him into her arms.

When she stepped back, Conrad took hold of both her hands. "Let's all just focus on getting Callie back home safely."

The door chimes sounded, and Mark and Paige walked through the doorway. Marnie greeted them with hugs, then stepped back to pull on her down jacket and slip her cell phone into her pocket.

Conrad kissed Ashleigh lightly on her lips and pulled her in for a reassuring embrace. "Call me if there is any change in plan. I'm not sure how late—"

"I'll stay here with Ashleigh until you return," Paige cut in.

"Thanks, Paige," he replied. "We're expecting another FBI agent sometime after midnight. The FBI assigned us another agent when we reported the ransom tape. His plane from Washington is due at O'Hare at twelve-oh-five."

Pocino ambled back into the room, a coffee cup in his hand, and shot a glance at Marnie in her jacket. Then, spotting Landes and Mark, he gave a grin and called out, "Ready to rock and roll?"

Mark nodded. "Let's go."

The moment the door clicked shut, the two women embraced.

"I can't tell you how thankful I am that you're here."

"I believe you just did." Paige's mouth curved up in a sad smile. "Besides, there's nowhere else I'd rather be at a time like this."

"There's so much I have to tell," Ashleigh said, trying to sort out where to begin. "But first let me check on Elizabeth and Juliana."

"How are they holding up?"

"Okay. We're trying to keep things as normal as we can. They're still camped out in Elizabeth's room, watching DVDs." She paused. "I need to give Erica a heads-up on Marnie's arrival, then check our sick ward. I'll meet you in the dining room. The TV crew is gone now, but we still have enough coffee to keep an army awake."

"For once I'll join you in a cup. I don't think it's likely any of us are going to get much sleep tonight."

As Ashleigh disappeared down the hallway, Paige drifted into the dining room and poured two cups of coffee, her mind flooding with questions and with concern for her friend. She'd noticed the dark circles beneath Ashleigh's eyes and the terror she was trying so hard to conceal. *Just how much can she take?* Only Ashleigh's optimistic outlook was holding her together, and Paige wasn't sure how much more it could endure.

Ashleigh gave a tired smile when she came into the dining room. "All is well," she said, picking up one of the coffee cups. "They're both asleep on Elizabeth's bed. I turned off the TV and left Juliana where she was—just pulled the covers over her."

"How is she coping, really?" Paige asked.

"Better. It's hard for her. She and Callie are very close. We've been trying to distract her, but she still has tears in her eyes. It's all so overwhelming. But Juliana bounces back to her usual positive self. When the TV crew was setting up, I overheard her talking to Marnie about choreographing a trio when Callie returns." The pride was evident in her voice. "Ever the optimistic child."

"Like mother, like daughter." Paige grinned. "What can I do to help?"

"Just pray that Callie is returned unharmed and that the next twenty-four hours are soon behind us."

"Our prayers are with Callie—with *all of you*." Paige reached out and placed her hand on Ashleigh's wrist. "But how are *you* keeping it together?"

"It's not a choice. You'd do the same." Before giving Paige a chance to respond, Ashleigh added, "Under the same circumstances, I can't picture you shattering into tiny pieces."

"I'm not so sure. I've had my share of trauma, and I'm pretty good at keeping things in perspective, but I've never been put to this kind of test."

"Paige, I second-guess myself every step of the way. One minute I think maybe we should have gone through with the TV segment. Maybe we should have as many people on the lookout as possible. The kidnapper doesn't want us to involve the authorities, but there was no warning about asking for help from the public." She sighed. "But from the start, we weren't sure how much support we'd get from the citizens of Chicago."

Paige gasped, putting her coffee down on the table. "You don't actually think the John Stewart's protesters—"

Ashleigh shook her head. "Not really. The protesters are not bad people. They're fighting for what they believe in. Both sides believe they stand for the better good. But people in this city have unjustly painted Conrad as a villain."

"But surely even the Fans of John Stewart's wouldn't aid in the kidnapping of a child."

"Of course not. That's why we agreed to go forward with the segment in the first place. We were counting on the innate goodness of the majority. To be perfectly candid, I think I was more afraid of how that kind of public appeal could affect Marnie. But when that ransom tape came in—"

"Ashleigh, please tell me about the tape. All April told us was that you'd received a tape from the kidnapper and that the contents shouldn't be leaked to the media."

Ashleigh nodded. "She told you all she knew. She doesn't know exactly what was on the tape." As she repeated the words her daughter had recited on the tape in an uncharacteristic monotone, Paige felt sick inside.

"So you didn't actually hear the abductor's voice?"

Ashleigh shook her head. "But Callie sounded so scared . . . The message the kidnapper made her read was chilling enough to turn my blood cold." Her fingers interlacing, Ashleigh stared down at her coffee. "If I could get my hands on whoever has taken Callie, I'd . . . I'd . . ." She rubbed her finger around the rim of her cup. "Well, I don't know exactly what I'd do, but anyone who would threaten a teenager with cutting off body parts has to be a real psycho."

"Do you think it could be the Kennedy kid?"

"We don't know, but it seems unlikely. He's the same age as the twins. His father thinks he was abducted too, and Nelson suspects his stepson, Rick. Apparently that kid's been in trouble since elementary school . . ."

As Paige listened to her friend, her mind jumped ahead. This kidnapper sounded dangerous and desperate. Ashleigh and Conrad couldn't perform the ransom drop alone; they would need the protection of the police and the FBI, and so would Callie. A sudden thought startled her. *Surely Conrad and Ashleigh aren't going to do as the kidnapper demands?*

By the time Ashleigh finished filling Paige in on all that had taken place that day—a day that felt more like a month—her coffee had gone lukewarm. "Ready for another cup?" she asked. To her surprise, Paige held out her cup.

"Walking on hot coals in pitch-blackness would be a lot more pleasant than this endless waiting," she said, placing the fresh cups on the table. "I can't remember ever feeling so impotent. But I'll do anything to get Callie back safely, even if it means fighting Conrad to do so."

"Hold on. Surely you can't be thinking of doing anything without the assistance of the FBI or the police. You have no idea what the kidnapper is capable of. Doesn't Conrad agree?"

"Of course. We aren't thinking of handling this on our own. Even if we were foolish enough to try, we're too far in. If we trumped up some story now, saying that Callie had not actually been abducted, no one would buy it."

Paige nodded. "Mark told me Callie's abduction was witnessed by someone other than Marnie."

"That's right. A young man who was leaving the Corner Bakery Café saw Callie being shoved into the van. He called 9-1-1. His report of the vehicle matches Marnie's."

"Didn't Marnie take a picture of the van?"

Now it was Ashleigh's turn to nod. "But she only caught the rear end. The young man got a better view of the side—there was a bakery sign on it." She took a sip of the hot coffee, and then set it on the counter."

"Ashleigh," Paige began, her brow knitting, "if you and Conrad don't disagree about having the authorities involved, what *are* you two at odds over?"

87

It had taken longer than expected to drive back from the city and exchange the Sienna for his old van, and only a faint trace of daylight remained on the deserted roadside by the time Rick tapped on the van's horn and pulled up behind the blue Civic. He inhaled deeply and set the cigarette on the lip of the ashtray. Without the aid of streetlights, this spot would soon be black as a witch's heart. Seeing no sign of the driver's-side door opening, he again tapped the horn. Nothing.

Cursing under his breath, he shoved the gearstick into park, left the motor running and the headlights on, and hopped out of the van.

In the dim light, he saw Sarah-Jayne's head lolling against the headrest. Either she was passed out or she had the iPod revved up to her usual earsplitting roar. He reached for the driver's-side door to wrench it open. It was locked.

All he saw were the white cords threading from her ears down to wherever the damn iPod was. He couldn't tell whether her eyes were open or not. Banging on the window with the side of his balled fist, he called her name.

She shot up from her slouched position and turned her head toward the window glass. For a few split seconds she just looked at him.

"Hey, we've got to get a move on."

The door creaked open at glacial speed. "Jeez, baby, I was beginning to think you forgot all about me."

"Yeah, right," he said, derision sliding off his tongue. "I had nothing else to do, so I stopped for a leisurely game of golf."

Shielding her eyes from the headlights that hit her square in the face, Sarah-Jayne squinted up through dull, red-rimmed eyes. "Huh," she said, pushing herself out of the seat. Then, blinking repeatedly, she said, "Sorry, baby, I didn't mean that." Her words were slurred. "But I was beginning to worry."

The stench from inside the car reached Rick's nostrils before Sarah-Jayne shoved the door shut with her elbow. Momentarily distracted by what he saw in her clutched fist, he demanded, "What do you think you're doing with those?"

She flung open her fist as if hot coals were wrapped inside, then stared down at the car keys in the palm of her hand as if she had no idea how they got there. It was a full three seconds and innumerable blinks before she got it together enough to speak. "Oops." An expression of chagrin covered her flushed face. "Sorry. Should I put them under the driver's seat?"

Rick rolled his eyes. "How many joints have you had?"

More blinking. "Jeez. I only had one."

"And what else?"

Her posture stiffened. "Sweet fuck all."

Rick bit back the words of reproach that shot through his head. "Look, sugar, in less than twenty-four hours, we'll be out of here. But I told you, the hours leading up to our getaway are crucial. We've both got to be on our toes."

"You saying we can't have *nothing* till then?" The skin between Sarah-Jayne's narrow-set eyes crinkled. "You never said that before. Don't think I can do that." Her voice rose and crackled with panic.

Rick reached out and pulled her into his arms. *Can't afford to have her freaking out now.* "Of course not, sugar. We have to cut down till we're across the border with the one and a half mil. We'll party a little tonight, but nothing after midnight. Okay?" he said, giving her a squeeze.

Tears trickling down her cheeks, she nodded. "I won't let you down," she promised.

"Now give me the keys." He stuck them in the ignition, where they would be easily found tomorrow, as planned.

Moments later, when they were in the van and barreling down the dirt road, Sarah-Jayne asked, "Do you really have to go in to work in the morning?"

Rick sighed. They'd gone over this to the point of tedium, but he controlled his temper and, as succinctly as possible, went over the game plan once more. "I've been very careful about not letting my dear old stepdad know where I work, but when he found Neil missing last night, you can bet your bottom dollar he called in the police. Probably reported that Neil was abducted and named me as the prime suspect. So I've got to check in at the construction site tomorrow morning. Can't take a chance of the bell going off too early by my not showing up." *When will she get it?* "I'll be out of there in less than a half hour. We're working on indoor jobs, so I can't count on the rain. Got some niacin." He patted his shirt pocket. "Discovered it after a binge. It's become my trusty friend for skipping a day of work and keeping my job."

At her puzzled expression, he explained, "It turns my face beet red, and with the flu bug on the rise, I'm positive the boss will send me home sick. Then if the PD comes snooping, it'll be too late. I'll already be . . ." He cut off at the sound of Sarah-Jayne's unladylike snores.

"Shit," he said aloud, and pounded the steering wheel.

In spite of the pain, Callie gritted her teeth and reached again for the bedspring above her. The distance between victory and defeat was no more than the thickness of a fingernail. She no longer felt the cold, nor did she think of her aching arm or the crick in her neck. Adrenaline surged though her body as she sat hunched on the lower bunk, working against time. She would not loosen her grip on the spring, no matter how much it hurt.

It had grown dark. The creep and his nutso girlfriend might return any minute. *I'm almost there. Please, please, please, don't let it slip back into place.* Taking a deep breath, followed by an even deeper one, she twisted the screw with the broken nail of her throbbing thumb. At last, she felt it slide. Relief flooded her as the screw released the metal ring. She easily pulled the other end of the spring free. Flopping onto her back, she looked up and whispered, "Thank you."

Her elation was cut short by a sound that jolted her upright so quickly, she banged her head on the underside of the top bunk. It was the unmistakable rumble of a motor.

They're back.

Pulling off the dirt road onto the overgrown patch of grass, Rick parked the van. The boat sat in total darkness, with not a single light on. His heart pounded against his rib cage. *No way those two brats escaped.* But could they have?

Grabbing the flashlight from the glove compartment, his heart rate slowed as he reestablished his grasp on reality and it dawned on him that the generator might not be working. Those kids were alone and all out of fight by now, in separate cabins, most likely curled up in a ball, awaiting their fate.

He nudged Sarah-Jayne until her eyes popped open, then reached across her to push open the passenger door.

"Okay, okay, I'm awake." A sheepish smile curved her chapped lips. "Sorry," she said for the umpteenth time.

Rick handed her the flashlight and squeezed between the two front seats, grabbing hold of the plastic five-gallon gas container on the floor behind them.

"My God," she shrieked. "What are you planning to do with *that?*"

CHAPTER

88

Huddled in the corner of the backseat behind Pocino, who was driving the rented Bronco, Marnie strained to hear what her dad and Uncle Mark were saying. At the same time, she was trying her best to become invisible. Her thoughts were all over the place, alternating between berating herself and giving herself a pep talk. She'd never felt so alone.

They said I wasn't to blame for all this, but that's what everyone's thinking. Her chewed fingernails looked terrible and her cuticles throbbed. But nothing she did could distract her from the pain in her heart. *Stop this pity party,* she chided herself. *Tonight you've got to show everyone you're not a total loser.*

A streak of lightning flashed, illuminating the interior of the SUV. It was followed by the distant roar of thunder, but no rain. The night was turning as dark as her mood. Shortly thereafter, to complete the dismal picture outside, rain began to tap loudly and steadily on the roof. It splattered across the windows. The thought of the meeting with her other mother's boyfriend made her skin feel hot and clammy. *What am I supposed to say to the man whose son pretended to be my friend just so he could kidnap me?*

Marnie caught a glimpse of Erica standing at the top of the steep stairs of Nelson's house. *My other mother.* The term echoed through her head. She had never thought of Erica in that way before. *What is happening to me?* She ran her fingers over the tiny scars on the inner side of her left forearm. What had given her such relief a fraction of an hour before, now filled her with shame. She'd broken her promise. She hadn't just hurt herself—she now knew that with certainty. *I'm so stupid. Mom doesn't deserve this.*

"We lucked out," Pocino said as he pulled into a parking spot directly across from the Kennedys' historic Victorian home.

"We're here," her dad said, turning his head toward Marnie. "You ready?"

Her throat constricted. She tried to respond, but when no words formed on her lips, she simply nodded and scrambled out of the car.

When Erica Christonelli appeared at the top of the concrete steps holding an umbrella, Conrad took a swift glance at Pocino and prayed he'd keep a civil tongue and his temper in check. For now Pocino would have to put the past behind him and deal with today.

Toddman leaned in close to Marnie's ear and said something. Conrad noticed a bit of tension drop from his daughter's face. "Thanks, Uncle Mark," she said. She pulled the hood of her parka up and gave him a quick hug. Then she ran halfway up the steps and ducked under the open umbrella Erica held out to her and into a long hug.

As they made a dash up the wet steps, Conrad turned to Toddman and asked, "What was all that about?"

"Our little secret," Toddman said with a grin.

Conrad noted that Pocino had acknowledged Erica with a curt nod as he followed the others through the open front door. When everyone had removed their dripping jackets, Erica introduced them to Nelson Kennedy.

Following the introductions, Kennedy turned to Marnie and said, "I've been looking forward to seeing you again, but not under such stressful circumstances." When Marnie failed to respond, Kennedy continued, "Please, everyone, let's go into the dining room."

Conrad observed Marnie's gaze as it flashed from Kennedy to Erica. *What does Erica know about the boy?* That thought lingered on Conrad's mind as they made their way through the living room. Taking in the interior—the breathtaking sculptured moldings, the Tiffany hardware on the windows of the dining room—Conrad registered that the exquisite building was utterly charming yet in need of some repair.

On the six-foot mahogany table was a silver tray with three carafes, one labeled COFFEE, another DECAF, and a third HOT CHOCOLATE. There were six mugs, a pile of napkins, an assortment of half sandwiches, and a plate of chocolate chip cookies.

Conrad was momentarily speechless. *This looks like the setup for a garden-variety ladies' luncheon.* No one else spoke. Finally, sensing that Pocino was about to explode, Conrad began, "Mr. Kennedy—"

"Nelson," Kennedy corrected, and he gestured to the chairs around the table. "Please."

"This is very nice, Nelson," Conrad said, also gesturing at the table. "But this is no social call. My daughter is missing and—"

"As is my son," Kennedy shot back.

Conrad and Mark sat themselves at the table, while Pocino remained standing.

"Yes, Neil too," Conrad continued. "And that's why we need to know what more you can tell us about the whereabouts of your stepson." Looking around this room, it occurred to him that most everyone in the room had been touched by abduction.

Marnie had taken a chair beside Erica, but her body language telegraphed a rigid unease.

Pocino finally pulled out a chair and sat down. "You mind?" he said, making brief eye contact with Conrad.

"Go ahead."

"Hold on, please." Kennedy held up a hand. His eyes shot from Conrad to Pocino. "Let me tell you what I've found out since you and Detective Senske were here earlier." He reached for his glass of water and swallowed a gulp. "The detectives who were canvassing the Cicero area located Rick's apartment—"

"The pad he shares with the girl from rehab?" Pocino asked. He pulled his notepad from his pocket and jotted something down.

"Yes. She goes by the name of Sarah-Jayne Smith. The detectives have not as yet figured out if that's her real name. But what they did find was that their apartment has been vacated. Appears they have no intention of returning." He took another sip of water. "The detectives and FBI agents are looking for anyone who might know them. They're also running down all the nearby construction sites. It'll take some time. I have no idea what name Rick goes by for his construction job, but I gave them some names he's used in the past. I didn't have any recent photos of Rick, but I gave them a snapshot that was in Neil's room."

He paused. "This construction job could be another of Rick's fabrications, but I doubt it. If it's all been some sort of ruse, he's gone to a lot of trouble to carry it off. I've seen him when he comes by for Neil—dirty coveralls, heavy work boots, a van full of tools. So the FBI is turning over every rock until they locate the right construction site. Any of the names fit, the FBI will plant someone on the site at the start of tomorrow's workday."

Marnie shot to her feet and glared at Kennedy. Her eyes went to Erica briefly before returning to Kennedy. "Why do you keep talking about your stepson? He's not the one who looked me up online. He's not the one who pretended to be my friend. He's not the one who made up a phony name. He's not the one who set up a time to meet me. What do you even know about your own son?"

The room fell silent.

Both Kennedy's and Erica's faces drained of color, but Kennedy quickly regained his composure. "Marnie, I completely understand your concerns . . ."

Marnie was right. *These crimes have to be connected.* Conrad was only surprised that his daughter had not blurted out those questions when they first sat down. But they had learned all they were going to learn here. When Nelson had finished talking, Conrad quickly brought the meeting to a close.

If this Rick shows up at work tomorrow, he thought, *we'll have no idea who took Callie. We'll have to wait for the call.* His heart sank to basement level. Knowing who the kidnapper was might not be enough. At this point, even more important than the *who* was the *where*.

When Ashleigh refilled her coffee cup a third time, Paige covered the top of hers with her hand.

"We just want Callie back with us," Ashleigh said. "The money isn't important, as long as we get her home safely." Taking a sip of the scalding coffee, she went on. "However, we know that the FBI's priority, in addition to Callie's safe return, is to capture the kidnapper and recover the ransom." She shook her head slowly. "The next several hours are bound to be the longest of our entire lives. We're in foreign territory, so obviously we need the help of the FBI and police. At the same time, we must be assured that they are keeping a low profile. We can't endanger Callie's life. If the kidnapper spots any form of law enforcement . . ." She did not dare to think what he—or they—might do.

"Have they located Kennedy's stepson?" Paige asked.

Ashleigh shook her head. Her stomach lurched as Pocino's words to Conrad echoed in her head: *The kid was a killer before he reached his teens.* "Let's go to the living room." Her nerves felt raw.

In the living room, she sank down on one of the sofas and kicked off her shoes. Resting her back against the upholstered arm, she swung her legs up on the cushions and made herself as comfortable as possible.

Paige dropped onto the sofa opposite Ashleigh.

"I'm not the only one second-guessing myself," Ashleigh said. "Both Conrad and I are on pins and needles about the kidnappers—their character, their state of mind . . ."

"So what is that you and Conrad don't see eye to eye about?"

"We are almost certain that the kidnappers—"

"You're sure there's more than one?" Paige interrupted.

"Someone had to be driving, because Marnie said the man with the mask jumped in back and the van took off."

"The *two* Kennedy boys?"

"We don't know. But based on what Pocino told us, I'm not convinced the younger brother was part of the ransom plan. He may also be a victim. We should know more when—"

"When the posse returns," Paige cut in.

"I sure hope so," Ashleigh said with a heavy sigh. "I keep reminding myself of what Dick Landes told me, that very seldom do ransom plots pan out. The culprits are usually caught." She didn't want to complete the negative thoughts thundering through her head. Kidnappings were abundant in the world of literature and films—but as often as not, the victims did not make it out alive. "The kidnappers seem to be insisting that I be the one to make the ransom drop."

Ashleigh heard her friend's intake of breath. "But surely you wouldn't go alone?"

Nodding, Ashleigh replied, "If that's the only way to get Callie back, I certainly would."

"But Conrad won't let you—"

"So you see the problem."

Rick lifted the five-gallon gas can from the floor of the van before turning back to Sarah-Jayne. *What's this drugged-out broad thinking?* Unable to keep the sarcasm from his response, he said, "It's for the generator, dummy, not for turning our guests into crispy critters."

The instant he'd said it, he felt like a real jerk. *What's wrong with me?* One minute he was crazy about the chick; the next he focused on her flaws. After this job was done, he'd sort out his feelings. Not for the first time, he realized she was no mental giant, but most of the time that worked for him. Her loyalty and her actions between the sheets, especially when their passion for weed and crystal skyrocketed them to the next planet, were all he needed to be content. But maybe she wasn't really so dumb. Maybe it was the drugs. He would have to think about that later. *Once we've got no gang after us, no money worries, I'll pull it all together.*

"The generator takes gas?" Sarah-Jayne looked up from gathering the hefty McDonald's takeout bags and the cardboard holder full of drinks.

He couldn't help himself. "Duh."

Sarah-Jayne's bushy brows shot up.

"Just kidding, sugar." He scrubbed his hands with a fresh wipe and reached for the flashlight. After cleaning off the base, he said, "Let's get going. Our guests must be starving."

A smirk rose on Sarah-Jayne's face. "Make sure you don't mix up the bags."

"Not a chance. I have better ways than crushed Halcion tablets to reach the land of nod. Besides, I'm horny as hell."

Once they reached the shore, Rick held the flashlight so Sarah-Jayne wouldn't make a misstep on her trek up the plank and onto the boat. He followed behind.

Sarah-Jayne heaved herself onto the boat, descended into the salon, and put the food and drinks down on the U-shaped table.

The floor shuddered as Rick skipped the last step and thudded onto the warped floorboards.

"You want me to take this to them?" Sarah-Jayne asked.

"No." Rick flipped on the lights. "Apparently the generator's still putting out," he said, "so I reckon our guests are sleeping or just sitting in the dark."

Sarah-Jayne's brow furrowed. "Hey, where are *we* supposed to sleep?"

Rick gestured to the table with the semicircular bench.

"You've gotta be kidding."

"Not to worry. The table folds down and makes into a double bed. But first . . ." He had to get his baby bro and the pampered little daughter of the big mucky-muck who was causing such an uproar in Chicago. "We need to make sure those two eat enough so they'll get a good night's sleep." He shot her a wink.

Limping in pain, Neil nearly tripped on the buckled floorboards in the salon. His knee now had a knot the size of a fist. His empty stomach gave off a vocal protest. He could hardly wait to dig into the fast food on the table, but he waited patiently for Callie to emerge from the head. "Hey, Rick?" he said.

"What do you want, kid?"

"Could you please untie my hands so I can eat?"

"Don't need your hands untied." Pressing his own wrists together, Rick lifted his own bacon cheeseburger to his mouth to demonstrate.

Neil felt his hands balling into tight fists. He bit his tongue and asked, "How about one of those wipes?"

Rick did not answer but threw him a sealed packet. It landed on the table.

"Thanks," Neil said, and struggled to tear off the wrapper. For as long as he could remember, his half-brother was never without a supply of them. Reaching back in his memory he tried to recall when Rick had first developed this fetish for continually scrubbing his hands. Filtered through his hunger, a splinter of a memory came to him: their father confronting Rick about the boatload of wet wipes he'd bought with what was supposed to be the grocery money.

The door to the head creaked open, and the memory faded.

Callie stepped out. She'd pulled her hair back in a ponytail. *But how . . . ?* Neil's eyes dropped to her hands, which were no longer tied. Her eyes scanned the room, then locked on his. "How's your knee?"

Neil shrugged. "I'll live. How are—"

"Hey," Rick broke in, "you wanna chat, or you wanna eat?"

Callie's eyes flashed over to his half-brother. They were filled with loathing. Her hands had balled into tight fists.

Fearing she might lash out, as he longed to, Neil said, "Let's eat. I'm starved."

Callie quickly dropped her gaze to the floor and unballed her fists. "Yeah," she said, "so am I."

"Well, isn't that sweet?" Rick waved them into seats across from each other at the table.

Sarah-Jayne glared at them, but said nothing as she pushed the paper plates holding the burgers and fries toward them and set large containers of soda beside each plate.

Callie was ravenous. She prayed that after she ate, she'd feel a lot stronger. Now that she'd pried the bedspring loose, she could set her escape plan in gear as soon as Rick and Sarah-Jayne fell asleep or passed out. She was thirsty too, but she feared that the creep and his girlfriend might have drugged their sodas as they had the hot chocolate the night before.

She dared not drink more than a sip to soothe her dry throat. "May I have some water?" she asked.

Perched on a bar stool at the counter, with juice from the burger dripping out of the corners of her mouth, Sarah-Jayne shot the creep a nervous look.

Rick stood before the table, eyeing them, and let out a gruff laugh. "Got no bottled water, princess. Don't think you want anything out of them rusty old pipes."

She didn't, but she was so thirsty that after a couple of bites of her hamburger, she fished out an ice cube and sucked on it.

"Whaddya know?" Rick jeered. "A teenager who don't like Coca-Cola."

Callie clamped her mouth closed. She wished she could wipe the sneer off the creep's face. Instead, she followed the script she'd written for herself. "I don't really like soda, but I appreciate you getting it for me," she lied.

Just then, she felt the room begin to spin. Her brain seemed to be shutting down, and she felt herself slumping forward onto the table, knocking over the Coke. The last conscious sensation she had was of something cold dripping down on the leg of her jeans.

It was late, but Marnie was not tired in the least. She was far too keyed up to even think of going to sleep.

Uncle Mark had left with Auntie Paige soon after the foursome had returned from Nelson's, but Mr. Pocino was still there in the suite. The meeting with the FBI, the Chicago PD, Mr. Landes, and her parents had been going on for over an hour. Curious to find out what was going on, she tiptoed on bare feet to the library door, which stood ajar.

"Helicopters?" she heard her mother ask.

The special agent from the FBI was saying something she couldn't make out. Then it seemed that everyone was talking at once.

"Hold on," Marnie heard her dad say. "We can do nothing to jeopardize our daughter's safe return."

Then she heard Mr. Landes's voice. It was calm and clear. "Of course not."

The FBI man broke in. "We will discuss that after the call comes in. In the meantime, my team is installing the tracking device in the briefcase. It will be under the hard lining and nearly undetectable . . ."

Then her mother spoke up, her voice rising above everyone else's. "I'm not crazy about going alone to deliver the ransom, but if that's what it takes, you have to let me do it."

Marnie's mind raced. Her parents would never let her be part of getting Callie back, but she knew that she had to. *Mom should not go alone. I've got to be with her.* It would be tricky, but an idea was taking root in her brain.

CHAPTER
91

At the sound of his cell phone alarm, Rick dragged himself out of bed. He'd been lying there awake for a good half hour already, not wanting to take any chances of arriving late for work. Not today, on his last day at that lousy job—his last day in the state of Illinois, which held nothing for him but danger.

Sarah-Jayne snored loudly, dead to the world. Rick set the sound up as loud as it would go on her cell phone and placed it on the pillow beside her. Then he set the travel alarm on the other side of her head along with a note written in bold letters: PICK YOU UP AT NOON. KEEP A CLEAR HEAD. WE PARTY TONIGHT.

He grabbed his overalls, pulled them on, and pushed his feet into his boots. Before leaving, he peeked into the girl's cabin at the stern and his brother's in the bow, relocking each of the cabin doors and making sure each heavy hook was in place. Both kids appeared to be sound asleep. He hoped to hell Sarah-Jayne had not overdosed the girl. He needed the little princess for the twelve-thirty call, and he needed her alive.

Callie awoke with a start and bolted upright. The sound of an alarm had pierced her deep sleep. Blinking, she tried to orient herself. *The boat . . . I'm on the boat . . .* The sound was coming from outside her door, most likely in the salon. It wasn't just *an* alarm, she realized; there was a chorus of alarms.

Dull light filtered through the thick plastic of the windows. Her vision was slightly blurred and her mouth was bone dry. She blinked again in hopes of clearing her head, then slipped out of bed and padded across to the cabin door. Resting her ear against it, she listened for any other sound of life. At the sound of someone groping about in the salon, she wondered which of her captors it was. Were both of them still on the boat? Hearing a string of profanity, she knew the skanky girlfriend was aboard. *But where's the creep? And when will someone come for me?*

Quickly brushing aside the thought of someone coming to her rescue, she concentrated on how she was going to rescue herself. She couldn't just wait. And the thought of her mother coming face-to-face with the creep turned her hollow inside. Swishing her tongue along the roof of her mouth, she tried to form a bit of moisture. They had to have put some kind of drug in her food rather than in the Coke. They'd probably drugged Neil too. Today she wasn't going to take the chance of eating or drinking anything she was given. Just thinking of all those hours she'd been passed out—all that time she could have been working to free herself—made her feel sick.

She rummaged beneath the mattress of the double bed for the bedspring she'd hidden there, wishing she had the night back.

Around nine o'clock the predicted storm hit and the intermittent rain became constant. This time the weatherman had gotten it right. Although most of Gino's work detail was indoors, the downpour prevented the safe delivery of drywall and other essential materials. The foreman at the construction site called it a day, sending the entire crew, including Gino, home.

Not at all unhappy about the turn of events, Gino dashed through the pouring rain to his Avalanche. He clicked the door open and took a second to look skyward and utter a silent *Thank you*. Raindrops bounced off his face and soaked his coveralls, but he was elated.

Today was opening day for De Mornay's.

CHAPTER

92

In front of the Christonellis' suburban home, Nelson Kennedy pulled up behind Tony Wainwright's red VW Bug, climbed out of the Highlander, pushed open his umbrella, and dashed around to the passenger door. Erica had already pushed it open.

The front door flew open, and Mike and Tony, clad in raingear, were heading out in a rush to meet him. Before Erica could ask what was going on, Mike stopped midstride and said, "We're not waiting around for the police anymore. We're taking matters into our own hands. Finding Marnie's twin is a priority."

Tony cut in. "I've got to help find this kid. I've had it up to here," he said, raising his hand to eye level, "with forever being everyone's number one suspect."

"Tony," Erica said, but she didn't finish. *What is there to say?*

"We've been noodling around on the Web since dawn," Mike said to Nelson. "We've got a lead on the place where your stepson and his girlfriend have been holed up in Cicero. Sarah-Jayne, if that's the chick's real name—"

"Hold on, Tony," Nelson said. "The police and the FBI already ran down Rick and his girlfriend's apartment. It leads nowhere. They've cleared out."

Erica's gaze was ping-ponging back and forth between the two men. She wavered, feeling as if she were ready to collapse.

Nelson reached out and steadied her by the elbow. Turning to Mike, he snapped his fingers. "Come back inside. It just dawned on me. I have an idea where Rick could have taken the kids. Can you locate any current maps of the outskirts of the city?"

Back in the house, Mike tossed his raincoat over the back of the sofa, and all three men headed to the office.

Erica's head pounded, but she was determined to help in any way she could. But before she could follow the men toward the computers, the phone rang. For a whole five seconds, she stood stock-still, making no attempt to answer it. Finally, she plucked up the receiver. "Marnie? Oh, precious, are you alright? . . . Of course you can. I can't wait to see you."

Viviana hustled up to the mezzanine, Dolly at her heels and her assistant, Delores, following a few steps behind. Not for the first time, Viviana was pleased with her new hire. The mature, meticulously attired woman gave off exactly the right image for De Mornay's, and fortunately she had no highfalutin ideas about designing clothing, as Erica Christonelli had years ago back in New York. Delores's only desire was to continue serving the fashion-conscious movers and shakers of the city. She was a perfect fit. Viviana hadn't had to explain the importance of keeping detailed information about sizes, colors, and other preferences of her clientele. Delores had her own little black book and quite an extensive patron list, which she'd brought with her from her last position at the Ferragamo boutique on Michigan Avenue.

Tail wagging, Dolly settled at Viviana's feet. With her pink collar encrusted with small Austrian crystals, and her fur, white as copy paper and flawlessly trimmed, the toy poodle was the ideal accessory for the upscale boutique, and she seemed to know it.

The floor-to-ceiling alcove, opposite the windowed wall, was filled with the preselected ensembles Viviana had chosen for the ladies who, she was certain, would grace De Mornay's this opening week. Many had been patrons of her Fifth Avenue boutique in New York; others she'd schmoozed before and during her opening-night extravaganza here in Chicago.

Behind the card labeled MAGGIE DALEY, she lifted the red, full-length evening gown by J. Mendel off the pole. She'd selected this one for the upcoming Governor's Ball, knowing it would be perfect for the effervescent, resilient blonde. Adding it to a matching dress and jacket from the Elie Tahari collection, she instructed Delores, "Run on down to the mayor's wife with these for now, and tell her I'll be right with her. First, I need to get the minaudière Stedman wanted for Oprah."

Although opening day so far had not been all that Viviana had envisioned, several famous personages had visited the boutique already, and it was not yet noon. Taking the beastly weather into account, it was exceeding her gloomy expectation early this morning, when she'd awakened with the steady patter of raindrops drumming on her bedroom window. At her suggestion, Gino had not stayed the night; she had wanted to get her beauty rest, which was something he was unlikely to give her. When she had awakened this morning, however, the imprint of his head upon the pillow beside her had given her a warm glow and made the gray morning not quite so dismal. *If only Gino hadn't been needed on the job at dawn.* She'd pictured him attending the opening in that Armani tuxedo he'd worn for her opening gala. All dressed up, Gino was even more charming than usual, and he would have been delicious eye candy for her patrons.

Thundering footfalls bounded up the stairs, and like a genie she'd conjured up from a bottle, Gino appeared at the top, outside her office. He had donned that Armani tux she'd envisioned, and a hunk of dark hair fell rakishly over his brow.

"What a wonderful surprise," she purred, as she ran to meet him. "I was just thinking about you." It occurred to Viviana that perhaps this downpour was not all bad. "You look positively yummy in that suit." *And even better undressed,* she thought with a wicked smile.

The Palmer House penthouse had been as busy as JFK during the holiday rush; otherwise, Marnie knew, she might not have had a chance of talking her parents into letting her visit with her other family. But right now, that was where she needed to be.

Last night Marnie had imagined herself waiting here at the Palmer House until the kidnappers called. Then she'd planned to sneak down and hide on the floor in the backseat of the car her mother would drive to drop off the ransom. But after she had overheard her dad's reaction, that plan had blown up before it took root. Her dad had totally lost his cool a few minutes ago, which almost never happened. If her mother had been around, she was sure he never would've exploded like that.

The argument he'd had with the FBI guy and Mr. Landes was fierce. "If there is no way around having Ashleigh make the delivery," he'd shouted, "it will be over my dead body that she leaves here without me." Then everyone was talking at once, until Marnie heard her dad's voice boom loudly above the others: "I won't get in the way. I'll conceal myself beneath a blanket on the floor in the backseat." Marnie couldn't believe it. That had been her plan all along.

Then she'd recognized Mr. Landes's voice taking charge: "Hold on. I think we can work this out so Ashleigh will be protected *and* you'll not be left out of the loop. You may recall Ray Billings, one of my agents who has worked with you in the past, is now in our Chicago agency. He's not a big man. He can easily be concealed on the floor. And Conrad, Pocino is arranging for a helicopter and a pilot. You'll get a bird's-eye view. You'll have to keep off the perp's radar, but we'll have you on ours."

It sounded as though her dad didn't like that idea, but that's what they were going forward with. So this Ray Billings would take Marnie's spot in the car her mom would be driving to the ransom drop-off. Marnie's plan was out the window—but she was already beginning to cook up a new one.

Now if only the driver would come to take her to her other family.

Juliana and Elizabeth were feeling much better today and had gone down to the Toddmans' suite to be with Nana Helen. But Marnie had more important things to do. Uncle Mark and Auntie Paige had been in and out earlier, but when the FBI agent with a briefcase came in, they had gone to their own suite too.

Everyone else had disappeared into the library, leaving the door only partially opened. She'd had her ear to the door, straining to catch as much of the conversations inside as possible, when Mr. Pocino arrived.

"What have we here?" the big man asked.

Whirling around, her eyes met Pocino's. "I'm going to Uncle Mike's," she said. "I'm just waiting for the driver."

His bushy eyebrows shot skyward, and he nodded. "I know this is tough for you. But it's all going to be okay. We are going to find Callie and bring her home." His gruff voice had softened, and he looked so sincere.

"Marnie," he said, taking her by the elbow, "since we have a few minutes, I'd like to talk to you." He pulled out one of the dining room chairs for her, then pulled out one for himself. He gestured for her to be seated. As he cleared his throat, Marnie dreaded what he might say. He wasn't like her mom—not at all. He wasn't the forgiving sort. In fact, she'd overheard his tirade when he'd first found out what had happened. *The last thing I need right now is a lecture about the dangers of the Internet. I'm already the sorriest teenager on the planet.*

"Your parents told me that you feel bad about what's happened to your sister, that you've buried yourself in a mountain of guilt. But we all make mistakes." Leaning in close, he said, "What I want you to know is that the kidnapper, who we now have a pretty good bead on, is a sociopath." He paused. "Do you know what that means?"

She nodded. She'd read about sociopaths in her health class.

"Whether or not you'd been the one to hook up—" He crinkled his broad brow and repeated, "Hook up? Isn't that what you call it?"

Marnie nodded. *Whatever.* She prayed that the driver would get there in a hurry or someone would call Pocino into the library.

"What I was getting at is, we are pretty damn . . . Sorry, I mean we're pretty certain that this kidnapping must have been planned quite some time ago. The kid you were communicating with was merely a pawn in the kidnapper's game. One way or another, this kidnapper would have found a way to abduct you or one of your sisters."

Marnie nodded again, but she knew he was just trying to make her feel better. *But why? And how does he know that this "Brad" guy isn't a part of it?* She had lots of questions, but the private investigator was in a position to answer just one of them.

"Mr. Pocino," she said, "is that briefcase the FBI guy brought in full of money?"

Conrad was wearing a path in the carpet when Pocino joined the group in the library. The FBI's net had not dragged in this Rick character at any construction sites this morning. Conrad desperately wanted Pocino to bring him up to speed, but he knew they'd have to talk privately. Conrad felt impotent as Special Agent Roy Porter painstakingly reviewed the plan once more, making sure he and Ashleigh understood every detail of the drop-off.

As much as Conrad wanted to prevent Ashleigh from being the ransom carrier, it was clear that he was not in control here. While it filled him with rage, he could not fight Ashleigh's logic. "Please don't try to stop me if the kidnapper demands that I must deliver the ransom alone," she'd said. "I'm not willing to risk Callie's life." Then, with an unwavering gaze, she'd added, "And neither are you." Only one thing had given him the strength to acquiesce: knowing that he and Pocino had set a backup plan in motion.

In addition to the tracking device in the briefcase, the rented car that Ashleigh would drive had been set up with two tracking mechanisms in separate locations. "That way," Porter explained, "if one tracking mechanism is detected, it's unlikely anyone would search for a second."

"Hold on," Conrad interjected. "Are you now suggesting we are dealing with a professional?"

"Not according to our intel."

"But isn't that kind of detection—"

"Today, all the bad guys have to do is go online. Much of what the pros have is available now to the amateurs. This guy is small-time, but he's creative. Remember, Senske and Murdock discovered that this Rick character drives a silver van, and the license plate on the silver van that he used to abduct Callie was false, leading to a black Buick. And the magnetic door panel signs used to disguise the vehicle as a bakery van are not hard to come by. So, we'd be willing to wager that he has more than a few tricks up his sleeve." Porter paused. "One thing does puzzle us, though. Not sure why the perp used his own vehicle. Why not a stolen car?"

An icy finger of dread shot up Conrad's backbone as unbidden thoughts crept into his mind. *Why would the kidnapper need a van?*

Taking the Homewood turnoff to I-94, Rick felt a lump forming in his throat. The traffic was bumper-to-bumper. He hoped to high heaven— if such a place existed—this was just a temporary bottleneck. He'd allowed more than enough time to pick up Sarah-Jayne and take her to the Sienna minivan, get back to the boat to make the call at the sched- uled time, and drive to the ransom drop. But timing was a key element; this must go off like clockwork. He squinted as huge raindrops pelted his windshield. *If this traffic doesn't let up, we're screwed.*

Then, as so often happens on freeways, the traffic cleared suddenly, and he picked up speed. Nearing his exit, he grabbed his phone and hit the speed dial for Sarah-Jayne's cell. She picked up on the second ring. "Be there in ten," he said.

When he met her up on the rain-soaked dirt road, in the spot where they'd been parking the van, he chuckled at her concern. "Of course it worked. I told you it would. The instant the boss caught a glimpse of my flushed face, he sent me packing. Couldn't afford to have a flu bug infect the crew." Once again the niacin capsule had been his salvation. *At least now I won't be reported as AWOL in case dear old stepdad has the police sniffing around Chicago's construction sites.*

Once inside the van, Sarah-Jayne riddled him with a jillion questions.

"Leave off, will you?" he told her. "It's getting late. I need time to go over what I'm going to have the princess say to her mom."

The ping of loose gravel from the unpaved road beyond the rest area rattled Rick's thought process. He whipped up behind the burgundy minivan, tension radiating from every nerve ending. He checked his watch and exhaled. *Plenty of time to get back to the boat to make that call. I've got to chill.*

Sarah-Jayne sat beside him, biting a cuticle. She had been silent like he'd told her, but she looked as nervous as he felt. She needed something to help calm her down. *Hell, we both do. And I know just what will do the trick.* There were no other vehicles in the area beyond the public bathrooms, and besides, even if someone took a short hike into this wooded area, no one could see inside the back of the van. Smiling to himself, he thought, *What's good for the goose . . .*

Pulling her to him, he gave her a deep-throated kiss and ran a hand up between her legs. Then, with a wink, he said, "How about a quickie?"

She grinned, and the anxiety evaporated from her round face. "I'm in," she said, running her tongue across her bottom lip. Then she dove between the seats for the back of the van.

Five minutes later, Rick was pulling on his jeans and reaching for his boots. As he scrubbed his hands with a wipe, he felt much less tense, and from the blush on Sarah-Jayne's cheeks, he knew she was satisfied too. "By sundown we'll be on our way, sugar." The thought of abandoning his van for the minivan was a concession he'd rather not make, but Sarah-Jayne had a good point: Minivans were far more common and less likely to draw attention. Still, he felt his pulse quicken as he placed the keys to the Toyota Sienna in her hands.

"You want me to go back to the boat with you for the call?" she asked.

"Of course not. We can't let the kids see the minivan."

"Why not?" Sarah-Jayne arched a pierced eyebrow. "I thought you said . . . You can't be thinking of leaving those kids alive."

The thought *had* been rolling around in his head, but . . . "Of course not," he said.

CHAPTER
94

Wiping the sweat rolling off her brow with the sleeve of her sweatshirt, Callie tried once again to straighten the bedspring. She set it under the heel of her boot and slowly shifted her full weight onto the spring. The last time she'd managed to uncoil and straighten the heavy spring, it had broken. Fortunately, the long end was more than enough for her purpose. She'd been so close. She would have had not only a tool she could slide through the narrow slit in the door to unhook the latch but a weapon too. Although she was thankful this door was not sealed like the cabin doors on cruise ships, she was still trapped.

The rain continued to drum on the roof and the deck of the decrepit old boat. Callie had no way of telling what time it was, but she felt the minutes evaporating. It must be close to noon by now. The creep would be back to make his call before twelve thirty, and probably his vengeful girlfriend too. *If only I could get the darn latch unhooked and get off the boat before—*

At the sound of a rumble she grew deathly still. It hadn't sounded like thunder, and there was no one else in this wasteland. At least, she didn't think so. *It must be the van.*

She slipped her sweatshirt back over her head and was ready to hide the screw beneath her mattress, until she had a second thought: *The creep will have to take me with him to collect the money.* So instead she tucked the screw under her sports bra, right where her phone had been, and then moved to the window, waiting for the creep and his girlfriend to come into view.

Rick picked up the bag of now cold Chicken McNuggets, pulled on the yellow slicker, and shoved the sou'wester on his head, feeling more like a Gloucester fisherman than someone who was about to become a millionaire. He hopped down from the van into a weed-filled area; mud splattered the leg of his coverall, and with it came a rush of expletives. *This fuckin' rain could throw a monkey wrench into my master plan.* But when his thoughts switched to the end game, he grinned. *If the princess's prissy mother gets wet, too bad. I'm not changing a motherfuckin' thing.*

Bowing his head against the unrelenting downpour, he trudged down the hill toward the boat. Several feet before he reached the plank, he sank deeper into the muck, so deep that he felt mud creep over the top of his boots. "Jesus H. Christ," he said aloud, his voice little more than a hiss.

The instant he hit the deck, he toed off his boots and tugged off the soaking socks, dropping them at his feet. "Chow time," he called out as he came down the companionway. He got no answer from either the bow or the stern.

First he unlatched Neil's door and tossed a bag of Chicken McNuggets onto the V berth. He felt like saying, *Enjoy your last meal,* but thought better of it. Instead, he barked out an order: "If you've got to use the head, do it now."

"This has gone far enough." Neil's face was a rosy red, his voice dry and raspy. "Is Callie okay?" Not waiting for an answer, he wiped the lenses of his glasses on his sweatshirt and said, "It's humid as hell on this stinking boat. It could sink any goddamn minute, but we're likely to die of thirst first. You've left us with no water." Neil rolled up the leg of his pants and pointed to his swollen knee. The area around the baseball-sized knot had already turned an ugly yellowish green. "And how about some ice for the swelling?"

"Sorry, Prince Charming, this isn't the Ritz-Carlton. We've got no room service, and I'm fresh out of ice." Pointing to the bathroom, Rick repeated, "If you've gotta pee, do it now. Your window of opportunity is closing fast."

Neil hobbled to the door and clung to the jamb for support. "What are you going to do with us?"

"Well, baby brother, you're not worth a thin dime, but the girl's a whole other story." With a sneer, he added, "Guess I should thank you for pointing out the opportunity."

"I did no such thing. You lied to me and took advantage of me. I never should have trusted you."

"That was your first mistake. Never trust *anyone.*"

"How about Sarah-Jayne? You trust *her.*"

Rick shook his head. "I trust no one but the man who stares back at me from the mirror. And sometimes that's a bit shaky." A quick glance at his wristwatch announced that it was twelve fifteen. He had no time to waste. "Now or never, buddy."

Neil limped toward the head, his bound hands grasping the walls every step of the way. Throwing open the door, he asked again, "How about Callie? You can't hurt her, Rick."

"So you're gonna be her knight in shabby armor?" Rick laughed. "Maybe if you'd shown a bit of gumption and become a team player, you'd be getting a piece of the action instead of ending up where you are now."

Holding onto the door, Neil raised his raspy voice. "I don't want any piece of the action. This is all wrong. You are an immoral SOB, just like Dad said." Before Rick could react, Neil lowered his voice and said, "As long as you get the money, you'll let us go, right?" His bravado had dissipated like the air let out of a rubber balloon.

"As long as everyone does what they're told, nobody gets hurt. You and the princess will be tucked into your own bed tonight by doting parents," he lied.

When Neil limped out of the head, he made his way for the salon table.

"Hold it," Rick shouted. "Not there. The princess and I have work to do. You'll be in your quarters for the duration." Rick held the door to the forward cabin open, then handed Neil a Gatorade. "Drink it or wear it," he said before latching the door.

Now for the little lady. He withdrew the Smith & Wesson revolver from the kitchen drawer, where he'd hidden it after Sarah-Jayne's assault on his brother—not to protect Neil, but to keep Sarah-Jayne from misplacing it. He didn't care about the pain his brother experienced half as much as he cared about the inconvenience of waiting for him to hippity-hop about the boat.

Callie's cabin door flew open with such force that it banged against the inside wall. An overwhelming wave of terror swept over her as she eyed Rick in the doorway. If only she'd managed to escape before his return . . . But she would have had nothing to protect her from the pelting cloudburst. And anyway, it was too late to think about that scenario. Although she hadn't made it off the boat, she must refuse to give in to defeat. *Only losers give up.* Pressing her palms together, she bowed her head and prayed for inspiration.

"You gotta pee?"

She shook her head.

"Eat this," he barked, tossing her a McDonald's bag, which she nearly dropped, and setting a bottle of red Gatorade on the dresser. "And make it snappy. We've got a phone call to make."

The very thought of food made her nauseous. Her tummy felt like a butter churn. She swallowed hard, gathering what saliva she could in her dry mouth. *Get a grip,* she chided herself. *You can't give in to panic now. Not when you're so close* . . . She inhaled slowly and exhaled just as slowly.

Silently, she watched Rick's every move. Without a second glance, he bent down and struggled with the rickety built-in drawers beneath the bunk bed. It seemed to take all the strength he could muster to pry one of the warped drawers from the equally warped wood surrounding it. It finally came loose, and he jerked it open and grabbed a pair of white gym socks. Callie stared down at the contents. *If only I could have managed to get the drawer open . . .*

When he looked up, her thoughts were cut short. He glared over at her unopened McDonald's bag. Not bothering to close the ill-fitting drawer, he said, "Eat or don't eat. I don't really give a good goddamn." Wearing a malevolent grin, he added, "Our time together is running out. Do what you're told, and you may see the sun come up tomorrow."

On that note, the door slammed shut behind him, and Callie heard the all-too-familiar sound of the hook locking into place.

Erica's head felt as if it were about to split apart. This was the worst migraine she'd suffered in years, and yet she couldn't let Marnie know. She wanted so badly to see her daughter and spend time with her.

The night before had been devastating. She felt that her daughter was slipping away. To see the baby she'd raised drawing away had set her nerves on fire. The alienation was more than she could bear. The closeness they'd always shared now seemed like a distant dream. Erica had to recapture that intimacy; she couldn't let it melt away. She couldn't help thinking, over and over, that fate had dealt them a horrific hand.

She cradled her neck, willing the pounding in her head to cease, as she stared out at the rain and waited for the first glimpse of her daughter so she could meet her with Mike's oversized golf umbrella. She was thankful that Marnie was safe and prayed that Callie and Neil would soon be returned safely too.

Nelson was frantic with worry over his son, but he was somehow managing to hold himself together and think clearly and constructively. He had some sort of idea about where his stepson might be hiding out, and for nearly an hour, he'd been totally engrossed in mapping out a plan. Tony Wainwright seemed as determined as Nelson to find the kids. Whether that was to clear his name or out of concern for the kids, she wasn't sure. The bottom line was that both men were determined to succeed where the police and FBI had so far failed.

Mike had been reluctant to leave the house. He'd told Nelson that if he could be of any real help, he was more than willing to let the project fall to the competition, but if he failed to present his website plan to Honda's management team and board of directors at the prescribed eleven o'clock meeting, he was bound to lose this plum of a job. So now it was just Tony and Nelson planning the next move, while Erica waited for Marnie to arrive.

She spotted the limo as it pulled up into the driveway. She gingerly rose from the sofa, picked up the umbrella, and moved to the door as swiftly as her pounding head would allow. But when she pulled open the door, Marnie was already on the porch stomping her booted feet and shaking the rain from her blonde hair.

Distracted and anxious, Marnie found it difficult to sit still while going over the events of the past couple of days with her mom. When Erica revealed that she had a debilitating migraine and excused herself so she could rest for an hour or so, telling Marnie not to disturb Nelson and Tony, Marnie felt a wave of relief. Her mom had been so apologetic that Marnie felt a little guilty, but not too much. Whether this was a good time or not, she needed to talk to Nelson about his lying son. *Is it possible that the boy who tricked me was also kidnapped? That he wasn't part of this horrible plan?*

As soon as Erica disappeared into her bedroom, Marnie marched down the hallway toward the office to confront Nelson, but she stopped short at the sound of raised voices. She stood beside the threshold of the kitchen, out of sight. *I'm beginning to feel like Huckleberry Finn, always listening to other people's secrets from the bottom of a sugar barrel.*

"Hold on." She recognized Nelson's voice. "I think I may know where Rick has taken them—someplace my late wife, Sandy, used to take him."

Who is Rick? She hadn't heard the name before. Could that be Nelson's stepson—the half-brother "Brad" had told her about? It had to be. *What kind of man has Mom brought into our lives? His own son's a liar, and his stepson's a kidnapper.* Maybe this Neil wasn't really the victim Nelson thought he was.

For a long moment no one spoke. Marnie heard the rustling of papers, and then Nelson said, "Rick told me Sandy, his mom, had taken the boat—the one where the shooting took place—off the beaten path."

Shooting? Marnie's forefingers shot to her lips as if to quiet her inward shriek.

"After the shooting, she'd wanted to avoid all the looky-loos. I had no interest in the boat or its whereabouts. Quite honestly, I didn't much care. Just witnessing the aftermath of that bloody scene was enough for me. All I knew was, the old boat was anchored offshore somewhere, on one of those quiet Chicago River offshoots.

"But when Sandy died and Rick ran away, I had to call the police. Without the Chicago PD's helicopter team, I never would have found the boat. Rick had pulled anchor and plowed into the shore. He never admitted it, but . . . Rick never took responsibility for anything. He always played the victim. Anyway, it was in a remote location, stuck in the mud. I doubt that it's seaworthy, so it's bound to still be there." He paused. "Somewhere near . . . here."

"What are we waiting for?" Marnie didn't recognize that voice.

Nelson responded, "I've only been there once, but I'm pretty sure I can find it."

"Let's hit the road," the other voice shot back.

Crossing the threshold between the hallway and the kitchen, Marnie saw that Nelson was shrugging into his jacket and the other man—the stocky man whom she met the night of the opening party at De Mornay's—was gathering maps from the table.

"Marnie," Nelson said. "When did you get here?"

"Nelson," she said, ignoring his question, "I need to talk to you. Mom said this isn't a good time but—"

"I'm afraid it isn't, sweetheart. We are—"

"Don't call me sweetheart." Marnie felt heat creep up her neck.

"Sorry, Marnie. I'm not sure, but I think I might know where your sister and my son are being held. We have to leave immediately."

"You do?" Marnie's heart beat so fast, she thought it might explode.

"I'm not positive, but I have a strong suspicion about where my stepson might hide. We've got to leave now. I'll let—"

"I need to go with you." Marnie took off for the foyer and grabbed her parka.

Nelson was right behind her with car keys in his hand. He took hold of her arm as she tried to slip into her jacket. "I'm sorry, Marnie. Tony and I have to be on our way. We can't take you with us. It could be dangerous."

When she started to argue, Tony tried to reassure her. "We're going to find your sister," he said, flipping open his cell phone and starting to dial a number. "And when we do, you'll be the first one we call."

Both men dashed out the door and into the rain, toward Nelson's SUV.

Marnie was furious. *Why won't anyone let me help?* She had to be there for Callie. She couldn't just sit still and let others clean up her mess. She watched desperately as the Highlander reversed and pulled out of the driveway, leaving Erica's car in full view, parallel parked at the curb.

Without a second thought, she darted back to the kitchen and pulled the Caprice's keys off the wooden rack.

All dressed up in his shoulder-binding tux in the middle of the day, Gino felt as if he'd been cast in an alien role. Yet without a word of complaint, he smiled and greeted Viviana's clientele cordially as they entered the prestigious boutique. Actually it was sort of fun. He hadn't had so much attention since he was a toddler. *Maybe Viviana was right. Maybe I should give acting a shot.* But as quickly as that thought surfaced, he dismissed the idea. He knew he needed physical activity to keep his body going and his mind fresh. *With all that downtime, I'd go stark raving mad.*

The vibrating cell phone in his breast pocket curtailed further speculation. Pulling it from his jacket, he checked the caller ID. It was Tony. Stepping outside under the awning, Gino flipped open the phone. "What's up?"

"Where are you?" Tony asked.

Hearing the note of anxiety in his roommate's voice, he said simply, "De Mornay's." But he couldn't resist asking, "Why?"

"We need to borrow the Avalanche." Tony cleared his throat. "I'll bring you up to speed as we head in your direction."

"'We'?"

"Me and Nelson Kennedy—you know, Erica Christonelli's boyfriend? To make a long story short, it appears that his son was kidnapped Saturday night along with the Taylor twin. Nelson suspects his stepson and thinks he may have a clue as to where he's taken the kids."

Gino heard what sounded like the slamming of a car door, followed by the roar of an engine.

"We need a four-wheel drive . . ."

As Tony filled him in, Gino came to understand the urgency in his roommate's voice. *It must be hell, always having his past thrown in his face.*

"Got it," Gino said. "Meet me at the house. I'll drive."

Even as she clenched her teeth to suppress a scream, Callie felt anger overshadow her terror. *Why does the creep insist on having Mom bring the money? What kind of trap is he setting?* More than ever, Callie was determined to stop Rick and his no-good girlfriend. *I can't let them hurt Mom.*

She fingered the jagged end of the bedspring, which she'd moved to the pouch of her sweatshirt, and envisioned catching the creep by surprise. She'd rake it down his pockmarked face, make a dash for the plank, rush down to shore, and push the plank away from the side of the boat, leaving him stranded.

A flash of lightning lit up the cabin. Seconds later it was followed by a clash of thunder that shattered her thoughts. Staring out at the unrelenting rain, she saw her idiotic plan being dashed to shreds. Even if she could execute it the way she'd imagined it and make her escape from the boat, she had no idea where she was or how far she'd have to slosh through the rain to reach any kind of help. And then there was the girl with the weird tattoos, who was most likely sitting out there in the van. Callie shivered, knowing that Sarah-Jayne would not hesitate to stop her anyway she could. On top of all that, with no protection from the elements, she'd most likely die of pneumonia.

Rubbing her upper arms to stave off the chill, Callie forced herself to stop envisioning the worst-case scenario. Willing her nerves to settle, she reached for the McDonald's bag. She sniffed the food for any sign of something added and told herself that it was probably clean. After all, the creep needed her now. Then she forced herself to eat. Hungry or not, she'd need every ounce of strength she could gather. She wasn't going to die of starvation—at least not anytime soon.

Noting that the seal was unbroken, she took several swallows of the Gatorade and grimaced at the icky taste. She had no idea how athletes could stomach it. This fruit punch flavor was even more sickeningly sweet than most, but she took another large swig, knowing that after so little to drink in nearly forty-eight hours, she was not far from becoming dehydrated.

"Hey, princess. It's showtime," the creep bellowed as he unlatched the door.

Startled, Callie dropped the bottle of Gatorade and stared in horror as the red liquid soaked into the pillow and gushed onto the floor.

CHAPTER
97

The door banged loudly against the inside wall of the aft cabin. "Showtime," Rick repeated. "Time to show—" He froze.

Blood. It was soaking into the pillow—into the blanket—onto the floor. So much blood. Rick sagged against the door frame as his world spun back in time.

He was a scrawny boy of twelve. A boy who loved his mother with all his heart. A boy who had no one in the world but his mother and would do anything to win her love. Do anything she asked. Do anything to see her smile.

The night before, he'd stolen the gun from their neighbor's garage—the one she told him she needed for protection. He'd found it in the bottom tool drawer, right where his mom had said it would be. That night he received a big hug from Mom. She told him that she loved him, that he was a good boy—words he'd longed to hear.

The next day she took him with her to Joe's boat. Though far from ritzy, the boat looked glamorous to his young eyes. Rick loved it when Mom took him to visit her friend. He thought it would be so cool to live on a boat, and since Joe's was anchored offshore, near a small marina, Rick got to take the dinghy back and forth. Mom stayed aboard the boat with Joe, giving Rick lots of time to tool around and explore, all by himself.

But suddenly that all came to an end. He was no longer a boy. His childhood came to a screeching halt with a vision of Joe sprawled across the bottom of the double bunk—a vision that formed again and again in Rick's mind. Rick had walked into the aft cabin. Blood was pouring from the hole in Joe's temple. Mom thrust the gun in his hand. Then everything went black. Had he passed out? The next thing he remembered was blood on his hands and soaking into the cuffs of his sweatshirt.

His childhood came to end that day, and no matter how hard he scrubbed his hands, they never felt clean.

The girl was rambling, saying something about Gatorade and an accident.

"Shut up," he shouted. Reaching in his pocket, he tore open the packet and began to scrub his hands. He couldn't think with her yammering away. He couldn't think . . .

Now get a grip, he ordered himself. "Forget about that," he said aloud, grabbing her by the elbow. He had to reclaim his authority. But as he led her from the mess in the aft cabin into the salon, he was gripped with uncertainty. Something about the vision he'd had was all wrong. Something about the memory was different. He hadn't been the one. He hadn't been holding the gun. *Is it possible? Was Mom only pretending to love me? What if I didn't shoot Joe?*

The thought might put a whole new perspective on things, but he wasn't sure. *I haven't killed anyone. Not yet.*

Callie stumbled across the threshold. The creep's grip loosened, and she caught herself on the door frame.

He didn't say a single word, just gestured toward the salon table. His indifference and faraway look somehow held a deeper menace than his abrasiveness had. *What is he thinking?* Callie fingered the bedspring in her sweatshirt pocket, dropped to the horseshoe bench, and slid in. She spotted what looked like a new cell phone next to a piece of paper, both of which were not quite within her reach. *My new script. If only I could get a chance to . . .* The thought died. Even if she risked giving her parents a clue, she had none to pass on—no idea where she even was.

Another roar of thunder shattered the silence. She'd seen no lightning. But what did it matter? She felt time running out, and she knew what she must do. The utter futility of making an escape from the boat was clear. It would be a dumb move. Now that she'd seen his face and knew his name, he wasn't about to let her go. Somehow she'd have to find a way to escape when she went with him to collect the ransom.

Still looking distracted, the creep shoved the paper in front of her. "When I put you on the phone, read this. And not one word comes out of your mouth other than those." He stabbed the paper with his index finger. "*Comprende?*"

A banging racket, followed by a slight rocking of the boat, seemed to catapult the creep back from that faraway place. "Cut it out, you sniveling little brat. One more peep out of you, and Big Daddy's pride and joy will be history." The noise stopped.

Callie had forgotten all about Neil. *What's going to happen to him? Is he coming with us to pick up the ransom, or is he going to be left behind?* She had no time to ask. The creep had tapped in a series of numbers on the cell phone, and now he was holding an index finger over his lips.

Out of the corner of her eye, Viviana noticed Gino standing a few feet away. He appeared to be waiting for her to finish her conversation with the reporter. It was unusual for him to intrude when she was engaged in business; he rarely interrupted even her idle conversation. He knew how thrilled she'd been that the De Mornay's opening would be featured in the next issue of the *Chicago Tribune* fashion spread, as well as in the next *Fashionista Chicago*. She reflected that he must have something important on his mind, something that couldn't wait.

"Excuse me," she said to the young reporter. "This will only take a moment."

Gino took her gently by the arm and led her to the patron counter, away from the reporter and the customers who were milling about the store. "I'm so sorry, angel, but I'm afraid I'm going to have to abandon my post."

Utterly taken aback, Viviana said nothing.

"Tony called," Gino went on. "Something has come up on the twin's abduction, and I have to go."

"I don't understand. What does this have to do with you, Gino?

"All I know is . . ."

Viviana's breath caught when he told her about Kennedy's son. "You mean Erica's boyfriend?" she asked. It was a rhetorical question. "It seems that woman is a catalyst for disaster."

"Now hold on, Viviana."

"I know, I know. That's unfair. But it seems that when things go wrong, she's always either acting the victim or lurking somewhere in the background."

"Angel," he said, "I've really got to get going. They need my four-wheel drive to check out the location where Kennedy suspects the kids are being held. They'll arrive at the house soon, and I need time to slip out of this monkey suit and into something more practical." He glanced around the salon, then gave her a chaste kiss on the forehead and headed out through the stockroom.

Viviana's emotions were in a tailspin. Why couldn't Gino just offer to lend Tony his Avalanche so he could remain here to be a part of her big day? But this thought made her feel self-centered, and she hated that feeling. She should be proud of Gino for supporting his friend, and for doing whatever he could to find the missing twin and bring her home.

Her thoughts turned to Callie, and she prayed no harm would come to the charming and talented teenager. Slowly, she began to feel better. *I'm a businesswoman, but I'm not heartless.*

Tearing her thoughts away from matters over which she had no control, she checked her image in the full-length mirror. Pleased that the stress pulsating through her body did not show, she rejoined the reporter.

It was exactly 12:30 PM when the phone sounded in the penthouse of the Palmer House.

No one spoke. The room reeked of tension.

Agent Porter and Dick Landes exchanged glances. Porter pointed to the phone beside Conrad and, as Conrad lifted it, picked up the receiver of the phone beside him.

"Conrad Taylor." His calm, steady voice belied the racing of his heart.

"Mr. CEO, you aren't running this show," a raspy voice rumbled across the phone line. "Put your wife on the phone."

Conrad bit back an angry retort. "Please, there's no question that you're the one who's holding all the cards. We've done as you instructed. We've got your money, and I'm ready to make the delivery."

"I'm not dealing with you, hotshot. Put your wife on the phone. *Now.*"

Reluctantly, Conrad handed the phone to Ashleigh, who sat statue still beside him. Dropping Callie's photo into her lap, she took the receiver. She hesitated for a brief five seconds while straightening her posture and taking a couple of short breaths. When she spoke, her voice revealed none of the trepidation that Conrad sensed was coursing through her every corpuscle. "This is Ashleigh Taylor."

"Nice to finally talk to you, Ashleigh," the raspy voice said. "It's okay to call you Ashleigh, right?"

"Yes."

"Now listen real good. I'm going to hang up, then call right back. If you care about your daughter, make sure no officer of the law is on the line when I call back. In fact, have them vacate the premises."

"Son of a bitch," Porter exploded the moment the line went dead. "Sorry," he said, addressing Ashleigh. "Don't worry. There's no way our suspect has access to the type of sophisticated equipment he'd need to detect a tap on the line. He's bluffing, trying to make you believe he knows. But he assumes you've ignored his warning and involved law enforcement. Anyone who watches TV, goes to the movies, or reads a novel is bound to jump to that conclusion."

Conrad watched Ashleigh's eyes widen at the blare of the phone, but she waited for the FBI agent's signal before she again picked up the receiver.

"This is Ashleigh."

"Hey, lady. Didn't I tell you to have the law take a powder?"

"Excuse me," Ashleigh said with a tone of indignation. "There's no law enforcement here," she lied, her tone steady. "We followed your instructions and—"

"Cut the crap, pretty lady. I'm not exactly the trusting sort, so listen carefully. Open the box that came with the tape. The combination to open the box is the numbers that correspond to letters on a telephone keypad. It should be easy for you to remember the code: 'Get our daughter back.' You dial 4 for *g*, 3 for *e*, and so on. Open the box, take out the cell phone, and use it as I tell you to. When you get a block or so from the hotel, pull over and punch the number that's programmed on the phone. Then I'll give you instructions for meeting up. Make sure you come solo—or the girl dies."

"Wait," Ashleigh's voice rose. "Let me talk to Callie."

"You'll get that chance when you call from the cell." The line was severed.

The color drained from Ashleigh's face.

"Did you get anything?" Still gripping the receiver, Ashleigh was pretty sure there hadn't been time for a trace, but she prayed she was wrong.

"Sorry," Agent Porter said, putting down his notepad. His expression was full of sincerity.

Landes spoke up. "It's a shame we couldn't break the code before the call."

Porter shook his head. "Our guys are good, but eighteen goddamn numbers, with the multitude of possible combinations? Was too tough to crack in the limited time we had." He tore the top sheet off the notepad, where he'd jotted down the keypad numbers corresponding to the letters of the unique code, and handed it to Sam, the tech team leader assigned to the task.

Conrad pulled Ashleigh into his arms. "God, I hate this. You don't know how much I wish—"

"I do know," Ashleigh sighed. The headache was back with a vengeance, but she did her best to ignore it. "But I'm *glad* it's me. I can't wait to hear Callie's voice, to know that she's okay."

Conrad hugged her tight before they turned their attention back to the box.

Sam spun the combination to the various numbers and attempted to open the lid. It didn't budge. "You sure you got that combination right?"

Porter double-checked the letters against the numbers on the phone pad and those he'd jotted down on the note. "*Get my daughter back.* That's right."

"What he said was 'Get *our* daughter back,'" Conrad corrected him.

Sam tried again. When he hit the 5 for the letter *k* in *back,* the lid sprang open, revealing a throwaway phone in a plastic baggie. "Got it," he said.

Landes glanced across to Porter—an unspoken request. Porter gave him a nod and turned his attention to the other agent and the detectives crowded around the table. As law enforcement talked over a possible plan, Landes took the phone from Sam and crossed the room to hand it to Ashleigh. "May I have your cell?" he asked.

She dug in her handbag, then dropped it into his outstretched hand. No one spoke. Neither she nor Conrad questioned the investigator; they watched as he punched in a series of digits and pressed TALK. When his own cell rang, he instantly flipped it open and just as quickly closed it.

"At the first sign of trouble, press here."

She saw that he had her phone opened to recent calls. By pressing the last call received, she would be taken directly to his line.

"Got it," she said, now eager to get started. She didn't like the tension transmitted through her husband's eyes, and she wanted to get this ordeal behind them as soon as possible. She squeezed his hand and gave him a peck on the cheek; then she picked up her handbag and headed for the door. Agent Porter was beside her, holding the briefcase filled with the money and the tracker inlaid in the hard surface behind the lining.

Turning back to Conrad, she said, "I'll be fine. But I'd better get down to the car before Billings falls asleep."

"Fat chance." Pocino chuckled. "But I'm sure as hell glad it's him and not me on the floor, squashed like a bug between the seats." Then, turning to Conrad, he said, "Time to hit the road. We've got a taxi at the ready, and the pilot's got the copter fueled and ready for takeoff from the Sheraton's helipad."

Ashleigh stopped in her tracks. "But the kidnapper . . . he specifically said *no helicopters*." Her voice rose of its own accord. She couldn't manage to keep the terror out of it.

99

Pocino and Conrad left the penthouse along with Ashleigh and Agent Porter.

"Don't worry," Pocino said, "we got a nice, safe helicopter with a big banner advertising Goodyear tires. The perp will be none the wiser." He didn't voice Porter's warning not to hover.

Though Conrad was uncomfortable about being able to make only broad sweeps of the area, it was the best they could do. They had to prevent suspicion, and Conrad swore he would make sure the pilot was careful. There was risk involved, but this whole affair wasn't exactly a walk in the park. Conrad refused to abandon this means of keeping tabs on his wife en route to the ransom drop-off and their daughter. There was no other way.

"The rented Lincoln's bugged. Landes will forward your driving instructions to us in the copter, so you're good to go," Pocino reassured Ashleigh. "Leave the big-time worries to yours truly." He thumped his broad chest.

Ashleigh wished she *could* leave it all to Ross. She was not prone to worry, but this was different. Her usual Pollyanna demeanor failed to kick in. She was so afraid—not for herself, but for her daughter.

After another brief hug, Conrad climbed into the waiting taxi along with Pocino as Ashleigh and Porter made their way to the Town Car.

Sliding behind the wheel, Ashleigh set her handbag on the floor in front of the passenger seat, but clung to the cell phone they'd retrieved from the box. When Porter handed her the briefcase, she placed it on the seat next to her.

"Billings?" Porter called through the open driver's door.

Billings's husky voice drifted in from the back. "Snug as a bug in a steel-plated rug."

After repeating the same instructions they'd gone over previously, Porter said, "When you're given the directions, repeat them aloud. Billings will text them to us."

Ashleigh merely nodded that she understood. Anxious to get started, she buckled her seat belt and turned the key in the ignition.

Porter gave her a reassuring smile. "You'll be safe, and we will have your daughter safe and sound before night falls." Before slamming the driver's door, the FBI agent muttered something unexpected, which warmed her heart: "God be with you."

Porter had said nothing about capturing the kidnapper, which was reassuring. While Ashleigh hoped he would be apprehended, the priority was getting Callie home safely.

At the first corner, Ashleigh pulled into the loading zone in front of the Corner Bakery Café and flipped open the cell phone. She pressed the programmed number and listened to it ring.

"So now our adventure begins." The voice was higher-pitched than the one he'd used on the phone in the penthouse suite.

Ashleigh briefly wondered why he felt a need to disguise it. "May I please talk to Callie?"

"Be patient, pretty lady. First we need to get you on your way."

"I'm not going anywhere until I hear my daughter's voice. Until I know she is safe." Her angry words surprised her. In the silence that followed, her blood turned icy cold. Had she made a big mistake?

Finally the high-pitched voice vibrated in her ear. "Maybe we should forget the whole thing, and you can slip back into your comfy life, where you have more control. After all, I understand you've got another kid just like this one."

There was a gasp in the background.

Could that be Callie? Or was that my own voice I heard? "Okay," she said, "what do you want me to do?"

"Don't get cute." There was a pause. "Do you have GPS?"

"Yes."

"Plug in North Kingsbury Street. It will take you to I-90, to the West Ohio Street turnoff. You'll take a right onto Kingsbury. When you get on Kingsbury, stop and give me a call. Your GPS is not likely to take you to our meet-up location."

"Okay. I-90 to West Ohio Street. Then a right on North Kingsbury." She projected her voice for the man lying hidden on the floor of the Lincoln. "Okay, I've resumed driving," Ashleigh said. "Now may I *please* talk to my daughter?"

"Of course, pretty lady. I'm a man of my word. And for your daughter's sake, I hope you haven't planned any shenanigans. If there is any sign of the law, your daughter dies."

"I . . . I understand." Ashleigh waited. A light rain fell on the windshield, but nothing heavy enough to run the wipers on anything but the lowest speed. She set them on delay then brushed away the tears that she had no power to stop. She heard indistinguishable voices on the other end of the phone and felt tension shoot through her veins.

"Mom. It's me."

It was Callie.

"Oh, sweetie, are you okay?" *What a stupid question. Of course she isn't.*

"Sort of," came a voice that was almost a whisper.

Ashleigh heard a soft sound that might have been a slap, and the high-pitched voice returned to the phone. "That's enough. Now call when you reach Kingsbury."

"Did you hit my daughter?" Ashleigh's voice rose, as if to match the man's on the other end of the phone. But there was no response. The line was dead.

Gino was waiting on the porch when Nelson's Highlander pulled up in front. He had slipped into a pair of Levi's, a sweatshirt, and his heavy boots, and he had a leather jacket slung over his shoulder. He was up for this adventure.

He was fond of all the Taylor kids. They were well mannered, down-to-earth, and friendly—not the spoiled brats he'd expected to meet. Actually, their parents were also pretty cool. When he'd mentioned to Viviana that they displayed none of the airs of the nouveau riche, she had corrected him by filling him in on their family backgrounds. While neither Conrad nor Ashleigh had endured poverty in childhood, both had achieved phenomenal success through their own hard work. They had not allowed themselves or their young family to be coddled by a life of privilege, nor did they appear to look down on others who had achieved less.

"Thanks, man," Tony said, as they walked briskly toward the Avalanche. "I owe you." He climbed into the front seat beside Gino.

Echoing the thanks, Nelson climbed into the backseat and said, "This might be a wild goose chase, but I don't think so. Take I-90 North."

As they headed down the Kennedy Expressway, Nelson filled Gino in on their destination.

"So," Gino said, puzzled, "your stepson keeps returning to the old boat where he shot the guy when he was a kid?"

"Don't know that for sure," Nelson admitted. "Haven't seen much of Rick since Sandy died and he ran off. Sandy, my wife—Rick's mother—was having an affair with Joe, the owner of the boat. Apparently no one claimed the boat after the shooting, so she used it whenever she wanted to get away."

"Joe was the guy Rick shot?" Gino asked.

"Yes. Won't go into the gory details, but Sandy often took Rick with her when she took off from time to time. Turns out, she took him to that man's boat more than once."

Gino was having trouble imagining the relationship between the courteous Nelson and his former wife, who sounded, at best, unbalanced. *I mean, who brings a child to a romantic rendezvous?* But it was none of his business.

"Rick was Neil's age when Sandy died," Nelson continued in a quiet tone. "He was angry and blamed me for not making his mom happy. The first time he ran away, I went after him. The police tracked him to the boat. Whether or not he ever returned, I really don't know. But it seems like a good possibility if he's the one who kidnapped the two kids, and my gut tells me that he has."

"Gino," Tony cut in, "we'd better pull off at the next gas station and fill up. Nelson has only a vague idea of where the boat might be moored. He's only been there twice—"

"Only once, actually. When I went to the boat after the shooting, it was anchored a short distance from a marina," Nelson cut in. "By the time Rick ran off, it had been moved to a remote area. Not sure who moved it. Rick didn't want to talk about it, and I'm afraid I didn't push. After I picked Rick up at the police station, he took me to the boat to pick up his things. I'm hoping that I'll recognize the roads—and that the boat wasn't moved again."

Gino had a sinking feeling in his chest. They were about to go off the beaten path in search of potentially violent, desperate kidnappers. Clearing his throat, he asked, "Has anyone been notified of your suspicion regarding this old boat?"

Both Nelson and Tony answered at once, saying more or less the same thing. "Not yet."

Gino didn't find their answer very encouraging. Considering what lay ahead, they would need all the help they could muster.

Marnie was scared out of her mind. Although she had passed the behind-the-wheel class, and David and her parents had let her and Callie practice their driving skills in the Lincoln whenever possible, she only had a learner's permit. But despite the terrors of driving on her own for the first time, it wasn't being caught without a driver's license that frightened her. Far worse worries lay ahead. Getting on and off the freeway was terrifying enough, but the idea of being spotted by one of the men in the Avalanche was far worse. Then there was the thought of her other mother waking up to find her and the Caprice gone.

Her stomach had jumped up to her throat when she saw Nelson stop his car in front of a house at the end of a cul-de-sac. She'd had nowhere to hide. She'd prayed that Nelson did not look in her direction and recognize her mom's car. Making a U-turn would have called attention to herself, so she'd parked at the end of the block and ducked down in the seat—but not so far down that she couldn't see what was going on.

Soon enough, Marnie saw someone who looked familiar bound down the steps of the house. It was Viviana De Mornay's boyfriend. Then the doors of the Highlander opened, and Nelson and the guy Tony got out and hurried across the driveway to the Avalanche. They all climbed in.

Marnie ducked clear down when she saw the Avalanche begin to back out of the driveway. The Caprice was so low and the Avalanche so high that all she could do was cross her fingers and pray once more that they wouldn't notice her.

She didn't let out her breath until she heard them pass by, and then she slowly lifted her head and turned the car around at the end of the cul-de-sac, hoping she wouldn't lose them. *There they are, just ahead.* But what were they doing now?

She followed them as they turned off and watched them pull into a gas station. Then she looked at her mom's gas gauge. It was less than half full. She didn't know how far she was going. Nothing to do but hope that it wouldn't run out.

Marnie parked up the street from the Arco station and kept the Avalanche in view through her driver's-side mirror. A mantra began to play in her head: *Please, please, please help me find Callie. Keep her safe. Don't let her hate me. And please don't let me run out of gas.*

CHAPTER
101

Pocino charged across the Sheraton's rooftop helipad and ducked under the whirling blades. Conrad, who was right behind him, hit a slick rain puddle and immediately regretted his choice of tennis shoes over boots. But that was the least of his concerns. He caught himself midslide, a few feet short of the helicopter.

"Take it easy," Pocino said. "Got no time for urgent care."

The strains of Kenny Rogers's "Lucille" blasted from Pocino's phone: *"You picked a fine time to leave me, Lucille . . ."* It played a few more lines before Pocino could pull it from the pouch on his belt loop and flip it open.

"Pocino," he shouted above the roar of the helicopter.

The investigator's brow deepened into a series of grooves. "You can't be more specific? . . . Okay, who else have you notified? . . . I'll take care of Landes and Special Agent Porter. You call Chicago PD and ask to be put through to the chief of detectives, Steve Young. If he's not available, ask for Detective Senske . . . No," he said, his impatience unconcealed. "Not likely to be in the station or off duty. Probably somewhere in the field."

Pocino slapped the phone shut. Answering Conrad's unasked question, he said, "That was Kennedy. He has a bee in his bonnet about his stepson taking the kids to some abandoned boat. Isn't sure about the exact location, other than it's an offshoot of the Chicago River. Don't think we can afford to ignore it, though."

Shouting up to the pilot, Pocino said, "You know anything about boats moored in offshoots of the Chicago River?"

Conrad felt the vibration of his cell phone, which he'd shoved into the pocket of his parka, before he heard the ring. He grabbed it and was relieved to hear Landes's voice reporting that Billings had texted Ashleigh's route and that she had talked, albeit very briefly, to Callie.

When he got off the phone, Conrad said, "Ross, I've got the route Ashleigh's been given so far. Turn the tracking of the boat over to the police, or maybe the Coast Guard. I want to stay close to Ashleigh. Even if Callie was being held on the boat, it seems unlikely that the abductor would bring the authorities straight to them. And if he leaves, I don't think he would leave her behind. He'll need her for the ransom exchange."

"Got it. That's the priority." Pocino began punching numbers into his cell.

The helicopter coughed and made an awkward dip before leveling off. Uneasy, Conrad wondered about the rain. He hoped they had an experienced pilot.

Callie raised her hand to her cheek. The blow had stung. But its hint of what might lay ahead was far more frightening.

Raising her chin, she met the creep's bloodshot eyes. "I'm sorry," she forced herself to say. It was a lie, of course. She wished she could have said more to her mom on the phone, and she would have, if she could have thought of a single thing that would help anyone looking for her.

"'Sort of' wasn't in your script." Rick jabbed the paper with his crooked index finger. "A straight 'yes' was what I wanted. You haven't been hurt." His look bore into her. "At least, not yet."

Callie swallowed past the lump in her throat. *What's he planning to do?* Aloud, she said, "Are we going to meet my mom now?"

"There is no *we*, princess. At least, none that includes you."

"What do you mean? You told Mom after she gave you the money—"

"Well, you're not much use after we get the money."

Callie began to shake. *I knew it. He's been lying. He has no intention of letting me go.* "But she won't give you the money if she doesn't see me."

"Is that right?" he said with a sneer. Then, dramatically raising both of his scrawny eyebrows, he said, "Is your mom Wonder Woman?"

Callie's heart sunk. She wanted to crumple to the warped floor beneath her booted feet. Her mother would be all alone when she met him. The creep, though rail-thin, was strong—a lot stronger than her mom—and then there was the overweight skank. She was jealous and hateful and would do anything the creep told her to do. Callie imagined her mom being overpowered by them. She couldn't let that happen.

If he plans to kill me, I won't go down without inflicting as much damage as I can. She fingered the bedspring in her pouch. Her stomach roiled as she thought of what she must do.

She would have to aim for his eye.

Rick saw the fear in the girl's eyes. She knew she was going to die.

But he was no longer as sure as he had been. The gun in the waistband of his jeans felt heavy—as heavy as the decision he now faced. Should he rethink his plan? *No point in killing one kid without the other, which would leave me with only two bullets.* But that wasn't his real concern, part of him realized.

His mind went into overdrive. The revelation on the boat replayed in his head. He hadn't killed Joe. *Mom tricked me. She tricked everyone. I wasn't a killer after all.* But no one would ever believe him now, so did it really matter?

Barreling down I-90, Ashleigh gripped the steering wheel so hard her knuckles appeared bloodless and feeling vanished from her fingertips. "That lowlife hit my daughter. I'm sure that's what I heard." She had to raise her voice, and it was awkward looking straight ahead while talking to Billings behind her.

"Hang in there," came his muffled voice, reminding Ashleigh of how uncomfortable the man must be. She wished it wasn't necessary for him to stay concealed . . . wished he didn't have to be there at all . . . wished that this whole thing was over, or better yet, that it had never happened.

Enough. Ashleigh sat up straight in her seat and focused on the road ahead. No point in thinking about what she had no power to change. She had to get her daughter back. He had hit Callie already—and who knows what other harm the abductor had done to her child.

But what frightened Ashleigh most was what harm he might do next.

As Gino topped off the Avalanche's thirty-gallon gas tank, Tony dashed to the window of the 7-Eleven and slid his credit card through the slot of the machine. Out of the corner of his eye he saw a green Caprice like Erica's parked up the street. He scrawled his name on the credit slip, then straightened up and took a closer look. *Holy crap. That* is *Erica's car. And the kid is behind the goddamn wheel.*

A punch straight to the gut couldn't have been more debilitating. *That stupid kid followed us.*

A moment of paralysis kicked in as Tony flashed through the various alternatives. *If I don't say anything and we find Kennedy's stepson, he could be armed and the girl could get hurt. But if I tell Kennedy I spotted the girl, he might call the whole thing off. We can't turn back now, but it's too dangerous to take a teenager along.*

Gino shouted his name and gunned the motor of the Avalanche.

Gritting his teeth as he jogged toward the truck, Tony made a decision. Right or wrong, he was going to keep his mouth shut. As far as he could figure, their route was fairly isolated. It was unlikely the kid would come across a single soul on the off-beaten pathways Kennedy described . . . *And without four-wheel drive, she won't get too far.* The kid would be stranded in that old Caprice.

With that frightening realization, he reversed his decision. Throwing open the passenger-side door, he said, "Afraid we have a rather big hiccup."

Rick pulled on his heavy work gloves, thankful the worst part of this ordeal was behind him. His decision was the right one, he assured himself.

Reaching down into the muck of the foul-smelling shore, he pried the end of the plank from the mud and pulled it toward him. He wasn't quick enough, though, to avoid the inevitable splash when the plank slid from its resting place on the boat above and fell into the water. Cursing, he made tracks up the slippery hillside as fast as he could manage.

This place was history. It had nothing but bad memories. Tossing his gloves to the ground, he headed for the van. This was one place he'd never again lay eyes upon.

When he looked back, the girl was standing at the railing. She was peering down into the muddy shore, knowing there was no way off the boat. Unless someone came for her, there was no escape. Rick was smart enough to know that. Sarah-Jayne would be pissed, but if he hadn't actually killed the crusty old boat owner who'd abused his mom, why should he kill two innocent kids? Nothing was to be gained by their deaths. While his stepfather was still breathing in and breathing out, he was sure to point a finger in his direction. By the time dear old stepdad figured things out, Rick would be out of reach—but if they pinned two murders on him, there would be an even wider net cast, and they might never escape.

Law enforcement would expect them to flee the country—and so would the mob. Rick knew damn well that there'd be traps laid out at every airport: not only detectives and special agents, but guns for hire too. Trying to fly out of the country would be a dumb move. On the other hand, no one would imagine their escape to Alaska. There wouldn't be time to get an APB out on their new wheels before he and Sarah-Jayne crossed into Canada. And then, soon enough, they'd cross back onto U.S. soil.

Why more people running from the law hadn't sought out Alaska was beyond him—no passport required, no currency exchange, no nothing. Hell, maybe he was actually one of many who'd figured out that all they'd need was some phony paperwork and an unknown auto to cross the Canadian border. And maybe the lack of press was due to the fact that these other lawbreakers hadn't been apprehended. They'd made their escape. They'd gotten their reward. They were home free.

Now it was time to reap *his* reward. He checked his watch as he slogged his way toward the van. Sarah-Jayne might be in never-never land by now; he'd given her the go-ahead to smoke as much weed as she wanted once she concealed the Sienna on the other side of the suspension bridge. He had plenty of time before the kid's mom was due.

The worst was over. The best was yet to come.

CHAPTER
103

Callie jumped back as the plank splashed into the water below, spraying the deck of the boat. The temporary relief that had flowed through her veins when she'd seen Rick push the gun back into the waistband of his Levi's had become a faded memory. That plank had been the sole connection between the old boat and the shore. Watching it sink below the surface of the murky water, she felt like crying.

She wrapped her arms around her and for a moment closed her eyes. Although she felt like giving in to the terror bubbling up within, that would get her nowhere. Her parents would tell her that she must be strong. Indulging in self-pity was deadly. She remembered her mom's response at her first dance convention, when Callie had complained about having to remain with her age group rather than join the older group of dancers who shared her advanced ability. "Life isn't always fair," Mom had told her. "What matters is what you do with the hand you're dealt"—or something like that. *Well, I've been dealt a whopper of a hand, so I'd better figure out how to deal with it.* Squeezing her eyes shut as tight as she could, Callie willed herself to get a grip.

A loud banging from below deck shattered her concentration. *Neil.* At least she wasn't alone. *How badly is he hurt?* Without another thought, she went down below and to the door of the forward cabin. The outside latch was firmly set, and the thumb of her right hand still throbbed from her efforts in removing the bedspring. It took her precious seconds to pry the heavy steel hook through the ring.

"You okay?" Neil asked the instant the door sprang open. He eyed her from head to toe.

Callie knew she must be quite a sight. She hadn't had a shower since before the opening of De Mornay's, nearly two days ago. The elastic band that had held her hair back in a ponytail had broken, leaving flyaway strands of hair in her face. Her hands were a mess and her clothes unclean, but that was the least of her worries.

Neil was in far worse shape. The material along the seam of the right leg of his Levi's was torn up to his thigh. He'd probably ripped it open to relieve some of the pressure on his swollen knee. But his sweatshirt was in far better shape than her own. What an utter waste of time focusing on the bedspring had been. And yet she would have gone crazy just sitting there, feeling as though she could do nothing that might aid in her escape. Now that she realized there was no need for the bedspring after all—the creep hadn't locked her back in the aft cabin—the irony failed to comfort her. *I guess I should just be thankful,* she thought.

She shoved the spring into the back pocket of her jeans, just in case.

"Excuse me," Neil said, clearing his throat and thrusting his bound hands in Callie's face.

"Sorry," she said. She fingered the spring before realizing she'd seen the creep toss a small knife into the small drawer beside the rusty sink. She pulled the drawer open. "Here we go," she said, plucking the small knife from the cluttered drawer and cutting him free.

"Thanks." Neil rubbed, slapped, and twisted his wrists to stimulate the circulation.

"We've got to find a way off this boat," she said, her tone emphatic. But she hadn't a clue how.

Neil hobbled across the salon and mounted the four steps to the deck, where he focused his gaze on the murky water below. When he turned to face Callie, she saw that one lens of his glasses was cracked.

"So," he said, "what do you suggest?"

The moment the words left his mouth, Neil regretted them. *He* should be the one to come up with a rescue plan. It was his fault that they were here in this godforsaken place. "Callie," he said, "I feel like such a fool for—"

"Stop. We don't have time for that kind of talk. Your brother probably—"

"Half-brother," Neil corrected.

"Okay, your half-brother." Callie's voice held an unmistakable note of exasperation. "If your half-brother returns after getting the money, he has no reason to keep us alive. Even if he doesn't return, he has no reason to let anyone know where to find us. Unless you want to stay here till we die of starvation or thirst, it's up to us to save ourselves."

"Look, Callie, if you're thinking of jumping or even sliding off the side of this old wreck, we'd be soaked to the bone in that freezing-cold water, and even if we made it out without drowning, our clothes would weigh a ton. We'd get hypothermia. It would be tough enough slogging uphill through the mud—"

"Cut it out. Stop thinking about what we *can't* do," Callie interrupted. "We know the obstacles—the challenges of the water and mud, how far we are from any kind of civilization. We know that. What we have to do is figure out what we . . ." Her voice faded and she sucked in her bottom lip. After a few long seconds, she shrugged, staring down at his leg. "Well, *you* can't even manage to get from one side of the boat to the other. So you need to help *me* get off this old tub without getting soaked to the bone."

She bolted back down into the galley and the aft cabin. She tore open the half-closed drawer beneath the bottom bunk. Suddenly she stood stock-still and let out a gasp.

"What . . . ?" Neil's voice dropped off when he saw what she held in the palm of the hand.

Wrapped in a plastic bag was one of those throwaway cell phones.

Ashleigh's nerves were on fire by the time she pulled up behind the blue Honda Civic that the kidnapper had described to her. Her car, as well as the Civic, sat well hidden beneath the overhanging branches of a large evergreen tree. The Civic stood empty. *Where is Callie? Is she nearby?*

The cell she'd been using for communication with her daughter's abductor rang seconds after she shifted into PARK. *How does he know . . . ?* "Now, pretty lady, this is where the rubber meets the road. You balk or make a single misstep, and your daughter dies. You do what you're told, and you get to tuck your little princess into bed tonight. *Comprende?*"

"May I talk to my daughter?"

"Watch it, lady. You're getting on my nerves. No time to chat until you complete a few crucial steps." He cackled. It was an evil sound. "Lucky for you, it's stopped raining. For now, at least."

"I'll do as you request. I just want to get my daughter home safely."

"Good. Now, first thing you do is take the money out of the car and set the container on the hood."

Ashleigh did as instructed.

"Now go around your car and to the passenger side of the Civic. The door's unlocked."

Still holding the phone to her ear, she leaned back into the car and grabbed her handbag off the passenger-side floor.

"Hold it," the high-pitched voice commanded.

She stopped in her tracks.

"You won't be needing no purse. Throw it back inside the Town Car."

Ashleigh hesitated.

"On second thought, throw that purse as far from the car as you can manage."

Puzzled, Ashleigh's eyes swept her surroundings.

"You know what they say about curiosity?" The voice was menacing. She did not respond.

"Well, we can't have you all stressed out, so just look to your left—to the hillside directly across from the gorge. That van belongs to me, and these binoculars bring you in good and clear."

Ashleigh shuddered at the sight of the van. She couldn't see any writing on the sides, but it was a light color, probably silver. It had to be the one that Marnie and the eyewitness had reported seeing at the scene of Callie's abduction. The road ahead, she realized, must lead up to that crest where the van was parked. There was what looked like a valley between them.

Ashleigh swallowed hard and then surreptitiously she slipped her own cell phone into the pocket of her jacket. Reluctantly, she tossed her handbag away from the car. She didn't dare speak directly to Billings, but spoke loudly so he could hear. "I threw my handbag away from the car. Now what do you want?"

"Don't go getting all snarky," he said. "I'll say this once. Go around and open the passenger door to the Civic. There's a duffel and a new cell phone in the plastic bag on the passenger seat. Grab them and take them back to the driver's side of the Town Car."

She pulled out the duffel and picked up the cell. Like an automaton, she moved back around the Lincoln to the driver's side.

"Now toss this phone we're talking on inside the Lincoln. Don't try any funny stuff. I can see every move. I'll call you back on the new cell. Do exactly what I tell you."

When she opened the door, she said as loudly as she could, without creating suspicion, "I've got the duffel, and the briefcase holding the ransom money is on the hood. Now you want me to hang up and put this cell in the car?"

Following his confirmation, she tossed the phone in the car and left the door open, hoping that Billings could hear her and text information back to Landes, who was somewhere—hopefully not too far off—with

Special Agent Porter and his team. She heard what sounded like a helicopter in the distance, but she dared not look up.

The new cell rang. She flipped it open.

"Here's where I find out what you're made of. Gotta make sure your priority is getting your little girl back in one piece—not preoccupied with catching the bad guy. If I find a single bug, I'll know you are working with the law, and your daughter dies."

Your daughter dies . . . Your daughter dies . . . Your daughter dies. How many times have I heard those words in the past few hours? Ashleigh swayed, struggling to remain steady on her feet.

"Now listen up. Open the briefcase. Face in my direction, hold up a stack of bills and let me see you fan through it. Repeat for each stack. When I tell you it's okay, drop 'em one by one into the duffel. Then turn and toss the briefcase in the car."

She did as he asked, knowing that there was no way to track the ransom money; the tracking device remained in the lining of the briefcase. The only way the authorities could track her now was through her cell. *And thank God, there's a tracker in my cell.*

"Now comes the tricky step. A real test of your love and loyalty." The kidnapper chortled. "Remember, I've got my eye on you. Any funny business, and you'll never see your daughter again. At least, not in one piece."

"Please," Ashleigh pleaded, "I'll do whatever you ask." She heard the whir of a helicopter close by, but again she dared not look up to check. She prayed they had spotted her and the abductor.

"Take off your jacket and throw it down on the ground."

"My jacket?" she repeated.

"Hey, is there an echo on that hillside? I said throw the jacket away from the car. You're not going to be standing in the cold for long. Now do it." He barked out the command.

There goes the cell. She tossed her jacket to the ground beside her handbag. The cold air bit through the arms of her sweater and penetrated deep into her skin. She snatched up the duffel again.

"Hold it." There was a sharp note to the raspy voice. "Now your sweater and trousers."

"What?"

"You have a hearing problem? I said, 'toss your sweater and trousers on top of the duffel.'"

Ashleigh's mouth went dry and she stood frozen in place. "Are you some kind of a pervert?"

"Look, lady. You're not my shot of gin. I like more meat on my women. But I've worked too hard on this payday. I'm taking no chances on being foiled by some concealed bug. This is not negotiable. You take off your duds. Show me you're not wired and there's nothing concealed. Then you can re-cover your skinny ass."

Ashleigh stepped out of her trousers, slipped her sweater over her head, and laid them on top of the duffel. She felt far more vulnerable than cold.

"That sick SOB," she heard Billings mutter.

Probably imagining the worst, Ashleigh thought.

Goose bumps ran up and down both arms as she crossed them in front of her.

"Ready for the next step?" The irritating voice crackled across the line. "To preserve your modesty, you can turn your back from my bird's-eye view. I gotta be stress-free about bugs, so unhook your bra and wave it in the air. Then slip right back into it."

She wanted to refuse, but he held all the chips. Unhooking her bra quickly, she waved it over her head, and in a flash rehooked it and reached for her sweater.

"Hold it," the pervert said. "Shake the sweater before you put it back on. Then turn your pants pockets inside out."

She was ready to explode with suppressed anger, but did as he commanded. "Now may I get back into my clothes," she said through gritted teeth. Even though Billings could not see her, she felt utterly humiliated. *If Callie's life weren't in danger . . .* Not waiting for his response, she quickly slipped back into her sweater and wool pants.

Again his voice sent a chill through every artery. "Now remove your shoes and necklace, and we're good to go."

Ashleigh stood frozen. She wore no necklace. There *was* a van on the crest of the hill directly across from her. That much was true, but how much could the fiend actually see? Maybe he had no binoculars, or maybe they weren't powerful enough to see everything. Still, she could take no chances. "I'm not wearing a necklace," she said. She wanted to say, *Can't you see that?*

"Now put the duffel in the Civic. Then you have one more job to do before you fire up the engine and we make the exchange."

One more job? "May I put my shoes back on?"

"No. The heels of shoes are too likely a place to insert a tracker. There are some slippers on the floor of the Civic that will work just fine." Again the obnoxious chuckle. "Now, you ready for the last task before proceeding to the spot where your daughter is waiting?"

"What do you want me to do?"

"This part is easy. You get back in the Town Car, start the engine, and drive to the lip of the hillside. Then slip the gear into NEUTRAL, get out of the car, and leave the door open. Then reach inside and slide the gear to drive. If it doesn't start rolling, give it a push from the rear end. And don't forget to jump back."

Ashleigh turned to stone. Raising her voice, she said, "You want me to send the Lincoln over the hillside?"

"That's right, pretty lady."

"I can't . . . I can't do that." Covering the mouthpiece and turning her back to the van, she said, "Ray—"

"Go ahead," she heard Billings say. "He's suspicious. Not taking any chances with the law. He thinks they'll find the car before they find you. His goal is to either throw them off track or distract them by faking an accident. Don't worry; this is a no-brainer. I used to be a stuntman. Unlatch the door locks before you set the car in gear. I know how to roll out with hardly a scratch. Do what he says."

"Are you sure?"

"Do it. *Now.*"

Taking her hand off the mouthpiece, Ashleigh waited until the kidnapper was finished speaking and then responded to the angry man's expletives. "I'm sorry. I'll do it. I'm just scared. I've never done anything like this before."

"You know, lady, you came damn close to losing a daughter there. In the next sixty seconds, I'd better see that car rolling down the hillside, or your daughter dies." The line went dead.

Now Ashleigh could speak directly to Billings, and her voice shook even more than her body. "I can't do this." But even as she said the word, she knew she must. That fiend had given her no choice. She slipped into the Town Car driver's seat.

"You can, and you will." Billings' voice was gruff. "Besides, since signing on with Landes, I'm getting soft. This is just what I need to bone up on my skills."

"You're a terrible liar."

"We've got to get your daughter out of that madman's hands."

Ashleigh looked up slightly, as if in prayer. *There it is.* She saw the Goodyear banner overhead in the distance. "Ray, when you text Landes, let him know I've seen the helicopter. If they have our location, maybe we shouldn't risk—"

"Don't worry. The copter pilot is a pro. He knows how to assess the risk. Everyone wants Callie home safe. Now, as Pocino says, let's rock and roll."

Ashleigh pulled the car up to the lip of the hill, flipped the switch to unlock all the doors, and slid the gear into PARK. "Ready?" she asked, and she stepped out of the car, still shaking. She swallowed past the lump lodged in her throat, shoved the gear into drive, and jumped back.

The car eased forward, teetered for a few seconds, and then plunged over the edge.

CHAPTER

105

Callie's fingers shook as she fumbled with the seal on the baggie. Finally she managed to slip out the small cell. She flipped it open.

The cell phone did not light up. "It's dead." Once again Callie felt the rug pulled from beneath her booted feet. She continued searching the drawers.

"What?" Neil's voice rose in alarm as he stretched out his hand. "Can I take a look?"

Callie handed him the useless throwaway, her mind spinning forward. Then she paused, looking directly into Neil's eyes. She gestured toward his knee. "We're going to have to do what we talked about. You're hardly up to becoming Sir Galahad, so I need to be the one to go for help."

He raised his eyebrows "Sure, Callie," he said. "You just jump off the boat, get soaking wet and freezing cold, and walk up to a pay phone on a nearby corner."

"Don't be so sarcastic. I have an idea."

"Signal's loud and clear," Pocino shouted above the whir of the helicopter blades. "The car must be concealed under that tree." He handed the binoculars to Conrad and pointed down to the overhanging evergreen beside the narrow roadway.

Conrad leaned forward, shielding his eyes against the glare reflected off the clouds. "Yes, I see. Slashes of white, through the branches of the tree." His jaw clenched. "Hey, the car's moving onto the dirt road."

"Let's not hover here," Pocino instructed the pilot. "No clue how close the perp is. We'll go out a ways, then turn back. It'll look like any legit advertising copter making a loop."

Conrad tried to keep his eyes on the white Lincoln. Now he understood why Landes had been adamant that the rented vehicle be snow white.

"Holy shit," Pocino roared suddenly. "Turn around."

In stunned silence, they watched as the Lincoln headed down the steep, rough terrain of the hillside.

Marnie's heart hammered against her rib cage. She was afraid she might pee her pants. Tony Wainwright had been jogging toward the Avalanche but had stopped in his tracks. *He's seen me, or at least he recognizes Mom's car.* She slumped further down in the driver's seat.

When she saw Tony turn back to the Avalanche, she felt a flicker of hope. It was driving away. Maybe he hadn't noticed . . . That thought died an instant later when the Avalanche pulled up beside her.

Nelson hopped out. "Lock the car, Marnie, and get in the Avalanche," he said, gesturing to the backseat. His tone left no room for debate.

Marnie swallowed, and then swished her tongue around the roof of her mouth. Nelson hadn't even asked why she had followed them. His stoic manner was impossible to read. She knew he was upset, but he said nothing. She wished he would shout at her, or at least say a word or two to justify the defensiveness she felt seeping from every pore.

The other two men—Tony and Viviana De Mornay's boyfriend—acknowledged her briefly, then quickly fell into conversation in the front seat. Their frustration was unmistakable, but their voices were low; she could only guess at the context.

Not able to endure another moment of unspoken tension, Marnie blurted, "I'm sorry you're upset. I promise not to get in the way. But I got my sister into this mess, and I can't just wait around. I know I shouldn't have taken Mom's car, but you wouldn't—"

"Marnie," Nelson broke in, "I understand how you feel. No one blames you. We excluded you only because we have no idea what we might run into. It could be dangerous. My stepson most likely has a gun . . ."

Listening to his rationale, Marnie realized that she'd been crazy to follow them. Still, she didn't regret it.

" . . . and when we locate the old boat, I want you to promise me that you'll stay inside this truck with the doors locked. Do you understand?" Nelson asked.

Marnie's nod acknowledged his command. *Yes, I understand.*

CHAPTER

106

Ashleigh stood glued to the rim of the dirt roadway where, seconds ago, the Lincoln had teetered on the lip of the hillside. Her mind's eye replayed the mind-boggling scene: Within seconds, the car had tipped forward, then gained momentum as it crashed through the plant life that clung to the edge of the bluff. And suddenly it was gone.

Her nails dug into her palm—the one not gripping the new cell phone she'd taken from the Civic. She prayed that Billings was the expert stuntman he'd claimed to be.

When the phone sounded in her hand, she flipped it open on the first ring.

"What are you waiting for? That rental is history. I'm sure your hubby is good for the money. Maybe he even took out insurance." The kidnapper cackled. "Now get going. The keys are in the ignition. Follow this road and turn right at the Y split. Then stop when you see my silver van. It will be parked directly in front of the suspension bridge." Then the line went dead.

Ashleigh flipped the phone closed and dashed to the Civic, risking a quick peek down the hillside. The Lincoln's rear door was open, but she could not see if Billings had rolled out. A silent prayer echoed in her head: *God be with you.*

Erica heard the blare of the phone on her bedside table and sat up with a start. Outside her window, the sky was darkening. *Oh my God. What time is it? How long have I been sleeping? Where is Marnie?* These thoughts shot through her head at lightning speed as she reached for the phone.

She fumbled with the receiver and then sat up, throwing her legs over the side of her bed. She was about to say hello when she heard that Mike had picked up. *Good—I'd better go find out what Marnie is up to.* She was about to put the receiver back in the cradle when she recognized Nelson's voice. He sounded upset, and his words made no sense. Mike was trying to calm him down. Nelson was saying something about . . .

"What did you say about Marnie?" Erica butted in.

"She followed us—"

"She *followed* you?" Erica parroted.

Nelson explained what had happened and tried to soothe their worries about Marnie. "She's in no danger at the moment. We had no choice but to bring her along. We're hot on the trail. We could hardly leave her alone here, and even if we could have talked her out of following us—Erica, she has no license. She has no business driving a single foot further. Besides, she's promised not to step outside the truck."

Erica knew her daughter too well to believe that, but before she could get over her shock and speak up, Mike cut in. "Keep an eye on Marnie," he said sharply. "She is not likely to just sit in the background."

Mike's words pierced Erica to the heart. He knew their little girl as well as she did. Marnie would not be safe, no matter what Nelson believed. She could very well get into a lot of trouble out there.

"If we locate the boat and all goes as we plan," Nelson was saying, "I'll drive the kids home in your car. Just hold tight."

Erica knew that was easier said than done.

Billings yanked on the door handle, pushed with all his might, and rolled from the backseat of the car. *Just like in the good old days . . .* It all came back to him, and he would have come out totally unscathed had it not been for the jagged rock that pierced his shoulder.

When he came to a stop and uncurled his body from its protective stance, the shoulder throbbed like hell, but otherwise he was okay. His gaze followed the white car as it plowed into a large boulder and tipped to the side. Quickly he flicked open the cell phone clutched in his right hand. He had only a fraction of a bar, but was relieved to hear his phone connect.

Pocino's husky voice barked, "Billings. You okay?"

"Roger that," he said.

"And Ashleigh." Conrad's voice rose above the roar of the helicopter. "Is she—"

The phone went dead.

"Son of a bitch," Billings said aloud. The spare phone—fully charged—was in the backseat of the Lincoln. Looking across at the hillside where the silver van had been, he saw it was no longer visible. He pushed himself to his feet and headed toward the Lincoln to retrieve the extra cell.

Before he'd taken two steps, though, he heard a tremendous rumble and saw sparks fly from under the hood. And then, with a *whoosh* of flame, the Lincoln exploded.

He'd have to design a plan B.

Conrad stared down at the remains of the Lincoln. Ashleigh couldn't be dead. He didn't feel that she was gone. And yet how could she have escaped?

Pocino elbowed him. "Ashleigh wasn't in the Lincoln. Look down there, at that blue Honda. She's behind the wheel."

Let it be true. Conrad strained to see the small blue car. "How do you know? You can't possibly see who's driving."

"Last text I got from Billings was about the perp having Ashleigh transfer the money into a duffel and drive a blue Honda Civic to the ransom drop. This isn't exactly a well-traveled road, you know."

"You'd better be right." Conrad watched the Civic as it made progress down the dirt track. Mud flew up from its tires. *Why not give her a four-wheel drive for this kind of road?* That momentary flight into the mundane made him cringe. "Hey," he called to the pilot, "can you dip down so we can take a peek into the car?"

"No can do," Pocino cut in. "Not if you want to stay under the perp's radar. But don't worry—I've got a plan."

CHAPTER

107

Erica sat motionless for nearly ten seconds—or was it an eternity? She *had* to do something. But what?

The thought of her daughter out there playing Nancy Drew sent shivers up her spine. Anything could have happened to her. A combination of fury and terror swept over her. *Thank God, Tony spotted her—and thank God, Marnie's no longer behind the wheel.* The thought of her daughter driving all alone into the unknown, especially without a license, sent a fresh wave of fear through her bloodstream.

When Erica looked up, she saw Mike standing in the doorway to her bedroom. He looked as defeated as she felt.

Ignoring the goose bumps that rose on her arms, she gathered all the strength she could muster and said, "I know Ashleigh has to be worried sick about Callie, but I've got to call her. Marnie took off while she was in my care. I can't take the chance that Ashleigh will hear about it from anyone other than me."

Mike nodded. He appeared drained not only of color but of every ounce of energy as well. In fact, he seemed to have aged over the past two days. "I feel like I've been thrown into a B movie without a script," he said, his voice tired. His words mirrored Erica's own thoughts.

She dialed the number for the Palmer House and asked for the Taylor suite. No one answered. She let it ring until it was picked up by a man who identified himself as an FBI special agent. Her mouth went dry, and she instantly hung up. Then she dialed Ashleigh's cell. It went directly to voice mail. Ashleigh's upbeat greeting made her think of happier times and filled her heart with empathy. The Taylors must be informed as soon as possible that Marnie was with Nelson and the others. Reluctantly, she dialed Conrad's cell.

———

Pocino fished the extra cell phone out of his jacket pocket. "How close can you get us to the spot where the Lincoln went down?" he shouted to the pilot.

"With this banner at our tail," came the answer, "we can't afford to dip too low or cut the engine, but—"

"Can you bring her in close enough to throw down a package?"

"There are some bubble packs in the seat of the back bench, along with a dozen or so mini-chutes."

"Got it," said Pocino, confident that Billings would catch on. He tucked the cell into a bubble pack and attached the mini-chute. "Ready when you are."

The copter swooped down. "On the count of three, drop the package," the pilot shouted. "One—two—three."

It didn't take long before they saw Billings scramble to retrieve the package. He ripped it open and, in the next instant, Pocino's cell beeped.

Not bothering with a greeting, Billings spoke before Pocino could fire off the question: "Ashleigh is in the blue Honda Civic, driving to meet the abductor," he said in his rapid, no-nonsense style. "We only got partial directions. The perp's giving them a turn at a time. I believe she's still following this road."

"OK, hang tough," Pocino said. "We'll forward your location to the local PD and have you picked up."

"Got it. I'll enlist their help in covering from the ground."

"Take no chances," Conrad's voice broke in. "Ashleigh and Callie are the priority. Apprehending the abductor and retrieving the ransom are on the back burner."

"Until mother and daughter are safe," Pocino added. *And after that, we'll take down this jerk.*

Neil hobbled after Callie to the aft cabin. She darted straight to the dresser drawers beneath the bunk bed and pulled one open.

"What are you doing?" he asked.

She pulled out two sweatshirts. "Duh," she said with the same sarcasm he'd shown earlier. "Sorry. But you were right. Getting off this boat without getting soaked to the core is impossible, so I'll need dry clothes. I saw some trash bags in the kitchen."

He stared at her in disbelief. "Callie, you can't just jump off the boat."

"Right," she said. "I can't. That's why I need your help. Now please listen while I tell you what I've figured out."

Neil rolled his eyes. Slumping against the doorjamb, he said, "Okay. Tell me your plan."

Callie explained as she made her way to the kitchen, pulled down a trash bag, and began stuffing in the sweatshirts. Then, leaning against the counter, she pulled off her boots and dropped them into the open trash bag too. She paused, and Neil noticed that her face was turning a deep shade of crimson. *Is she . . . blushing?* Then he realized what she had in mind.

"This is no time for modesty," she said, stepping out of her jeans. "I need to keep these pants dry." She seemed to be talking more to herself than to him.

Neil stared at her as if she'd gone mad.

"Hey, this sweatshirt covers more than my bikini." Her tone was defensive.

"Callie. This is crazy. I can't let you jump off the boat with—"

"Don't fight me, Neil. I know what I'm doing." He could tell she was lying, but she seemed so sure. "Besides, I don't plan to jump. I don't think the water is deep enough, maybe only up to my knees. So we can tie our two blankets together, and you can hold one end and lower me down."

"What makes you think that will work? You're a dancer like your sister, not a gymnast. You'll probably land face first in the mud if we try it." He noticed the surprised look on her face. "I got to know your sister pretty good online."

"Well, just look at you. You can't make it three steps without holding on to something." Before he could issue a protest, she rattled on. "I had a lot of training in gymnastics, but I won't be needing that. What I need is good strong legs, and ballet has made my legs as strong as any pro football player's. So don't treat me like some weak, helpless damsel in distress."

Neil had to admit, she sounded more confident than she had since this ordeal first began. His gaze settled on his swollen knee, and he remained silent for several long heartbeats. Finally he said, "I don't like it, but you win. I'm afraid you might be right about Rick not telling anyone where we are. So we'll try your plan. What do you want me to do?"

The two of them spent the next few moments working together. After knotting the blankets, they each took an end and pulled it tight, throwing their entire body weight into the pull.

When Callie was ready to make her descent, she took a last look at Neil. He looked pathetic. She could tell his masculine ego was crushed. Not only that, but he was also looking at her through shattered glasses. And his freckled face looked pale as an albino's.

"It's going to be okay," she said. *Why am I mothering him? Neither of us would be here if he hadn't trusted that creep in the—*

Awareness of the darkening sky hit her, and she didn't finish the thought. She'd seen a small flashlight. But where? For an instant she closed her eyes, trying to conjure up the image. Then it came to her: in the top right drawer. She retrieved the flashlight and, reopening the trash bag, tossed it in. Then, rummaging through another drawer, she found a knife.

Neil extended his hand. "Let me wrap that so you won't cut yourself." He quickly wrapped a plastic bag around the blade and handed it to her.

She added it to her supplies and retied the bag so her things would not fly out and so the water wouldn't trickle in, but loosely enough that she could untie it without a struggle. "Okay, let's get started," she said.

Callie took hold of the firmly knotted blankets that Neil had wound around the base of the anchor winch. He was holding onto the end as if *his* life depended on it. "As soon as I get my footing, I'll give you a wave. Then you can tie this," she pointed to the trash bag, "to the end and lower it to me." Then she was over the side and heading for the murky water below. As she grew closer, she redoubled her efforts to grip the blankets with all her might, more thankful than ever for her strong dancer's legs.

CHAPTER
108

The Civic sluggishly made its way up the narrow, muddy incline. Ashleigh's tension mounted as the Y junction came into view. When she turned right, the band of anxiety compressing her chest squeezed even tighter. She saw only the road snaking ahead. No suspension bridge.

The cell phone rang.

"Where are you?" the shrill voice barked into her ear.

She told him what she saw out the windows, realizing that she was no longer in his sights. This might have given her a hair of relief had it not been for the awareness that she was no longer on anyone's radar. Her own cell phone lay on the side of the road, in the pocket of her jacket. How would they find her now? All she heard as she drove forward was the splash of mud and gravel pinging off the fenders. *Where is the helicopter?*

"Well, pretty lady, you've almost arrived. My silver van is parked in front of the bridge now. When you see it, stop and turn off your motor."

"I'd like to talk to Callie," she said.

"You would, would you? Well, I'd like a Lamborghini."

The line went dead once again.

The way Rick figured it, this was going to be a chunk of cheese. Even if the Taylors had alerted the law . . . *Hell, of course they have.* But it didn't matter; he'd thought of everything, covered every contingency. No one knew these back roads like he did. Plus, there'd be no alert on the wires for a burgundy Toyota minivan. They'd hit the freeway while the cops were standing around scratching their heads.

His cell bleeped. If it was the Taylor dame wanting to talk to her kid again, he'd scare the bejesus out of her—let her know who held all the chips. But when he checked the caller ID, he saw it was Sarah-Jayne.

"Hold tight, sugar. We're less than five minutes away from our big payday."

"I was starting to worry, baby. I took a nap, and when I woke up I saw it was nearly dark."

"Not to worry—" He cut off at the roar of a helicopter overhead and looked up. It was close by. Had his warning been ignored?

Callie was hip-high in slimy water when Neil lowered the loosely tied trash bag. As she grabbed for it, she wondered if she was indeed a lunatic. *Cut it out,* she reprimanded herself. *Don't think, just move.* She lifted one bare foot, then the other, hoping she wouldn't cut her herself on the jagged stones beneath her.

Once she stepped from the murky water to the muddy shore, she realized she should have taken one of the towels and a ton of the creep's wet wipes. *Don't think about that.* But she realized that she had to do some fast thinking. She'd planned to wear both sweatshirts for warmth, but decided she'd be better off using one as a towel. Better to be dry than layered.

With her back to the boat, she pulled her wet sweatshirt over her head and tossed it to the ground. Then she dug in the bag and pulled out a sweatshirt, using it to dry herself as best she could. She then pulled on the second sweatshirt and slipped back into her jeans.

The next part was a lot trickier. Trying to keep her balance, she dried her left foot and tugged the first boot on. She teetered and nearly fell to the mud, but caught herself. *Thank you, Ms. Daryl, for making me work that ballet bar.* Callie quickly repeated the maneuver with her right foot.

Finally, she dug into the bag to retrieve the flashlight before turning back toward the boat. Her spunk dipped when she realized she could barely make out Neil's silhouette at the boat rail. How much time had gone by since Neil's evil half-brother had stranded them out here in the middle of nowhere? Not knowing where they were was enough of a challenge in the daylight. And soon it would be pitch-black.

Conrad's pulse raced. Leaning forward on the copter's bench seat, he fixed his gaze on the intermittent flashes of blue: the Civic winding up the narrow dirt road. All too aware of how dangerous the rain-soaked surface had become, he felt his heart sink lower in his chest. *Without the transmission from her cell phone, there's no way of tracking Ashleigh's exact location.*

The pilot continued to keep him and Pocino current with continuous updates on their coordinates. That failed to bring much comfort, though. And as Conrad heard Pocino forwarding the pilot's updates on Ashleigh's exact location to Landes, he fought hard against utter despair. "I've lost sight of the Civic," Conrad said, anxiety coloring every syllable. "With us here in the air, and with Landes, the FBI agents, detectives, and other members of law enforcement keeping a low profile on the ground, miles away, how can we possibly protect Ashleigh and Callie?" He knew his question was rhetorical.

Being forced to maintain a steady speed to keep the damn Goodyear banner from dragging made it virtually impossible to monitor Ashleigh's movement as closely as Conrad knew was necessary. *Whatever possessed me to allow her to get in that car and take off without me?* But even as Conrad damned himself for going along with this insane plan, he realized he had no power to stop Ashleigh once she'd made up her mind. And when it came right down to it, because the abductor had Callie, he held the power. With no alternative plan on the horizon, Conrad had been unwilling to veto any plan that had a chance of saving his daughter's life.

He heaved a long, slow sigh. *Now, not only is my daughter in danger, but my wife as well.* Balling his hands into fists, he damned the Fates.

Soon, though, he came to his senses and forced his mind from those negative thoughts. He could not allow them to invade his rational mind. Clearing his head as best he could, Conrad willed himself to remain alert and positive.

His cell phone bleeped. The caller ID told him it was Landes. He hoped to hell the FBI had kept tabs on the Civic, and at the same time he prayed that they had not moved in prematurely—which could place either Ashleigh or Callie in jeopardy.

Landes put Special Agent Porter on the line. "Mr. Taylor," he said, "with this rain, it's too risky to continue helicopter surveillance. Your pilot has been instructed to land."

Callie shivered. An icy cold seeped deep into the marrow of her bones. Thank God, the rain was fading into a light drizzle. And yet even the effort it took to slog through the matted, long grass and mud to the area where the van had been parked had not warmed her. Her muscular legs now seemed no stronger that a couple of strands of spaghetti.

The flickering of her flashlight turned her mind away from the uncharacteristic weakness in her limbs and toward the danger that threatened. She thought about turning off the flashlight to save the battery for when the night became totally dark. After stepping into a hole and nearly falling, however, she rejected the idea, hoping she would reach the road before the flashlight blinked out and she was unable to see the uneven ground. Without the little flashlight's beam, she knew that later, in the pitch-blackness, she could fall over boulders as well as into holes both deep and shallow. And if she encountered some form of wild animal, she wouldn't see it until it was too late. She had no idea what she might run into and didn't want to think about it, but the thought of stepping on a rattlesnake came unbidden. She cringed. No telling what might be lurking out here when it grew dark.

A dim illumination in the distance gave her hope, and yet Callie had no idea how far she would have to walk before she reached it. Maybe a mile—maybe a whole lot more. But from where she stood now, there was nothing else to light her way. She had to remain alert, step by step, and not give in to the fatigue.

She focused on searching for a long stick that could act as both support and weapon. With so few resources available to her, it seemed like a smart move. At last she found one, thank God—just beyond the parking area, and hopefully a long distance from the boat. The flashlight finally flickered out soon after she reached what seemed to be the road. The stick was not too long, but long enough to prevent her from stumbling over the larger rocks or falling into any of the road's pits and gullies.

Wiping the raindrops from her cheeks, Callie kept one thought at the front of her mind: She must get far, far away from the boat in case her captors returned. She had to reach help. She had to let her parents know she was safe. She had to send someone back to rescue Neil. But she was so tired and so cold, she wasn't sure she could make it to that distant glow. *I have no choice. If I quit, the creep wins.* If she knew anything, it was that she wasn't cut out to be a wimpy loser.

As this encouraging thought slipped away, she froze midstep. Headlights were coming down the deserted road. They were headed straight for her.

It had to be Rick and his girlfriend. *Does that sicko have the money? Is he coming back to kill us? What will he do when he finds Neil alone on the boat?*

Callie's speculation came to an abrupt halt when an image of that creep flashed before her mind's eye. Earlier, when she'd stared into his ugly face, she'd felt as if she could see the wheels of decision whirling in his head. If anything went wrong when he went to pick up the ransom money, he would have to keep her alive. *But now, if he has the money . . .* If only she hadn't seen so many movies.

As the headlights drew closer and closer, she broke free of her trance. Dropping to the ground behind a group of boulders lining the roadway, she prayed as she'd never prayed before.

CHAPTER
110

The instant Ashleigh crested the hilltop, the silver van sprang into view through her rain-spattered windshield. With damp, shaking hands, she turned the steering wheel toward the side of the narrow, winding road. Pulling up behind the van, she struggled to engage the emergency brake and then, without thinking, flipped off the headlights. Plunged into darkness, she instantly turned them back on.

She longed to dash straight to the van, to fold her arms around her daughter, to make sure Callie was okay. Setting her jaw, she managed to restrain herself. It would be extremely unwise to do anything to set off the power-hungry loose cannon who held Callie's life in the balance. Instead, Ashleigh waited impatiently for the cell to ring.

"Have a nice trip, pretty lady?" The voice that reached her ears was filled with malice.

"Where is my daughter?"

Ashleigh heard a malevolent laugh. Then she saw a tall man with long blond hair spring from the driver's-side door of the van, cell phone in hand. Still talking into the phone, he said, "Get out of the car with the duffel. Then look across the bridge."

Ashleigh did as he commanded. The light drizzle and darkened sky impaired her vision and added to her sense of foreboding. At the far side of the suspension bridge was a figure, but Ashleigh couldn't make out any features. "You said my daughter would be with you. You said you'd get the money and Callie would be returned to us at the same time. I need to see her up close." Ashleigh hoped her voice didn't betray her fear.

"You *are* seeing her, but that's as close as you get before I get the dough. She will walk across the bridge as soon as you hand over the duffel."

Ashleigh felt as if her body had transformed into an ice sculpture. When she heard the whir of helicopter blades, her body temperature dropped several degrees more.

"What the fuck," the thin man hollered. "I said no copters. Your daughter is toast."

"No," Ashleigh lied, "if there's a helicopter, it has nothing to do with us." In a flash, she picked up the duffel and dashed forward.

"This is the second time it's passed. You telling me a helicopter just happens to be flying around here after sunset? Fat chance. I wasn't born yesterday."

"Here's your money," Ashleigh said, throwing the duffel at his feet and looking around wildly. "I heard something too, but I didn't see any helicopter. I saw one earlier—it was trailing some sort of advertising banner." She paused, wary as a cat. "As far as I know, the FBI and the police department aren't into advertising." Now less than a few feet from the skinny young man, she could see his pale, pockmarked face. Ashleigh felt weak in the knees. *He has to believe me.*

Then her mind shifted to the men in the helicopter. *What is that pilot thinking? He's put Callie in jeopardy.* She couldn't figure it out. Why had Conrad and Pocino allowed him to get so close?

"Jesus Key-rist," Pocino roared.

Conrad's heart jumped to his throat as they flew above the glare of car headlights. He was almost certain they belonged to the blue Civic. And at last it had come to a stop.

After Chicago PD had instructed him to land due to the nonstop rain and darkening sky, the pilot started heading toward the flat area where Pocino had a Bronco at the ready. They had little choice for an appropriate landing spot—fortunately, it was only about a quarter mile from the bridge. Conrad had wanted to make one more sweep of the hills near the rest area, but the pilot dared not risk it as dusk set in.

"I'm already pushing it by not turning on the headlights," the pilot had said.

Conrad knew he was right. His fear of being spotted was paramount; a promotional helicopter would arouse suspicion in this deserted area at night, especially in inclement weather. But now their efforts at going unnoticed had all been a waste. Surely the kidnapper, if he were anywhere nearby, had heard the copter as it roared overhead.

"Look, I'm sorry," the pilot said. "I cut the roar of the engine down to the minimum, but there's no way to silence these machines."

"I know, I know," Conrad conceded. He just hoped they hadn't further jeopardized the lives of his wife and daughter.

Rick eyed the woman in the light of his flashlight, which he directed at her face as she grew nearer. She might be telling the truth, but maybe not. He could afford to take no risks. He had to get the hell out of here and on the road.

This rich broad would do anything to get her kid back. That was no news flash. *Lucky girl. Maybe if my mom had given a rat's ass about me, I wouldn't be here.* He shrugged the thought away.

The woman frowned, but she didn't say anything until he grabbed the duffel. Then her hand shot out, grabbing his wrist. "I want to see my daughter."

Yanking his arm free, he said, "Hey, lady, you're not running this show." Ignoring her enormous brown eyes, which sparkled with tears in the glare of his flashlight, he said, "We do this my way, or your daughter dies."

"Stop saying that," she shouted. "I gave you the money. Now—"

Rick withdrew the revolver from his waistband. "Not another goddamn word. Get the picture? Your daughter is alive and well for the moment, but you try any funny business and you'll be picking out a casket." Again the thought came to him: how lucky the kid was to have someone who cared so damn much. He supposed the same was true of his wimpy half-brother, who at least had that nerd of a father to love him.

Rick's thoughts turned to the mother whose love he'd craved. The mother who had said she loved him, then let him take the rap for murdering her boyfriend. But he didn't go there for long. Hell, the past was crappy, but at least it was history.

The future is what I've got to wrap my head around.

"You lying SOB," Ashleigh shouted, and she grabbed for the duffel with both hands. The figure on the other side of the bridge had vanished. "I want to see Callie now."

"My, my," he snickered. "So now I'm a son of a bitch? I resent you talking about my mom like that."

Ashleigh swallowed hard, using all her strength to hold on to the duffel. "You know this has nothing whatsoever to do with your mom."

Wrenching the duffel from her grip with one hand, and holding the gun tightly in his other, he knocked her to the ground with the back of his forearm. As he backed away and tucked the gun into his waistband, though, she sprang from the muddy ground, not bothering to assess the damage. Again she lunged for the bag. She didn't care about the money . . . but he did. All she wanted was Callie's safety. The duffel was the only link between them.

Again he yanked the duffel out of her hands. This time he threw it to the ground and kicked it out of reach. Then he caught both of her wrists in one large, callused hand, pinning them together. "Settle down." His voice resembled a bark. "Got no time for this. I can shoot you here, and by the time your little girl gets home, she'll be attending her mom's funeral." He paused, maintaining the pressure on her wrists. "Or you can cool it, and you both might live to see the sun rise tomorrow."

The phrase was chilling, but at least it wasn't the grating, terrifying refrain *or your daughter dies.*

The figure she'd seen moments before had vanished from the bridge. *Where is Callie?*

Then, before she knew it, he was dragging her to the rear of the van, where he reached inside and withdrew a roll of duct tape.

When Ashleigh saw that Callie was not inside the van, she panicked. "Where is my daughter?" she demanded. Then, taking a different approach, she asked, "Please, may I see my daughter?" Except for the constant murmur of drizzle, the night was deadly quiet.

"Sure," the kidnapper said. "But as I said, you ain't running this show. You'll see your precious daughter when we're on the road and I know it's safe." He wound the tape around her wrists.

Ashleigh held her wrists at an awkward angle, doing her best to keep them from being taped together too tightly. She hadn't missed the reference to *we*. "What do you mean? You said—"

"I know what I said. Don't worry your pretty little head over it." He tossed the duffel into the van.

As he spoke, Ashleigh noticed, he did something strange: He withdrew a foil packet and opened it, then began scrubbing his hands with the moistened towelette. Opening a second and then a third packet, he continued scouring his hands. Like a chain smoker, his actions seemed to be done unconsciously. Then, pulling the gun from his waistband, he wiped it down too.

Ignoring his bizarre antics, Ashleigh asked, "How do I know that Callie is safe?"

"You don't. But she is. Trust me."

"How can you expect me to trust you? You lied about the exchange, and you could be lying about Callie's well-being too." Ashleigh's voice rose. She no longer cared about this man's anger. "*Was* that even my daughter on the other side of this bridge?"

With an unsettling laugh, he dragged Ashleigh to the Civic, opened the door, and shoved her inside. "Your daughter is on the other side of *some* bridge, but you won't be seeing her right away." Then, pointing the gun at her head, he said, "Stay put, or this will turn into a real ugly scene."

He slammed her door shut, sloshed through the mud toward the van, and slipped behind the wheel.

Ashleigh searched the car. She had to free her wrists. The car keys might cut through the tape, but with her wrists tied together, it was impossible to maneuver. Instead, she swung the door open and attempted to use the corner of it. But the tape didn't budge or tear in the least. If only the automaker hadn't done such a good job with the smooth edges.

Following the van with her eyes, Ashleigh gasped when she saw the thin man swing it crossways at the far end of the bridge and leap out. *Where did he go? Is he abandoning the van?* There had to be another vehicle. But where?

A moment later, she saw taillights receding into the darkness. *Is Callie with him?* She couldn't make out the vehicle or even a color. She couldn't even guess whether it was a car, a truck, or another van.

Rick leaped from the van with the bulky duffel and jogged to the burgundy minivan. "Payday, sugar," he sang out as he stuffed the duffel in the backseat.

Sarah-Jayne threw herself into his arms. "Knew we could do it, baby." Then she began singing, "*We're in the money . . .*"

Rick turned the key in the ignition and headed for freedom.

Squinting through the rain-mottled windshield, Nelson shouted, "Straight ahead. I see flickers of light. This has got to be it."

Marnie leaned forward, straining to see through the windshield of the Avalanche. At first she saw nothing but darkness, and then a few speckles of light appeared in the distance. Nelson had said there would be a boat, and now it was only about a city block away from them.

As they grew closer, Tony shone the giant flashlight out the passenger window, swinging it from side to side. "I think we can park over there," he said, gesturing to the left and handing the floodlight to Nelson.

Nelson quickly rolled down his window and, ignoring the light mist, lit up the area to their left.

"This is the spot. The copter set down here, and then the police cars showed up. It seems like a lifetime ago."

"So this is where your stepson shot the guy?" Gino asked.

"On this boat but not this location," Nelson said. "This is where we found him the first time he ran off, after his mom died."

Marnie's heartbeat went into overdrive. She spotted tire tracks. There were deep impressions in the mud—they had to have been made recently. She'd watched enough episodes of *CSI* to know that.

Turning to Marnie, Nelson said, "Stay inside the truck while we check out the boat." He paused, looking her straight in the eye. "Understand?"

Marnie nodded that she understood his request.

"We'll let you know what we find. Just make sure the doors remain locked."

No way. Marnie wanted to protest, but it was smarter to say nothing. She didn't want to lie to her mom's boyfriend; nor did she agree to his terms. She knew she must say something. "How are you going to get to the boat?" It was an honest question. The headlights lit up a path—but between the shore and the cockeyed old boat, there was a lot of water.

Using the corner of the car door, Ashleigh jabbed frantically at the tape stretched between her wrists, over and over and over . . . It stretched a little but refused to tear. *I have to find Callie before it's too late. He's got Callie, and now that he's got the money too . . .*

She stifled that thought, but another shot to mind. *The cell phone.* Scrambling back into the car, she fished awkwardly for the disposable phone on the floor where she'd dropped it. She flipped it open and set it face up on the seat so she could punch in the numbers to Conrad's cell.

She had to pause for a moment. *Oh no.* Without autodial, she had to recall her husband's number.

Pocino jumped down from the copter before the propellers came to a full stop.

Conrad was ready to follow when his cell phone blared. He dropped back down on the rear bench and pulled it from his jacket pocket.

"Ashleigh," he said, flooded with relief. "Are you alright? Do you—"

"Conrad, please, just listen." She spoke quickly, her breaths coming in sharp intakes. "I'm at the top of a hillside beside a suspension bridge. Your helicopter flew over about ten minutes ago. The kidnapper has blocked the far end of the bridge with his van. He took off in the opposite direction."

So the kidnapper has another vehicle. That came as no surprise to Conrad.

Pocino poked his head back into the copter. "Come on. No time to waste."

Conrad stretched his arm out toward the impatient Pocino. "Did you see what he was driving?" he asked Ashleigh.

"All I saw was a set of taillights. But Conrad, he took off in the direction the helicopter came from. There's no way to drive after him from here—the van is in the way. Can the helicopter land on this side?"

"Hold on." He relayed the message, and Pocino got on the phone with Landes, who was on the ground nearby with Agent Porter. Landes said he would contact Billings, who had managed to hook up with the local PD. The news would soon be out to all law enforcement. Maps of the area were at the ready, so the police and the FBI should be able to block all possible exits.

But now it was thoughts of Callie that weighed heaviest on Conrad's mind. *Is she with that fiend?*

"We've got to find a place to land back on the other side of the bridge," Conrad shouted to the pilot. Then, turning to Pocino, he said, "You take the Bronco, figure out how to reach the other side of that suspension bridge, and call me."

"Will do," Pocino shouted back over his shoulder as he lumbered toward the Bronco.

The helicopter took to the air again, heading back to get Ashleigh. After explaining the plan, Conrad flipped his cell closed. Events were unfolding at lightning speed, but he had to remain calm. All he cared about was getting his family home safely.

His phone gave a shrill bleep, announcing that he had voice mail.

Callie heaved herself up from behind the boulders. The vehicle heading in the direction of the boat was not the silver van. *Could it be help?* She wanted to believe it was, but doubt clouded her thoughts. *Should I make my way back toward the boat?* She stood as still as a statue, trying to decide what to do.

Finally, she made up her mind. She'd overheard the creep and his disgusting girlfriend talking about changing vehicles. It could be them. Maybe they were returning to kill her and Neil.

With renewed energy, Callie wiped her muddy hands on her jeans and headed off in the direction from which the truck had appeared.

The pilot had the coordinates logged, so the copter reached the area in no time. It was on the opposite end of the bridge from where they'd seen the headlights, marking the spot where Ashleigh had met with the kidnapper. Thank God, there was a fairly level place to land.

As the copter set down, Conrad let out an audible sigh. Through the mist, he spotted his wife making her way around the van that was blocking the bridge. As she ran across the bridge toward them, his heart ached.

Before she had closed the distance between them, she called out, "Have you heard anything?"

He told her about the voice mail. "We know where Callie was being held." *But now that the kidnapper has the money, he may be going back.*

"Conrad, we've got to find Callie before he hurts her—"

"Oh my God." The sight of Ashleigh's taped wrists blotted out her words. Conrad gently lifted her hands. Even in the dim light thrown off by the helicopter, he saw that her wrists were red above and below the duct tape, and there were specks of blood on her skin and the pale blue sweater. *What might have happened to her if the kidnapper had taken the cell with him?* He refused to think about it. Though he was relieved to know that Ashleigh was not in the hands of that sicko, his guts wrenched as he looked out into the vast blackness of the area. *Callie is out there somewhere . . . but in what condition? She's so young and all alone. How is she coping?*

Now that Ashleigh was safe, their priority was to find Callie. He cringed at the thought that more manpower might be allocated to catching the kidnapper than rescuing his daughter. *I hope to hell I'm mistaken.*

Gino was the first one to reach the shoreline, Nelson and Tony on his heels.

"Neil," Nelson shouted. There was no answer. Cupping his hands around his mouth, he hollered at the top of his lungs. "Neil, it's Dad."

More lights flashed on from within the boat. A head popped up from below. Then a figure emerged onto the deck, slowly making headway to the rail. The ground was mushy, but at least the rain had stopped.

Tony swung the floodlight toward the boat rail.

The figure shielded his eyes with a forearm. "Dad? Is that really you, Dad?"

Nelson looked heavenward for a fraction of a second to thank God before shouting, "Yes. I'm here to take you home, son."

"Is the girl with you?" Tony called out.

At Neil's response, Nelson's heart took a nosedive.

A staccato volley of questions and responses shot back and forth for a few seconds before Tony said, "We've got to call the Taylors. Does anyone have a number for them?"

"I have Conrad's number." Nelson pulled out his cell, punched the keys, and handed his phone to Tony. Then he turned back toward his son, standing on the deck of the lopsided boat. "How do we get to you?"

Neil explained about Rick pulling the plank down into the water when he left.

"I'll call 9-1-1," Gino said. "We better alert the police ASAP."

For a split second, Nelson contemplated plunging into the murky water, but he instantly came to his senses. He didn't have the strength required for a one-man rescue even if such a thing were in the realm of possibility. From this side of the water, there appeared to be no way to board the vessel.

Nelson's mind reeled as his son filled them in about the plank that had been the only way on or off the old boat. The area was totally deserted. Shining the flashlight into the murky, black water, he saw no sign of any boarding plank.

"I've got an extension ladder in back of the truck." Gino shouted. He turned to Tony. "Give me a hand."

"Sure thing." Tony handed Nelson's cell back to him, a faraway expression on his face.

"What's wrong?" Nelson asked. "Did you reach Conrad?"

"Got his voice mail," Tony said. "Even tried to get hold of my nemesis."

Gino gave a mirthless laugh. "Pocino?"

"You got it. But Pocino's cell also went straight to voice mail. Left messages on both lines. Just hope they pick up before they hand over any ransom money."

Tony turned to follow Gino back to the Avalanche, contemplating the best way to tell Marnie the news. Nelson had promised he'd keep her informed. The cliché *I've got good news and bad news* shot through his head. Well, that *was* the case. The good news was that her sister was not in the hands of the kidnapper. The bad news was that Callie was missing and there was no telling what she might run into all alone in this wilderness.

The hum of an engine in the star-filled sky curtailed further thoughts. In seconds the area was flooded with artificial light, no less bright than the searchlights engaged for the opening of De Mornay's two nights ago.

Gino, who had pulled the extension ladder from the back of the Avalanche, leaned it against the back fender and dashed toward the helicopter as it settled on the flat muddy surface. Conrad Taylor sprang to the ground, then turned to assist Ashleigh. Ducking under the propeller blades, the Taylors made their way toward Gino.

No point rehashing regrets, Tony thought, hanging back from the helicopter, *but it'll be a long time, if ever, before I'll feel at ease in their presence. Particularly Conrad's.* But baggage or no baggage, he knew this was the time to pool their resources. Finding the twin before anything else happened to her had to be everyone's priority.

At that, Tony's thoughts darted to Marnie. *Why is she still in the truck?* With all the hubbub of the copter landing and her parents' arrival, surely she would have gotten out of the truck by now. Unless she'd fallen asleep—which was as likely as Conrad inviting Tony into his circle of friends—something was very wrong.

Tony spun, jogged to the Avalanche, and threw open the door to the backseat. "Son of a bitch," he shouted. "Marnie's gone."

A loud steady roar from above caused Marnie to look skyward. It was a helicopter. Bright lights were directed to the ground, piercing the black night that surrounded her. A wave of relief washed over her. Callie could not have gone far. With those bright lights, they would find her.

A knot had formed in Marnie's stomach when she heard that her sister was not on the boat. She had leaned across the top of the front seat of the truck and watched through the windshield as the three men had made their way down the steep grade toward the boat. As soon as they'd gone a few yards, she had slipped out of the car and trudged down the hill after them.

The mud made it tough going, but it also muffled any sound. And anyway, the men were focused on the boat, so it was unlikely they'd look back. In the still night air, she had heard nearly every word: Nelson's loud voice as he'd called out to his son. The son's voice as he'd told his father how he'd dropped Callie down in the smelly water. Marnie was totally dry in her down parka, yet she'd felt the bitter cold all the same. Callie must be soaking wet. She'd probably end up with pneumonia—if some wild animal didn't get her first. Marnie's stomach roiled when she thought of it.

And here was Brad—Neil—who'd been nice and dry all this time, chilling out on the inside of the boat, safe and sound. Marnie balled her hands into tight fists, not able to forgive or forget how he'd deceived her—not even using his own name. If not for him, none of them would be living this nightmare. She'd love to dump *him* into the grimy water and see how he liked it. It made her sick to listen to Nelson making such a fuss over him, treating him like an innocent victim when he was the evil instigator.

But this was no time for revenge. She had to find Callie.

So Marnie had retreated up the hill, hoping the men were too busy to notice her. The mud was slippery, and the only light away from the boat area came from the headlights of the Avalanche, which were aimed too high to illuminate the ground. She'd slid more than once and feared that she might reinjure her weak ankle, but she had kept going. Until the helicopter had suddenly appeared overhead, flooding the area with glaring white light, and she'd realized that now they had a chance at finding her sister amid the dark wilderness surrounding them. That's when she breathed a sigh of relief.

But an instant later, her breath caught in her throat. The whir of a motor was growing louder, and she was again veiled in darkness; the blinding light had moved closer to the ground. Marnie sucked in her breath. The copter was landing. They weren't going after Callie at all. They must be here to help Nelson's lying son.

Slipping back into the Avalanche, Marnie quickly rummaged through the console until her fingers ran across a small flashlight. She grasped it and flicked it on to make sure it worked. It was small, but the light was bright.

Suddenly, she heard male voices. Someone was heading back to the truck. Impulsively, she grabbed the umbrella, slipped out the door on the driver's side, and crossed her fingers, hoping that the tiny flash of light from the door opening had gone unnoticed.

She hunkered down on the driver's side of the car and tried to make herself disappear. In a crouch, she began crab-walking the length of the truck and then stood and headed for the road they'd come in on. When she looked back over her shoulder, she saw that the men had not glanced back in her direction; they were bolting toward the helicopter.

When they found out she was missing, all hell would break loose. *But I'm already in a truckload of trouble. I've got nothing to lose.* And maybe if she was the one who found Callie, everyone would begin to forgive her. *Maybe I'll begin to forgive myself.*

Those were her thoughts as she planted one foot in front of the other on the uneven terrain. Step by cautious step, she was beginning to feel more confident. *Callie isn't just my sister; she's my* identical *twin. I have a better chance of finding her than anyone.*

Weak in the knees, Ashleigh felt paralyzed. "Marnie's *gone?*" Tony Wainwright's words echoed in her head; she tried but failed to process the idea. She felt Conrad's hand at her elbow, steering her toward the Avalanche.

"What do you mean?" Conrad's voice shook with rage.

Even in the reflected light from the helicopter's floodlights, Ashleigh saw the color rise from Tony's neck to his face and his hands clench into fists. "Mr. Taylor," he began, "did you get the message that Marnie had followed us in—"

"Yes," Conrad cut in. "But the message said you and Kennedy would keep her safe. Why would she be left alone with no—" Halting midsentence, Conrad said, "There's no need to lay blame. What's more important is finding my daughter—both of my daughters."

"They couldn't have gone far." Tony's voice was steady and rational.

Conrad failed to respond. He opened the back door of the Avalanche and said, "Ashleigh, please stay here, out of the cold, until Pocino gets here with the Bronco." Then he pulled out his phone and began punching in a number.

Feeling numb and disoriented, she slid in without a word. She was not dressed for the cold, and the slippers she wore were so big, they threatened to fall off her feet.

Gino poked his head inside the truck and cast his gaze from side to side, as if he thought Tony could be mistaken about Marnie's disappearance.

Tony came to the open door and reached out and touched Ashleigh on the arm of her sweater. "I am truly sorry. We thought we were doing the right thing when we found that she'd followed us. Since we didn't know what we might find on the boat, we thought your daughter would be safer locked inside Gino's truck—"

"I understand," she said, making no attempt to stem the flow of tears down her cheeks. Her heart ached, but Conrad was right: Laying blame would help no one.

"Oh my God." Tony's voice rang with alarm as he stared down at her wrists. "What happened—"

"Tony," Gino interrupted, "while Conrad contacts the police, we've got to cover some ground between the truck and the road we came in on. As you said, Marnie couldn't have gotten far. Callie has most likely been searching for the same route, and she may have found it by now."

"Right," Tony said, hefting his large flashlight. "I've got this, so I'll take off now and start searching. Gino, follow in the Avalanche—but first, give Nelson the ladder and tell him that we've had to change our focus. We'll get his boy off that old tub, but for now his kid is safe. The twins have got to be our priority."

Ashleigh's mouth was dry. Her world had again tilted off its axis, and she found it hard to breathe. They had spent the last forty-eight hours worried sick about finding Callie, and now Marnie was also missing.

Ashleigh stared into the darkness. Both of her twins were out there somewhere. Over and over, she thought, *Please, keep them safe.*

Callie looked up as the sound of a motor pierced the silence. Next came a blinding light from above. *A helicopter?*

Without a flashlight, Callie had been relying on the light of the moon and the stick she was using to steady herself. But the drifting rainclouds frequently covered the moon's face, and the uneven ground was treacherous in spite of her stick. So far she'd encountered no wildlife or reptiles. She had been praying there were no rattlesnakes. Had Rick only been lying to terrify her? He'd done a pretty good job of that.

Finding her step as she picked her way up a sloped embankment, she finally reached the top. Now all of a sudden, in the glaring spotlight, she could see a swath of wild grass in the hills surrounding her.

The kidnappers wouldn't be in a helicopter. Maybe it was the police or FBI looking for her. She whirled around as it passed overhead. Then she ran down the embankment and into the middle of the road, waving her hands in the air, praying someone would look down and come to her rescue.

The rush of despair that had washed over her moments earlier lifted. *Whoever is in the helicopter has to have seen me. It's landing.* She was about to dash toward the bright light—the spot in the distance where it seemed the helicopter would be landing—but curbed her excitement and instead took cautious steps. *This is no time to break a leg.*

Before taking another step toward the helicopter, however, her heart caught in her throat and then came to a full stop.

A backlit figure was coming toward her.

It was no animal; it stood upright on two legs and had a flashlight. The figure was headed in her direction.

Callie scampered away from the road, back into the thick shrubbery and tall grass, and searched frantically for a place to hide. Momentarily terrorized, her mind was awash with contradictions. The helicopter had just landed—its passengers couldn't have reached her already. Who was it, then? Was it the creep?

Here, on top of the embankment, there were no large boulders to hide behind, yet she dared not run into the darkness. Without another thought, she dropped, flattening herself against the wet ground, preparing to slide unnoticed over the lip of the embankment. Darkness was now her only hope.

Marnie slogged along. She was making steady progress toward the dirt road—the only access to the old boat, as far as she knew. She was thankful she'd impulsively grabbed the umbrella, realizing she couldn't have done without it. It made a perfect walking stick for this uneven terrain. *I must be getting close to the roadside.* She hadn't seen any car headlights yet, but she knew that the area would soon be filled with police cars.

Slow down, Callie, wherever you are. I need to be the one to find you.

Marnie took a deep breath and cupped her hands around her mouth. "Callie. Callie," she screamed as loud as she could into the silent, cold night air that surrounded her. Her throat felt raw, but taking in three short breaths, she again cupped her hands around her lips. She began to holler her sister's name, but she stopped short.

"Marnie?" came a voice, hesitant but clear. It was a voice she would never mistake—her own voice as well as that of her twin.

It was Callie.

But where is she? Marnie swung the beam of the small flashlight in the direction of the sound. There was no sign of Callie. No sign of anyone. Marnie scanned the area ahead of her and called out again while walking in the direction of the voice.

There. She saw the top of Callie's head near the spot where the ground sloped down to the roadside. Her heart leaped with joy, and casting all caution aside, she ran toward her sister.

Callie struggled to her feet, rubbing the mud from her hands onto her even muddier clothes. In the next moment, the two sisters were on the roadside hugging each other, happier to see each other than they'd been in years.

Marnie stepped back and looked her sister up and down. She was a mess, but she was alive.

Soon they were both talking at once, their questions overlapping, neither twin leaving room for any kind of coherent response from the other.

The girls had barely registered the wail of sirens in the distance or the headlights rapidly approaching before a Bronco screeched to a stop a few yards from them. The door swung open, and the unmistakable form of Ross Pocino was soon charging toward them.

"Holy mother of God," he roared, pulling both girls into a teddy bear–like hug. Then he prepared to let them have it. "If you ever even think about—"

"Thank God." The disembodied voice was nearly on top of them before they recognized Tony rushing toward them.

Pocino stepped back, wiping the mud from his parka. Tony stopped in his tracks. For a moment no one spoke, and then everyone was talking. No one was listening.

In the blink of an eye, the area exploded into a hive of activity. A myriad of headlights and searchlights swept the roadside and beyond. It was bright as day, and they were encircled by a cacophony of police cars and ambulances. But when the Avalanche pulled up and parked in front of the Bronco, and Conrad and Ashleigh Taylor stepped out from the back, a silence fell.

Callie's face lit up and she ran to her parents.

Marnie stood riveted to the wet ground beneath her feet.

CHAPTER
115

As if in a daze, Ashleigh slipped from the backseat of the Avalanche, raising a forearm to shield her eyes against the blinding glare of a rotating searchlight. Her feet touched the ground, but she was unsure they would hold her.

Conrad steadied her by the other elbow. "It's not a dream," he whispered in her ear. "Our girls are safe."

"Mom, Dad," Callie cried out as she ran to them.

Ashleigh threw her arms around her daughter. Conrad waited a moment before taking a step forward. He tucked a strand of hair behind Callie's ear and wrapped his arms around both his daughter and his wife. For a moment, time stood still.

Ashleigh was about to inspect Callie from head to toe when she caught a glimpse of Marnie, who hung back on the opposite side of the road. Her stomach did a slow roll.

"Eww." Callie pulled back. "I got you all muddy, Mom."

Distracted, Ashleigh gazed down at her light blue sweater, now caked with mud. She couldn't care less. "Sweetheart, what really matters is that you're safe. Both of you." Then, without missing a beat, she called out to Marnie. The kidnapping had been nearly as horrific for Marnie as it must have been for her sister. Now, as Ashleigh looked from one twin to the other, she thought that Callie's recovery might be the less difficult one.

Marnie hesitated for a moment. Then she slowly crossed the road to join her family.

"I'm so, so sorry," Callie and Marnie said in unison, their gaze taking in both parents. Then, simultaneously, their eyes widened in surprise before meeting briefly. And when they burst into laughter, the tension evaporated.

Conrad smiled and pulled Ashleigh close. "You were right," he whispered. "I guess there really is more to this identical twin thing than meets the eye."

Tony watched the happy family reunion but did not approach. He couldn't help wishing he'd played a bigger role in the twins' rescue. *Without Nelson, we'd all have been up a creek.*

With that thought of Nelson, Tony's mind switched into gear. He called out to Gino and jogged over to the Avalanche to ask about the situation back at the boat.

Ray Billings stepped away from a nearby police cruiser and joined Tony and Gino at the truck. "I'll ride with you," Billings said, and he climbed into the backseat of the truck while holding one shoulder protectively. "They said they'd follow and lend a hand," he added, gesturing with his free hand toward the two officers who were getting back into the police car that had delivered him to this spot.

When Tony opened the passenger door, he heard someone call his name.

"Hold it, Tony." Conrad Taylor was approaching.

Oh shit. What does he want? Tony stood, his hand wrapped around the door handle, his body tense with expectation.

Conrad extended his hand. "I want to thank you for the part you played in the rescue of both of my daughters."

Tony swallowed and let out a breath. "I didn't really do anything. Nelson is the one who knew about this place."

"That's not the way I see it. I'd hate to think what might have happened to Marnie behind the wheel of that car had you not spotted her."

In all the confusion, Tony had forgotten all about the shock of finding the other twin following them earlier that evening. It seemed like days ago. "Glad I could be of assistance," he said, shaking Conrad's outstretched hand. "Now we've got to get Nelson's boy off that boat."

Before heaving himself inside the truck, Tony saw the twins being herded into the ambulance with Ashleigh and Conrad following. He slammed the door shut while Gino slid behind the wheel.

"Give Nelson a call," Gino said. "He's sure to be coming unglued by now." He slipped the truck into gear. "Callie said his kid had a pretty messed-up leg. I told the paramedics we'd most likely need another ambulance on standby."

They drove to the flat area where they'd dumped the ladder when they discovered Marnie had taken off. There was no sign of it now.

Jumping from the truck, Gino flicked on the flashlight and scanned the area. The light revealed deep grooves in the damp ground, leading in the direction of the boat. "Nelson must be dragging the ladder himself. Let's go," he shouted, "before he has a coronary."

Tony and Billings took off after Gino, heading down the slippery slope.

CHAPTER

116

Viviana felt a warm glow as she thanked her assistant for helping to make this a special opening day. Coming to Chicago had been the right move. She felt optimistic about the future. The backlash from the Fans of John Stewart's had in fact been a blessing for her. She was sure their boycott of Jordon's had driven many patrons to her boutique—patrons she planned to cater to, to ensure that they kept coming back.

The moment she heard the front door click closed, though, her thoughts turned from business to Gino and the missing Taylor twin. It was growing dark, and she'd heard nothing from her adoring Adonis. She debated calling his cell but quickly dismissed the idea. *He said he'd call as soon as he knows anything.* As long as she had to wait, she decided, she might as well go over the day's receipts.

A few moments later—or was it a few hours?—Viviana's heart leaped at the sound of a key turning in the lock below. She'd lost all track of time.

"Viviana?" A strong masculine voice shot up the stairway. Gino bounded up the stairs to the mezzanine—two at a time, by the sound of things.

Slipping on her shoes, Viviana flashed her most provocative smile. She quickly slid out of her chair, meeting him halfway between the door and her desk. When she threw her arms around his neck and pressed her body close to his, all of her coherent thoughts flew out the window.

Stepping back from a long, penetrating kiss, she rested her slender, tapered fingers on his broad shoulders. "Did you find Callie and the boy?"

Gino gave her a tired smile and filled her in as best he could, but she kept interrupting for clarification.

"Hold on," she said, "how did Marnie get involved?"

As he concluded his explanation, he added, "Since Nelson had to ride in the ambulance with his son, I dropped Tony off back at the gas station. He's driving Erica's Caprice to the Christonellis' house. I told him I'd pick him up there after he had a chance to fill Erica and Mike in on all—"

"What did Nelson have to say about his son's involvement?"

"Angel, my information is pretty sketchy. There are so many layers, it will take days, even weeks, to sort it all out." He chuckled and shook his head. "By the time I left the Taylors, it was clear that even the twins didn't know the whole story."

"What about the kidnapper?"

Gino shrugged by way of an answer, as they heard his cell phone shrill.

Viviana listened to Gino's side of the conversation.

"Got it," he said into the phone. "Give me about twenty minutes."

Viviana waited for him to disconnect before repeating her question. "Did they catch the kidnapper?"

Gino nodded. "Don't know the specifics, but Pocino received a call from Landes, who was tracking the situation from the ground. It seems that once Pocino was able to give the FBI the coordinates of the ransom pickup, they blocked all the exit routes from the area."

"And how did they know the location of the ransom pickup?" Viviana was having trouble putting the pieces together.

"Pocino and Taylor picked up Ashleigh there, in a helicopter," he said, squeezing her hand. "As I said, my info is sketchy at best. But right now, I've got to get a move on. I told Tony I'd pick him up at the hospital."

"Hospital?"

"He's driving Erica over to Northwestern Memorial."

Viviana gave him a look of confusion.

Gino explained, "Erica's pretty shook up. She insisted on joining Nelson while his son is being checked out, so Tony offered to drive her there."

"Got it," Viviana said. "I'll go with you." Although she'd been utterly exhausted before Gino dashed in, the minutes the words were out of her mouth, she knew without a doubt that she was too wired to go to sleep. Besides, she did not want to be left on the outside when the complicated stories began to unfold.

Ashleigh had been relieved that they were not required to go to the police station after the hospital. But their temporary home at the Palmer House had been turned into a beehive of activity. Between the constant stream of phone calls and the endless questions, they had been kept busy all night, and now it was well after 3:00 AM. There was no telling how long the questioning might have gone on had Conrad not taken charge.

"Excuse me," he said to Chief Young, "my daughters—*all* of us—are utterly exhausted. For now, we've given you all the relevant information we have." He'd glanced away from the Chicago detectives and FBI agents and over to the girls. "Further questioning at this time is becoming counterproductive. After a good night's sleep, we'll all come down to the precinct and answer any other questions you may have." Then, shifting his eyes to Callie, he said, "Tomorrow, they will need you to identify—"

Callie said, "Dad, I'm not tired. I can do that now."

Conrad shook his head.

Chief Young said, "Thank you, Callie, but your dad is right. This Rick character has been apprehended, so you have no need to worry. He's being questioned now, and a positive identification can wait until tomorrow. Right now, you need to get cleaned up and get some sleep." Turning back to Conrad, Young checked his watch. "How about one o'clock tomorrow?"

"Can I go too?" Marnie asked.

Ashleigh's stomach roiled. She wanted to say no, but she wasn't sure if that was the right thing. She couldn't imagine that Marnie had more to contribute. After all, she'd had no contact with Neil's half-brother.

In the end, her indecision meant little. "We will need to talk with all of you," Young said.

At eleven o'clock Tuesday morning, following the interminable rescue the previous evening and the late-night examination at the hospital, Nelson reluctantly climbed the steps of the Chicago PD precinct on South Michigan Avenue. Neil hobbled up the steps beside him with the aid of crutches. Special Agent Roy Porter of the FBI had called the night before and asked him to come to the precinct and to bring his son with him. It did not sound like a request.

Both Chicago PD and the FBI would undoubtedly be going through the accounts of the abduction ad nauseam with both Neil and Callie in the coming days. Nelson would have preferred to stay home with Neil—after all, he was no longer legally responsible for his stepson—but felt it was best to get this over with. Erica, who had taken another day off work, had driven with them to the precinct. She was looking for a place to park the car and would wait for their call.

Nelson had been shocked to learn that Rick's girlfriend was dead. He had no clue about the where or the how. All he knew was that his stepson had been apprehended and the girl had died.

Neil had told him what he could, but of course Neil knew nothing of what had transpired after Rick had left him stranded on the boat. He had told Nelson that Rick had a gun—the one the girl had used to bash Neil's knee. Although the leg hurt like hell, there was no infection and she hadn't hit the ACL, so the doctors believed it would heal with no lasting damage. That was a relief.

As he and Neil made their way to the chief of detectives' office, Nelson caught sight of Rick. He was slouched in a chair in front of a steel desk in one of the cubicles, his head in his manacled hands. He did not look up, but Nelson noticed that his body shook.

Nelson hurried by and pointed toward the open office door, wanting to shield Neil from a glimpse of his half-brother. He was thankful when they sat down, their backs to the outer office. Neither of the boys was aware of the other's presence.

Chief Steve Young introduced himself to Nelson and Neil and then introduced Special Agent Porter and his partner. The men seated themselves. In response to their questions, Neil repeated much of what he'd told the detectives and the other FBI agents the night before. But when they asked about Sarah-Jayne, he unexpectedly raised his voice and tried to get to his feet. "She was mean, a dopehead," he said, biting down on his bottom lip, "but Rick dug her. He wouldn't kill her."

Nelson reached out and laid his hand on his son's arm.

"Neil," Agent Porter said, "what we need to talk with you about is the kidnapping. We will deal with Sarah-Jayne's death separately, since you were not there when she died."

When they got up to leave, Chief Young said, "One more thing, Mr. Kennedy. Your stepson has asked to speak with you."

118

"Why do you have to stay and talk to Rick?" Neil complained. "He's a liar."

"You'd rather I didn't?" Nelson had excused himself to assist his son in making his way through the precinct and down the steps. Erica would be waiting for Neil at the curb in front of the station.

Neil stopped and leaned heavily on his crutches. "Dad, I really don't know. Rick is a scumbag, just like you warned me. He takes drugs, and he played me for a fool. I hate what he did and how he made me feel, but . . ."

"But what?"

"He could have killed Callie and me, but he didn't. And I *know* he didn't kill his girlfriend."

Why is he protecting Rick, after all he's done? But this was no time to explore his son's unexpected defense of his half-brother. "We'll discuss this when I get home." Nelson helped Neil into the car, gave Erica a peck on the cheek, and forced himself back up the precinct steps. He was dead tired, with pain shooting through every nerve ending. If he didn't get to rest soon, he'd be debilitated for days. But that wasn't exactly something he could share with the chief of detectives.

Buried in his own thoughts, Nelson did not notice the Taylor twins and their parents climb out of the limo that had pulled up beside Erica's Caprice.

At the sound of footfalls heading his way, Rick lifted his head and turned toward the doorway. In less than a heartbeat, his eyes locked with those of Nelson Kennedy. "I didn't kill Sarah-Jayne." His voice was loud and directed at his stepfather. "I didn't kill anyone. Not now, and not when I was a kid."

"Right," Nelson said as he nodded to Chief Young and slipped into the other chair. His tone was mocking. "It was all a big mistake, and you were an innocent, misunderstood boy."

"Didn't expect you to believe me. The fact that I wasn't the one who shot Joe doesn't matter. He deserved to die. Anyway, that's all dust under the bed by now. But no way did I kill Sarah-Jayne."

Getting right to the point, Nelson asked, "Since I'm not likely to be your greatest ally, why did you ask to see me?"

"I need your help."

"Excuse me. You've terrorized my son—"

"Hold on," Rick said, raising his cuffed hands. "Neil is my half-brother." Still holding them up to ward off any sort of rebuttal, he continued. "I know I've always put the emphasis on the half, but the truth is—"

"Don't give me any crap about brotherly love. I don't buy—"

The chief of detectives rose to his feet. "I'm sorry, Mr. Kennedy. This doesn't seem to be going anywhere."

"Wait," Rick said, his gaze flashing to Nelson. "If you'll just listen, I'll cut to the chase." Rick's voice was low and shaky. He seemed on the brink of tears. "Sarah-Jayne had a heart of gold. It's just that—well, she was brought up in a bunch of different foster homes. Nobody gave a damn about her, except me." He glared into his stepfather's eyes. "In that way, she was kind of like me. But even though you never gave a damn about me, you never had the guts to find me another home either. You—"

He cut off again when he saw Nelson about to spring from the chair. *That's not going to work.* If he failed to get Nelson's help, he was a dead man. "Sorry. That was uncalled for," Rick said, putting on his most remorseful expression.

"Sarah-Jayne and I got hooked on crystal, and we got involved with some real bad dudes. If I didn't get hold of a lot of cash, I was dead meat." Noting that neither Nelson nor Young was about to shut him down, Rick jumped ahead. "Bottom line, I thought we had a foolproof plan. I never planned on hurting anyone—it was all about the money. Hadn't counted on the law getting wind of our location in time to block the exits. We miscalculated . . . big-time.

"Anyway, when we heard sirens screaming up our escape path, we dumped the car off by the side of the road and headed down the ravine. I knew a place where we could hide till things cooled down . . ." He hesitated, his red eyes pooling with tears. "It was black as a witch's soul in there. I told Sarah-Jayne to be careful, but she wasn't really . . . well, focused, and it was dark. She tripped. When I tried to help her up, she didn't say anything. At first I didn't know what happened . . ." He began to sob, unable to go on. *I need to . . .* His head turned to and fro as he desperately scanned the small office.

Young jumped in. "When the FBI team came on the scene—"

Rick pulled himself together. "Please, Chief," he said, "I'm almost finished." He sucked in his lips, then took a breath. "When I took hold of her hands, they were like dead weight, but they were warm, and I thought . . . I thought she was alive. I thought she just needed help, so instead of hiding when I saw lights scanning the roadside near where we left the car, I called out to whoever was there." He gave a sigh and closed his eyes. "Until the FBI agents got down beside us with their flashlights, I didn't see all the blood. I didn't see that she'd hit her head." He paused. "I didn't know she was dead." His eyes quickly scanned the office once more. "Chief Young," he asked, "do you have anything I can wipe my hands with?"

Young frowned. Then, ignoring the request, he said, "The girl either fell and hit her head on the rock, or"—he looked from Nelson to Rick—"she was hit with the rock."

Rick sprang to his feet. "I'd never hurt Sarah-Jayne. She's the only one who ever cared whether I lived or died. My own mother didn't love me. She killed her own lover and then set me up to take the fall."

Young stood and rounded his desk. With one large hand, he pushed against Rick's chest, and Rick toppled back onto the chair. He looked down at his handcuffed wrists as if he were noticing them for the first time. "I really need a towelette."

Nelson rose, took a small packet of Kleenex from his pocket, and tossed it to Rick. "I'm sorry for your loss," he said, "but what does all this have to do with me?"

Chagrined, Rick looked up. The Kleenex was better than nothing. He tore it open and began wiping his hands as best he could. "I know you want me punished. I deserve to be punished—for the kidnapping, for scaring the bejesus out of you and the girl's parents, for costing the taxpayers a ton of money. I know all that. I won't pretend that I've had some big epiphany and now I know the error of my ways. I did what I had to do to save my own neck, but I screwed it up big-time and now Sarah-Jayne's gone. I don't much care what happens to me, but . . ." Catching Nelson's glare, he knew his time was running out. "Nelson. Like it or not, I am related to your son by blood. You once loved our mom."

"Where are you going with this?" Young asked. "You told me you had information that could aid—"

"I do. Here's the deal. If I'm put in prison, I won't last a week. My life isn't worth all that much, but I don't want to die on the floor of the kitchen or in the yard of some state prison."

Nelson shrugged and again began to rise. "You always were the king of drama, Rick. I've heard enough."

"Wait. I told you I got hooked up with some real badasses. They've got connections everywhere, including inside the prison system. The word goes down that I didn't pay my dues, I'm history." He hurried on before either his stepdad or Chief Young could bring the meeting to a close. "I've got enough information to bring down a whopper of a drug ring that's operating across the nation. One that's infiltrated most of the high schools in Chicago, and even some of the middle schools."

Nelson looked disgusted, but Rick knew he had piqued the chief's interest.

"What does this have to do with your stepfather?" Young asked.

"The head man for the high school trade is Robert Herrera."

Nelson leaned forward, and Rick knew the name had struck a chord. But before he could insert a single word, Rick said, "Hold on. Let me finish. Herrera's in his early twenties, but he looks like a teenager. He's currently posing as a junior at Calumet High—"

"What?" Nelson's face was as red as the stripes on the American flag hanging in the corner of the chief's office. "You're lying. He and Neil are in charge of the layout for the school newspaper."

"Don't get your jockeys in a wad," Rick shot back. "Neil is clueless. He's hardly one of the players." But Rick knew who the players were, which just might give him the bargaining power he needed.

CHAPTER

119

After several nights with little or no shut-eye, when Ashleigh had finally dozed off the previous night, she'd been no more aware of the passing of time than had the bed beneath her. Although she hadn't heard Conrad when he'd left this morning, she had a vague awareness of his gentle kiss on her forehead before she'd drifted back to sleep.

"It's so random," Juliana was saying as Ashleigh made her way into the suite's living room. *Random* had become Juliana's favorite buzzword. Padding across the room, Ashleigh saw Juliana in animated conversation with Paige.

Juliana was the first to notice her. "Mom," she cried out, leaping up from the sofa and flying into her arms.

Ashleigh held her tight—so tight that Juliana squealed.

With a giggle, Juliana said, "Is this what it means to squeeze the stuffing out of someone?"

Kissing her on the forehead, Ashleigh laughed. "Missed you a whole bunch, pumpkin."

Paige joined their merriment as she rose from the sofa. The two women gave each other a warm, wordless hug.

"Thank you so much," Ashleigh said.

"Hey, it was my pleasure. Spending time with Juliana this morning gave me the opportunity to see *Charlotte's Web*."

"I bet that was a thrill," Ashleigh said, rolling her eyes.

"Actually, it was. Since Mark was brainstorming with Conrad over the upcoming meeting with Alan Grey and a couple of his John Stewart's backers, Mom and I were able to enjoy the film with Juliana." She grinned. "It was well done. Mom said she remembered reading the book to me when I was little. While that memory is unlikely, we made a nice *new* memory."

"It was a really good movie, but it made Grandma Helen cry." Juliana folded her arms in front of her. "Now, tell us what's going on."

Obviously her precocious daughter felt left out. Although Ashleigh and Conrad kept her up to date on her sisters' safety, they had spent little time with her since the kidnapping.

"Where is Elizabeth?" Ashleigh asked.

"Mom." Juliana's voice was little more than an exasperated whine.

Ashleigh pulled her in close as Paige reported the latest. "Elizabeth said you had told her all she needed to know for now, and since Juliana needed time with you and her dad, Elizabeth offered to stay with Mom." With a sheepish grin, Paige admitted, "Guess she knew I was dying for firsthand information." A frown crossed her smooth brow. "You look like you could use a cup of coffee."

"It shows?"

Paige didn't respond. "Have you eaten anything?"

"I'm not hungry, but you're right—I could use some coffee." She was still reeling over the fact that she had slept until nearly eleven. "Have you seen your sisters?" she asked Juliana.

"I tried, but Callie pulled the covers up over her head and Marnie told me to get lost."

"She did?" Ashleigh asked, frowning.

"Well," Juliana said, grinning, "not exactly. She said to let her sleep. But that's what she meant."

Ashleigh shook her head. "Ever since Saturday night, I've felt as if I'd been dropped down the rabbit hole." Addressing Juliana she said, "My little love, give the girls a break. They've been through a lot. Callie stayed up long after everyone left last night. She fell asleep soaking in the bathtub."

"Bathtub? Callie never takes baths."

"Well, after being on that stinky old boat, I guess she felt like she needed more than a shower."

"Mom, why don't we go in the kitchen? You can get some coffee and I can get a root beer."

Ashleigh was taken aback. "A root beer?"

"One root beer isn't going to rot my teeth, is it? I already drank milk today." Then, anticipating her mother's objection, she raised her hand like a traffic cop. "Come on, give me a break. It's not every day that my sister gets kidnapped—and returned safely. Milk just won't—"

"Okay. I get it," Ashleigh said, trying hard not to show her amusement. "Can I get anything for you?" she asked Paige.

Soon the three of them were seated around the kitchen table, and Ashleigh began telling them about their day at the precinct. "Forgive me if I repeat." She went on to tell them what she and Conrad had learned about Nelson's stepson.

"Have you met Nelson yet?" Ashleigh asked.

"No. But I understand he is a highly respected architect."

Ashleigh nodded. "It's most likely the architecture that prompted him to join the Fans of John Stewart's." Tossing up her hands, she said, "But let's not open that can of worms. What's important is—"

"Hey, Midget?" The voice of one of the twins filtered into the kitchen.

Juliana was no longer interested in anything other than joining her sisters. "That's Marnie," she cried out. "May I be excused?"

"Sure," Ashleigh said, glad to have some time alone with her friend.

"How did she know it was Marnie calling her?" Paige asked. "I've learned to tell the girls apart when I see them together, but their voices sound absolutely identical. Or is that just me?"

"No, it's not just you. I can't tell their voices apart either—but I know that was Marnie." When Paige continued to stare at her, she explained. "Only Marnie calls Juliana 'Midget,' never Callie."

Paige nodded. "But now that we're alone, tell me how you and the twins are coping with all that's been going on in the past few days."

"Well," Ashleigh said thoughtfully, drawing out her words, "the analogy that springs to mind is what happened in the aftermath of the L.A. riots."

120

With her elbows on the table, Paige leaned forward, resting her chin on her folded hands. "Okay," she said, "you've piqued my curiosity. What connects Callie's abduction to the L.A. riots?"

"Remember the boarded-up display windows at Bentleys Royale?"

Paige nodded.

"On those signs, the store's sales promotion staff had written 'Out of something bad, let's make something good.'"

Again, Paige nodded, but she was still confused. *Where is Ashleigh going with this?*

"Well," her friend said, "at first Callie and Marnie were filled with questions for each other—and also with guilt for their part in making the abduction possible. Each seemed to realize how much of a loss she would feel if something happened to the other twin."

"That's terrific," Paige said. But from the expression on Ashleigh's face, she saw that the tide must have turned.

Swallowing hard, Ashleigh continued. "Since that first night, though, they have done nothing but blame one another."

"So they are currently at war?"

"Yes and no. It's impossible to explain. Whenever Conrad and I are ready to step in, they become the best of friends and suddenly we are the enemy."

"How—"

"Maybe I'm overdramatizing. Actually, now that Callie is out of the hands of danger, some things have become easier. Before Callie was found, we had to tiptoe around Marnie and her delicate psyche. She was so close to the edge, blaming herself for everything . . . We were afraid our disapproval would tip the scales in the wrong direction. She told us she wished it was her and not Callie who'd been kidnapped, and she thought we felt the same."

Paige shook her head sadly.

"You know how I feel about placing blame, but the twins must take responsibility for their actions. Now that they're home safe and sound, we've had to come down pretty hard on both of the girls."

"Both? But Callie—"

"She knew better than to take off on her own. Especially here in the city, at night. And Marnie—well, there's no denying that what she did was wrong. But she just tries to turn the tables and say she never would've been forced to take Erica's car if . . ."

Taking another sip of her now cold coffee, Ashleigh made a face. "Enough of our trials and tribulations," she said. "Easter is in four days. . . ."

Conrad's head was swimming by the time the presentation was finished and Alan Grey had left the conference room. Grey had brought with him two Asian investors who had flown in from Japan and were scheduled to depart on Friday. The Jordon's management team was still in a state of shock; they had been unaware that the investors' goals had shifted. The original plan of purchasing the entire former John Stewart's division had been abandoned. Their current offer was for the landmark store only. A one hundred percent cash offer.

Conrad glanced down at his watch. "We'll take a ten-minute break before we discuss the pros and cons of this proposal," he said.

"Be right back," Mark said.

"Sure. Then I'd like to bounce a couple things off you before we reassemble." Although Conrad knew in his heart what was in the company's best interest, he was glad he'd asked his former partner to sit in with his management team. But he was also thankful for a few minutes to himself. He needed time to wrap his mind around the facts and figures Grey had presented.

The leader of the Fans of John Stewart's was every bit as dedicated to his quest for the best as Conrad was to his. The problem was that their views were polar opposites.

Conrad felt the weight of the towering stacks of data that his nemesis had piled on the conference room table. Grey had done his homework. Neither Conrad nor his savvy management team doubted the validity of Grey's exit interviews, which confirmed that eight out of ten shoppers in the city overwhelmingly preferred the John Stewart's brand over Jordon's. *Hardly a news flash,* he thought. But that alone was neither earth-shattering nor insurmountable.

Conrad had never dreamed it would be smooth sailing. Change was always difficult. The road to acceptance took time and understanding. But who would have dreamed he'd encounter such well-organized resistance? And yet, as confident as he remained over the power, dedication, and ability of his management team to bring their vision of a truly national department store to fruition, how much time could they afford to invest? How long would it take to produce the profit they must bring to the bottom line? Profit, not a dream, was what he owed to his stockholders.

His eyes raked over the stack of more than sixty thousand signatures from both here and abroad, protesting more than just the name change. It was also impossible to ignore the effects of the well-organized boycotts of Jordon's this past holiday season. A thirty percent drop in profit for this region was nothing to sneeze at.

They had more than eight hundred Jordon's department stores and forty Carlingdon's stores to look after. *Is it best to hold on to the landmark John Stewart's location, or to cut our losses and concentrate our time and resources elsewhere?*

Mark Toddman's return to the conference room cut off further speculation. There was no more time for contemplation. It was time for a decision.

Neil leaned on his crutches and lifted his foot onto the ottoman. He tried not to fidget as Erica leaned down to tie his sneaker. In the past few days, he felt like he was getting to know her, and in spite of all he'd read, she really wasn't so bad. *And she seems to really care about Dad,* he thought. There was no denying that, but her relationship to the twins and their parents was really weird.

He'd tried every which way to wheedle out of going to meet the Taylors, but nothing he said had made a dent in his dad's resolve. Today was going to be painful and embarrassing, but maybe his dad was right. He was bound to come face-to-face with them during Rick's trial, maybe even before that. Might as well get the first meeting over with.

And yet that flash of pure hatred that Marnie had cast in his direction before walking into the police station yesterday chilled him to the soul. The twins really were identical. But Neil had no doubt that the one who'd given him a brief smile and a little wave was Callie, so the other had to be Marnie. If only he could write her an e-mail or a text before they met. But what could he say that wouldn't sound totally lame?

The Taylors' suite was abuzz with activity by the time Conrad walked through the door.

He stopped short at the dining room entry. Elizabeth was filling water goblets, and Conrad saw that the dining room table was set with seven place settings for lunch. They would be meeting with Nelson Kennedy and his son—the boy who, thanks to his daughters' naïveté, had been responsible for all the turmoil of this past week. An upheaval that had resulted in the death of a young woman.

The twins and Juliana, looking freshly scrubbed, dashed up to meet their father. They were clad in jeans and tank tops, their hair damp and pulled back in ponytails. He noticed the game of Rummy Tiles on the floor of the living room and was thankful that his girls were doing something together rather than being into their own individual worlds, either talking on their cell phones or sending text messages. After giving them each a hug, he asked, "Where's Mom?"

Juliana hitched her thumb in the direction of the master bedroom. "She's taking a shower."

Conrad shrugged out of his suit jacket and walked into their bedroom, then called his wife's name.

With a hairbrush in hand, Ashleigh poked her head out of the bathroom. "All yours," she said as she came to him. Wrapping her arms around his neck, she gave him a kiss, then said, "This next chapter is about to come to an end."

"But does it have a happy ending?" His brows became a dramatic arch.

"I sure hope so." Ashleigh gave a light laugh. "Juliana and Elizabeth are going down to have lunch with Helen."

"And we're having a luncheon for the kid responsible for turning our world topsy-turvy."

"I thought a meeting with the Kennedys would be less awkward if I had food brought in from the Corner Bakery Café."

"Leave it to you to make the kid responsible for kidnapping our daughter feel more comfortable." He gave a weary smile and shook his head, then squeezed her tight and pulled her in for another kiss.

"Love—" she started.

"Okay, I realize this isn't a kid with evil intent, but without his—"

"I know," she cut in, "but he was as much a victim as Callie was." She paused, "There's something I didn't mention. Erica will also be with them."

Conrad groaned. *Is there no end of innocent victims?* "Okay. Guess we may as well clear the air with everyone at the same time."

"That's what I thought." She smiled. "Erica and Marnie have some issues to resolve before Easter, and since we are returning home Sunday night—"

"Ashleigh," he said, "you didn't invite them for Easter, did you?" He braced himself.

"No, love. With a few exceptions, I agree that our time for attempting to be one big happy family has come to an end."

"The exceptions being . . . ?"

Ashleigh shrugged. "High school graduation." Then a grin broke out on her gorgeous face. "Weddings, grandchildren's birthdays . . ."

"Okay. Got it."

The melodic door chimes began to peal.

"Go ahead and change your clothes," Ashleigh said as she headed out the door.

Despite her typical optimism, Ashleigh was prepared for tense moments around the lunch table. Off and on, the air in the penthouse suite was filled with raised voices spouting accusations and recriminations.

Just as Ashleigh saw that things were getting out of hand and was about to step in, Conrad took over. Firmly planting his hand on the mahogany table, he stood and said, "Enough."

Nelson leaned forward, his eyes riveted on Conrad. Erica reached out, placing her slim hand on his, her gaze also focused on Conrad.

"This is no time for the blame game," Conrad continued, glancing across to Ashleigh.

Blame game. She smiled at his use of her expression.

"What happened is no one person's fault." He looked from one teenager to the next. "All three of you played a part." Then, resting his eyes on Neil, he said, "Perhaps your half-brother would have come up with a plan to kidnap one of my daughters on his own, but—"

"I know," Neil said, before Conrad could finish. "I was stupid, but I didn't—"

Holding up his hand, Conrad said, "Stop. I'm sorry. There's no point in discussing the what-if's. We all know exactly how this played out, and each of you knows the role you played." He paused, again making individual eye contact with each teenager. "What I hope you take away from this experience is the knowledge that you are the creator of your own lives. You and you alone have one hundred percent responsibility for your own actions."

There were nods around the table.

For a few awkward seconds, silence permeated the dining area. Callie broke it, saying, "Mr. Kennedy, Rick was constantly scrubbing his hands raw with wet wipes. Has he always done that?"

Kennedy shook his head, then seemed to consider the question further. "Not always. It seems to me that it started just before he ran away the first time—after the shooting on the boat. It became an obsession."

Callie had told them about "the creep's" odd behavior. But Erica, who had not said more than a few words since entering the suite, jumped in with her theory. "I can relate to that kind of obsession."

All heads turned toward Erica. But for a long moment her gaze focused only on Marnie, then dropped to the table. Erica cleared her throat and said, "It's no secret that I once had a drinking problem."

For several seconds, it was so silent in the room that the ticking of the clock seemed thunderous.

"That was the worst period of my entire life . . . before losing Marnie."

Ashleigh froze, uncertain where this was going.

Erica looked up. Her eyes drifted to Conrad, who sat stiff as a toy soldier, and then to Ashleigh. "Sorry, I didn't intend to turn this into a melodrama."

Nelson moved his chair a bit closer to Erica's.

"Well, Mom," Marnie said, "you never had any obsession for washing your hands."

Erica met Marnie's eyes. "No, my obsession was not for washing my hands. My obsession was scrubbing the kitchen counter and walls. My hands were red and raw from the cleaning materials."

"I sort of remember that," Marnie said, "but—"

"Precious," Erica said, "obsessive behaviors aren't the same for everyone, and seldom do they make a lot of sense. I think my obsession for cleaning came out of my guilt for not providing a decent place for you to grow up in. I didn't want you to smell even a trace of alcohol."

She paused and looked directly at Nelson. "Rick started his obsession with the wipes right after he shot the man on the boat. You said he never seemed to feel any remorse, but maybe he did feel guilty. Maybe he wanted to wash his hands clean of the memory of holding that gun."

"Oh my God," Nelson murmured. "The blood. When the police arrived, his hands were covered in blood."

CHAPTER
122

Viviana sat on the sofa, her hands gently stroking Dolly's silky fur, but her mind was far from being at rest. Tomorrow was Easter, and the more she thought about it, the more she realized that she had no desire to share the day with a lot of people.

Dolly licked the back of her hand, nuzzling even closer. A flash of inspiration struck Viviana, and suddenly she knew exactly what she wanted. It was time. Easter was the perfect occasion to show her lover that he had won her ultimate trust.

Padding into the bedroom, she placed Dolly on the velvet cushion of her tiny four-poster doggy bed. It pleased Viviana each time she saw the royal crown design of the canopy formed by the four posters with their matte-gold finish. Dolly scrunched into a curve of the cushion and settled her chin on her front paws. She looked up at Viviana for a moment, then laid her head back down and closed her eyes.

Viviana smiled, her thoughts turning to Gino. She dashed into the bathroom and turned on the large Jacuzzi and lit the candles around the tub, creating the perfect ambiance for love. Then, catching a glance of herself in the mirror, she plucked a couple of combs from the bottom drawer and swept her hair into a casual updo.

A few minutes later, when she heard a key in the lock, she quickly slipped off her robe, tested the temperature with her big toe, and slid into the fragrant water.

"In here," she called out.

"Umm," Gino said as he sauntered through the doorway. His dark eyes sparkled in the candlelight. "Do I detect an invitation in those dreamy mermaid eyes?"

"You do," Viviana said, beckoning him closer. Then she hesitated before asking, "What would you think of calling off our Easter dinner at the Taylors' suite?"

"Fine with me," Gino said, cocking a dark brow rakishly. "But if we're going to stay in the bath all day long, we'll have to figure out a way to keep this water from cooling," he said as he stepped out of his trousers and pulled his sweater over his head.

Once again, Gino's bronzed physique took Viviana's breath away. His taut abs and broad chest distracted her for a long moment. All rational thought threatened to vanish into the steam. But as he stepped into the tub, she forced herself to focus. "What do you think of having Easter with Mason?"

When Gino did not immediately respond, Viviana feared he didn't remember—after all, in recent weeks he'd stopped asking about her son. Her heart plummeted.

But in the next breath, she felt his muscular arm slide around her waist. "Thank you," he said softly into her ear.

"Thank you?"

"Yes. Meeting your son is important to me. But I knew you'd let me in only after I gained your trust. And your trust is worth a thousand Easter baskets."

When Gino lifted her onto his lap, she felt his desire. She trusted this man more than she'd ever trusted anyone, and she planned to enjoy every moment they had together, for however long it lasted.

Marnie was excited as she shimmied into her new skirt. As long as they had to dress up for Easter, it was great that she'd found this long black skirt to wear with her cashmere shell. She'd been told that the champagne tone of the sweater accented her dark eyes. And she wanted to look her best.

This morning she'd have a chance to talk to Neil—without Callie there. Though she knew it sounded lame, in a way Marnie really wished she'd been the one who'd been abducted—and not just because she felt guilty. Nothing bad had really happened to Callie in the end, right? After finally meeting Neil, her anger had dissolved a fraction—or possibly more. Her mother's mantra drummed through her head: *You can't live your life in reverse. You can't live your life in reverse. You can't live . . . .*

Marnie brushed her hair and ran the straightener through it, then pinched her cheeks before heading to the door.

Callie—and probably Juliana too—was still in bed and sound asleep. If she weren't a part of two families, that's exactly where Marnie herself would be. But she couldn't blame her parents for not inviting her other family to Easter dinner, and in some ways, it was better to be part of two Easter celebrations. It was nice not to have to share attention with her sisters all the time.

The other day, when she'd seen her *other mom,* nothing had been said about her sneaking off with the car, nor had Erica said anything when she'd called to tell Marnie about this morning's Easter breakfast plans. It was as if the whole thing hadn't happened. But Marnie hadn't talked to Uncle Mike yet. She knew she couldn't count on him to be silent about last Monday and the danger in which she'd put herself and maybe everyone else on the road. *I can handle it,* she thought, and suddenly she felt warm inside, knowing how many people cared about her.

"Ready, Marnie?" her dad called from the entry of their suite. He was wearing his sports jacket.

Marnie felt the surprise jump to her face. "Are you driving me?" she asked.

"No. The limo is waiting downstairs. But since Mom and Elizabeth are busy with the caterers, and we haven't had much time together in this past week, I thought I'd ride along."

Oh boy. What now? Marnie had heard enough about the dangers of the Internet, of meeting strangers, and of driving without a license. *I got it. And I'm sorry about most of it.*

On the way down in the elevator, her father commented on the renovation of the Palmer House and pointed out some of the details Marnie hadn't noticed before. In fact, she'd noticed very little this week.

When they'd stayed here the year before, Marnie and her sisters had gone on a tour with Ken Price, the director of public relations, who knew all about the hotel and its history. Mr. Price had brought the Chicago fire to life by showing them pictures of the first Palmer House, which Potter Palmer built for his young wife. History was usually boring, but learning about the people who made it was fascinating. Mr. Price had told them that the hotel burned down only seven days after it opened. *Imagine how painful that must have been.* Marnie remembered a lot of what he'd told them about the impact Potter and Bertha Palmer had on the city of Chicago and the nation, but as she slid into the backseat of the limo, her mind centered on avoiding another lecture.

The best way to distract her father was to get him talking about department stores, but since coming to Chicago she'd had information overload about Jordon's and John Stewart's. Besides, even if she could think of a good question, her dad would see right through her ploy.

However, Marnie soon discovered she had nothing to worry about. After a comment or two on the nice sunny day, her father asked her how serious she was about becoming a writer. Maybe he was just trying to make conversation, but he seemed truly interested and expressed no negative opinions. He didn't even say anything about what might and might not be acceptable subject matter. She was surprised when he suggested that she might like to begin looking into the best colleges that would help her fulfill her dreams.

"Don't you think I need to concentrate on graduating from high school first?" She giggled.

"You'll be surprised how quickly these next two and a half years will flash by." Reaching out, he squeezed her hand and gave her one of his killer smiles. "We'll talk more seriously about this in the summer."

The limo pulled up in front of the Christonellis'. The driver parked behind a gold Lexus, then dashed around to open her door.

As Marnie and her dad made their way up the walkway, it occurred to her that throughout the ride he had been as intent as she was on avoiding any unpleasant conversation about the past week. He wanted her to enjoy the Easter holiday. And that's exactly what she wanted to do.

Mike Christonelli dashed down the walkway and threw his arms around Marnie, lifting her off the ground and giving her a whirl. "It's so good to see you, precious. We've missed you so much. This house gets pretty lonely every time you leave."

"Thanks, Uncle Mike. I miss you too."

As Conrad extended his hand to the stocky man who had shared the first years of his daughter's life, his stomach clenched.

"Thank you for allowing Marnie to share Easter morning with us," Mike said. "It means the world to Erica and me."

"Yes, it does," echoed Erica, who was a few steps behind him. After giving Marnie a quick hug, she looked to Conrad. "Would you like to come in?"

"Thank you, Erica, but I've got to get back." Glancing down at his watch, he noted that it was nine thirty on the nose. "David will pick Marnie up at quarter to two."

"We'd be glad to take her back," Mike offered.

"No need, thank you. The driver will take Marnie back into the city." Conrad did his best to provide them with a smile. "Enjoy your Easter."

As the limo drove away, Marnie noticed that Nelson's Highlander was parked behind her mom's Caprice in the driveway. Uncle Mike's and Bill's cars were probably in the garage. But what about the two cars at the curb? The red bug had been here last time, when she'd taken her mom's car, so it was probably Tony Wainwright's. But she'd never seen the Lexus. It was parked directly in front of the house. Six cars meant at least seven other people. Hardly what she'd imagined. She was anxious to talk with Neil—just the two of them.

Unbidden, a song her mother liked popped into her head: "Que Sera Sera." Whatever will be, will be.

And then, as she reached the front door, it hit her like a bolt of lightning. *I have two sisters and two mothers. No one has a problem when I say "my sister," even though it might mean Callie or it might mean Juliana. So what's the big deal if I call both Ashleigh and Erica "mother"?*

She stopped dead in her tracks, and Erica almost ran into her. "Mom," Marnie said, turning to face her, "would you be hurt if I used the same name for you and Ashleigh?"

"What?" Erica looked truly confused.

"I mean if I stopped dancing around and just called you both 'Mom' all the time?"

Erica smiled. "Of course not, precious. I know it's been awkward. I told you from the beginning, Ashleigh is your biological mother, and calling her mother takes nothing away from me. In my heart, you will always be my daughter and I will forever be your mother."

They'd had this conversation too many times to count, but slowly Marnie was beginning to think that maybe she *was* really pretty lucky. Another of her mom's analogies came to mind—the one about looking at the glass as half full or half empty. *Well, maybe I can change my view.*

When Marnie stepped into the living room, she was greeted by the group assembled there.

She returned their greetings and wished them all a Happy Easter, but was momentarily surprised to see Mitchell Wainwright. The rented Lexus must be his. Instantly she began to pull the threads together. *Of course.* Tony was Mr. Wainwright's son. She hadn't seen the resemblance at first, but now that she saw them together, she saw what her mother meant. The two men had the same strong jawline and bright hazel eyes.

"You clean up real good," Tony teased.

"Thanks," she said with a smile. "And sorry I—"

"Forget it." Tony gave her a wink.

Erica joined Nelson and Neil on the sofa and gestured for Marnie to sit in one of the chairs that had been pulled from around the dining room table. But when Marnie noticed Neil's crutches balanced on the arm of the sofa, she realized she was not yet up for idle chitchat.

Mike had taken off for the kitchen—the perfect excuse. "Be right back," Marnie said. "I need to say hello to Uncle Bill."

The two kids had taken off to borrow a couple of chairs from a neighbor, and the others were either in the kitchen or the dining room, involved in the last-minute preparations for a breakfast for eight. This gave Tony the opportunity he'd been waiting for.

"I could use some air, and you're most likely dying for a smoke. How about taking a short walk around the neighborhood?" Tony suggested.

His father eyed him skeptically but rose from the armchair and followed him outside.

At times like this, Tony wished he hadn't given up smoking. That would have given him something to do with his hands. Observing his father as he slowly extracted his cigarette case from his inside pocket, Tony attempted to pull all those well-rehearsed words from his memory bank.

"It appears you have something on your mind," Mitchell said, selecting a cigarette and tapping it on the outside of the case.

"I do." Tony's voice was strong. He was relieved to note that the tremor he felt deep within was not reflected in his tone. The flicking of the switch of the old Ronson lighter, which his father had used for decades, threw him off course. "I'm surprised that thing still works."

"Wouldn't be caught dead with one of those Zippo gadgets. But it's getting pretty difficult to find the wicks for Old Faithful." He ran his finger across the sterling silver shell and slipped it back into his pocket. "But I don't imagine we're having this father–son tête-à-tête to discuss the preservation of the classic cigarette lighter."

"Dad, all the words I've been going over in my head are nothing but a blur, so in plain ol' English . . . I've got to get something off my chest."

"Look, Tony. I told you I'm sorry. I shouldn't have asked if you had anything to do with the kidnapping. You didn't deserve that. And from all I know, you have a right to be proud of yourself for your part—"

"This has nothing to do with the kidnapping. I didn't do much, other than maybe prevent a second one. But that's beside the point."

His father's gaze did not waver from his as Mitchell took a drag on his cigarette, then slowly exhaled.

"What I need . . . what I'd like, is more than your tolerance."

"Meaning?"

"Let's lay all our cards on the table. I know my lifestyle, or rather my sexual preference, is abhorrent to you. You don't accept it; you merely tolerate it."

"If you expect me to be *excited* about the fact that you choose to be attracted to other men, and that the Wainwright name will come to an end with—"

"That's just it. My sexual preference is not *a choice*. And it's not about what you or Mom did or did not do. It's just who I am."

Mitchell waved his hand in the air. "I've heard all that bullshit. I've even read up on it over the past couple of years, but I don't buy it. We all have a choice."

"Is that right?" Tony stopped dead and turned to face his dad. "Can you tell me when you decided to be straight? Can you recall that exact moment?"

Their eyes locked, and Mitchell flicked his cigarette into the gutter. "Don't be ridiculous. I didn't have to decide. I *am* straight."

"Thank you. My point exactly." Tony's eyes stayed fixed on his father's.

Mitchell shook out another Marlboro and tapped it on his case. Could Tony be right? Could a person's sexuality be part of who he is—part of his DNA?

"Look, Dad, if I actually had a choice, do you think I'd have chosen to be gay? It's a rough road to travel."

"Life is no roller-coaster ride for any of us. We all have our challenges. The bigger the challenge, the tougher we become."

"And you are as tough as they come . . ."

Mitchell was about to jump in, but Tony's next words caught him off guard.

". . . the kind of toughness I admire. Even when I was a naïve, vengeful reprobate, I looked up to you."

Looked up to me? Hell, the kid tried to destroy me.

Tony hurried on. "I know I didn't show it, but truth be known—a truth I wasn't even aware of at the time—what I was after was your attention. I'd failed at winning your love and acceptance, so I was hell-bent on destroying you."

"And pretty damned successful at it." Mitchell chuckled, then instantly became serious. "We'd better hotfoot it back to the Christonellis'." Patting Tony on the shoulder, he said, "I can't pretend to understand the gay or lesbian lifestyle. I've got to admit that when I see same-sex couples showing affection in public, it turns my stomach." He cleared his throat. "Then again, I don't much relish public affection by heterosexuals, either."

Stopping midstride, he locked eyes with his son. He knew what was needed, and it was long overdue. "You've come a long way, son.

Your intelligence, I never doubted. But I know I wasn't there for you when you needed me most. That time is lost forever, but I want you to know how gratifying it is to see how you've turned your life around." They resumed walking and picked up their pace, but Mitchell was not finished. "Over these past few months, I've tried very hard, but as far as I attempt to stretch my mind, I haven't developed an understanding of your . . . lifestyle.

"But son, I know firsthand the devastation of going through life without a father's acceptance. Your grandmother tried her best to make me aware of the vicious, demoralizing cycle within the Wainwright family. I'm talking about the unsatisfying father-son relationships we seem to inherit. My own mother encouraged me to be a catalyst for ending this pattern. I can't promise any instant flash of enlightenment or a swift about-face, but I do promise to give it my best shot."

Still, he wondered, *How will I handle it if Tony develops another intimate relationship with a man?* But despite his self-doubts, Mitchell Wainwright meant every word of what he'd said. He hoped his son believed him.

Inevitably, the breakfast conversation revolved around the kidnapping and the dangers of teenagers on the Internet or of giving them too much freedom at too young an age.

When Erica began clearing the breakfast dishes, Marnie started to get up to help, but her mom gestured for her to stay seated. "Stay and visit. Tony and I have this under control, right?" She threw Tony a glance. "And Bill and Mike have a special surprise coming."

Turning back toward the table, Marnie asked, "What's going to happen to Rick?" She knew that the police or maybe the FBI had recovered the money, although for some reason they were holding on to it for a while. But that's all she really knew about this still-unfolding drama.

"We're not certain," Nelson said above the clatter of dishes.

"He's working on some sort of plea bargain," Neil jumped in. "Rick said this guy I've been working—"

"Neil." Nelson's voice boomed above his son's. "That is not something we can discuss."

"But Dad, I was just telling Marnie—"

"'But' nothing. Remember what you were told. We can't say anything until the detectives tell us exactly what, if anything, we can share."

Neil seemed to shrink into himself.

Nelson looked around the table, making fleeting eye contact with each individual. "Rick has connections to some sort of drug ring that's operating in high schools and maybe even some middle schools. That's all we can tell you. We were told that any leaks could jeopardize the case."

Marnie looked up as Uncle Mike and Uncle Bill entered, each carrying a tray filled with crepes smothered in chocolate and whipped cream.

After serving the elaborate breakfast dessert, they slipped into their chairs and joined in the conversation.

Marnie hadn't thought she was hungry, but she was delighted that Uncle Mike and Uncle Bill had made their special crepes—her favorite food in the whole world. Especially since she knew they had done it just for her.

"Well, Nelson, I know your plate is pretty full," Bill began, "but have you heard anything about Alan Grey's proposal?" Bill had been a merchandise manager for John Stewart's before it became a casualty of the Jordon's takeover of the Hay's Company retail empire. Now he worked for Jordon's, but he remained a closet member of the Fans of John Stewart's and all it stood for. He had not been able to jump ship, as Erica had, when he found himself at odds with the Jordon's philosophy. Approaching his fiftieth birthday, with no other job offer on the horizon and a mortgage to pay, he'd stayed on under Jordon's management.

"It's a no-go. Rumor is that—" His eyes shot across the table to Marnie.

Marnie's back stiffened. No one here understood her dad's dream, and she didn't know enough to defend it. Still, she had to say something. She glared at Nelson. "I know you're with that group that hates my dad."

"Marnie, that's not true," Erica said, her voice wavering. "Nelson doesn't hate your father, he just disagrees—"

"I saw Nelson's picture in the paper. He was with all the protesters, holding up a sign and passing out flyers." She remembered the photograph: hundreds of protesters marching around the John Stewart's store on Main Street. Many were dressed in costumes. Some of the women wore dresses and bonnets that her mother had said were the type that would have been seen in the 1870s—the early days of John Stewart's. The dresses were made of yards and yards of material and were worn with tons of petticoats. There were also some men in old-fashioned suits, but it was the women's costumes that fascinated her.

Nelson raised his hand as though he were in school. "Hold on. Your mom's right. The protest is not an attack against your father. We have a great love for—"

"Excuse me, Nelson," Bill interrupted. He sounded nervous. "I wasn't thinking. This is not the time to be discussing this."

"Uncle Bill," Marnie said, "I'm not a little kid anymore. I know you and Mom feel the same way as Nelson, even though you—"

"Hey, I happen to understand both sides of this conundrum," Bill replied. "Preservation of tradition versus progress and change. I could be devil's advocate for either side, but it's not something that we can settle or even have an impact on today."

Mitchell Wainwright's words tumbled out before Marnie could reply. "It's Easter, everybody. Let's play nice. How about going on down to the basement for another Ping-Pong challenge?"

"You're on," Tony said. He was on his feet in a flash. "But let's take care of these dishes first."

"Not a priority," Mike said, joining him. "Who's up for a game of pool?"

At the moment, Marnie wasn't interested in going down to the basement. She wanted to talk to Neil, who had not followed the others from the table.

She was about to ask her mom where she'd moved the board games when Neil said, "How about going outside?"

Marnie glanced around. Only the three of them remained in the dining room. Her pulse quickened. Neil was looking straight at her, his crutches tucked under his arms.

CHAPTER
125

Callie was helping Elizabeth and Juliana assemble the Rummy Tiles pieces when she looked up to see Ross Pocino and Dick Landes, who had stayed on in Chicago to help unravel all the circumstances of her kidnapping. Her mom, grateful for the part the two men had played in reuniting the family, had invited both of them to the Taylors' late-afternoon Easter dinner.

Callie's stomach lurched, and question after question tumbled through her brain. What else had Rick told the police and FBI? And why did he kill his girlfriend—or was it really an accident?

"The door was open, so . . ." Pocino explained.

"Please, come in and make yourselves comfortable," Ashleigh said as she glanced down at her watch. "Marnie will be here any minute, and we plan to eat at three."

Everyone soon fell into companionable conversation.

Paige, who sat beside Ashleigh on one of the sofas, groaned. In a soft, whispery voice, she said, "I don't know what to do with Mom."

Ashleigh gave a light laugh as she observed Helen coquettishly batting her long eyelashes at Renzo, who had stopped by with April and Kyle to wish everyone a happy Easter. "Cherish her, Paige," Ashleigh replied. "And don't worry. Your mom is a delight. Besides, Renzo is eating up all the attention."

"You're absolutely right. We love having Mom in our lives, and she certainly gives us cause to keep the gray cells working." Paige grinned. "By the way, didn't you say you invited Viviana and Gino?"

"I did, but she begged off. She's taking Gino to meet her son."

"Her *son*?" Paige asked, a clear note of surprise in her tone.

"Oh, did I forget to mention that? I only learned of his existence a few months back."

Paige was speechless for a few seconds. Then she asked a string of questions. "When? How old is he? Where does he live?" Uncharacteristically, she giggled. "Sorry. This blows me away."

"Viviana had kept it a total secret until recently, but it seems she no longer cares who knows, so I'll tell you what I know."

"Who's the father?" Paige frowned. "Couldn't be Sloane or Wainwright. She wasn't out of public view long enough—"

"No. She had the baby when she was a teenager, long before she came to Bentleys Royale, and long before we knew her."

"So why didn't anyone know? Had she given the baby up for adoption?"

"No." Ashleigh quickly filled Paige in on what Viviana had told her: that the boy was severely autistic and that she had placed him in a facility in Southern California until a few months ago, when she moved to Chicago. She recently had him moved to a nearby facility.

"My God, Ashleigh, her son must be almost as old as Gino."

"No," Ashleigh grinned. "Her son is *older* than Gino. Paige, I think Gino was actually the catalyst for Viviana's candor."

"Only Viviana could pull off something like that. I just wonder how long it will last.

"I think shedding that veil of secrets has done her a world of good. Since she met Gino, she seems to be happier and more relaxed than she's been since I've known her."

"Do you think she plans to marry him?"

Ashleigh shook her head. "I doubt it. You know, she—"

The thought was left unspoken, because the door to the penthouse suite burst open and a breathless Marnie dashed in.

For a fraction of a second the room fell silent. Then, as always, everyone seemed to be talking at once, returning all the wishes of "Happy Easter" until Ashleigh ushered everyone into the dining room.

When they were all gathered around the table, Elizabeth led the Easter prayer and they were soon engrossed in various conversations.

Callie, who was seated beside Dick Landes, took the opportunity to ask him some of her questions.

"Well, Callie, there's a lot I don't know at this point, but I will share what I do know—anything that is not privileged information. Rick Schmitt did not kill his girlfriend. Her death was an accident."

"How do they know?" Callie asked. Then she quickly added, "They argued a lot on the boat."

"The rock that Sarah-Jayne hit her head on—the one that has been identified as the cause of her death—was not a loose stone as was thought originally. The jagged point was all that the police officers saw at first. They immediately taped off the area to preserve the crime scene. It wasn't until after the ME—"

Juliana, on the other side of Landes, leaned forward. "That's the medical examiner."

He smiled and nodded.

"Is it like on *CSI*?" Before he could respond, she said, "Nobody gets to walk around the crime scene until the ME says so. Right?"

"Yes, little lady," Landes continued in his quiet way. "When you're out of school, come and see me. We could use someone with your bright analytical mind at the agency."

Juliana giggled and sat back in her chair.

"After the ME was finished, the forensics team found that the jagged rock the young lady fell on was actually a small piece of a boulder that was deeply imbedded in the ground. So deeply that it took the good part of an hour to unearth it."

"So there was no murder? The trial will be just about the kidnapping?" Callie asked.

"Well, Callie, there may not be a trial."

The other conversations had halted. Callie and Marnie looked at Landes in stunned silence.

"What do you mean?" Juliana asked as her pale complexion colored. "They aren't going to keep the creepy kidnapper in jail?" She'd obviously conjured up her own picture of the man who had taken her sister. "They can't let him out of jail. He could kidnap someone else. Maybe even try to get Callie again."

Pocino cut in. "No matter what happens, Rick Schmitt will be nowhere near you or your family." The blustery investigator had everyone's attention. "There's a lot up in the air. But this Rick character has some information that can potentially save a lot of lives."

"What?" Callie's voice rose. "He is pure evil. He's no Good Samaritan."

"It's about drugs in high schools, right?" Marnie offered.

Landes and Pocino spun their gazes in her direction and spoke at almost the same time.

"Where did you hear that?"

"How did you know that?"

Marnie told them what little she knew, and Landes gave an audible sigh. "That's right, Marnie. Mr. Kennedy was correct in telling you nothing that might jeopardize the case that the DEA will be attempting to build. If Mr. Schmitt—Rick, the creep, or whatever you choose to call him—cooperates fully and his information is reliable, he will most likely be placed in the Witness Protection Program."

"And he won't be punished for what he did to my sister?" Juliana asked.

"Girls," Conrad jumped in, "what Mr. Landes is trying to tell you is that Callie's kidnapper has valuable information. Information that could save hundreds or even thousands of teenagers' lives. If that's the case, and law enforcement is able to keep drugs from being dispensed in the high schools, more good can be gained by putting the man into witness protection than by sending him away to rot in prison."

"Being in witness protection can be its own sort of prison," Landes added. "The person has to start all over. He isn't allowed to talk to anyone from his past life . . ."

No one spoke as Landes explained.

Silence reigned even as the catering staff cleared the table in preparation for dessert. In an obvious attempt to lighten the mood, April broke the silence. "Uncle Conrad, tell us about Jordon's and the future of the John Stewart's building." She grinned and held up her right hand as if making an oath. "Off the record, of course."

Conrad gave April a warm smile and a rakish wink. "Well, Miss Future Investigative Reporter, off the record, what have you heard?"

"As I'm sure you know, rumors are rampant about the sale of the landmark store."

Shaking his head, he said, "Not going to happen."

April squeezed Kyle's hand, and a knowing look passed between them. "Did you actually consider the offer?"

"Of course. With a business enterprise as large and vital as Jordon's, we can't afford to ignore any viable opportunity. The sale of the headquarters store housed in the historic John Stewart's building was not viable. It would be detrimental to our long-range plan. We cannot run a national department store business with multiple names, and the former John Stewart's landmark location is a vital part of our long-range plan." Conrad picked up his cup and finished the remaining coffee, suddenly aware of his daughters' rolling eyes,

He stood and placed his napkin on the table. "Now, we've spent far too much of this beautiful day discussing the kidnapping and the state of the modern retail business. Shall we have dessert served in the living room, where we can watch the recaps of the Easter Parade on the TV?"

As they all filed into the living room, Conrad's gaze took in his four girls. As long as they were all safe, his glass was far more than half full. He was up to any challenge.

In the sanctity of the steamy shower, as the hot water pounded every nerve ending, Ashleigh closed her eyes and reflected on the past week. What a disaster—and yet, she could not help but count her blessings. Her family was safe and her friends nearby. Paige and Mark had changed their Easter plans, remaining in Chicago with April and Kyle rather than having everyone travel to the Toddmans' home in Texas to celebrate the holiday. It was like old times.

Everything seems to be falling into place. But as Ashleigh reached for the towel and stepped out of the shower, her mind turned to Marnie. She appeared to be getting along with her sisters and seemed happy enough to return to them for Easter dinner. Ashleigh hoped it wasn't just her daughter's pleasure at seeing April and Kyle. There had been no more talk about Marnie wanting to live with the Christonellis, but Ashleigh and Conrad had discussed the fact that the crisis might not have totally passed. Marnie could be biding her time until August, when she would turn sixteen and would be allowed to choose with whom she wanted to live.

And yet over the past few months, ever since Ashleigh's ungraceful tumble into the bushes, it seemed that Marnie was finally beginning to bond with them, her biological family. Ashleigh couldn't remember when Marnie had stopped avoiding addressing her by name or using the awkward "Mom Ashleigh." *She calls me "Mom" now—all the time.* She also called Erica "Mom," but that didn't matter to Ashleigh in the least.

As she towel-dried her hair, Ashleigh peered into the steamy mirror and decided to forgo the tedious task of drying her thick mane. Pushing open the bathroom door to dissipate some of the steam, she reached into the drawer, pulled out a scrunchie, and tied her hair back. Slipping into her robe, she felt her husband's arms wrap around her. But before either had an opportunity to utter a single word, there was a knock at the bedroom door.

"Come in." Conrad sighed as he stepped back from his wife.

Ashleigh followed him into their bedroom as Marnie threw open the door. "Please listen," she began. "I know what I want to do this summer."

This could signal trouble, Ashleigh knew, but she refused to jump to the worst-case scenario. Gran's words replayed in Ashleigh's head: *You are as strong as your greatest challenge. And with every challenge, you gain strength.*

Conrad settled into the armchair. Ashleigh sat across from him on the edge of the chaise longue, patting a place beside her for Marnie to sit.

Marnie remained standing. "Please, let me finish before you ask even one question."

Ashleigh and Conrad nodded. Conrad looked amused, but Ashleigh's stomach was doing a tap dance. *Is this about living with the Christonellis again?* Although Conrad did not believe a judge would allow a sixteen-year-old to make a decision that was against her best interest, Ashleigh wasn't sure. In any case, she knew in her heart that winning a lawsuit did not equal winning a battle. She hoped it wasn't going to come to that.

"I spent some time getting to know Neil this morning. He really is kind of cool. He's smart, and I think—"

"Marnie, you don't know anything about—"

"Please, Dad. This isn't what you think. Let me finish, then I promise I'll be a good listener."

Ashleigh stared up at her daughter. She sounded so reasonable, so unlike her usual seat-of-the-pants-thinking self. And yet Ashleigh feared they might soon be blindsided.

"Don't get all uptight. I don't have a crush on Neil. He's too skinny. I feel like a clumsy cow beside him."

Her daughter's slim figure conjured up no such image, but Ashleigh knew the feeling from her own girlhood.

"But we like a lot of the same things. He wants to be a writer, and so do I."

A writer? But Marnie had always been a dancer, even before coming back to live with them at age eight. Up until a few months ago, as far as Ashleigh knew, Marnie had been more interested in the performing arts. But apparently writing had become more than a passing fancy.

"I've been thinking about it for a while, and after talking with Neil, I think we could help each other."

"Might as well get it out into the open," Conrad said. "If you are asking if you can come to Chicago for the summer, the—"

"Dad," Marnie said with an impatient stamp of her bare foot, "no. But please, let me finish. I know writers don't make a lot of money. Not even enough to support themselves at first. So what I wanted to know is, since I'll be sixteen this summer, could I work part-time for Jordon's?"

"Which Jordon's?" Ashleigh asked, her heart in her throat.

"Well, I sure don't want to come anywhere near this city, especially with all the dumb protesters. And I really don't want to be here until Neil's half-brother is far, far away. Besides, Neil and I can work together over the Internet." Her hand instantly shot up to stop any protest. "He's not a stranger now. You know where he lives, and you know his dad."

"Actually," Conrad said, "I believe having a part-time job this summer would do both you and Callie a world of good." He paused before saying, "You know my philosophy: In order to learn how to manage money, you must have money to manage."

Marnie flopped down beside her mother. "I'm really sorry it's taken me so long to know how lucky I am."

Stunned, Ashleigh could not think of a single response. Conrad too, she noticed, had been struck speechless by Marnie's out-of-the blue candor.

"I was jealous of my sisters. I felt left out, Mom, when you guys talked about vacations and funny things that happened before I knew you. I was jealous of Callie for having so many friends, and I was jealous of Juliana for being the youngest and so darn smart. I made a big deal about having two moms, and I felt sorry for myself. What I didn't think about was how much I have that most kids don't—that even my sisters don't."

Her eyes drifted from Ashleigh to Conrad and back again. "Sure, I missed out on a lot of stuff by not growing up with you guys, but I

wouldn't want to give up knowing Mom and Uncle Mike and Bill."
Marnie sucked in her cheeks and locked her eyes on the chandelier. A
grin started to creep onto her lips. "Okay, so I call you and Erica both
'Mom.' *I* know who I mean, and *you* both know who I mean, so why
did I have to make it a big problem?" Then, unable to control the grin
spreading across her face, she turned to Conrad. "Well, *you* might have
a problem knowing who I'm talking about. But you'll just have to deal
with it."

"Touché. I can deal with that."

Pulling Marnie toward her and wrapping her arm around her
daughter's slim waist, Ashleigh said, "You were only eight years old—
younger than Juliana—when you found out you had a twin and a little
sister. You had a whole family that you knew nothing about. It's no
wonder—"

A smile lit up Marnie's creamy complexion. "Well, you're stuck with
me now. At least, till I graduate."

Ashleigh smiled too. She felt the merry-go-round stop spinning—the
one they'd all been riding for nearly sixteen years. Marnie was home
at last.

The rumor linking the department store to a dinosaur—soon to become extinct—is simply untrue. The model is not broken. After several years of decline, department store sales are slowly rebuilding.

The world of retail in the twenty-first century has become a Pandora's box: Once you open it, you find much more than you ever bargained for. The wants and needs of shoppers around the globe vary from one extreme to the other. Just try posting a question about shopping preferences on your choice of social media outlets—Facebook, Twitter, Myspace, whatever your poison—and you're sure to find, as I did, varied responses clearly indicating that no one size fits all.

While many of us greatly miss that very special home for shoppers—the regional department store, which houses scores of fond memories for some—others embrace the convenience of the Internet and are reluctant to step outside their own sanctuary to do their shopping. In our fast-paced techno-world, we have gained a great deal in terms of the shopping experience, but at what price? No one can deny that life is rapidly changing for today's shoppers. The idea of "window shopping" with a friend or family member has lost its luster, and even the expression is starting to fade. While change is inevitable and indeed makes our world a better place, we must not become victims of change. We must evaluate and accept what we have no power to change, while continuing to fight for what we truly believe must not change.

Across the nation, thousands upon thousands of shoppers lament the loss of those special times when they would join friends or family for a day of shopping and lunch at the tearoom of their favorite regional department store. I have fond memories of announcing my plans on these

DARLENE QUINN

sorts of days, along with the time of my expected return. When I was very young, nothing interfered with those sacred hours spent shopping—no one could reach me. When I was a bit older, with children of my own, the only interruption was concern for the home front, which could be allayed by simply making a call from one of the nearby pay phones located in every department store, mall, gas station, and convenience store, as well as on many street corners. Those were the days before today's cell phones, of course, when few people owned a mobile phone (and those that did exist were housed only in cars or large briefcases). We were not accessible 24/7. We shopped at our leisure and made a day of it.

Today, a person without a cell phone is an anomaly, and it would be just as difficult to find a public telephone. Department stores too have undergone many transformations over the past decades. For stores where you can find any and everything under one roof, profits have suffered; they are being squeezed out by large specialty stores and budget prices.

To resolve this problem, many upscale players have shifted their product offerings toward the high end. Whether the market will allow this shift is yet to be seen. In recent years, several department stores have gone through a redistribution of space and goods, cutting down on less profitable items and giving more space to what sells best. This is a logical but potentially dangerous solution. At what level of specialization will a department store give up on its formula and lose its reason for existence? Will the loss of identity lead to a loss of sales and the eventual closing of its doors?

Meanwhile, department store shopping is getting more and more complicated. The biggest challenge, not only for department stores but throughout most of retail, is the lack of differentiation, the me-too-ness and sameness that have plagued retailing for years. In an effort to stave off rounds of price-slashing that will allow them to compete over the same brands, savvy merchants are developing and relying on merchandise that can be found nowhere else. Committing to these exclusive lines is far more profitable than relying on national brands, since the retailer can mark these items down at its own pace rather than being forced into premature markdowns in response to the competition.

One version of the exclusive line is tricky, however: celebrity brands, which are growing in popularity. A marketable celebrity who has an authentic vibe and caters to a particular customer base can be potent. And while these celebrity items offer the advantage of being unavailable elsewhere, they can be dizzyingly hard to keep track of. Which store carries X celebrity brand? Cindy Crawford and the Olsen Twins are at JCPenney, Jennifer Lopez and Marc Anthony are at Kohl's, Donald Trump and Madonna are at Macy's . . . Each line must fit a specific slot. For example, for Macy's to bring in a celebrity or brand name, the line must hit a "white space"—a category or a customer base that is underserved. Madonna's Material Girl, a fast-fashion preteen line, was brought in to fill this type of void.

The downside of celebrity lines is unpredictability; a star can wane in popularity almost overnight, and a scandal can hurt sales. Also, there's a disturbing trend toward half-hearted sponsorship of these lines; many celebrities lend their name to clothing without being picky about the manufacturer, choosing an accessible price, or promoting after the initial buzz wears off.

Designer labels can be exclusive offerings too. A special color, material, or style may be available in only one venue or in just several items. For instance, Saks has the exclusive on the taupe color of a Christian Louboutin ankle boot, while a metal-heeled boot in beige is only at Neiman Marcus. Even Home Depot is getting in on the action, with an exclusive line of Martha Stewart hardware, paint, and furniture.

The idea of selling products that consumers wouldn't be able to buy in other stores has been part of the retail landscape for some time now. During the recessions in the first decade of the twenty-first century, as we saw purchases being cut dramatically, some vendors were being eliminated from the store mix. Designers became more than willing to work differently if that's what was required to stay on the racks, and exclusive lines became a way for retailers to strengthen ailing brands. For instance, Liz Claiborne fell into trouble when it was ubiquitous, but JCPenney turned it into an exclusive brand in 2010, and it has become a strong seller there.

Exclusivity is smart thinking for retailers. It takes them out of being a commodity seller of goods at the lowest price. According to the *New*

York Times, in 2009 at Macy's, 42 percent of total sales were from exclusive merchandise; at JCPenney, the figure was 50 percent; at Kohl's (in 2010), 48 percent. Saks's proportion is lower, about 10 percent, but the store plans to raise this figure to 20 percent.

Throughout the recession and its aftermath, Nordstrom outperformed its peers with ten consecutive quarters of double-digit sales growth. However, Nordstrom is not immune to today's fast-changing retail environment. The majority of today's consumers are engaged in obsessive online comparison-shopping. Since most open their wallets only for must-have products, retailers are stocking merchandise shoppers can't find elsewhere. Gone are the days when we had the same four department stores as mall anchors, all offering the same brands. Since a third of Nordstrom's $10 billion in annual sales is generated from ladies' apparel, the company has taken on the challenge of spicing things up. The forward-thinking president of merchandising, Pete Nordstrom, recently cut a deal to sell clothes from Topshop, the London-based retailer known for producing trendy, midpriced styles known to defy characterization. It's not the sort of fashion people expect to find at Nordstrom. It is a risk that could draw new customers—or turn off existing ones. This partnership is an inexpensive, low risk way for Topshop to expand its presence in the United States and for Nordstrom to lock up an exclusive.

Savvy retailers around the globe are seeking exclusive lines to drive sales. By depriving rivals of specific goods, these retailers make it harder for today's discount-addicted consumers to compare prices. For instance, designers Tory Burch and Diane von Furstenberg recently announced partnerships with Target and Neiman Marcus, respectively, to produce collections of limited-edition holiday items.

One of the most radical proponents of the strategy is JCPenney. Straying from the usual department-store setup, Penney's plans to devote selling space to as many as one hundred branded boutiques.

Nordstrom's approach is less risky. While Topshop goods will have a high profile in stores, the British chain will not be running its own enclosed boutique. Topshop's appeal is being tested in fourteen cities of varying sizes. In September 2012, Nordstrom started selling Topshop (and Topman for men) clothes online.

It remains to be seen whether this experiment will be a success; if it is, perhaps some credit will go to the online shopping community that has helped introduce the British brand to a broader market.

There is no doubt that the Internet is changing the retail experience and, with it, how we shop. Beloved brick-and-mortar stores are feeling the pressure of the prices and the convenience that e-commerce retailers offer. This has become a key focus for major department stores (Sears is the largest operator by market share, closely followed by Macy's). They are expanding their online networks to achieve global presence and reach a wider audience. They are improving their website functionality to better compete in cyberspace. While highlighting the benefits of shopping in-store, they have added the ability to return items purchased from their websites in stores to avoid shipping costs. By opening outlet stores, they are attracting price-conscious consumers.

Do you avoid department stores in favor of smaller boutiques and online retailers? Are you unable to find what you are looking for? Are you simply overwhelmed by the hundreds of thousands of square feet of merchandise, and the lack of customer service? Retailers are seeking answers to your conundrum. Harrods in London has launched its own free iPhone app that includes an interactive store guide using GPS. Customers are able to locate anything in the store in an instant. Menus to all twenty-nine restaurants within the store are included in this app. There are also links to the Harrods Twitter feed, a history of the company, and much more.

In the near future, all Macy's locations will be outfitted with free wireless Internet service. Since the company earned back its S&P investment-grade rating after two years, CEO Terry Lundgren has announced the launching of its Search and Send program. This allows shoppers to order products from better-stocked Macy's locations in other parts of the country. While it sounds a bit like shopping online, in-store shoppers avoid shipping charges.

With 850 department stores in forty-five states, in Guam, and in Puerto Rico, Macy's (along with Bloomingdale's) is dedicated to serving each of its regional communities. To satisfy the wants and needs of its customers across the nation, the company has formed sixty-nine separate teams of merchants to buy for various geographic areas. Thus you are not likely to find the same merchandise in each Macy's store. For example, if you live in an area of the country where winter clothing is out of season and are planning a trip to the East Coast in midwinter, you will love the convenience of the Search and Send program. Yet for the younger population, will department-store shopping ever trump shopping in trendy boutiques or online? Will technology-driven changes attract new and younger shoppers?

While researching this piece of fiction, I spoke with a number of fantastically dedicated individuals who held diametrically opposite views as to what was in the best interest of consumers across the nation and in the city of Chicago in particular. What I realized above all else is that change is never easy. Often we resist because we do not wish to step away from our comfort zone to embrace the unknown, even when the specific unknown may offer some great advantages. Often the past holds something precious that truly should be preserved and that we must not let go. And often the pendulum has swung too far in either direction and we must strive to find middle ground.

What I found in Chicago was an enormous amount of good, logical rationales for both points of view. What I did not find were any "bad guys." The truth is, there is tremendous passion in the Windy City, as there has always been in the retail world at large.

As I write, the holiday season is approaching. Our mall parking lots are jammed. Consumers are headed for department stores, trendy boutiques, and specialty stores. How many will make purchases on the spot? How many will return home to compare prices or values online? How many will pull out their cell phones and compare values while in the store?

In our changing world of expanding shopping choices, many of us take advantage of multiple forms of shopping. However, I continue to believe in the value and longevity of the department store.

Readers, please send me your thoughts at www.darlenequinn.net.

READER'S GUIDE

AUTHOR Q & A

Q. Is there one character you identify with most in this novel? Do you have one such alter ego in each of the novels you've written to date in the series?

A. Ashleigh is the character I identify most closely with. Although her personal life is not at all like mine, she holds the same position in Bentleys Royale that I held in Bullocks Wilshire. She tends to think like I do and responds much as I would, particularly if I had the gift of hindsight.

Q. What was your inspiration from the beginning of your "webs" series for having Ashleigh and Conrad have twin daughters? Do you read about the studies conducted among twins? How have the results of those studies influenced the characters you've created?

A. When I wrote *Webs of Power*, I had no idea I was writing a series. However, by the time my first novel went to press, my characters had become as real to me as my own family, and I found they had more stories to tell. I had read a novel and then a nonfiction book about identical twins who had come together much later in life. The concept fascinated me, so I gave a set of identical twins to one of my favorite couples. I did a great deal of research on identical and fraternal twins. When I first began *Twisted Webs* (which became far more twisted than I envisioned), I was looking forward to implementing some of my research about "twin talk"—a special language twin babies who are brought up together are known to create for themselves. However, that plan flew out the window when Mario kidnapped one of the twins.

Q. You write natural dialogue for characters whose lives differ greatly from your own. How have you cultivated an "ear" for the way people from all walks of life speak with one another?

A. Many of my characters are drawn from the men and women I worked with in the world of retail. Other characters are created through observation of the personalities and actions of others outside of that arena. In *Webs of Fate*, I created a character very much like my best friend and matron of honor. It made the dialogue between her and Ashleigh very easy and natural. While the personal lives of my characters are pure fiction, the professional lives and personalities of the movers and shakers in the world of department stores are a composite of those I have worked with in my own retail career.

Q. This fourth novel shows a darker side of what human beings are capable of doing. Was it hard for you to create Rick, who kidnaps his half-brother in *Unpredictable Webs*? Did you struggle to make him multidimensional and thus a more sympathetic character?

A. Since I am an insatiable reader, new ideas are always taking root. I had no role model for Rick. His character was formed as I was writing. I needed a villain but had no clear idea of who he might be. While setting the stage and asking myself a lot of "what if" questions, Rick sprang to life. In order to provide a number of twists, I made Rick the stepson of Erica's boyfriend. My minor in college was psychology so I am aware that no character is all evil or all angelic. I dislike stereotypes and cardboard characters; consequently, I found that working in Rick's bit of humanity came easily.

Q. Have you chosen to create homosexual characters for your novels simply to be as representative of our current society as possible, or do you have a hidden agenda in presenting likable, talented, and loyal men who are gay?

A. The world of high fashion retail would falter without the number of talented gay men in the industry. Glenn Nelson (who has only a cameo role in this novel) is a mirror image of a terrifically talented buyer whom I worked with at Bullocks Wilshire. By the way, I ran into my role model at a book signing in Palm Desert. He loved the fact that he was a character, but told me that he was disappointed that in *Twisted Webs* Glenn was not at the Christmas Party in the epilogue. I could not write about that industry without including gays. However, like heterosexuals, they are not all good. While most of my gay men are talented and intelligent, in *Webs of Fate*, the two men who were behind the embezzlement and the kidnapping were gay. One was a very angry and vengeful young man.

Q. You've moved fashion maven Viviana into a new role in this novel, that of cougar, without making her a laughingstock. Is there a special place in your heart for women of her age because of your proximity to the societal pressures put upon women in Hollywood and Beverly Hills?

A. I love this question. Viviana's personality is similar to that of the Bullocks Wilshire director of fashion merchandising whom I worked with and who now has an upscale boutique on El Paseo in Palm Desert (akin to Rodeo Drive in Beverly Hills). My husband and I had breakfast with her when I was doing some book signings in the desert area. She had read *Webs of Power* and recognized herself, and she asked, "Was I really that bad?" However, she also loved being a character.

In my novels, Viviana is vain, power hungry, and manipulative—the kind of woman you would love to hate, but somehow do not. Because of her vulnerability, most readers are drawn to her. Viviana is also intelligent, beautiful, and tenderhearted. So, I was delighted to find that the real woman behind my creation not only loved the book but also wanted to give me more input.

And, in talking to my role model, I discovered that my character was even more like her than I realized. Let me explain.

In *Webs of Fate*, I created a scene based on an extravaganza that I knew had taken place after I resigned from my position on the management team of Bullocks Wilshire to aid my severely deaf daughter in her last year of high school and to travel with my late husband. I knew that the Bullocks Wilshire sales promotion staff had hoisted a ten-story balloon replica of King Kong onto the roof of Bullocks Wilshire for a "Hurray for Hollywood" black-tie fund-raiser. I talked with the former sales promotion executive and got all the information I needed to make the scene authentic. Knowing Viviana's personality as I had created her, I thought she would be opposed to having that image tied in with Bullocks Wilshire, so I had her objecting to and trying to sabotage the plan. What I found out at breakfast is that that is exactly what this former director of fashion merchandising did. Her plan of sabotage was better than the one I had originally created, and since the manuscript was then only in first draft, I used her plan. It is so much fun when you get something exactly right.

During our breakfast meeting, she also suggested that Viviana would be even more interesting if she became a cougar—just as she had.

Q. What one message in particular do you want readers to take away from the themes and subthemes within *Unpredictable Webs?*

A. While there is no overt message in my novels, most of my savvy readers read between the lines and come away with knowledge that our destiny is not determined by what happens in our lives so much as what we do about whatever challenges come our way.

Q. Are there other issues you grappled with as you wrote this novel that might make good starting points for discussion among your fans or book clubs?

A. When I began this novel, my thoughts were that Marnie would be the twin who was kidnapped. I had not anticipated Callie's intervention. How might the story have changed if Marnie had been the victim? How might it have played out if both girls had started out to Starbucks together?

DISCUSSION QUESTIONS

1. At the heart of *Unpredictable Webs* are the relationships between parents and children. What was the author trying to say about how intrusive parents Ashleigh and Conrad, Paige and Mark, and Nelson should be in monitoring what their daughters and sons are up to, especially during their offspring's teen years?

2. How critical a role does sibling rivalry play in the novel? If Callie and Marnie and Neil and Rick had been closer to one another, could the story possibly have played out in the same way?

3. What advice would you have given to Ashleigh when she was listening to Marnie confess to cutting herself? How might the author have written the scene if Marnie had shared this intimate detail with Conrad instead?

4. Which character would you most want to have lunch with? Why?

5. What would you say Ashleigh's greatest strength is, both as a wife and as a mother? What, on the other hand, is her greatest weakness? Did her maternal love impede her from making a wise decision at any point in the novel?

6. Were Rick's threats to the lives of Neil and Callie plausibly conveyed? How would permanently injuring or killing either one or both of them have changed the outcome of the novel?

7. In this fourth novel by Darlene Quinn, Mitchell Wainwright attempts to be reconciled with and to understand his gay son, Tony. Would the story have unfolded differently if Tony's role in finding and rescuing Callie and Neil had been larger?

8. Did the author convey Helen's circumstance—that of an aging woman with a degree of dementia—with humor and compassion? Did Helen's desire to become a cougar enhance or detract from the story line?

9. When you discovered, just as Rick did, that he hadn't shot and killed his mother's boyfriend, Joe, how did you react? What kind of mother could allow her innocent child to be tried for such a crime? Should any of that backstory be factored in during Rick's trial for kidnapping?

10. Describe the different kinds of prejudices that emerge in the novel. How did the biased characters express their opinions, either in word or deed? Did the victims of those prejudices share anything in common?

11. The author portrays Erica as a recovering alcoholic and Nelson as someone who suffers with the chronic pain of fibromyalgia. In your opinion, does this make them more sympathetic characters? Do their frailties play a role in their budding relationship? Do they influence their parental behaviors?

12. Where do you see Viviana and Gino going at the end of this novel? Do you think Marnie and Neil will continue to grow their friendship? Will it be possible for Nelson and Rick to overcome their misunderstanding of one another and actually have a meaningful relationship?

www.ingramcontent.com/pod-product-compliance
Lightning Source LLC
Chambersburg PA
CBHW050610110726
47899CB00001B/49